I0580152

MY BARE LADY

SCORNED WOMEN'S SOCIETY SERIES BOOK #1

PIPER SHELDON

WWW.SMARTYPANTSROMANCE.COM

COPYRIGHT

This book is a work of fiction. Names, characters, places, rants, facts, contrivances, and incidents are either the product of the author's questionable imagination or are used factitiously. Any resemblance to actual persons, living or dead or undead, events, locales is entirely coincidental if not somewhat disturbing/concerning.

Copyright © 2019 by Smartypants Romance; All rights reserved.

No part of this book may be reproduced, scanned, photographed, instagrammed, tweeted, twittered, twatted, tumbled, or distributed in any printed or electronic form without explicit written permission from the author.

Made in the United States of America

Print Edition
978-1-949202-13-7

DEDICATION

To J.R., always

CHAPTER 1

SUZIE

In the drop-down mirror of my car, I puckered my lips to add another coat of lipstick. My complexion was flawless and my eyeliner smooth despite my shaking hands. My whole face was perfectly primed, painted, and plumped. Not that nobody ever looked at my face for very long.

I might be bad at most things but at least I looked good doing them. I guess, at some point, we all just start playing to our strengths. And my strengths are dancing on a pole and looking fine. There's not a person in Green Valley that'd argue with that. Suzie Samuels and stripping go together like bacon and grits. But not after tonight.

I hoped.

The thrum of activity at the G-Spot hit me before I even left my car. The bass vibrated the dashboard almost enough to cover my own wobbling insides. I smoothed my hair one last time. I'd spent an hour straightening and then curling it into the perfect waves for that just-out-of-bed look. My outfit was a complicated crisscross of elastic straps all over my body meant to emphasize my dancer figure. It was a twofold benefit; the material helped protect my skin on the pole and the straps held a lot more cash than a G-string.

Plus, I looked damn hot in it.

I sauntered toward the door with my most eye-catching sway because Ka-Bar sat on a stool outside. I wasn't part of the Iron Wraiths Motorcycle Club anymore, in fact, I'd gone to their rivals, the Black Demons, but he'd always been good to me, so I gave a little show. Plus, acting real sexy tended to calm my jitters. It was a cold October night and I fought to keep from shivering.

"Hey, Ka-Bar." My five-inch platforms wobbled in the gravel leading to the door but I didn't falter.

Ka-Bar looked like most of the Iron Wraiths; tattooed, scraggly beard, and leather from head to toe. A giant knife tattoo taking up the length of his arm and the dog tags around his neck distinguished him. He looked me up and down and licked his lips like he wanted a taste.

"Hey, gorgeous." He leaned in for the kiss I ghosted over his cheek. "Little early for your shift?"

"Well, I never get to see you when I come in later." I leaned out of his embrace noting the familiar smell of exhaust, sweat, and smokes.

"Shucks." He put a hand over his heart.

"Also, I need to talk to Occum before I go up." I shrugged like I wasn't sick to my stomach thinking about it.

I was high up on the Black Demon's Motorcycle Club food chain but I was still just a stripper. Stripping was supposed to be temporary, a means to an end after I made some bad life choices. One life choice named Jethro Winston. But I wasn't thinking about him right now.

"He should be in the office." Ka-Bar thumbed toward the building. "Meeting with some suit from the city as we speak."

"No shit?"

"Yeah, something for the new renovations. Heard it wasn't going well. He's a real hard-ass."

The same renovations I was here to talk about. I wanted to ask more but didn't have the chance. Two regulars walked out of the bar; Rooster and Cueball. The Iron Wraiths insignia on their vests was as good as waving a gun in the air. I recognized their swagger as an attempt to hide sloppy drunkenness. G-Spot was neutral territory for several of the local MCs, including the Black Demons and the Iron Wraiths. It's the only place the MCs tolerated each other, far as I knew. Everywhere else they'd pick a fight over the color of the sky. Here, business was business and us women were business.

"Look at this one." Rooster—named for his short red mohawk and hooked nose—looked me up and down. These bikers weren't exactly blowing any minds with their nicknaming skills.

"Where were you, baby? I'd pay extra for some time with you," Cueball added. Cueball was—you guessed it—pale with a shiny bald head and round enough to roll down the Smokies.

What I wanted to do was roll my eyes and tell them their wedding rings weren't just for decoration. But Occum's rule for dancers was "shut up and look pretty," so I couldn't go pissing off his clientele. And Lord knew I was already on thin ice for my sharp tongue and quick temper.

I smiled and tried to go in past them. If I couldn't say nothing nice … I'd kick their bikes later.

"Come on now, how much for a quick BJ in the parking lot?" Cueball was so drunk his eyes couldn't focus on me as he asked.

My teeth ground together. I knew everybody thought dancers were hookers but we weren't. At least, not all of us.

"You can't afford me, sweetie." I winked.

"Hey, aren't you Short Fuse Suze?" Cueball asked. I knew they'd recognize me sooner or later. I was almost a Wraith girl a million years ago. "Careful. You know what she did to Jethro Winston."

"I don't care. I still want a piece." Rooster just about had me in his grip when Ka-Bar got 'em.

He was faster and stronger than these drunks would ever be. He had the redhead face-first against the club exterior faster than you could say Mississippi mud pie.

"No hands." His voice was cool but the threat was clear.

"You can't fucking touch me," Rooster said, his cheek smashed against brick.

Cueball looked back and forth, fists balled and ready for action.

"You know the rules. Get your asses home," Ka-Bar warned.

Rooster stood up and shook out his leather jacket. "Don't forget who you're fucking with. Razor's gonna hear about this."

My cheeks burned. I dug my fake nails into my palms to keep from clawing their eyes out.

"Big mistake." Cueball spat on the ground as they made their way toward their rides. When he was a safe distance from Ka-Bar, he shouted something about me being a cocktease.

I picked up the stool Ka-Bar had been sitting on and lifted it over my head, fully intending on nailing the suckers as they hightailed it out of there.

"Easy girl." He grabbed me around the waist, pulling me back out of sight. He ripped the stool out of my tense grip.

"Just one good smack. Teach 'em a lesson." I glared after them until their rumbling engines were out of earshot.

Ka-Bar rubbed my shoulder. "Don't get any ideas, Short Fuse."

Set one bike on fire and suddenly you had a reputation. Okay so maybe I had been thinking about setting them on fire. If I couldn't do that I'd whack 'em with a stool.

"Mother clucker," I swore under my breath.

Ka-bar raised an amused eyebrow at me.

"I'm trying this new thing where I don't swear as much. And come on, he's Rooster. It's funny."

"I sure miss your crazy antics." He shook his head. "Get in. You're shivering."

Making him smile helped ease my tension but my fingers still trembled as I ran them through my hair. I should be used to this behavior from men. I'd been ogled since thirteen when my natural Ds sprouted overnight. Still, it was nice to have Ka-Bar around when men got ugly. Not all the Iron Wraiths were so bad.

Inside, bass thumped through my chest to "Bad Girls" by M.I.A. All around, girls in thongs and bikini tops served drinks, danced, and ground themselves on the customers. The air was heavy with smoke so thick the dim lights created a reddish halo on each table. It took shampooing my hair twice after every shift to get the smell out. The vibe here was dirtier than the Pink Pony but guaranteed a good time for the right price. My palms tingled as I made my way through the crowd toward Occum's office. Busy was good. Busy meant more money and hopefully a good mood.

I was about to bust into the main office when a loud bang through the door made me jump. It had sounded like a fist slamming down on the desk. Occum did that a lot when he got worked up. I was very familiar with that sound.

"That's not gonna work," Occum growled.

Whoever was in there was doing fine work pissing him off. I shot a quick glance over my shoulder to see if anybody was coming. His office was way in the back where the music hardly reached so hopefully nobody would catch me being nosey. I tiptoed closer to the door in between a stack of lumber and a stepladder.

"The work you laid out doesn't align with what you detailed in this report. When you've updated the blueprints to show the true structural changes being made, I'll review the site again. If the work is satisfactory at that point, then I'll sign off on the structural modifications." The voice was calm, not as deep as Occum's but smoother, and oddly confident considering it sounded like Occum was two seconds from steaming out his ears. There was something about it that caused a tiny shiver to go down my spine. It was flat but rich. There was no catch at the end of his sentences like he was asking a question the way most folks talked around here.

He was a Yankee.

Color me intrigued. I moved closer to listen. This man better be careful. One, because Occum was likely to get violent and two, I didn't want him getting my boss all riled up. Not now.

"Those changes'll cost a hundred grand easy," Occum spoke dangerously slow.

"At least," the stranger responded.

The office chair creaked and I pictured Occum leaning back, staring at the ceiling with fists clenched behind his head.

"How much is this going to cost me?" Occum asked.

There was a slight pause. "I believe you just estimated. Though to be honest that sounds on the low end to me. You're cutting corners.

Or you could just update the blueprints to reflect the actual changes being made and add a few safety precautions like—"

"How. Much. Do. You. Want?"

There was another pause. My ear now pressed flat against the door.

"I can recommend a company but I don't have a crew myself."

I covered my mouth to hold back a laugh. Either this guy was thick as molasses in winter or he had cojones the size of bowling balls.

"I want to pay you off so you'll sign the goddamn papers and I can finish this fucking remodel!" The sound of a chair slamming back into the wall had me jumping back about a foot. "How much do you want?"

"I'm sure you aren't suggesting I risk my career and reputation for a measly payoff." The voice was closer this time when it spoke so I tucked myself against the wall and out of the way in case he came out.

"Fuck you. I'll find someone else to pay."

"Good luck. I'm the only certified building inspector within two hundred miles with the authorization to sign off on this." There was another shuffle and the voice was closer. "And no person with any morals would sign off on the shoddy work I see here."

The door opened so abruptly after that bold statement I jumped and hid my face to the wall. I didn't know why. I never hid myself. If anything, I showed too much of myself but for some reason, I didn't want this stranger seeing me or knowing I had listened in. His confidence in the face of Occum was unsettling; his voice, a little too intriguing.

He brushed past me with a polite, "Excuse me, ma'am," taking care not to touch me, which was tricky with the construction material taking up all the hall space.

He muttered something about fire hazards before melting into the darkness of the bar. I couldn't tell much from his retreating figure; his dress pants and collared shirt were a little too fancy for this place. His hair was salt and pepper, but that was about all I could see. Shoulders back, his stride was as cool as his voice had been, confidence oozing as he disappeared. My jaw hung slack like a largemouth bass.

Then his words registered. I was half tempted to chase after him just to smack him upside the head. "Ma'am"?! Me? I was equal parts confused and offended. My outfit hardly covered my nipples and he called me something we call ol' Mrs. Albensi when we saw her at the Piggly Wiggly. I'm not a ma'am, I'm a miss. I'm still in my twenties! Technically. Though, my hangovers were lasting a little longer these days and I did pluck a grey hair this morning.

I debated chasing after this stranger to give him a piece of my mind when Occum shot out the office.

"Goddamn!" His face was twisted with rage.

That's when I should have skedaddled but I was stuck like a bunny on a state route—too afraid to move and about to be roadkill. Occum's head was shaved completely bald but what he lacked up top sprouted from his face like Rip Van Winkle. The thin tip of his beard reached all the way down to his belt buckle.

He spotted me still half turned facing the wall. "What in the hell are you doing, Short Fuse?" Before I could make up an answer he added, "Get your ass on stage, right now."

For somebody with a reputation for talking too much, I struggled to find words. "I need to talk to you."

Now wasn't going to be the best time to talk to him but the words had tumbled out after days of preparing them. I guess that's why everybody told me God used a teaspoon to pour my brains in and had shaking hands.

He had been looking down the hall after that ballsy fellow but this caused him to snap his head toward me. "You want to talk? What about, nail polish and blowjobs?"

I ran my hand down his arm and squeezed his sinewy bicep. His cologne was overpowering this close. "I was thinking—"

"That face ain't for thinking." He pushed me off his arm. "I have important clientele here tonight and I promised them a show. I've had enough backtalk from people for one day. Now get moving before the next song starts or I'm gonna have one of my new girls dance and you can bus tables."

I blinked back the hurt at his words. I batted my eyelashes and smiled to sidetrack his tension. "Okay, sugar. Whatever you want."

"That's my girl." He smacked my bottom as I walked away and headed toward the changing rooms.

I'd talk to him after my set. I wouldn't lose my nerve. This was my life. I had gotten myself here with my bad actions and I was paying for them. I wasn't fit for anything proper, but maybe I could have this one thing just for me.

CHAPTER 2

CLIFFORD

I was meticulous about my hand washing despite the rage pumping adrenaline through me. I glanced at my bland expression through the splashes of God-knows-what on the mirror. I performed my counting mental exercises until my heart beat at a normal pace.

The froth of bubbles was the perfect consistency and evenly distributed as I scrubbed clean. I'd felt dirty for hours now. Of course, there wasn't a dryer in sight, nor a paper towel roll. The only option was an old-fashioned towel loop where the rag was a rainbow of putrid oranges, browns, and yellows. This whole establishment had been nothing but a disgusting disappointment from the moment I crossed the threshold.

After seeing what happened here, I was sure there was no surface untainted.

That barbarian thought that I could be bought. He'd thought I didn't understand his fumbling bribery. I'd given him a chance to back out, to realize how fruitless his attempt would be, but he was too thick-skulled to recognize the opportunity.

What would it be like to take the money, to be crooked and betray my own moral code? The things I could do with that bribe. The

9

research I could get funded. But I stopped that train of thought before it derailed. Imagine-the-headline was my favorite way to stop bad decisions.

"UT Professor Found Guilty in Strip Joint Payoff Scheme."

Nope. Not worth it.

Outside I still looked the unflappable professor, bow tie in place, my hair in need of a cut but at least combed back a bit. My beard was trimmed a respectable length. Not like the rest of these men. I aggressively shook my hands around to dispel the water droplets and carefully opened the door with my elbow to get out.

I needed to leave before I caught a rash.

The exit was in sight when the music stopped and the lights all dimmed save for one spotlight focused on the main stage set up in the center of the room. A hush fell over the crowd, like everyone took in a deep breath at the same time. A quick guitar strum filled the air shortly followed by the thrumming tempo of a foot-stomping beat. On stage, a woman materialized from the blackness. She walked forward confidently. The same woman I tried to see in the hallway but who had averted her face from me. I had that effect on women. Especially women like that—women who captured the audience of every man that they passed.

My workload nagged at the back of my mind. Time to leave. Papers waited to be graded, grants needed to be applied for. I didn't have time to deal with a backwoods hillbilly trying to buy me off for a side job I didn't want or need. And yet, my feet remained planted.

A dark cove near the exit beckoned. I crossed my arms and settled into the dim area to watch her unseen. No harm in watching her dance. If she took off her clothes, I'd leave. The music had a life of its own. It existed to highlight her movements and seep under my skin. The tempo of the bass drummed down my chest and out through my extremities.

With every stomp of dark tempo, she glided her way toward a gleaming pole in the center. Her hair flowed like a living entity as she tossed it around. Onyx waves reached just to the top of her luscious...

I cleared my throat and shifted my feet.

As the melody built, her movements became more exaggerated and complex. She dropped to the floor suddenly, arched her back, crawled, writhed, flipped her head, and spread her legs, all with intention and fluidity. She was sexuality incarnate. The area around the stage filled with men and women surging forward, waving their cash and trying to get it in her outfit. Occasionally she made her way to them to allow them to slide bills against her glistening skin.

She was flawless. She was a beacon of pure light in this grotesque pit of hell. Her sloping waist, her creamy skin—all perfected to allure men. She was a siren with cash crashing at her feet like boats against rocks.

Good God, she even made my thoughts poetic. Pathetic.

The chorus started and with a small head start, she jumped to the top of the pole in an outstanding act of pure athleticism. The sultry voice blaring through the speakers sang of rivers and mouths and sex and power. Goosebumps prickled my arms and neck.

Her body spun around the bar completely unaffected by gravity. She ran and flowed and never stopped collecting the attention of everybody around her. It looked effortless, but immense strength powered those smooth curves.

I was transfixed. It wasn't just the way she mastered the room. It wasn't just how her choreography perfectly correlated with the entrancing music. It wasn't just her sex appeal. It was that unwavering gaze and focus on her task. To the rest of the room, staring blatantly at her admirable—ahem—assets, she was an object, but I recognized the barely controlled passion roiling under her skin. What would it be like to be that strong? Not just physically, but strong in a way that allowed her to bare her soul to a group of greedy strangers. My passions were locked away safely inside me and yet she put it all out there. Such bravery and passion.

In certain moments, I swear she looked right at me—quick, stolen glances that shot a bolt of adrenaline down my spine. Perhaps this was a skill she learned to earn more tips, as the money was out in droves now, peppered over the stage and her sweating skin. But I swore she saw me. Saw through me. To the things I didn't want seen. I stepped back further into the darkness knowing my concerns were irrational but unable to tear my eyes off hers. I was stronger than this. I was thoughtful, pragmatic, and not a victim of animalistic natures and poetic fantasies.

Though she occasionally snapped the thin strips of material that made up her outfit in a playful tease, she never took any clothes off. She didn't need to. She'd managed to capture the attention of every person in that room with her movements alone.

My body reacted despite my rationale; heart pounding, skin aflame. I needed to leave. I wouldn't be like the rest of these people.

The song crescendoed and in a show of strength, she launched herself back to the top of the pole once again. A small gasp escaped from me but the music drowned out all noise. She performed a trick that made her appear to fall down the entire length of the pole, tumbling over and sideways, limb over limb, only to catch herself at the bottom using only her thighs. She hung upside down, panting, dark hair sprawled out around her and her gaze set on me. Her eyes were a brilliant emerald, unlike any color I'd ever seen. They were luminescent in the stage lighting. Even across the hazy bar, they were transcendent. Glowing. Fixated on me.

Nobody else.

I swallowed but it wasn't easy. The song ended and the lights went out. The crowd went wild. Several moments passed before I gained control of my faculties again. With that control came the shame of watching her. The understanding that just seeing her perform was enough to make me forget who I was. That couldn't happen.

I got out of there as fast as I could. The entire drive back to Knoxville my chest heaved at an alarming rate; my body remained a mass of tension. Her hypnotic gaze flashed repeatedly in my vision no matter how often I tried to shake it loose.

Thankfully, I'd never see her again.

CHAPTER 3

SUZIE

I left the stage sweaty and satisfied. That's more than I could say for the last few sexual experiences I've had. "Like a River" by Bishop Briggs was a risky choice over the usual crowd pleasers but her demanding voice and that hungry tempo hit nerves. I'd put on one hell of a show and made more money than expected. Sometimes the music spoke to me and my body moved in just the right way so the crowd ate it up. More than speaking *to* me, it spoke *through* me. It made me feel like I was more than a stripper. It made me want to be something extraordinary.

Not that I'd ever tell anybody that. I could just imagine the look of one of the Black Demons as I explained how powerful and alive I felt when I moved around that pole. They'd likely tell me to shut my trap and spread my legs.

I organized my bills, flattening and stacking from singles to the fifty. The fifty I folded up and hid in the thick strap under my boob. Despite everyone calling me dumber than a bag of bricks, I knew enough to keep some cash hidden. That should get Daddy through the week. I made my way back to Occum's office.

Occum took over the Black Demons right around the time I came looking for help about eight years ago. He ran the G-Spot and was in the process of upgrading it from a dive bar with strippers to a fancy nightclub—also with strippers. He was only sort of rough before he busted faces to get to the top. Now, there was a cruelty about him that made my skin itch. But he was the boss so if I wanted change, I went through him.

Still panting from my routine I pushed into the office. Maison was in his lap, arms wrapped around his neck. She was new and eager to prove herself by shoving her tongue in his ear. I hid a shudder. I had been there only a few years ago. Thank God I'd moved up the ranks because I could still recall the smell of sour cigarettes in his uncombed beard.

"A couple of guys just sat in your section," I told her. It may or may not have been true.

She stuck out her lower lip to Occum. He roughly pushed her off his lap. He smacked her ass loudly as she walked away. She giggled but I recognized that hidden wince. Those booty shorts didn't cushion against the sting of a flat palm or pinch.

"Shoo," I said and waved her away with one hand and dabbed sweat off my neck with a towel.

She scurried out of the room. Maison might call me a name now, but at least she didn't have to do something she may regret later. I wish I could tell her that she didn't have to prove herself that way, that there were other ways to earn your value, but I wasn't exactly a showcase example myself.

"Next time. You knock." Occum leaned back in his chair and adjusted his jeans.

"Sure thing, babe." Men had to be stroked just right. Especially their egos.

I laid the bills out in front of him, still damp from being thrown on stage, covered in beer or various body fluids.

"That it?" he asked.

"'Course," I said.

"Good night." He flipped through the cash, counting it out. He gave a small frown of approval behind his scraggly beard. He took half the cash.

"Hey, what gives?" I spoke without thinking.

"Excuse me?" He stilled on his way to the safe behind the desk and looked up at me with yellow eyes.

They didn't call me Short Fuse Suze for nothing. I couldn't stand by and let him take half the money I worked my booty off for. Usually, he only took twenty percent.

"I got bills."

"You mean you gotta support your daddy's habit."

"I need that money." I smoothed my hair into a twist over my shoulder. It wasn't any of his damn business.

"Yeah, well your real family needs it more. This is for keeping your top on. You know what they're paying for."

I ground my teeth. I had tried to get away with staying dressed. I wore an outfit that was basically like being naked but it still wasn't enough. Even though I made more tonight than most of the other girls did in weeks. I bit my tongue. Better blood in my mouth than blood on the ground. I stared longingly at the bills. The things I could do with that money. The money I earned through sweat and bruises and rough hands.

"About that." I bit back the overwhelming desire to yell at him, remembering what my main goal was here. "I heard about the VIP stage you're building."

"What did you hear?" He leveled me with a look.

"That it's gonna be upstairs, in the new level. That'll be like a Vegas show."

"Right." He stroked his long beard, face unreadable. "And?"

"I was thinking—"

"And isn't that the problem. What did I tell you about that?" He quirked a smile at his own joke. One I'd heard a thousand times.

I squared my shoulders and plowed on. I'd been working up to this for some time. Even if I was scared shitless, I had to ask. "What if I stopped stripping down here and I put on a real show. I have some real good dances, actually, I've got lots of fans on Instagram—"

"No stripping?"

"I wouldn't get naked, not completely, but I'd put on an actual show. I could do big dance numbers with the other girls, have fun costumes, stuff like that."

"Short Fuse. You're my main girl." He patted his lap. "Come 'ere."

"Thanks." I flipped my hair off my shoulder and started twisting it up into a knot to get it off my sweaty neck. I didn't show any hesitation as I went to his lap but dang, I was so tired. I didn't want to do the flirting thing tonight. I was so tired of the games.

"You're damn good at what you do. I expect the best from you."

I fell into his lap and threw my arms around his neck, making sure to press my breasts into him. "Thanks, babe."

"It's because you're my number one girl that I give you the most important assignments."

I smiled but my stomach twisted. He wasn't answering me about the VIP room. I'd been working up to ask about it for weeks and he brushed it off without consideration.

"I need you to help out your family now. I need you to step up."

"Okay. You know I will."

"That's my girl." He pushed back my hair causing it to fall out of the bun I just created and tugged my head toward him.

There was something in that grip. A little voice deep down inside, the one I had learned to ignore a long time ago, warned me to get out. He grabbed my hair into a fist and yanked back my head so our eyes were locked. It stung enough that my eyes watered.

"The G-Spot is our home. All these people that work here, all your family in the Black Demons, they rely on it. And," he ran his free hand down his face, "the Man wants us to fail. They hate that us working folk are busting our asses and finally making our way up in the world. So they're putting bureaucratic red tape all over the place."

His rant was mostly to himself, but when he looked up again his face hardened with focus. I didn't know what he was building toward but I wish he'd just tell me already.

"Now don't worry your pretty face over the details. Just know the Man doesn't like us. He's trying to bring us down. I work hard to protect you and the girls. I do things to protect this family..." He trailed off with a shake of his head. "Like I said. I need you to do something. You're a good girl and so I know you won't let your family down."

"Just tell me what you need, baby."

"There was a suit in here tonight. Tryna to tell me that my work's not up to snuff. That we aren't working hard enough and that just ain't fair. He wants to make a dime off our hard work."

I knew exactly who he was talking about. I thought of that man again. The one who hadn't worn a suit but was dressed totally different than most of the men in this place, with that little dorky bowtie. He was intriguing. He had watched me on stage so intently. Couldn't take his eyes off me. But it was the way he focused on my eyes that stuck with me. He had strayed briefly to study my moves but he always came back to my face. His attention drove me to push harder, be sexier, feel more. Normally up there, I didn't think—I just felt.

Suddenly, I didn't want to be here on Occum's lap waiting to hear his plans for me. I didn't want anybody telling me what I wanted or needed. I wanted the attention of a man like that. A sophisticated and classy man. But I kept all that to myself because I was torn. Occum was real upset but that man seemed like he was just trying to do right. He seemed like he was just doing his job. But maybe I wasn't thinking straight. I'd been fooled by a man before.

"He must want his cut but he isn't taking cash." Occum ran dirty fingernails down my arm. "But every man has a price, you understand."

His finger traced across my collarbone. There was a time where this action would have had me purring under his attention but now my stomach soured. I was trying to change, be better. No more swearing. No more stripping.

"Occum, I want to help…" But what? I didn't finish. I didn't want to know what he was getting at.

"Good." He released my hair and gently kissed my forehead. "So you'll go to him. You'll give him whatever he needs to get this renovation moving."

The dread in my gut solidified into a block of ice that shot through my veins.

I knew what he was really asking me to do. Despite what everyone said, I wasn't an idiot. I wasn't that type of girl. Sure, I've had good times with a few of the guys, but that was always my choice. That was what I wanted to do. This. What he asked me, this felt awfully close to that line I promised myself I would never cross.

"I can talk to him but I d-don't—" I couldn't get the words out.

Occum had some of the girls doing things under the table—literally—but he never asked that of me. I thought I was above that. I thought. And wasn't that my problem? Thinking. I've been told my whole life I was too pretty to worry about thinking.

"Oh, look at you." He rubbed a thumb over my bottom lip. "I can smell the smoke. Don't think so hard. This is easy. This is what you're good at. Look at you. You're gorgeous. You're made for this."

For what, exactly? I focused on his hard stare as it bore into me. I pushed away the scary and overwhelming thoughts that tried to pull me under. Better when I didn't think at all. I knew that.

I nodded slightly.

"You want to go back to the Wraiths? You want them to collect what's owed to them the old-fashioned way? The way I see it, you have it pretty good here. Don't you want your big stage?"

I nodded.

"I need you and the best girls. I'm throwing a private party."

I didn't know I was available for assignments. My schedule was pretty full between the club and keeping my social media accounts up to date. I had almost five thousand followers on my Instagram and not all of them were men. Women were always asking for health and makeup tips. I wondered if I could ...

"Suzie, goddammit! Pay attention. I swear to God, you're no better than a bitch in heat at a dog park." Occum was in a no-lip mood so I smiled pretty for him. "I'm throwing a private party for some very important people. Very important. Very intimate."

"Okay," I said. "You want me to dance?"

"Yeah. Black Demons rented out a hotel. One of those big rooms."

He meant a banquet hall, but I wasn't about to correct him.

"Why not here?"

He chewed the hairs on his bottom lip and the coarse sound made my stomach turn over. "This is a big show. For all the regulars and VIPs. You don't need to know any more than that. That man's gonna be there. His name is Clifford Rutledge. He's a professor at UT. You're gonna dance for him in the private booth."

"Oh okay," I sort of drug out the word because Occum looked real desperate. "Just dance for him? Get him to sign off?"

"Of course. Do what comes natural."

What comes natural? Dancing came natural, nothing else. But I could get a man to agree to things. I could do it without crossing my own lines. I needed to get that stage.

"Okay," I said.

His chin dropped to his chest and he glared up at me without lifting it. At that angle and the dim lighting, he looked like a demon straight from hell. "Good," he rumbled. "I don't need to remind you of life outside this MC. Nobody having your back. No money. Wraiths breaking down your door and your daddy's other leg. You don't want to fuck this up, Short Fuse. Not if you want your own stage. Haven't I taken care of you?"

I nodded as best I could under his grasp.

"I put my neck on the line for you. Razor and the Iron Wraiths own this town but I've kept you safe from them."

I swallowed.

"You know Razor came sniffing 'round for you again. Asking for his cut. I kept him away but it cost me."

"When?" I asked.

I hadn't seen Razor. I had hoped I was close to paying off my debt to Razor. It weighed me down like a lead blanket, day and night, for eight years now.

"Don't worry about it." He waved off my question. "Here're the facts you need to worry about. Your daddy's a drunk. Your momma left. Dropped you without a thought. The Black Demons saved you. We protected you, and continue to do so, from those scum in the Iron

Wraiths. We want you safe. Not like the family that supposedly shares your blood. We took you in and protected you when nobody else cared."

He was right. Alone I was dead; with the boys I was at least protected.

I took too long to answer so he kept talking.

"You're my main girl. I'm going to keep you safe and take care of you. I'm going to give you the VIP stage so you can dance for top dollar. You need to do your fair share too. We all do."

I blinked up at him. "Really? You promise the VIP stage?"

"Of course. You're the first girl I thought of for it."

I didn't want to seduce this stranger, but maybe I could find another way. Maybe I could talk to him. I didn't have a choice. Not really.

"Okay," my voice was weak as I said it. "I'll do my best."

"That's my girl. Now head on home. Rest and clean up. You got a big task ahead of you."

I swallowed down what felt like my lunch trying to make a reappearance. I could do what Occum asked of me. I didn't have to sleep with that professor guy. I could find another way. I'd gotten plenty of men to do my bidding without sleeping with them. This was some nerd who'd probably never been laid. How hard could it be?

CHAPTER 4

CLIFFORD

"It's just this idealistic vision of America, where everybody has the ability to 'pull themselves up by their bootstraps' and be a success. I mean, come on, that's not feasible for every person. It all depends on a combination of ethnicity, socio-economic background, gender, attractiveness, et cetera. From the moment you're born labels are applied to you."

My best friend, Jack, and I talked as we walked from the bus stop. Or rather, I talked and Jack nodded occasionally. It was the start of October and the air had just begun to bite. I had the collar up on my coat and Jack had his hands tucked deep into his pockets as we hustled toward our destination.

"If I could just show each person on a funding panel their own inherent biases, I know that I could prove my point and get what I need to finish my research."

Jack chuckled. "You don't have to tell me. I get it."

"Of course you do." I relaxed. I had been getting worked up. My shoulders were almost at my ears when I forced them down.

"Is that what you told the dean today? Is that why you're all wound up?"

My stomach soured at the mention. I groaned.

"Didn't go so well?"

"She reminded me the original research stipend is almost out." The tension from the week returned.

"Any other options?"

"We talked about possible grants I could apply for. Some that I already applied for. She wants me tenured here but there isn't money for my type of research. It's not flashy enough. Not in so many words, but that was the gist. The current administration isn't interested in government funding programs to help the less fortunate."

"Damn. That sucks. What about your research?" Jack asked.

"I'm not sure. I may have to put it off for a few more years. Take on a couple more classes until I can find something." I let out a breath counting down from five. It would have been so easy to take that money from the bikers.

"Someone will fund. This always happens. It comes down to the wire. You've got months. Something will come through."

I appreciated his attempt. "Maybe."

"We're going tonight for the potential investors. Just talk to them like you practiced with me and you'll be fine. Don't get nervous. You got this." Jack slowed to a stop and studied the surroundings. "Wait, are you sure this is the right place?"

Neither of us had heard of this hotel in Old North Knoxville. The neighborhood was less than reputable but the hotel itself had decent reviews online. Despite that, something was off about this invite from the get-go. But it came to my staff email address and promised investment opportunities. Distantly, bass thumped and a hint of sweet tobacco reached me. Jack had been bribed into coming as my moral support by the promise of free appetizers and drinks. These university fundraising mixers were often boring but our house was almost out of food, so it didn't take too much convincing.

I pulled out my phone and double-checked the email. "Yes, according to the GPS this is where we need to be."

We had both dressed in nice slacks, pressed shirts, and blazers—though somehow Jack looked dapper and I just looked old—but already it was clear we were both overdressed. Our heads turned to follow a group of scantily clad young women who walked past. They turned back to giggle as they caught us staring.

"Huh," Jack said, and I nodded agreement with his assessment.

We studied them for a moment longer. I cleared my throat and he shook his head. There was no signage to mark the event. I made my way to the front desk to ask, only to realize I wasn't sure what to ask. Normally, these events had some cheeky name like "Funding our Futures" or "Titrating Liquid Assets." But just as I was about to ask, a local congressman headed toward a back hallway. If anybody had money, it was this guy. Jack and I exchanged a glance, obviously having the same idea. We tagged behind him as he headed down a carpeted hallway and toward the sounds of rumbling bass, sporadic laughter, and yelling. We were led to a pair of double doors. Grabbing a handle each, we opened the door and walked straight into a den of iniquity.

"Holy hell," Jack said on a breath.

We didn't get much past the threshold before our progress slowed to a stop. We took in the scene in front of us.

Women.

Women everywhere. Mostly undressed. They strutted around carrying trays of drinks. They lounged in the laps of men smoking cigars. They danced on a makeshift stage in the middle of the room.

"I repeat, holy hell."

I nodded, again, in agreement.

At one point the room must have been some sort of respectable banquet hall, the kind you'd expect to host a wedding reception or bar mitzvah, but now it looked like walking into the dirtiest biker bar in all of Tennessee. Aside from small yellow lamps on the dozen tables and the main lights that circled the stage, an unidentifiable red glow filled the room. It truly looked lit from the pits of hell. Seductive, bass-heavy music filled the room.

"My asthma is not going to like this." Jack coughed and waved a hand in front of his face.

"There's no way smoking is allowed inside. This room violates several health codes. In the state of Tennessee, if the establishment isn't twenty-one and over at all times then smoking is strictly..."

I trailed off as a topless woman walked up to us carrying a tray of beers. She had small silver tassels barely covering her areolas so as she walked, they alternated spinning like propellers on a jet.

"Gentlemen, come in. Don't be shy." Her eyes flicked back and forth between Jack and I and caught on him a second too long. This reaction upon seeing him was not uncommon. He was strikingly tall and almost everybody that met him found him handsome. I fought hard to keep eye contact with her. Jack had given up completely and studied his shoes.

"Thank you." I grabbed a beer for myself but Jack shook his head once at the floor. "I'm sorry, but is this the fundraiser?" I asked.

"You bet, darlin'," she said sweetly. "Take a seat and enjoy yourself. One of the girls will be around to serve you shortly." There was a little too much emphasis on the word *serve*.

"I'm sure they will," I mumbled.

After she walked away, Jack turned to me wide-eyed. "I'm out."

"It's a bit nontraditional, I agree. But there are, in fact, free food and drinks, as promised. And a lot of men in this room have deep pockets."

Jack moved backward toward the exit. I was forced to follow him.

"Look around you, man. There's not a single brother in this room," he said with his lips hardly moving.

As he spoke I was surprised to find he was right. Aside from the entertainment—which varied in all ethnicities and combinations of skin and hair color—the room consisted of mostly white, middle- to upper-class males. I frowned. I hadn't noticed. But there were often things I didn't notice that Jack did, that he later pointed out to me. Another unspoken bias in American culture.

"I'm pretty sure there's a skinhead in that corner. No, don't look." Jack whispered and his gaze never moved off my face. "I'm getting out before I'm taken out tied to the back of some truck."

I would have chastised him for his judgmental comment but I had to agree. Though it wasn't completely rational or tangible, my gut twisted. Normally, I'm not one to listen to my body's more base impulses, but many studies have shown that right before a disaster or attack a person sometimes *felt* a warning. My mind flashed a headline:

"UT Professor Caught at Local Prostitution Ring."

"You're right. I'll leave with you."

Jack was already out the door when something had me stopping. It was as though someone had called my name from across the room. An awareness I couldn't explain. I scanned the area again, noticing even more questionable attendees, until my gaze landed on the stage.

It was her. The dancer from the other night, whose green eyes haunted my dreams.

Her arms were clasped above her head on a pole that stretched from stage to ceiling. Her back pressed against it as she moved up and down, up and down. Her enthusiasm was nowhere near what it had been the first time I saw her. She moved as though she were going through the motions, none of her previous passion burning through. She wore her hair down again and onyx waves trailed down around her. She was hardly covered in what could have been a purple bikini.

As I watched her, her gaze flicked up to mine. She straightened. She scanned the room quickly and then came back to me. Her eyes widened and her head tilted to the side like she was trying to tell me something. I looked behind me. There was nothing but wall. That look was meant for me.

"Let's go, man." Jack's agitation grew.

She flipped around the pole quickly, did a few moves—but her focus was soon back on me. She was definitely trying to get my attention. Why me?

"Yeah, uh, actually..." It was irrational. It was pure instinct and I hated to even consider it but the choice was made before I could think clearly. "I'm going to stay. I need to uh—I need funding and that woman did say we were at the right place. Maybe I'll find an investor."

Jack shook his head. "You're on your own for this."

"I understand." I scratched at my short beard and set my beer down on a nearby high top table. "Do you, uh, want me to make sure you can get a car okay?"

Jack sniffed and lifted his chin. I thought he would scoff at my question, insulting as it may be to a man's ego. If we were closer to the university I wouldn't have been worried but a few sketchy looking bikers kept glaring his way. Maybe we were both overprotective after growing up in foster homes together, but having each other's backs was second nature at this point. He shifted on his feet and quickly scanned the room. Something he saw in that short time decided his answer.

"Yeah, sure. Thanks."

After Jack was in a rideshare and on his way home, I went back to the party. The woman was no longer on stage. I searched the room and told myself I would just keep an eye out for her for a few more minutes before heading home. Jack warned that he'd call the police if I wasn't home by midnight.

I found a mostly empty table on the periphery of the chaos and waited in the shadows. Across from me, a heavyset man bobbed his head to the music.

"Nice party," he said as his gaze clung to the retreating figure of a server.

I grunted something noncommittal.

I felt his gaze move to me as I continued to watch for that woman who'd been occupying my thoughts since I first saw her—despite my best efforts. He stuck out a hand. "I'm Ted Buffount, of Buffount Cattle."

I reached out mine and shook his in return. His grip was callused and strong as though he spent years working with them, but his expansive middle and designer clothes spoke of successful retirement.

"Clifford Rutledge. I'm an adjunct professor at the University of Tennessee."

"Go Vols."

I nodded with a smile at the typical reaction to my declaration.

"That's my alma mater. Nice to meet ya. I knew you looked like good people." Ted tilted his head like he couldn't make out what I was doing here. Albeit, my general appearance did not fit in. My pressed shirt was at odds with all the dark jeans and gleaming belt buckles. I still couldn't make out who hosted this event, but a disturbing hypothesis was forming. It certainly wasn't the school. The man looked at me like he was waiting for more.

"I'm doing research at UT, specifically on the socio-economic impact on access to government facilities and mass transit with a specific emphasis on education and healthcare."

"I see." He nodded politely. "Relax a little, Cliff."

"Clifford."

He laughed jovially. He had one of those old south accents, like his words were dipped in molasses.

"Okay, Clifford it is."

Familiar humiliation increased my heart rate. He had been trying to make polite small talk and I had shut him down with my awkward correction. Why was small talk socially acceptable? It should be outlawed. People should only be allowed to discuss important matters. Everything else was a waste of energy.

Yet, it was how the world ran. I thought of colleagues who were offered multi-million-dollar investments for their research from a chance meeting while tailgating. I couldn't imagine the Herculean effort that would take. I had made it this far. I had changed everything about myself; I could do this too. I could play the game.

He sat back, spreading out his arms on the accompanying chairs on either side. He continued to bob to the music, seemingly unbothered by my social faux pas.

"I'm uh, actually doing some pretty interesting research right now."

"Oh, yeah? What about?" Ted turned his head toward me but kept his eyes on a girl who was smiling at him from across the room.

"I'm interested in proving the theory that many Americans are bred with inherent bias and that many opportunities in one's life are afforded based on how you are perceived by each person you interact with. But primarily it breaks down to, specifically in my field, the understanding and impact of public transportation and government-funded scholarships and other types of programs." I rubbed my hands together, then stopped myself. Jack told me I look like a praying mantis when I did that and it freaked people out.

"Try again, son." He raised an eyebrow at me.

I calmed myself down and forced myself to mirror his relaxed disposition. "I want to prove that the way we judge people based on their adolescent environment directly impacts their success in life."

He lifted his chin in understanding. "How're you going to do that?"

I scrambled. All my work heretofore had been research-based. Testing my hypothesis was the next step but money was required first. "Ah, well, unfortunately, my funding will run out before stable findings can be published. I need time and capital to—"

"Look my friend, you seem really...smart." Ted held up his hand. "But I already had one sales pitch tonight. I'm just here for some fun."

"Sales pitch?"

"Yeah, Occum. Trying to get me to invest in his, uh, business. I assumed that's why you were here too. Though now talking to you, I see I was wrong."

I shook my head. Familiar humiliation flooded me. I was an idiot. The pieces fell into place. The biker wasn't giving up.

"Why are you here?" he asked.

"I shouldn't be," I mumbled.

"Clifford Rutledge, you said?" Buffount asked appraising me.

I nodded.

"Occum mentioned some renovations. You're the inspector?"

I frowned. That wasn't even remotely right, but I had already mucked up this situation. I nodded without commitment.

"Pulling double duty as a professor? I don't get it."

"Lack of resources. The only other certified PE, er, Professional Engineer, moved out of state. I stepped in to help."

"Gotcha." He scratched at his chin. "Excuse me. I gotta see a man about a horse." He got up and left.

I groaned and dropped my head back. So much for that. And to know this was Occum's doing? Best to leave before he found me again. This night had been a total waste. Though, I did get to see her again. Not that I cared. Not that I continued to search the room for her. I was going to leave now.

After just one more minute.

CHAPTER 5

SUZIE

It was an ambush. That man, Clifford Rutledge, had no idea he was being thrown into a viper pit when he came here tonight. I tried to get his attention the second I spotted him. I wanted to warn him that Occum was gonna throw whatever he could at him, namely me. But he was stuck talking to Titty Teddy—a regular at the G-Spot, not-so-affectionately called so for his taste in the largest-chested women in the club. I wanted to avoid those grabby hands if I could.

Occum had me dancing and working the room so I couldn't warn him directly. I warred with myself. I had a job to do tonight. But I also knew I couldn't let this man be played. I wasn't sure why I felt the need to warn him, except that he struck me as a good and honest man —even if he didn't know how to dress.

I walked around getting drinks and making small talk with the men until finally, the Professor was free. I just needed to pass by and talk to him. No big deal. I talked to men all the time.

"Hey, Short Fuse," a regular called out, distracting me. "Get me a whiskey."

I would not hit the customers. I would not hit the customers.

"Sure, doll." I flashed a quick smile.

After delivering the drink for no tip, I headed back toward the Professor. If I could just get a moment with him, maybe I could find a way to convince him. My stomach churned at what he might ask for in exchange.

Occum was talking to Titty Teddy himself when he spotted me headed toward Clifford. He abruptly ended their conversation and cut me off before I could get to him. I exchanged a glance with Clifford before focusing on Occum.

"What are you doing?" Occum blocked my path with his arm, keeping his face friendly.

"I was going to talk to the Professor, like you asked."

"I didn't say *talk* to him." As he spoke, he stepped forward, forcing me to walk backward until the bar hit my back.

"I just meant, I was gonna go get 'em." My nerves were getting the best of me. I could hardly focus on my performance all night. As soon as I saw him, my knees just about gave out. I could hardly speak.

"Wait a minute. I got other plans for you."

"But you promised—"

"I know what I promised." Occum grabbed my upper arm and squeezed. "Don't forget who you're talking to."

I swallowed and bit my tongue to keep from making things worse.

"There's a room over there." He pointed to a door off the main hall. "Go in there and wait. Don't speak, Short Fuse, or so help me."

I sucked my lips back in.

"I'll send in your man. If he doesn't want you, I'll send in another girl he *does* want. He isn't leaving here until he agrees to sign off. Do you understand?" His fingers dug deeper into my arm.

I nodded.

"Whatever he wants. Whatever his tastes. You give it to him."

Tears burned the back of my eyes. I lifted my chin and swallowed back my fear. I refused to let Occum see any of that.

"I don't give a shit if he wants to tie you up and wear your panties. You do it, whatever he asks. You get me that goddamn signature."

"Okay," I managed to croak out. I wanted to fight back. I wanted to tell him no, but my fear muted my anger.

"Don't disappoint me. You won't get a second chance."

My legs were about to give out. I wanted to curl up in a ball. I wanted someone to hug me and tell me it would be okay. I used to be able to rely on Occum for at least a little support. He'd been so angry and mean lately. I rested my head on his chest. He sighed and it ruffled my hair. He wrapped his arms around me and I felt so much relief I thought I might start sobbing.

"It's okay." He held me a minute longer and I blinked up at him.

"I'm sorry. I'll get that signature. I promise." Even as I said the words, I knew I wouldn't be able to come back from this.

"You understand what's at stake here don't you?"

"Yes."

"That's my girl." He kissed the top of my head and pushed me toward the room.

"Give him a minute. I'll bring him to you," Occum said.

I glanced to see that Titty Teddy was back at the table and the two were lost in conversation. I'd lost my chance to warn him. Any hope of talking to him was gone.

My heart hammered against my chest. I wanted to stop stripping. I wanted to dance on my own stage. But I didn't know if I could do what I needed to make that happen. I just prayed Clifford Rutledge would sign off because I had no other options. Every step brought me closer to a line I never thought I'd cross. But this was my life. My choices had all led me to this point. There was no changing those facts without doing what Occum asked. I had to live this role a little longer if I wanted to be someone new.

But it didn't change the fact that with every step toward that room, I felt like I was giving something of myself away I could never get back.

Clifford

I had scared off Bouffant only to realize that I hadn't even been invited to woo investors in the first place. I had been invited to be bought off. Again. This reeked of bikers, not academia. My head fell back. The moment I saw the passionate dancer, I should've known I was wrong about everything. Had I really thought she wanted me? That it was just a coincidence to see her again? I'd let myself hope, and that was my first mistake. I wished I'd left with Jack.

Buffount returned a few minutes later surprising me from my musings. He smiled and held up a fresh drink as he settled into the same relaxed position as before. I felt his gaze flick to me several times.

This night could still be rectified if I could just be a smoother talker and try to convince him to invest in my research. We sat in silence a while longer. I debated what the proper course of action was when the dark-haired dancer reappeared. Occum had backed her toward the bar; her face was pale but there was a stubborn set to her chin.

Instantly, my heart hammered against my chest. My slumping posture morphed into rigidity as I tried to casually watch their inter-action without seeming obvious.

"That's Short Fuse Suze." Ted grinned knowingly at me. I cleared my throat. "Go talk to her. She's a girl just like any other," he said.

I studied the full beer I held. "I, Uh." Suze. That's her name. I hadn't expected that. Ridiculous.

"She won't bite. Unless you pay extra." He chuckled.

"I wasn't—I—"

"I saw you. She's a real looker. She'd be putty in your hands if you talk all that academic mumbo jumbo to her."

I shook my head not able to think clearly, embarrassed at having been caught staring. His large hand engulfed my shoulder and shook it until I made eye contact with him.

"Listen, girls like that don't have a lot going on upstairs. A couple of four-dollar words and she'll do anything you ask. If you catch my drift." He winked at me.

"A girl like her?" I fought to keep my face neutral.

"You know, fine as hell but dumber than a box of rocks."

"How do you discern that just by looking at her?"

He gave me a patronizing look. "She isn't dancing here tonight because she likes the workout. Some girls play to their strengths."

Rage spiked my adrenaline but I held it at bay. Hearing the typical preconceived notions from this man had me unaccountably furious. "She's likely a product of her upbringing. She's just as capable as anyone here to make something of herself."

"Right." Ted snorted. "And I sprout wings at night and fly around town."

"She was not given the same opportunities as you and most of the men in this room."

"Now listen here, I made my own fortune. You hear me?"

"No. I'm sure you worked hard for your success, but you also had the advantage of being a white male."

"Excuse me?"

I shook my head to clear it and took a moment to collect myself. "Would you give that woman a job if she came up to you?"

"Probably not. We're a family company."

"Explain why you said that."

His brow furrowed. "Like I said, some women are made for fun."

My fist clenched involuntarily. The idea that people could be treated so casually as objects had always boggled my mind. Who decided who was of value and who was expendable? The hypocrisy caused me to lose track of my point. I could make the connections in my head but, as always, I couldn't find a way to accurately communicate them.

Maybe he sensed my frustration because he changed the subject, "Tell me, what's the research you want to do. What's your end game exactly?"

"By proving my theories, I'll have tangible evidence to bring to the state board to show the impact that programs like free public transportation could have on the chances of success in a life. It could change everything. It could change how children are raised, by equalizing the playing field. Or at least getting closer to it. It could improve towns, resulting in a benefit to society as a whole."

"This sounds like some socialist stuff and I'm not on board with that."

"It's not that simple. We aren't talking about designating the path someone would follow only increasing the opportunities so that people can have the freedom to choose their own path. But I'll need the time and money to organize statistics and do studies." I relaxed my hands down at my sides. No praying mantises here.

"I get what you're saying." Buffount sat forward with his elbows on his knees and studied my dancer, er, the dancer, still talking with Occum. "So you convince me I'm wrong." A slow smile spread over the man's face. "Yeah, I like this. You get that girl there, the one you been drooling over, to convince me that I was wrong about her."

"What do you mean? How?"

"I don't know, you're the genius." He lightly punched my shoulder. "Find a way to show that she's where she is based on prejudice or whatever bull you were spitting and I'll fund your research."

"You're serious?" I focused fully on the man now.

He slid a cocktail napkin closer to him and pulled out a silver pen from his pocket. "Why the hell not? I donate to the school every year anyway." He started to scrawl across the small square. "Maybe I can get a library or something. Show up those bastards at Shaw Dairy. Them and their fancy statue." He mumbled the last part mostly to himself.

"What are the conditions exactly?" My throat was tight and a weird feeling crept up my spine.

"You transform that girl over there from stripper to someone I'd hire. No better yet, an academic like you. I'm having my big annual Christmas ball down at The Ranch in December. You bring her and if you can pass her off to all my friends that she's a legitimate professor-type, then I'll fund your research."

"But she's a person." This couldn't be real. He spoke as if debating buying a lotto ticket.

"Yeah, so? I'm not asking you to hurt her. If you're so confident in your ability to transform her life, then you'd see you're doing her a favor. According to your own words. Change her white-trash talk.

Change how she dresses and carries herself. Stuff some knowledge into that pretty little head. You'll be giving her opportunities she never had. If that's all it takes to be a success. You do that and convince my friends she's a woman of high social standing and well-breeding, then I'll believe what you say is true. Otherwise, I hold fast that if she wanted to, she could change her life but chooses not to."

"This doesn't make sense—" I shook my head, getting ready to stand.

"How about a million?"

I blinked rapidly. I swallowed down shock keeping my face as close to neutral as possible. Was this for real? That much money...I could be funded for a few semesters with research assistants. My heart raced at the possibilities and he talked like it was pocket change. This was a woman's life however, not statistics cooked up in a lab.

"I—I—Straight towards research?"

"Sure."

"You'd have to go through the university. Make it official, makes sure one hundred percent of funds are allocated toward research and not overhead." I'd been burned before by not specifying.

"Sure. Whatever. You draft up the contract. Just make sure I get a wing or a classroom or something."

"I need to think."

"Seems to me like you need to think a little less and do a little more."

"Why would she agree to it? I wouldn't lie to her," I said.

"That's for you to figure out." He glanced at his watch. "Look, if you're not interested..."

"No. I am. I think. I just need more time."

"I don't got all night, boy. I may change my mind without all this good time atmosphere around me."

The napkin had his signature and the unbelievable offer written in blue ink, bleeding through the napkin. It was right there. All I had to do was grab it.

"You're serious? That much money? You don't even know me."

"I know a man the second I meet him. If you want it bad enough, you'll do it."

When I looked up again, my gaze immediately found Suze. Occum had a hold of her upper arm, his grip strong enough to indent her soft skin. I blinked back anger and half stood.

"I'm serious about this offer," Buffount pulled my attention to him. "But I won't wait forever. You have until tomorrow."

"Excuse me, Mr. Rutledge?" A woman dressed in lingerie tapped my shoulder. "Mr. Occum would like to speak with you."

"Looks like you're up," Buffount said. "He does a hard sell. Make sure you know what you want going in."

Momentarily distracted by the interruption, I turned back but Suze was nowhere to be seen.

"I'll call you," I said to the man, not sure I meant it but feeling the need to end the conversation.

The shocked confusion that had settled over me during that surreal conversation melted into frustration as I followed the woman to a side door. I couldn't think about the potential funding right now. I had to deal with a crook who wouldn't take no for an answer.

CHAPTER 6

SUZIE

*C*lifford Rutledge walked into the private room and my carefully constructed internal pep talk went out the window. My hands and toes went numb. Shit was getting real—er, this was one clucked-up situation. Behind him, the door shut and clicked loudly. His face changed from apprehensive to glaring. Occum sat with his arms spread wide over the back of the small velvet couch, one leg crossed over the other. I was tucked back into a corner so he couldn't see me at first, despite the room being only a few square feet.

"Mr. Rutledge, so glad you could meet us."

At Occum's greeting, Clifford's mouth turned down and he scanned the room. When his gaze landed on me his eyes widened slightly before he slipped on a cool mask of disinterest. I recognized that move to self-control, because I did it all the time.

I smiled. He frowned.

Okay, that wasn't the start I'd hoped for. In fact, instead of looking even remotely happy to be there, he seemed seconds away from flying off the handle. His fists were balled with arms crossed tight across his chest. His chest rose and fell quickly.

"What's this about? It's unethical to have contacted me as though this were a university function."

"I did no such thing. You were invited to a party, nothing more. Now take a seat." Occum gestured to the portion of booth between us.

"No." Clifford turned to leave but the door was locked. "This is illegal. I'm being held against my will. Open this door."

My heart started to race. I didn't think the professor was necessarily gonna be happy, but I didn't think he'd be this ticked off either. A vein in his neck was all but popping out though he kept his voice calm. Occum looked as cool as ever though, slowly stroking his long beard.

"I can tell you're a man of strong moral fiber. That's admirable," Occum said. "But every man has his price."

Occum gestured to me. I stepped forward.

"You think you can throw her at me? Like that will change my mind?" His words were calculated but licked by fire. "I'm not interested in anything she has to offer."

Heat of humiliation traveled up my chest. Of course, he wouldn't want someone like me. He wouldn't want to lower himself to my level. My own rage started to simmer. That anger gave me courage.

"Occum?" I stepped closer to both men, keeping my demeanor cool but inside I was crawling with angry fire ants. "Why don't you let the two of us get acquainted for a bit?"

Occum looked back and forth. I gave him a small but assuring nod. He stood.

"That's a great idea. Short Fuse here is my best girl."

"I said I'm not interested." The words were low and even.

Occum squinted as he assessed the other man. "I got plenty of girls to choose from."

I'm sure the color drained from my face. If this man didn't go for me...I didn't know what I'd do. My anger was flushed away with a wave of panic. Clifford studied me. My heart was pounding in my chest. He had to choose me. I only had one shot at this. I poured all my heart into staring back at the man, praying he could hear me. Please pick me. *Please.*

He may not be interested in me or what I had to offer but our eyes had clashed like this before. It was like an invisible power line connected us. I poured all of my emotion into it just like I had on stage that night. A thousand hours passed as he held my stare.

"It's not going to change anything," he said eventually.

I let go of a slow breath, tingling with relief. Occum's mouth pulled into a slow smile.

"We'll see about that." Occum stood and went to the door.

"You can't just lock people in rooms until they agree to your terms." Clifford stood back to allow him to use the key.

Occum turned a cold smile in his direction. "Watch me."

He was out the door before the other man had time to react. Clifford beat on the door with all his rage. "Open this door!"

"You can beat it until the cows come home but Occum isn't coming back until he gets what he wants."

"This is absurd. You cannot lock a man against his will." He stopped his banging to look at me. "How are you not more outraged?"

I shrugged. I mean, it wasn't great, but I was pretty much used to this behavior from the men in my life. "He's just proving a point."

"I'm calling the police."

He reached into his pocket. My hand was on his arm to stop him. "Wait. Can we just talk for a minute?"

This close his face looked younger than I originally thought. He was actually quite handsome behind the frown that wrinkled his forehead. Sure, his eyebrows needed plucking and his salt and pepper hair was in desperate need of a good trim, but cluck, he was handsome. His dark eyes flicked back and forth between mine.

Something hardened in his gaze as he watched me.

"I'm not interested in what you have to offer."

I pushed back the anger from that comment. I was wholly unused to being refused but punching him square in the nose wouldn't get me anywhere. This wasn't about my pride. This guy wanted logic.

"If it's not me it's gonna be another girl, or another way."

His fist dropped from the door to hang at his side. He took a deep breath and actually seemed to be listening to what I had to say.

"Let's just talk," I added.

"Talk?"

"Yeah. I've heard good things about it. You use your mouth to form words and those words make sentences."

"Clever." His voice was flat but I swore he looked at me a little differently, like I'd surprised him. I gently tugged him by the wrist to the sofa. He fell into it, a sorta shocked look covering his face, but doing it anyhow.

"He can't lock us in here," he said but his protest was half-hearted.

"Shhh." I pressed my fingers to his lips.

"Wh-what are you doing?"

I pulled back and stood before him, letting him take in my body. The purple suede of this getup made my eyes pop, not to mention what it did for my figure. I always got the best tips when I wore it. But his attention remained locked on my face. He genuinely had no physical interest in me, far as I could tell. What the actual cluck?

The lights around us dimmed and slow, sensual music started. Dancing for men came with the territory. I'd done it a thousand times. I had no idea why it felt like my knees might give out at any minute. I took two steps back and began to rock my hips to the slow tempo.

"I thought we were talking?" His arms gripped the couch next to his legs.

I lifted my arms into the air gathering my hair up along the way. It dropped slowly as I continued to sway, feeling the long waves fall softly on my shoulders. I closed my eyes to absorb the music and make for a better performance. I couldn't see his reaction, or more so, his rejection. The song was "OT" by Niykee Heaton. I chose it for the naughty lyrics, the sexy tempo, and the sultry voice. Now I let it take over me. My hips moved, hands traveled, and to be honest, I felt it.

At the climax of the song, I opened my eyes again. His focus moved from my hair to my face to my hips, then shot to the ceiling when I caught him staring. He let out a slow breath. His mouth moved like he was counting down. So maybe not totally immune to me after all.

I sucked in my lips to keep from smiling.

"Suze—"

"It's Suzie, actually."

"Suzie," he repeated then brought his gaze to study my face.

"Nice to meet you, Ford."

"Ford?"

"Suits you." I shrugged.

I smiled. He frowned.

Okay, so that's what we did then? He was not going for this. Time to up my game. I snapped at the waist and bent forward to run my hands up my legs, starting at the straps of my heels, slowly moving up my calves, past my knees, rubbing my bottom, hips, and stomach. Just as my hands were about to cup my breasts, his gaze moved to the ceiling again.

"Can you please stop? Just stop. I'm trying to think."

I froze.

Okay, so the good news was he wasn't gonna be seduced. But the bad news was he wasn't gonna be seduced. Despite the foreign feeling of total rejection, I was also immensely relieved. Unfortunately, that didn't change the fact that Occum had demands. I glanced to the camera in the corner. The little red light was flashing.

Cluck. Cluck. Mother clucker.

Coming back in front of him, I bent to whisper in his ear. "He's watching."

"What?" He leaned back to look me right in the eyes. They moved between mine. Our faces were close enough that his breath tickled the strands of hair at my ear. Goosebumps prickled down my neck.

"I get that you don't want me, but we have to go through the motions or we're never getting out of here."

He blinked at me but closed his mouth with one small nod.

"Play along."

"What? How?" His Adam's apple moved up and down with a loud swallow.

I slid into his lap. My knees hugged him as I draped my arms over his shoulders and started grinding myself to the music. The heat from his body lit me up from the outside in. Immobile, he seemed to be fighting some internal struggle.

"Touch me, Ford," I whispered.

"This is a bad idea." His voice came out strangled as he lifted his hand.

CHAPTER 7

This was a very bad idea. My hand moved up Suzie's thighs. She ground against me, undulating and provocative. She was very, very good at her job.

The atmosphere of the room had shifted. When I had first walked into the room and saw her, my wariness had flipped to rage. We were pawns in his game. She was being used by Occum and if not her, then another. I was still mad. Somewhere. Under the heat of our bodies, and the sweet clean smell of her hair that brushed over me.

"Take this off," she tugged my blazer off my shoulders. As her hands moved down my shoulders her eyes widened with surprise. "What do you do in your spare time, Professor?"

That was inappropriate. She shouldn't call me that. I should push her off me.

"I rock climb."

I helped her tug my jacket the rest of the way off. I was on fire. She squeezed my biceps as she licked her lips. Could she be feeling the heady power of our physical connection as well? Her cheeks were high with color and, though I tried very hard not to notice, her nipples were beaded under the suede material of her top. It was obviously a tactic for seduction. Rationally, I understood this. Yet, my arms flexed under her perusal to their own accord.

When she moaned with approval, my inner caveman picked up his spear and beat his chest with pride.

"You're supposed to be touching me," she whispered.

I hadn't realized that my hands were back to gripping the velvet of the couch. My body could clearly not be trusted to make its own decisions right now.

"I still think that's a bad idea." It was more important than ever to remember why I was here, despite the act for the camera.

Suzie's face when Occum suggested another person for me said enough. For whatever reason, she had been chosen for this task and she was afraid. Seeing that fear in her made me act irrationally—something I abhorred doing.

She grabbed my wrist, bringing me back to the here and now. She moved my hand to the smooth slope of her waist.

"We can keep it PG-13," she said as she thrust again, undoubtedly feeling the state she'd put me in. What programming did she watch where this would be considered PG-13?

Her skin was warm and soft but muscles flexed just beneath. What might it be like to touch her everywhere? Where was she softest? I had been studying the curve of her shoulder when I lifted my gaze back to hers. Her chest was rising and falling quickly. Her gaze moved to my lips. She licked her own.

"Ford." That name was a whisper on her lips. It triggered something in my brain that crackled down my spine.

The music hummed through our bodies; with her on top of me, we were completely connected. The heat flushed her neck. She'd stopped rocking. We both sat perfectly still except for the mutual rise and fall of our chests. The song stopped and our labored breathing was audible.

She leaned so slightly forward I would have hardly noticed except I was watching her lips so carefully that I could tell they were a fraction closer. What it might be like to taste them? I never felt raw attraction like this. It caught me unaware. It felt so real.

But it wasn't real. She was doing her job. Well.

"UT Professor Caught with Stripper," flashed through my mind.

"Suzie." I stood, gently pushing her off my lap. "I'm not signing off on that work."

She stumbled to steady herself. Whether it was an act or not, she was taken aback. In an instant, her face changed from stunned to furious. Her nostrils flared and her brows sharpened enough to cut. Her mouth opened to speak. I couldn't listen. I held up an arm to stop her.

"No. I know you're supposed to give me what you think I want but there's nothing you can say or do to change my mind."

Her arms crossed over her chest. Her lashes fluttered as she took in my words. Her hands smoothed through her hair and she flicked her gaze to the corner above my head.

"Why are you being so difficult?" Her words were a harsh whisper. "Fine. If I'm not good enough just take the money and leave." Her ears burned red. "What's it going to take, for crying out loud?"

"It isn't about money." Some deep instinct urged me to comfort her. I fought it, as I fought all superfluous emotion.

"It's your pride then? Can't back down now, can you?" She pushed hair back from her face.

We stood facing off. I counted back from ten as I waited to calm down. Pride had nothing to do with it. Aside from maybe pride in doing my job.

"The blueprints didn't match the tour he gave me."

"So what?" She threw her arms out to the side.

"You don't understand, there were—"

The door slammed open. Bright light filled the room. Suzie gasped and her hands flew to her chest when Occum walked in. Then her face visibly relaxed, like she was willing herself to calm down. Occum was unreadable as he took us in standing inches apart. She stepped back and lifted her chin.

"I made my instructions clear," he said. "This is not a time for discussion."

I eyed the door. I could shove past him and make it out of there but I didn't know what would happen to Suzie.

"I tried to do this the nice way." He pulled out a long knife from the holster under his leather vest.

"These tactics are getting ridiculous," I said. Occum thought his intimidation could work on me. He didn't know what I'd already survived.

"Occum, babe, things were going well." Suzie stepped between us. Kept her voice calm and charming.

Her action was unexpected. Why would she care if I got hurt when I was the one who wasn't doing what he wanted? I clasped her shoulders to move her to safety but Occum was faster than me. He grabbed her by the hair and ripped her away from me and into his grip. Time slowed down in that moment, but I still couldn't stop him.

"You had one shot to do this," he spat at her, raising the knife to her throat.

"I—I—," she gasped. Her eyes were wide but she didn't struggle.

He wasn't threatening me. He was threatening Suzie. As far as he was concerned she was the one who failed. Not me. Maybe he knew he couldn't get away with hurting me, but…

"What the hell is wrong with you?" I reached for her but the blade twitched.

Suzie gasped and I forced myself back. I couldn't make this any worse for her.

"She knew the consequences if she didn't do her job." Occum's voice remained infuriatingly level.

Suzie's face was devoid of all color. Her eyes were wide and unblinking.

"This is absurd, you can't just—"

Suzie yelped as he squeezed her tighter.

"F-fine. I'll think about signing. But-but I need time." A stupid idea formed before I could stop it. "I want her. To come live with me. Till Christmas."

"What?" he said but loosened his grip.

"I need a research assistant."

"Research?" His eyebrows lifted. He looked between the two of us. "Is that what you call it now?"

Suzie watched the exchange with an increasingly confused expression. I didn't have a plan. I wasn't thinking. I just knew I couldn't let her get hurt.

"Yes," I said. "Three months. She comes to live with me. Exclusively." I added on and almost winced at myself.

"Exclusively?"

"No G-Spot. No stripping. No others."

For the first time since he grabbed her, Suzie looked like she was gonna speak but I gave her a subtle shake of my head while Occum used the blade to pick his teeth, lost in thought.

This was insane—this whole night was—but maybe I could protect her and get what I needed, too. I would have to talk it through with her, but now was not the time—even if she thought the worst about me in this moment. Her pallor had a greenish tint. Of course. Who wouldn't be sick at the thought of essentially being sold like cattle?

"Sign now. Prove it," Occum said. "I brought the papers." He touched his leather vest with the thumb of the arm around her.

"Let her go first."

Occum shoved Suzie away. She stood staring between us, arms wrapped tight around her middle.

"Now sign," Occum growled.

"No. I said three months. I don't know that you won't take her away right now."

Occum seemed to play out his options. "Three months?" he asked again.

"Yes." I repeated, growing increasingly angry. This whole situation was surreal. With effort, I evened out my voice and unclenched my fists to diffuse some of the rage bubbling to the surface. But I couldn't sink to his level. I had to outthink him. There was no way in hell I would sign off that work, but I could buy us some time.

"What about her cut from stripping?" he asked.

"I have a research grant. Money for costs. Whatever she normally makes will be covered."

At this, Suzie's jaw fell open. Occum slowly grinned. He slid the knife back into the leather holster. He was going for it. He was actu-ally going for it.

Shit, he was going for it.

The realities of what that entailed would have to be analyzed later. I wouldn't be able to relax until Occum was out of this room.

"Looks like you did your job after all." He grinned at Suzie.

Suzie didn't speak, but her attention was carefully split between me and Occum. He needed to leave. Now. I wanted to break that man's face, but her life was at risk.

He clapped his hands together loudly. "Okay, well I'll let you two lovebirds work out the details later, on your own time. Short Fuse, get back out there and finish your shift."

Occum slammed his way back out of the room. Suzie and I exchanged a look. "I can explain."

"We need to talk," she said at the same time.

"I know, it's not what—"

"Not. Now. Give me your phone." Her hands shook as she reached for my phone and tapped at it for a moment. "Meet me at this place around nine tomorrow morning. I put in my number too."

She shoved the phone roughly back into my hands. We stayed like that for a fraction of a second, my hands around hers, eyes locked. Her mouth opened as though to speak but she snapped it closed again and left without another glance at me.

I slumped back onto the couch. "What the hell have I done?"

CHAPTER 8

CLIFFORD

Suzie was late for our meeting. At half past nine, my self-indulgent annoyance started to melt into worry. What if Occum had done something after I left last night? He had agreed to the arrangement pretty easily all in all. Money talks I suppose, and he was used to trading women like commodities. But what if she wasn't okay? Or worse yet, what if she decided against being used as a pawn in this weird struggle between her boss and me?

The diner was nice, at least. It was decently busy early on a Sunday morning. A few tables were occupied and a few singles sat at the counter. One waitress buzzed around the diner nonstop as she called out orders to a fry cook in the back. The coffee was superb and the drive to Green Valley from Knoxville was straight forward and quick. So I had been in a neutral mood until her tardiness pushed me decidedly toward cranky. Lack of consideration of other people's time was disrespectful. And being angry at her was easier than reflecting on my own actions, a little voice deep inside pointed out. I ignored that voice.

I took out my wallet to throw down money for the coffee when Suzie finally strolled in. She wore cut off jean shorts and a tank top despite the fall weather. Her cowboy boots were seasonally appropriate, at least. I didn't miss how all sets of eyes watched her saunter across the restaurant toward my table, some with interest, but most with visible disdain or disgust.

"Hiya, Ford." She came in on a cloud of perfume and noise. She slumped into the booth across from me slapping her bag down. "Colder than a witch's titty out there." She shuddered dramatically. "Why the frown?"

I had been frowning at the people staring at her and whispering. I was about to tell them to mind their own business.

"You're late," I hadn't meant that to be the first thing I said but her laissez-faire attitude riled me up. And why did she have to say my name like that? Like it was a sigh of relief. After last night. After everything, she strolled in like nothing had happened.

"Yeah. My bad. I ended up getting home after three this morning. My dogs are still barking." She looked around and waved down the server. "Daisy's Nut House has the best coffee and doughnuts in all of Tennessee and anybody that says otherwise gets socked in the face. Hey Beverly."

"Hey, Suzie." Beverly swung back around the table. "Shouldn't you be at church?"

Suzie looked up at me and then to Beverly. She popped her gum loudly. "Went last night." She winked. "I'll have a coffee and a cinnamon crunch doughnut. And a chocolate. Oh heck, and a frosted." She glanced up from the laminated menu to tell me, "I burn a lot of calories dancing."

Beverly tutted before asking me, "Want anything to eat, sugar?"

"No, thank you." I'd already eaten. Hours ago.

Beverly sniffed looking at Suzie with haughty attitude before going back to the doughnuts. Suzie seemed unaware of the other woman's judgment. She toyed with the menu and stacked sugar packets and looked everywhere but at me. We sat in awkward silence. How does one gracefully proposition a stripper into being the subject of a social experiment this early on a Sunday morning?

"Y'all enjoy," Beverly set down the food and coffee.

"Thanks, Bev." Suzie stuck her gum on the side of her plate.

Beverly walked away mumbling something about the Sabbath day.

After a minute of picking at her doughnut, Suzie said, "Maybe we should have gone somewhere else besides Green Valley. Not everybody appreciates my...career choices."

Her cheeks were red as she spoke, and what I initially took as oblivious disinterest may have been masking anxiety. Suzie exhibited classic signs of posturing to cover up the fact that she was nervous. She likely felt the judgment coming off the other patrons as strongly as I did. It was almost tangible.

"The coffee is very good here," I said.

When she looked up, her mouth quirked into a half smile. My heart thumped loudly once before returning to its cave of solitude. She took a large bite into one of the doughnuts.

"This might be the perfect segue to discuss our meeting." I cleared my throat. "Last night was..."

"Wild, right? Sorry about that. Occum's a little crazy, but mostly harmless."

I blinked at her. She had a knife to her neck last night. I couldn't fathom how she could possibly claim that. I was about to launch into a series of examples of how wrong that analysis was, but reminded myself of our purpose. Most of what she said and did was an act. It was difficult to discern fact from lie when a person was always pretending. Likely, last night had shaken her to the core as much as it had me.

"Right. Be that as it may, we are now bound by a contractual agreement. Albeit a verbally binding one."

"What?" She looked up and her eyebrows came together.

"My research. I wanted to explain my intentions."

She swallowed a large bite down with effort, her eyes widened. "Wait, there really is research?"

"Yes, of course. What did you think?" I glanced around wondering if anybody was listening. "Wait, did you think I was asking for..."

She made a gesture like that was exactly what she thought. She slumped back and crossed her legs on the seat.

"Thank cluck. That's a relief. To be honest, I was late because I wasn't gonna come. I didn't know if you were gonna want me to live with you to play into some crazy kink, like dressing up like your mother or something."

"What? No! I—wait. Have you done that?"

"Not me." She shrugged. "But there are some unusual tastes around here." Her eyes widened meaningfully. "Well, anyway. Thank goodness you weren't serious about living with you. Rather ballsy to lie right to Occum's face though. That's not gonna end well."

"I was serious. I do need a, um, research assistant." Though I may have stretched the truth about signing off. I just needed some time to formulate a plan of action.

"Why did you say it like that? You hesitated."

"I didn't hesitate."

"You did." She crossed her arms, chest blazing red. "Is this a sex thing or not?"

"Suzie. No." I leaned forward and whispered, "And keep your voice down. That woman over there looks like she's about to have a heart attack."

She glanced over her shoulder. "Oh, don't worry about Scotia Simmons. Her face always looks like that. What's the deal then? What do you need me until Christmas for?"

"I've been offered substantial funding to continue my research if I can satisfactorily produce a real-life example validating my thesis."

I had called Bouffant that morning needing more than ever to see if he had been serious in his offer. And though he sounded groggy and slightly reticent, he agreed to send the necessary paperwork to the school first thing Monday morning. Having this confirmation was such an intense weight off my shoulders I had almost forgotten about the biker holding a knife to Suzie's throat last night. Almost, but not entirely.

"Okay," she said exaggerating the vowels. "And where do I fit in?"

"You are my sample subject."

"Meaning?"

No time like the present. Just put it out there. I clasped my hands on the table between us. "I propose you spend the next twelve weeks living with me so that I can use you in an experiment on inherent social bias. After which, by Christmas, I would present you to a group of observers to see if you have successfully passed yourself off as one of the scholarly elite."

She'd been in the process of using a sugar packet to gouge a piece of food out from between her teeth when she stopped to stare at me. "Say what now?"

"I propose you spend—" I started the same speech I prepared overnight but she held up a hand.

"Yeah, no, I got the gist. I'm just processing the crazy that came out of your mouth."

The awkwardness of this topic caused the tips of my ears to grow warm. "I have a roommate too. If that helps." One who was still angry at how little information I gave him last night.

"Sure?" her head shook back and forth.

"It isn't—it's not a sexual arrangement. I'm not interested in that." She frowned with skepticism but I kept speaking, "I would be interested in adjusting some of your physical attributes and idiosyncrasies in an effort to present you as an academic to a man on a ranch."

"Come again?" Her voice was lifting along with her eyebrows. "You want to present me to a man on a ranch after you change my outfit? Listen, I appreciate that you think I'm smart enough, but I'm not hanging right now."

My concentration stuttered. Her presence had the effect of a strong wind on a stack of papers. I needed to catch my thoughts and organize them. "I'm explaining myself poorly."

I looked up when she grabbed my hand.

"Take a deep breath and start over." She shrugged. "It's just me. Short Fuse Suze, Green Valley's best dancer." Her gaze bounced around my face like she was worried.

I took her advice and restarted. "Do you like being a stripper?" I tried a different approach.

She frowned. "I'm a dancer. I enjoy dancing." She considered her answer. "Most of it."

"Is that the profession you'd like to have long term?"

"I guess. I dunno. Where you goin' with this?"

I pressed further. "Why do you do what Occum tells you?"

She frowned and crossed her arms. "He's family and family looks out for each other."

I tried again. "Funding secures my tenure. That's what I want and dream about every day. That's the goal I'm always working toward. What's yours?"

She braided her hair over one shoulder only to comb through it and start again. "Well, I was hoping to stop stripping." She flicked a glance to me like she was waiting for the other shoe to drop.

"I'm not passing judgment. I'm genuinely curious."

She considered me. She uncrossed her arms to pick at a spot on the table. "I want to be a real dancer. I'd like to have my own Vegas style show. I won't have to take off my clothes. I could come up with real routines. A couple of the other girls said..." She trailed off. "It's stupid. I just thought...I mean, I guess, that's what I want. But it's whatever. Occum said I could stop stripping if I..." She focused on the table.

"If you get me to sign?" I finished for her.

She nodded.

"I have an investor. He said he'd fund my research substantially if I could pass you off as one of the academic elite. A professor, like me."

"Me?" She started to chew on her thumb until she caught herself and sat on her hand.

"Yes."

"Well, that's easy." She shoved another chunk of doughnut into her mouth. "I can grasp my pearls and speak fancy with the best of them," she said around a mouth full of food.

"It's more than that. It's etiquette lessons, conversation topics, language, education in several areas. Obviously not as deep as someone with an actual degree, but enough to make it believable. And of course, your accent."

"I don't have an accent. You're the one with an accent." She crossed her arms and it emphasized her cleavage.

I quickly looked up to her face. "To many people, the regional Southern accent is often interpreted as uneducated."

"Well, shit, I am uneducated."

"And swearing is another thing you'll want to work on."

She squished up her face. "I'm working on that. Okay, I think I get it. So you want to spend the next few months making me classy so you can show me off at this party?"

"Yes."

"And then you'll sign?"

I hesitated. She sat up straighter. "That's what you said!" her voice grew high-pitched. "You can't change your story now."

"I can't in good conscious sign things off as they are now."

"Ford, you promised." She was even louder now. "Verbally binding. You said it."

"Shh, I know. Shh. I know what I said." I moved to her side of the booth. My hands reached for her shoulders to calm her but I balled my fists, reminding me to keep my hands to myself. She watched the actions with skepticism. "All I'm saying is that he will need to update the blueprints or make some safety changes. That's an easy fix. We have time to get that done."

"Okay." Her frown was in place. "If I'm about to change my whole life for your career, you better not screw me over on this."

"I won't."

We held each other's gaze. We were so close. I was reminded of last night and things I wouldn't let myself think about.

"Pinky promise," she said holding up her pinky.

I put mine in hers. "Pinky promise."

Her long eyelashes fluttered as she leaned forward to kiss her hand. I frowned, feeling ridiculous but I followed suit. Our faces were inches apart.

She watched me closely.

Her eyes were even more startlingly captivating this close. How could someone walk around life looking this beautiful all the time? How did she get anything done? She crackled with passion. Being near to her was risking getting burned.

I straightened to put distance between us and cleared my throat. She studied me and slid the last doughnut towards me.

"Thank you." I took a bite and chewed as she grinned at me.

My heart was racing like this because of what was at stake. Nothing more.

I admit I had my own preconceived notions about Suzie's capability to undergo such a change, but those were based on my own past insecurities that I projected upon her. Of all people, I especially understood what changing a person could accomplish.

She was unrefined, uncultured, crass—and she was my only hope. I shoved the rest of the doughnut in my mouth.

CHAPTER 9

SUZIE

$\mathcal{T}$he chick who picked me up was so hot I instantly distrusted her. Her hair was a shade of red that nobody was actually born with. But her roots were perfect, so it was definitely her natural color. She had an impeccable style that was biker/boho/pinup-girl chic that made my lounger jumpsuit feel cheap by comparison. It shouldn't work but it did on her.

"You Suzie?" She asked examining me over the top of stupidly cute sunglasses.

"Yup." I was glad that at least my hair was on point and my eyelashes were real.

"Sweet. I'm Gretchen LaRoe. I'm your ride."

My reflection in the car frowned. When Ford and I discussed how all this would work I told him I had a car but Daddy needed it. Not that Daddy went anywhere but the bars. I didn't tell Ford I had no way of getting to his place and decided to just use one of those rideshare things. I guess I'd expected some fancy all black sedan with a driver who wore dark glasses and never spoke—maybe all sexy-like with tattoos and big muscles. Anything but a redhead in a Honda Accord who snapped her gum loudly when she looked me up and down.

It felt weird to have someone drive me around. I wasn't sure if I should sit in the back like Ms. Daisy or what.

"Need help with the bags?" she asked.

There wasn't much—a suitcase and my work bag filled with essentials like makeup and dry shampoo. Sad how my whole life from this trailer could fit into a couple of bags. She got out before I could respond. Her fur vest and flawless skin were way too sophisticated for this town. She looked like she belonged in LA.

She tossed my stuff into the trunk. "Cute pants. Your ass is banging."

"Thank you." I blinked at her. "I know."

I still couldn't believe this was happening. Maybe I was in shock. When Occum threatened me that night, I didn't think he'd actually hurt me. But then Ford came up with this crazy scheme. Everything happened so fast from then I hadn't had a chance to think about it all that much. I was used to living in the moment though. No point in planning ahead.

The trailer screen door slammed and my heart sunk. Daddy must've heard me, hangover or no. He barreled out of the trailer in a stained wife-beater and his tighty-whities.

"Oh Lordy," I muttered to myself.

Gretchen raised an eyebrow. "Your dad?"

"Yeah. Give me a minute."

She snapped her gum again and shrugged. I stepped toward Daddy with my arms out like he was a wild raccoon. "Go back to bed."

He glared past me and frowned at Gretchen. She checked her phone unfazed.

"I knew you'd leave. I knew one day." His red, mushroom nose flared as he spoke. "Just like her."

"I told you I'd be back in a few weeks. And I'll still come check in on you every week and go grocery shopping."

I didn't look at Gretchen because I didn't need to see her judgmental eyes. Her with her perfect stupid style and me with my white trash trailer and drunk dad.

"Yeah right. That's what your momma said too. Tell me how that turned out." He held a hand over his bloodshot eyes to protect them from the midday sun and looked at the car and Gretchen again like he was trying to place who she was. Daddy barely knew what the internet was; there was no way in hell I was about to explain ridesharing.

Behind me, the trunk slammed shut. This was humiliating and I just wanted to go already. "Daddy, I gotta go. You'll be fine. And go put pants on. We talked about this."

In more movement than I'd seen from him in years, Daddy ran down the metal steps and grabbed for my hand. "No. No." He tugged as he swore. "You can't go. You just gonna leave me to fend for myself?"

I tugged back. "Daddy!" But I was so caught off guard I fell on my backside into the gravel. "Dammit."

"You can't just leave me."

"I'm not leaving you."

"Okay, that's enough." Without warning, Gretchen came around the car holding a baseball bat raised above her head. "Drop her or I'm breaking your knees, old man."

My dad did as he was told and stepped back. "She's my little girl. You got no right."

"She wants to leave."

He flinched at her words. I hated that look. Like he couldn't understand why life kept taking everything from him.

"It's okay." I looked between the two of them. "It's okay. He's going inside now."

She didn't lower the bat and her gum snapped a bubble loudly. Her eyes were unreadable under the giant shades. Of course, Mrs. Albensi chose that moment to come out of her trailer. She had a cat under each arm and wore the same mustard-colored polo and white polyester pants she always wore.

She gestured with a cat—Shortcake, I think—toward the bat. "Whack him upside the head. He's got it coming."

"Mrs. A, mind your business." I put a hand on the bat and pushed it down. "I promise. He's harmless."

My dad frowned at that. "Sure, I'm just an old man. Used up. Nobody wants me. Nobody cares about me. I'll just go bring a toaster in the tub with me."

"We don't have a tub, Daddy." Or a toaster, actually. "And I'm saying for the last time, I'll be back by Christmas. And every week till then. You'll be fine."

He crossed his arms. He glanced to Gretchen who was repeatedly smacking the bat into her palm and staring him down. Mrs. Albensi hovered on her small cement pad, greedy for gossip to tell the neighbors.

"How'm I gonna make it to Friday?" he asked me in a quieter voice. "The house is dry."

I let out a sigh. So that was what this was really about. Honestly, I was surprised he had put up so much of a fight; not even Occum fought to keep me. I reached into my bra and pulled out a twenty. "You gotta make this last until the end of the week. That's all I got till then."

He examined it with a frown and grunted. "I don't know."

Next to me, Gretchen took a step forward. He pocketed the cash and walked quickly back up the stairs. "Okay, that's fine. I'll see you Friday with more."

"That man still needs a whoopin'," Mrs. Albensi grumbled as she went back into the house.

Daddy swore something about the flammability of cats as he walked back inside. Gretchen tossed her bat into the backseat and got in the car. I did too.

We didn't speak as she drove the winding road toward the city. She didn't seem bothered by the silence between us and bobbed her head to the country station. For whatever reason, I couldn't handle the idea of her thinking Daddy was just a mean drunk.

"He's usually more weepy than angry. He's just mad cause I'm leaving for a few weeks."

She held up her hands for a hot second before putting them back on the wheel. "You don't owe me an explanation. I've had my fair share of drunks."

I frowned.

"I don't mean anything by it. This part of the country, most people are either drunk or high to beat the boredom. He'll be fine when he sleeps it off."

"Right," I said. He will sleep it off. Until the next time.

"So you headed to classes?" She pointed to the map on her phone attached to the dashboard.

"No." I laughed.

"That's UT ain't it? Go Vols!" She made a hand gesture that may or may not have been offensive.

"Yeah, but no, I'm not a student." I snorted.

She turned the music down. "Why's that funny?"

"Not a person 'round here thinks I'm smart enough for school."

"I don't give a fuck what other people think. I didn't ask them," she said.

I smiled because, to be honest, she reminded me of a sassier version of myself—which I hadn't even thought possible.

"You don't have to tell me though," she said when I took too long to answer. "I was just making conversation." She turned up the radio.

I wasn't sure how to talk about it. I wasn't used to talking to people at all, especially not women. The sad fact was the only people I talked to were lonely men who wanted to use me as a therapist. Even with the other dancers, it was just about routines or tips to help with calluses and such.

"I'm just gonna try living with this guy for a little bit. It's sort of complicated," I finally settled on.

She glanced over and turned the radio back down. "Isn't it always. Well, you don't owe me or anybody else an explanation."

I bit back another smile. "You're making it hard for me to hate you. And I really want to hate you for those sunglasses and your hair."

She laughed a quick, "Ha! That's great. Because normally I have the opposite effect on people."

"Me too." I couldn't help but smile with her.

We fell into silence again and I wished I were the type of person who made friends easily. Not everybody wants to hang around after they learn what I do for a living. If she knew, she'd not be so chatty. After a few more minutes of silence, Gretchen spoke up again.

"You ever just get so sick of how people talk?" She asked out of nowhere. "Hearing the same damn stories over and over? Like some people are just video game characters and only have so many lines of pre-programmed dialogue."

I thought about her question, random as cluck as it was. She glanced over at me again.

"Yeah," I said. "Sometimes at work, I hear the fellas tell the same story over and over every night." The pick-up lines were always the same too. The drunken boasts. I couldn't actually remember the last time somebody caught me off guard. Except Ford. He'd definitely caught me off guard.

Not for the first time since Daisy's I thought of him and his confusing behavior. It was like he wanted me but he was ashamed of it. It made my stomach sour every time I thought about it, so I pushed those thoughts away.

Gretchen continued on. "Right? Like, don't you have anything better to talk about?"

"Yeah. I once heard this guy who comes to my work tell at least five people about how he needed a filling. Nothing happened with the filling. He just needed one. That was it. That was the whole story. But he told every single person who talked to him."

"Exactly." She laughed and hit the steering wheel. "Like, do you think we all care about your dental hygiene?"

"Sometimes I want to yell, 'Nobody cares!'" I let out a breath. Daddy did that too. He'd tell anybody that looked at him how Momma left. And that was over twenty years ago. My mouth kept running. "But then I sort of end up feeling bad for them because if they have to tell strangers about the little stuff it means they don't have nobody else to tell." I couldn't believe I said that. My cheeks heated. I didn't know why I was so honest but her rawness brought it out in me.

She was too quiet and I waited for her to call me an idiot. I'd punch her in the face and jump out of the car.

But eventually, she just said, "Huh. That's a good point. I didn't think about it like that. Maybe I should be more patient."

Tension released from me when I realized she wasn't going to make fun of me.

"But also some people are just boring," I added.

"God save me if I ever live that life." She prayed to the roof of the car.

She pulled off at the next exit and I felt like I was a world away from Green Valley. A giant cement sign for the University of Tennessee in old-fashioned script introduced the area. Massive, fancy buildings were lined with manicured lawns and planted flowers. Every block had a new, interesting looking building with signs like "College of Agricultural Sciences" or "Haslam College of Business."

"This is all one school?" I asked as she drove through streets packed with students. Each new turn added to the knot currently twisting up my insides.

"Yeah. Pretty campus, huh?"

I swallowed down a sick feeling. I'd lived my whole life less than an hour away and I'd never been here during the day. I'd gone to a few parties that I hardly remembered but I didn't want to think about that. I'd thought this would be an easy request. Change my outfit and act classy, no biggie, but now I realized how wrong I'd been. I was gonna stick out like Reverend Seymour at the Dragon Bar. Not that Reverend Seymour would ever be at the Dragon Bar because he knew where he belonged. I was so anxious now I couldn't sit still.

We turned off the main road toward residential housing.

"Oh look, we're getting close. This is a nice neighborhood."

I nodded, taking it all in but unable to speak. I didn't fit in here. My clothes that made me feel sexy at home seemed tacky and out of place here.

"Looks like you're just around the corner." She turned the car and stopped in front of an older two story. "This house is amazing. I love the classic Victorian architecture. That plaque on the porch means it's a historic home."

I nodded, too in awe to speak. This couldn't be where Ford lived.

He was a teacher and he had a roommate. I pictured a run-down student house like the college party I'd gone to—hardwood floors stained with beer and no furniture.

But even from the car, it was easy to tell the house was as beautiful on the inside as it was on the outside. The gray siding was highlighted by a bright blue front door with matching window trim. The front room had big bay windows just made for a giant Christmas tree to fill it in winter.

With leaves sprinkling down from the surrounding trees, the heavy clouded dark sky, and the uncarved gourds and pumpkins on the front porch, it was a perfect autumn scene. My heart clenched in my chest. This home was beautiful—way nicer than any home I'd ever lived in.

I wasn't going to fit in here. I needed to be back with the boys and the bars. This was a mistake.

"You okay?" she asked.

I nodded my head but I gripped the car door handle like it was keeping me from spinning right off the earth.

"Go on. I'll help with the bags."

She was out of the car again before I could answer. I wasn't ready. The car felt safer than going in. The Black Demons were a little scary sometimes, but at least they knew me.

Gretchen tapped my window. "You okay?"

"Yeah." I gathered courage I didn't feel and got out.

"You don't have to tell me anything, but you don't look so good." She squeezed my hand and it was so unexpected I turned back to look at her. "You tell me if you aren't safe. I'll take you straight away from here. The bat was just the beginning of the weapons I've got packed away."

Her words made my throat tight. "No. No, I'm fine. I guess it's different than I thought."

She studied my face intently.

"Okay. But if for one second you feel like you want some company you call me." She grabbed a card from her back pocket and handed it to me.

I didn't know drivers had cards. It said, "Gretchen LaRoe - Fashion Consultant, Driver, Landlord, and all-around Badass," and then her phone number. I snorted.

"You like that? You feel free to call me if anything gets weird."

"Okay."

"Also, if you're ever bored or in Green Valley again, call me. I'm in a club that meets every other Thursday. We meet at different places, so just let me know if you wanna get out. You should come. You'd get along with all of us. I got a good feeling about you."

I nodded but didn't take my eyes from the house. I was only half listening. "A book club?"

"Well, sort of." She shifted her eyes away. "We'll talk more soon. Seriously, call me if you need anything."

She squeezed my hand and I felt battle-bonded with her. She was safety and Green Valley and everything I knew. My throat was too tight to swallow. If she only knew who I really was—the things I'd done—she would never have said all that.

I squeezed her hand one last time, feeling such an odd connection with this stranger before letting go, knowing I'd never see her again. I grabbed my stuff from the trunk and headed toward the front door. There was a soft yellow light coming through the windows and a tall figure moved around inside. I climbed the front steps and prayed for courage.

CHAPTER 10

CLIFFORD

I shook out the umbrella on the front porch and heard laughter from within my house. A grumble escaped me. It had been a lousy day. Technical issues caused a delay in my class. The rain persisted until my coat was soaked through. A student asked for an extension because his Tinder date went all night and couldn't I "help him out, man to man." The refusal resulted in him calling me a name under his breath. All I want to do was come home to a quiet house, listen to some nice jazz, and read in my study undisturbed.

But that wasn't going to happen because she was in there. And she was laughing with Jack. They were in there laughing together, having the time of their lives while I sloshed off wet loafers. I left my coat and bag on the hall tree and made my way toward the gaiety.

Around the corner to the kitchen, I found them in the breakfast nook.

"And then this armadillo went chasing after him...It was the wildest thing I'd ever seen." Suzie could hardly speak she was laughing so hard, and Jack was silent with laughter, hunched over holding his gut. "He kept running and running...this wild animal was running straight at him...we all just watched because, to be honest, he's kind of a jerk cop sometimes."

"An armadillo?" Jack shook his head, wiping his eyes.

"Yeah, someone told him they had leprosy or something."

She took a deep breath. Her long legs were extended onto the bench where Jack sat, but not quite touching him. Empty plates and half-drunk glasses of wine sat on the table in front of them. When Jack finally looked up, he spotted me waiting in the threshold.

He waved and Suzie turned.

My frown deepened. "Leprosy isn't a joke. There are several cases a year because armadillos are the only other carriers besides humans."

"Hiya, Ford." She sat up straighter, legs dropping to the floor.

"Ford?" Jack slipped on an amused grin. I waved him away. I hadn't decided how I felt about the nickname yet. "I thought you hated nicknames?"

"It's not a nickname, it's an identity," Suzie said without seeming to be aware of the truth to those words.

Her astute observation surprised me. A thought to analyze later, when I wasn't worked up.

"I see you ate already," I changed the subject.

"Yeah, we just cooked up pasta and sauce." Suzie stepped to the sink. "We saved you some. Want me to nuke it up for you?"

It smelled amazing. I wanted to sit and eat but there was work to be done and I had already interrupted their fun. The laughter had already stopped and the room had palpable tension. Some people slip so easily into conversation. I always feel like the needle busting the bubble.

"Shouldn't we get started? With our limited timeline, we should be working in the free time we have."

She tucked her hair over her shoulder and glanced to Jack. To Jack. As though he had any say in our plans. To me, she said, "Sure, grumpy britches."

"I brought home some textbooks to read."

"Ugh. Okay." Suzie had been about to scoop me some pasta but dropped the spoon and went to sit down. She crossed her arms and slouched back. "Reading is stupid."

"I'm going to pretend I didn't hear that," I said. Jack snorted. "We need to discuss your educational background."

"Well, that'll be a very short conversation."

"When did you graduate high school?"

"This is chicken-sh—this is stupid. I don't have to answer these questions." She stood up cheeks bright red.

"It's important to understand what I'm working with."

"Who," Jack corrected me quietly.

"I didn't mean—" I glared at Jack. "Don't you have papers to edit?"

He raised an eyebrow at me before slowly squinting his eyes. "Nope." He crossed his arms behind his head and kicked up his feet. "I want to hear more about this experiment you are doing."

I hadn't told Jack all the details because there wasn't a way of explaining that didn't come off a little unclear ethically.

My stomach growled and I crossed my arms over it. "There isn't anything to say."

"Suzie made it sound like there was. You didn't tell me you got funding."

I moved to wipe down the counter where someone had spilled parmesan cheese grumbling an affirmation.

"Suzie also said you're giving her a makeover? I didn't know you had the skills."

"Well, it sounds like Suzie told you everything. So we don't need to discuss it."

"Who peed in your Cheerios?" Suzie asked. "If you're mad at me about somethin' don't take it out on Jack."

"I'm not mad." The pot I had picked up to wash clunked loudly into the sink basin.

"Clearly." She gestured to the sink.

They both chuckled.

"It's not a makeover." I snapped. "I plan to change her clothing and general appearance but I'll also endeavor to modify her accent and teach her basic engineering concepts."

Suzie sucked in her lips and all the fun left the room again. I hated that I was being so short. Why did it feel like it cost so much to be relaxed? But this was my Suzie. No. Rather, it was my research. It wasn't a joke. I took a deep breath and counted.

"Sorry, man, I was teasing."

I glared at Jack. "My research isn't a joke."

Suzie looked between us and said, "I gotta go use the little girls' room. I'll be back." She scooted out of the room.

Jack crossed his arms and sat back to frown at me. "You know I think your work is valuable. Why're you really upset?"

I scratched the back of my head and let out a sigh. "I don't know."

Jack got up and moved around the kitchen, a minute later he put a plate of food in front of me. "Eat this and tell me your plans."

I did as told. After my hunger was blunted, I told him about Ted Buffount and his proposal. I didn't mention the signature or the misleading blueprints, afraid to see my own concerns reflected in his face.

"Okay." Jack looked up and then shook his head. "I guess I don't see how it all ties together."

"It was sort of organic. One minute I was fumbling through my pitch, the next he was offering money. He judged her from the second he saw her. It perfectly highlighted those inherent biases that I was talking about. If I can prove to Buffount and his friends that she is an academic based on changing a few things typically associated with class and intelligence, then he will believe me that the odds are stacked against some people. He'll pay for my research so I can be eligible for tenure."

"Where does that leave Suzie after all this?"

"What do you mean?" That itching sensation crept up the back of my neck again.

"You're going to dress her up and take her to fancy parties and rub elbows with the elite in society and academia and then what? She goes back to dancing for money and getting tossed around by bikers?"

The image of Occum threatening her flashed through my head. Would he hurt her? What if she held up her end of the bargain and he still refused to make the changes? She seemed to think he'd never actually hurt her.

I shook my head. "She'd be given an opportunity to change her life. Make something of herself."

Jack frowned deeper. "What if she doesn't want that? What if she wants something completely different?"

I scoffed. "I highly doubt that."

"I don't know. Something about this doesn't sit well with me. You don't love it either."

I couldn't meet his gaze. "He offered me a million dollars, Jack. A million dollars and I could make a real impact on people's lives. I could give whole towns a chance. I could keep people like Suzie from ever having to be on the path she's on. I could help kids like us who grew up with absolutely nothing and nobody believing in them."

He made a sound that we both made when we thought about our past—a combination of a grunt and a growl. Jack and I were the only people who knew the ugliest parts of our childhoods. He had his own trauma he'd recovered from. All of this was so much bigger than Suzie, or Jack, or even me.

"I know. Your work is important. I like her, is all."

If liking her made me lose sight of my goal it was a risk I couldn't take. I had to keep a professional distance. Everything I've felt for her thus far was attraction. A voice deep down tried to point out that I'd not felt this level of attraction before. I ignored that voice. The future was too important. I pushed back the empty plate.

"This will be good for her, too. She could actually make something of herself."

Jack frowned. "Just be careful. She seems like she's been dicked around too many times."

I nodded. The pasta sat heavy in my gut. I hadn't meant to sound like such a prick.

"This will be good for everyone," I said, and I meant it. The ends justified the means. Suzie would be fine at the end of all this and I could change the world. Or, at least a small corner of it.

CHAPTER 11

SUZIE

$\mathcal{I}$ eavesdropped on Jack and Ford from the hall, gripping the wall behind me as I fought the urge to throw up my dinner. *Make something of herself.*

He thought I was trash. He thought that I was nothing. This wasn't a surprise to me. That's what everyone thought of me. He was no different. That's what I got for eavesdropping.

I'd show him who was trash. I thought of where I could hurt him the most, but something stopped me. A little voice inside wanted to prove I wasn't Short Fuse Suze. I was here to clear my debt and get my VIP stage. Nothing more. He could change my clothes all he wanted but everybody would always treat me the same, so who cared. I would just get through this and get what I wanted. I'd read his little books and play his little games, but this was all a waste of time.

I crept silently back a few feet before I stomped down the last few stairs and into the kitchen giving them plenty of time to hear me coming.

"This house is frickin' amaze-balls," I said perkily.

Jack smiled at me but Ford only examined the table with focus.

"Isn't it?" Jack got up and collected the plates. "I had a professor who was moving out just as I achieved tenure. Clifford and I were foster brothers and had been rooming most of our lives at that point. I couldn't afford it alone and we had a good thing going, so here we are. Ford is a clean-freak, like me."

"Cleanliness is godliness," Ford grumbled.

"Germs are the enemy," Jack said with mock seriousness.

Boy, they were in for it with me. I could already see Jack chasing me around with a bottle of Lysol. I ran my hand over the granite countertops that were modern but still managed to fit with the whole vibe of the place. There were little details everywhere I couldn't get over, like tiny potted plants, colorful pieces of art, and appliances I didn't recognize. Who knew people lived so low-key classy?

"What's this?" I pushed down on a handle in a glass jar and it came apart. I made a face and set it down.

Jack smiled. "A French press. Makes for better coffee."

I nodded, impressed as I examined all the things. I eventually made my way back toward the guys. "Where do we start?"

"Clothing," Ford said. "We will go clothes shopping as soon as possible."

"I don't need any new clothes." My cheeks burned.

Maybe he had extra cash for things like that. It's hard when every extra penny you earned went to a motorcycle club or your bottomless father. I chewed on my lip.

Jack flicked a glance at me and then back at his roommate. "You know, I bet there are plenty of places to find super cheap clothes, like Goodwill."

I made a face, I couldn't help it. I had champagne taste on a Coors Light budget.

"The mall will have better options. It won't cost too much. Maybe a couple hundred tops," Ford said.

"Oh, is that all?" I snapped.

Maybe Mr. Fancy-Pants could drop that sort of money without thinking but I wasn't able to. I felt my blood start to boil. I was about to French press that coffee maker on his face.

Ford must have picked up on my sarcasm because he finally

glanced at me. I stood with my arms crossed and I'm sure I appeared about two seconds from a fight.

"I forgot to mention that all fees incurred during this experiment will be covered. The clothes, the books, whatever we need to purchase, is all part of the experiment fees."

Jack and I stared at Ford. Then at each other. We were mirrors of open mouths and wide eyes. We turned in unison back to Ford. "How am I just learning this?" I asked.

At the same time, Jack asked, "How much?"

Ford frowned, before providing a staggering number. Like a month's worth of shifts at the club.

When Jack and I looked at each other again, we were smiling like demons at an orgy.

"Well shoot. Let's go shopping."

Jack tagged along when we left the house, which was totally fine because I liked him more anyway. He was funny and nice and he didn't look at my tits like they should be under a nun's robe. He was the opposite of Ford in every way. It was amazing they got along so well.

Jack suggested an ice cream stop for fuel before shopping. We went to this place where they spread your ice cream out onto frozen marble and scraped it up with what looked like a paint scraper to make these little rolls of ice cream. I thought it was sort of a rip off because they were rolls of ice cream for more money instead of a whole cup. But Ford paid using Rich Dude's money and it tasted clucking good.

"I think I like yours the best," I said as I dug my spoon into Ford's cup. It was a chocolate something or 'nother and it tasted like the German chocolate cake from Donner Bakery.

He made a sour face and slid it away from me. "Well, you wanted the peanut butter disaster, so you have to eat that. Also, it's impolite to just dig into other people's food."

"Oh, excuse me." I rolled my eyes.

Jack was enjoying his sherbet with gummies. It sounded gross, but just to put salt in his grits, I dug my spoon into his and made a big show of eating it.

"Mmm." I licked the spoon with way too much tongue and groaned. "Sticky and sweet."

Ford frowned and his leg started jumping up and down. I smiled at Jack and he laughed into his cup shaking his head.

"Please take your elbows off the table and sit up straight," Ford snapped at me. "If we're using research money, we're using this as an opportunity to learn."

"Fine." I did as he told me and sat ramrod straight. I crossed my ankles and pushed my knees together like when I went to church as a kid. I started to fan myself and put on a thick Southern belle accent, "Oh me, oh my, I just cannot contain myself around such handsome specimens of men." I ran my hand down each of their arms and made big ol' doe eyes.

"Suzie," Ford said in a deep warning voice.

"Ford," I copied with a frown.

"This is my life's work. Try to take it a little seriously."

I felt a little ashamed. I knew how it felt to have people look down on the things that made me happy. People like him, actually. But I'd be better than that. I would show that I understood. So I corrected my posture. "Okay, I'm real sorry."

He looked at me like I still might be yanking his chain so I made my face serious. I held out my hand, palm down and limp, like I'd seen in movies toward Jack. "How nice to meet you Mr....ah, what's your last name?"

"Jones," he provided.

"Jack Jones?" I asked.

He shrugged. "Suzie Samuels," he said with a smirk. "Maybe we were meant to be Marvel characters."

"I'll have to take your word on that one. Well, Mr. Jones, it's so lovely to meet you this fine autumn day. Please, tell me more about your line of work."

I tilted my head to the side sweetly and listened intently. Jack looked to Ford, who nodded with approval.

"How'd you do that?"

"What?" I turned to answer Ford's question.

"Your accent is gone. How did you do that?"

I thought for a moment. I hadn't done anything. I just thought about how I wanted to sound and did it. "I don't live in a swamp. I know how Yankees sound. Believe it or not, we have those fancy moving pictures in Green Valley."

Jack laughed and Ford narrowed his eyes. "You did the deep south accent as well. How'd you do that?"

I shrugged. "I dunno."

"Don't slur your words. 'I don't know.'"

I rolled my eyes. Of course, he had to criticize me.

"What other accents can you do?" Jack asked after he swallowed another spoonful.

"I don't know," I emphasized slowly while throwing shade at Ford.

"Try a British accent."

Ford sat back and crossed his arms.

"'Ello, gov'ner," I said, then added, "Please, sir, can I 'ave some more."

Jack cackled with laughter and I found I really liked to make people laugh when it was on purpose.

I kept going. "How's about you give me a lift in ye carriage, back to yer fine establishment." I didn't remember what movie I quoted, if it was a movie at all, but they seemed to like it.

"Okay, now less cockney, more posh." I musta made a face because Jack added, "Like Prince William and Harry."

"Oh shoot, shoulda just said that." I cleared my throat and thought for a second, replaying the interview where Harry had talked about Meghan Markle and it was so flipping adorable. "Good sir, you cannot possibly expect me to..." I struggled for a word and thought of the conversation with Ford a while back. I placed my fingertips to my chest, and spoke, making it up as I went, "I'm interested in focusing on manipulating her ingrained idiosyncrasies to prove my theories about inherent biases in our culture."

Ford had said something along those lines at some point. He wasn't British but he did talk like he had a stick stuck up his—

"Bravo." Jack clapped.

I stuck my tongue out at Ford. He blinked at me, a little crease between his eyebrows and his mouth partially open. Take that, sucka.

"Well, we could do this all day or we could go shopping." Ford wiped his mouth and threw his crumpled napkin in the cup of ice cream.

I looked longingly at the ice cream he hadn't finished. "Hey, I woulda eaten that."

"Actually, I'll have to skip shopping. I have to go teach." Jack stood up and stretched. "This was fun though."

I appreciated the toned muscles of Jack's stomach. He'd make a terrific dancer. His long, lean body was built for a pole. Would that be offensive if I told him that?

"You better show me what you bought tonight." He bent and kissed my cheek before waving a goodbye to Ford and leaving.

I lifted my hand to my cheek. Jack liked me. He had said so. He knew I was a stripper and yet he liked me. He never made me feel uncomfortable or stupid either. I liked him, too.

I found Ford was glaring at me and I dropped my hand from my cheek.

"Let's go home. I have work to do." He shoved up from the table and walked out. I collected the trash and puzzled over his behavior. It was almost like he was jealous; but he must see that Jack didn't like me like that. Maybe it was because Ford thought I was trash. He'd made that much clear.

"What about shopping?"

"Another time."

"Yes, sir," I mumbled and followed him out the door.

I thought he'd been pleased with my attempts at accents but he was back to being grumpy. I didn't want to spend time with him anyway. I couldn't do all the work. He'd have to make an effort. It was going to be a long twelve weeks.

Thwump!

My hair flew back from the poof of air caused by the stack of books dropped in front of me.

"Let's start here." Ford pulled up the chair next to me, his frown in place as he studied the names of the books on the spines facing him.

This was my hell. It's not that I hated reading; it's just that I had a hard time focusing. I always have. I'd rather be moving and dancing. I cracked open the first book and flipped through hoping for some pictures but saw only walls and walls of text.

"Remind me of your educational background?"

"None of your business." I cross my arms. "I don't have time for this. Let's do something else."

"Reading is crucial to development. Not only for the knowledge ascertained but the world experience. Fiction, non-fiction—it doesn't matter. Knowledge is power. When did you graduate high school? What classics have you read?"

I pushed back from the table. "This is stupid." My hair was in waves and I played with it to avoid looking at him. "Can't you just give me the CliffsNotes?" I could just Google it later. But even reading the wiki pages made my eyes cross. I was not a reader. Was that so hard to understand?

Ford looked up at me before glancing at his watch. "We don't have time for this. Have you ever tried audiobooks?"

"No."

"We can try that later. That can be your homework as we move on to other things."

Dread caused me to slump in the chair. "Homework?"

"I'm going to assume, as you're avoiding the question, that you didn't graduate high school."

A small pressure in the base of my skull started to grow. I wanted to grab this table with all these stupid books and flip it over.

"No," I admitted and heat burned my cheeks.

"Did you get your GED?"

"Ford. I'm too stupid for this."

He shook his head. "You aren't stupid. Not having an education makes you teachable, not stupid. I've seen how quickly you learn. Now stop avoiding the questions. GED?"

"Yes," I growled. "I worked at the Pink Pony for a while. The owner, Hank, insisted I had to." What a waste that was. But he wouldn't let me work until I did. I tried going to community college for a while but the travel killed me and any money I had needed to go to other people. An old pang of embarrassment swelled in my chest thinking about that guy in one class who asked how much I charged when he found out how I was paying for school.

"Excellent." He pulled out a tiny notepad from his pocket and jotted something down in deep cursive I couldn't read from this angle.

"What is that?" I pointed to his notes.

"Just things I want to make sure we accomplish these next few months."

I chewed my lip. "What's the point? What could I learn in this amount of time?"

He sighed and closed his notebook. He folded his hands over it patiently. "Our primary objective is to pass you off as a scholarly elite. You'll not have to be an expert in anything, but passable in everything. Basic education is a must. We'll need to focus on wardrobe, accent, vocabulary, and how you carry yourself."

"Is there anything about me that can stay?"

His gaze moved from my head to my feet. "No." It moved back to my hair that I twisted around my fingers. "Your hair is fine. Very healthy and clean."

"Well, knock me over with a feather. That almost sounded like a compliment." In truth that made me smile because my hair had always been a point of pride for me. I never had extensions and I took real good care of it.

"You should probably keep it tied back though. It's…distracting." He frowned and opened his notebook again to jot something else down.

"What does that mean? How can my hair be distracting?"

"Keep it up and out of the way. You're always fidgeting with it. It says a lot. When dealing with strangers and first impressions the less you give away with body language the better. The mystery can keep the suspense alive. They'll assume more, rather than less. Especially if you don't talk. You talk, and it gives you away."

My fists balled up and I wanted to pummel his face. I'd show him my roots. I'd kick him to next week with my favorite biker boots.

"Stop frowning. This isn't the time to be oversensitive. We both knew, going into this, the main objective was to change you. Unfortunately, for us, you'll have to speak though."

"So now what?"

"Now, we'll focus on elocution. The ability to provide lucid, grammatically correct English will speak more to your education than years of schooling. The accent stuff is cute but you need to be able to maintain a conversation, not just quote movies. That will imply education. Others will take you seriously if you speak clearly and enunciate your words fully. No charming Southern phrases." The snide tone of the way he said "charming" told me he found them anything but. "No cutting off words. No adding additional, unnecessary words."

"What do you mean?"

"Like 'real pretty' instead of beautiful or using curse words. Less is more. Instead of adding futile words, just take the time to find the correct ones. Take the time, period. Think before you speak. I suspect that alone will be your biggest challenge."

"You're a real asswipe, you know that?" I glared at him. Real pretty and beautiful had different meanings. Didn't Mr. Professor know that?

"Case in point." He dragged my chair closer. "If you're going to insult me, do so with decorum. Do so in a way that will make the person have to think to figure out if they've been insulted."

"Like what?"

"You clearly have not been burdened by an overabundance of education."

I paused, then fought a smile. "That's pretty funny." I sat back and let out a slow breath. "I need a drink."

"We haven't even started."

"I know, but you're already annoying me." I crossed my arms.

I knew that we'd be doing this, but it was humiliating to know that everything about me needed to be fixed. Oh, except my distracting hair.

"Hmm. Try again," he said. "Feel free to insult me. Get it all out."

I turned and our knees bumped. I wasn't exactly sure what he meant. But if insulting him was part of the work, I could get behind that.

"Your condescending tone makes me want to claw your face off."

"Better…" He tilted his head side to side as though mulling it over. "But not great. Work on it."

"Gladly." I smiled sweetly.

"Let's move on. Read this with me and then say it out loud."

He slid the notebook and turned to a page where large block letters filled half the page. He started and I joined in with him, "Around the rugged rocks the ragged rascal ran."

He looked expectantly at me. "Okay, now you."

I repeated the phrase. He studied my mouth closely and frowned. "No."

"What? I said it!" I didn't like how close he was and how his mouth moved slightly as I spoke.

"You mumbled it. Think of the words you're saying. Enunciate." As he spoke the last word he moved his mouth dramatically.

"Around the rugged rocks the ragged rascal ran."

"Again."

"Around the rugged rocks the ragged rascal ran."

"No. No. You aren't listening." He grabbed my hand and placed it on his chin.

His short beard was prickly and his skin was warm. This close, his scent surrounded me. It was spicy and clean, like a pine Christmas candle, but not so strong. There was an earthy smell underneath it too, like chalk or something. I liked it.

"Feel how my jaw moves," he said. "You're very observant and quick to learn. Watch my lips."

His compliment caused my heart to skip. I'd never been described as quick. I'd been called fast though. I cupped his chin with both hands, our faces less than a foot apart. It was shockingly intimate. I smirked at the silliness of this situation.

"Around the rugged rocks the ragged rascal ran." As he spoke, the muscles of his cheeks worked up and down, moving my hands with him. Who knew his jaw was so sharp and strong? His full lips moved with purpose.

I licked my own lips.

"Did you feel that?" he asked in a soft, scratchy voice.

I nodded once. I felt a lot of things just then. My hands dropped to my lap.

He lifted his arms and I stilled. He brushed my hair back off my shoulders and cupped my chin as I had just cupped his. His large hands reached almost all the way around my throat and his thumbs rested on my chin.

"Now, try again."

I spoke the phrase slowly and deliberately. As I did, his mouth moved along with me. His thumb hovered above my lips, grazing my bottom lip as I finished.

We sat staring at each other. My gaze moved from his frowning lips to his furrowed brow. "Good." He spoke hoarsely, cleared his throat then added, "Better."

I made a sound somewhere between thank you and "ungh."

"Let's try this tongue twister." He blinked away and placed his notebook between us. He studied the page for several seconds. "Okay."

I looked to the page and read alongside him. "Grey geese in a green field grazing."

"Now you."

"Grey geese in a green field grazing."

He frowned.

"What?" I asked.

"You aren't trying."

"I am tryin'!"

"Try-ing" he emphasized.

I groaned and threw back my head.

"You are more capable than this. Put effort into it and stop giving up before you start." He sat back. "And stop chewing on your thumb."

I tucked the thumb that had been in my mouth into my palm. "I want to take a break."

"We just started."

"I'm tired."

"Too bad. You have about thirty more of these tongue twisters to get through. Once I see serious improvement then you can take a break."

"You are being ridiculous." I overly emphasized each word.

"Better." He pushed back and stood up. "Now keep going. I have papers to grade."

"Oh, that's convenient."

"I can't sit here and handhold. You're going to have to work for this, Suzie. If you want to be better, you'll make yourself better. Otherwise, you'll find excuses to fail."

My mouth fell open.

"I, for one, think you are more than capable."

My trout mouth could think of nothing to say.

He frowned. "And I'll load up some audiobooks on your phone so you can listen to them tonight while you paint your nails or whatever it is you're doing up there." With that he left the room—his favorite thing to do after frowning.

When Jack came home I was still sitting at the table but I had my head down and was gently thumping it over and over again. A hundred stupid phrases were swirling in my brain.

"Did he break you?" Jack asked from the doorway.

I kept my head on the table but turned to him. He was eating an apple in the doorway.

"I hate him," I said.

"No, you don't."

"No. I really do."

"He's not so bad." He came closer and peered over to see what I was doing. "What's this?"

"Torture."

Jack smiled. "You're as dramatic as he is."

I groaned and closed my eyes.

"Six sick hicks nix six slick bricks with picks and sticks," he read from over my shoulder without missing a beat. "Damn. He isn't messing around."

"That one's just plain offensive," I grumbled.

"There's always a method to his madness."

I sat up and pressed the heels of my palms deep into my eye sockets until I saw stars. "Will you help me hide his body?"

He chuckled again and I bit back a smile.

"Where is the dungeon master?"

I stretched my arms overhead. "Hiding in his office. Making me do all the work." I was sick of sitting still. I needed to get up and moved around. "I'm surprised he didn't strap me to the chair."

"That's next week."

I shot my head toward him.

"Kidding, kidding." He wrapped his finished apple in a paper towel. "Mostly."

"I hate him, Jack. I hate Clifford B. Rutledge. What a stupid name."

"You don't hate him."

"Yes, I do."

"You hate that he's challenging you. You hate that he's not letting you distract him with your womanly wiles."

I frowned because that felt a little too close to the truth.

"No. I hate that he's an arrogant asshole that thinks if I knew the definitions to some four-dollar words then suddenly I wouldn't be such a loser."

Jack raised a sassy eyebrow at me. He hid a grin and I could tell he thought this was funny.

"It's not funny, it sucks," I said.

"I know for a fact that Clifford doesn't think that way about you."

"Then what's his deal?"

Jack shrugged. "He has high expectations for people he cares about." He raised an eyebrow as he let that sink in.

I opened my mouth to argue but then closed it again with a pout. High expectations? I didn't know that I had ever been held to any expectations before. I think I've always had the opposite.

"What's the word for the thing where everybody assumes you're going to be a fuck up your whole life?"

"For me, that was called 'childhood.'" He played it off as a joke but there was some deeper issue there. He changed the subject before I could dig. "At some point, you have to decide to stop letting other people define you and decide what you want to be for yourself."

His words mirrored Ford's. It would be easy to raise my hackles and get defensive. It was my natural response. But maybe I really could decide who I would be. Maybe I really could choose to be a lady of class instead of a stripper from Green Valley that lights bikes on fire. Ford said I was a quick learner; he believed in me. Jack acted as if my success was a given. I wanted to prove someone right—rather than wrong—for the first time.

"Dammit." Despite the ache in my backside from sitting so long, I pulled the book back over. "Fine."

"Atta girl."

"Six sick hicks nix six slick bricks with picks and sticks."

"There you go." He nodded with an impressed frown. "Now a hundred more times and maybe he'll let you leave the table."

CHAPTER 12

CLIFFORD

I knew it wouldn't be easy. That's why I allotted so much time for these lessons, but I hadn't expected Suzie to be so mulishly stubborn. After the disaster of last weekend, I developed a syllabus for the next few weeks. I couldn't improvise with her. The silly accents were a fluke but we needed to get serious. Bouffant had called to check the progress of our lessons. She was a quick learner, but we hadn't done anything but elocution.

Music had been blaring from her room for hours, rattling the windows until I was sure the homeowners association would call us. Whatever she was doing resulted in intense thumps that had the dining room chandelier swaying. I gathered my patience and made my way to the guest room.

I beat her door with a fist. After a minute of no response, I knocked again and opened it.

"Can you please turn that down—"

She was spread-eagle on the carpeted floor facing the door. Her cleavage was exposed as she leaned in half to stretch to one foot. Her cheeks were flushed with exertion and tiny hairs framing her face stuck with sweat to her skin. Her workout clothes consisted of a brightly colored sports bra that couldn't contain much of her and tight athletic pants.

"Ford?"

"What are you doing?" I asked unable to move from my position just inside the door.

She leaned forward and pressed something on her phone that made the music stop. "What am I doing?" She snapped her legs together and got to her knees. "You're the one barging into my room."

"I knocked." I looked down to where she was on her knees just a few feet in front of me.

I swallowed.

I stepped back at the same time she scrambled to stand. "Well, if I don't respond, assume I don't hear you and knock again."

"You shouldn't be listening to music that loudly. This is an old neighborhood. Our neighbors are in their eighties and would report me to the HOA at the first sign of rule breaking." They already assumed Jack and I were a couple and gave us begrudging stares that only got better when we hauled up their trash cans each week. I kept that much to myself.

"Fine, I'll turn it down." She grabbed a towel from the floor and dabbed her cleavage with it.

I stared resolutely past her and noticed her room.

"Good Lord, what have you done in here? You've only been here a few days."

Her comforter was half off the bed, the sheets twisted off one corner exposing the mattress. Bras, shirts, and various and sundry items were strewn over every surface, as though her suitcases, which sat open on the floor in the corner, ate too much and spewed the contents. Tiny brushes and tubes of creams and pastes were leaking out on the surface of the antique vanity that had come with the house.

She followed my gaze around the room and shrugged. "I've been told I'm not super tidy."

"Tidy?" I ran a hand through my hair. "It looks like you were attacked and used whatever you could find to defend yourself."

"Okay, okay. I get it." She folded the towel she'd been using and set it gingerly on the bed. As if that could help. Like putting sunscreen on a third-degree burn.

"Is that one of my tea towels?" I groaned. "It's like this room is the end of the wormhole where all the missing socks of the world disappear to."

"Okay, Ford."

"I mean seriously, where do you even sleep?" I gestured to the bed where more clothes and various corded hair tools occupied the only corner that wasn't twisted up. "Do you hide under the bed? Sleep standing upright in the closet?"

She stood to block my view of the room, with arms crossed and a serious glare contorting her features. "I get it. I'm a slob. Is there a reason you came up here?"

I could see I'd gone too far but, my God, how did somebody live like that? I focused on why I had come up, ignoring the clawing desire to tidy up. "I made dinner."

Her eyebrows shot up.

"We're going to have your first etiquette lesson on table manners," I clarified.

"Oh." Her shoulders slumped.

"Don't look so excited."

"No. Really. I am," she said deadpanned.

"This isn't a vacation. This is about change."

"Yeah, yeah. Let me change," she emphasized my repeated word. "And I'll be right down."

I had just finished setting the table when she appeared in the doorway. Her hair was still damp but in a soft braid over her shoulder. Her jeans were skintight and paired with an equally skintight cream sweater that left a large strip of midriff visible.

I cleared my throat and gestured to a chair. I had spent an hour cleaning and setting the table. The silverware and napkins were set with care and the accompanying dishware was precisely aligned.

"Dang, Ford. Looks swanky." She brushed right past me and went to the table pulling out her chair and slumping into it.

"Wait, wait. You're already failing."

She had a glass of wine to her lips and stilled. "Shit. What?"

"First of all, please refrain from swearing, at least while at dinner."

She rolled her eyes but came back over. "Sorry. I'm working on that. Mother clucker!"

My cheeks burned. "Feel better?"

"Just getting it all out of my system." She smiled sweetly.

"You know saying similar sounding words as a replacement defeats the point. All words are subjective to the culture, so it doesn't really change the meaning. Best to leave it out altogether, at least in the company of people. When you are alone you can cluck until the chickens come home."

She rolled her eyes but I swore she had to fight to keep from smiling.

"Secondly, please come over here. Let's pretend you've just arrived as my guest. We've already made all our initial greetings. You should wait for the host to dictate where to sit and when. Make sure your phone is off and away."

"Fine." She melted out of the chair with the insouciance of a teenager and shuffled in bunny slipper-clad feet back toward me.

"Nice shoes, by the way."

"Har. Har. Sorry, I didn't know I'd be dining with the Queen of England." She stopped in front of me with arms crossed and head tilted expectantly.

"Or you would have worn those cowboy boots?" I wished I hadn't said it as soon as the barb left my mouth. And as a barb is meant to do, it cut her. Her eyes shuttered and she straightened.

"Aren't you as sweet as watermelon on a summer day."

"I shouldn't have said that."

She shrugged. "Truth be told, those are my classy 'take me serious shoes.' Most of my shoes are platform heels." She toyed with the sleeve of her sweater, not meeting my eyes.

"Listen, this isn't about having fun. But it doesn't have to be awful. Etiquette has its place."

"Oh yeah?"

I led her to her chair by gently directing her with a hand on her lower back. "Table etiquette isn't about being a snob or trying to prove you're better. It's about having respect for your host." I scooted her chair in. "Etiquette highlights character. Or lack thereof."

I snapped out her napkin before bending to lay it across her lap.

"Thank you," she said. Her brow was furrowed and her mouth was open in a little "o" shape. I'm not sure what I had done to elicit that reaction.

"You're welcome." I cleared my throat.

I went to the chair across from her. She sat straight up, not moving. Her gaze moved over the setup on the table but wouldn't meet mine. I had made her uncomfortable and now she wasn't sure what to do.

"Table manners are all about not drawing attention to yourself. The more refined you appear, the more comfortable the other guests will feel."

"I feel super comfortable," she said dryly.

"Let's begin." I dished out food for myself before passing the dishes to her.

For all her grace in movement on the bar, she was loud and clunky in other areas. Every scoop of food clanged loudly against the serving dish. Every bowl was set down with a thud.

She frowned when she looked at me. "Now what?"

"Try to make as little noise as possible."

"Sorry," she said, not sorry at all.

"What did you do today?" I asked watching as she stuck her gum from her mouth on the edge of her plate.

"Worked on a new routine." Her frown grew as she stared down at the cutlery. "Shit, er, I mean, cluck, I mean, ugh! Ford, what fork should I use?"

"Always start from the outside and move in. The far left fork is for salad."

"'Kay." She frowned again. "I'm not having salad."

"At a formal dinner, they would likely bring out courses and clear the cutlery associated with it. Also, don't chew gum. Ever."

"Fine." She rolled her eyes.

"Sit up."

"Oh."

"Elbows off the table."

"For crying out loud."

"No talk of religion or politics, or anything crass."

"So, I shouldn't tell you about the mysterious stain I found in the bathroom of the G-Spot?" The tines of her fork audibly grazed her teeth as she took a bite with a grin.

"No." I made a show of setting my knife along the top edge of the plate when I wasn't using it. "What are your thoughts on closed-access academic journals and the business of publishing in academia?"

Suzie piled a mouthful of mashed potatoes into her mouth. "Wha—?"

I closed my eyes and counted backward from ten. "Please don't speak with food in your mouth. Also, there's no rush. Take your time, taking small bites so you can still talk if you need to."

"I don't want to talk. I want to eat. I'm used to cramming in meals between sets."

"Conversation is critical to good table manners. You have to learn to keep it flowing easily so that everybody feels included."

"Is that why you're such a Chatty Charlie all of a sudden?"

I nodded once.

"Well, I don't know what you're talking about. Oh, but I did hear something juicy about Jackson James."

"I don't know who that is. Is he a friend of yours?"

This time Suzie blinked at me like I spoke around a mouthful of food. She set her fork and knife down, and to her credit she did so as gently as she'd seen me do. She dabbed the corners of her mouth with her napkin.

"Ford, what's the point of all this? I'll never be able to hang in a conversation with people like you. The only current events I know revolve around Green Valley. I know about hair and makeup and shit, er, stuff you don't care about. We're from different worlds."

Though she spoke with anger, her cheeks were flushed and her eyes kept shifting to the side. I never meant to embarrass her. I set my silverware down as well.

"People are universal. You don't have to over think it. The truth is, you don't need to know much. Most people inherently want to discuss themselves. When in doubt, just ask people about their lives. Surface things, career things. You don't want to accidentally tread on toes or have them feel like they're being interviewed, but simple questions get them talking."

She looked up to the side and thought. "I can do that. I actually do that all the time when I'm working the floor for better tips. You wouldn't believe the stuff these guys want to get off their chests. I have heard some things over the years." She shook her head like she was trying to free them from her mind.

"How long have you been dancing?"

"Oh man, since I was legal." She cut delicately into a piece of broccoli. For as vulgar as she could be, I was astounded at how quickly she learned to mimic the nuances of my movements; the gentle lift of her pinky as she sliced, the delicate cut into her entree. "How long have you been teaching?"

"Since I finished my undergrad. I received my Ph.D. at the Georgia Institute of Technology and then I transferred to the University of Tennessee almost a year ago as an adjunct professor on a research stipend. I'm working toward tenure now, teaching mostly 101 Engineering classes."

"Oh yeah, you said that. That's why you want the money."

"That's part of it."

"What does that involve? Tenure?"

"I teach classes, write papers for publication. I'm on thesis review boards. There are a lot of facets. I support requests for the city, but only because I'm the only licensed PE in the area."

"PE? Like gym?"

"No, sorry. Professional Engineer. It's a type of certification. I got mine post-grad as a way to make extra income. There was only one other person certified for Green Valley and he moved out of state."

When I looked up from my food, she was watching me closely. She blinked and refocused on her plate. "Why do all that? What's so great about tenure?"

"It means security and respect." My fork scooted into the gravy pouring over the edge of my mashed potatoes and pooling onto my plate. "Then, I can slow down a little. Before tenure you push, push, push trying to get to the next level."

"It sounds exhausting."

"It can be. But it should be rewarding. If I can help change the future or make an impact it'll be worth it. After all the years of working nonstop, I'll be able to breathe."

I stopped talking abruptly and looked up. She was staring at me with a face I hadn't seen yet. Her chin was in her hand, elbow resting on the table. I cleared my throat, abashed at the raw honesty that had leaked out.

"Elbows off the table."

She obeyed. "It's okay, you know," she said without looking up.

"What is?"

"To have a little fire in you."

I scowled at my plate. I was talking about work. I wasn't passionate. I wouldn't let myself be passionate about anything. Control. That's what I was about. And I didn't like how she looked at me. Like I was interesting.

"I have to work." I pushed back from the table abruptly. "I'll clean up later."

She stood up when I did. If she spoke, I didn't hear her, because I was behind the door to the study in record time.

***

"Out with it," I called up from my desk where I was writing yet another grant begging for money as elegantly as possible.

Jack had paced past my office enough times to make track marks in the floor.

"You need to give her a break." He came into the room and folded himself into one of my chairs.

"She isn't progressing quickly enough."

"You know different people learn different ways. She's a physical person. Sitting there reading from a book isn't doing anything."

"What do you suggest?"

"Did you ever take her shopping?"

"Why should she be rewarded for lazy behavior?"

"Ford." Jack gave me a look I didn't like.

"Oh God, not you too."

"I like it. Fits you."

"Yeah, yeah." But I didn't tell him to call me by another name.

"Get her out of the house. She's gonna crack being locked up like this. I know you agree."

"Fine. But only because her clothes are..."

"Distracting?" He provided for me.

I shot him a disgruntled look. "If anything happens, it's your fault."

Jack grinned. "What could possibly go wrong shopping?"

***

Stupid shopping. Stupid Jack and his stupid ideas. Stupid short, repetitive sentences.

"Hey, Grumpy Face?" I looked up to see Suzie standing in front of me snapping her fingers. "Didn't your mother ever warn you your face would freeze like that?" She pressed a finger in between my eyebrows and some of the tension relaxed out of me.

"No," I said. My mother only gave orders, things like "find my pipe" and "don't tell the police about the people from last night" but those weren't refreshing anecdotes.

Then I noticed Suzie's outfit. "What are you wearing?"

"You said casual clothes." She twirled and stopped with her rear end facing me. She stood up on tiptoes and arched her back, as though it needed any more emphasis.

Her very well-sculpted derriere filled out a pair of cut off shorts —and then some. Her full cheeks peeked out from the ripped bottom hem, like an apple ripe for biting. Her top was a skin-tight white shirt with thin straps doing nothing to cover her black lace bra.

She continued to strut in the mirror, turning side to side and cupping her breasts to lift them. "I think it looks good. You don't like it?"

"I think it's great." This came from the gangly teenage boy who waited for his mom in the chair across from me.

"Thanks, doll." Suzie smiled. In the reflection of the mirror, she focused on me and her smile fell away. "See, he likes it."

I glared at him until he went back to playing on his phone.

"The goal was to get casual clothes for day-to-day activities. You look like you're about to go to a barn dance to get laid."

"You're just uptight." She snapped her gum with a loud pop.

Right then, the teenager's mom came out of the dressing rooms. She took one look at Suzie and clucked her tongue. I gave Suzie a pointed look as the woman yanked her gawking son away.

"Fine." She blew a large bubble before sucking it in with another loud pop. "What did you have in mind?"

"I don't know. Stop chewing your gum like a cow chews its cud. And no bubbles. No popping either."

She pulled her gum out of her mouth and stuck it to the face of my watch.

"Better?"

I snagged a tissue from the register nearby, peeling the gum off to throw in the trash. I wiped the surface until it gleamed perfectly again. Suzie stood with arms akimbo, tapping one foot impatiently. I tried to think about what my students wore but honestly, I never paid attention. "We should have brought Jack."

"Like he would know?"

"No. But he'd charm a salesperson to help."

"True. Girls don't like me. I don't know why. Probably jealous."

A blush spread on her chest. I had insulted her again. I replayed what I said but wasn't sure. I noticed she said ridiculous things like that the more upset she was.

"Don't misinterpret me. I think the choice is very flattering to your figure. It's just not right for our purposes."

She glanced up at me. "Oh. Okay." She looked in the direction of where the lady had been.

"And she was definitely jealous," I said it without thinking. I didn't know why. Except it was likely true. Or she was another person judging Suzie with only a look. Like I had. No, like Bouffant had.

That woman could keep her looks and sighs to herself. "It's those looks and comments that we are trying to avoid. She is judging you and has no idea what you're capable of. Prove her wrong."

She rolled her eyes but her mouth quirked into a smile. It was rare when Suzie directed her smiles in my direction. She often yielded them as a weapon on other men but I had yet to be the receiver of a genuine one. It was heady stuff. When her eyes locked on me it was as though the things I did and said mattered. It made me want to be better.

"Thank you for saying that." She placed her hands on my chest and she gently backed me to the waiting area again until I dropped into a chair.

My mind instantly jumped to the last time she pushed me into a chair, her hands running up my thighs, her hips grinding over me. My pulse began to race with hope despite my brain's pragmatism. She wouldn't do that here. Right? What would the point be? But I mean, if she felt it necessary, who was I to stop her? There went those wild thoughts again.

She smirked at me. "I'll be right back. I'm just messing with you. I got other clothes."

I cleared my throat, unable to speak. There was nothing pressing to say at that moment anyway. I shifted in my chair and adjusted my tight pants.

Since it was just us now, I called out, "You don't have many girl-friends?"

"Not really," she called back. "There're some girls at the club that I get along with okay enough. But I don't have time for friends."

I added "make friends with women" to the growing list in my notebook.

She stuck her head out. "I know you're not adding that to the list."

I tucked the notebook away.

She tracked my movements. "Hey, what about you? Where are all your friends?"

"I have Jack."

"That's one."

"One best friend is more than enough."

"He's your best friend?" She grinned. Her dark locks brushed against white shoulders as she leaned out of the doorway.

"More like a brother." I trailed off as my gaze moved to her exposed skin. Did the bare shoulders mean she was naked? Was her bra draped carelessly across the floor? What was she doing in there? What would she do if I came into the room and pulled the door closed behind me? Would she stop talking if I pushed her up against the wall and kissed her?

"UT Professor Caught Performing Lewd Sex Act in Department Store."

I swallowed. I was no better than most men. My attraction was getting worse the more time I spent with her. What I found crude and off-putting at first, I now understood as a front. Everything she did was an act to protect herself by playing into society's expectations.

"That's sweet." When I looked back up to her face, she was still smiling but with a heated look in her eyes. I couldn't remember what we had been discussing. I bent over and focused on fixing the cuff of my pants.

She came out a few times in various combinations of pants and skirts and tops with sweaters and scarves that suited her nicely. They were modest but appeared fashionable. With every outfit, her smile grew at her reflection.

"This stuff isn't too bad is it?"

I nodded.

"And I'll be a lot warmer. And look, pockets! Pockets everywhere." She slipped her hands in the long cardigan and twirled.

I smiled. It couldn't be helped.

"You'll need a formal dress for the party," I said, ready to wrap up. I had grown too comfortable with openly staring at her body. Her figure was a piece of art and every article of clothing suited her.

"Oh, it's only October. We'll have to come back. These dresses won't work."

"Excellent." I stood up and rubbed my hands together. "We're done."

"Not quite. You had your way with me. Now it's my turn." She shoved the stack of clothes into my arm.

"Phrasing," I mumbled unheard.

She led me to the men's department and loaded her arms up with clothes I would have never bought for myself. She shoved me into a dressing room.

"And you will show me every single outfit. Every. Single. One."

"This is humiliating," I growled through the door.

"No, this is fun." She cackled an over-the-top villain's laugh.

I ended up indulging her. It was easiest to let her win on some things. Battles need to be chosen. Also, I liked the way her eyes moved over my body when I came out in dark jeans and a fitted tee. I would never leave the house in it, but seeing her look me up and down bolstered my ego.

"Looks good, Ford. Looks real good." She looked away and then added, "Those clothes are very flattering to your figure." She stepped forward and ran her hands down my shoulders and picked off a piece of lint. "For a nerd, you sure have a lot of muscles."

I rolled my eyes. "You're very judgmental of educated people."

She tapped a finger on her bottom lip, ignoring my observation. "We just need to do something about those eyebrows and trim up your hair and beard."

"You do know how to ruin a compliment." But secretly I was proud of her self-correction. In fact, this whole shopping excursion had proven that she was a damn quick learner. I was a damn good teacher too.

"How old are you?" she asked breaking through my thoughts.

"Why?"

"No offense, I thought you were older than me. But in these clothes..."

"I'll be thirty next June," I said.

Her face paled. "Oh my God."

"What?" I looked down at myself again. "What's wrong?"

"I'm older than you."

I couldn't help the laugh that coughed out of me. "What?"

"I need to sit down."

"How old are you?"

"I turn thirty in January."

I scoffed. "Well, you're ancient then." But my tease did little to change her face. "Suzie, thirty is not old."

"No, but it's older than you."

"And?"

"I don't know." Her look was still far away. "I don't know why, but it bothers me."

"Get over it." I jostled her with my shoulder.

She jostled me back hard enough to make me stumble. "Fine. Let's go. First, we have to go pay. And by 'we' I mean you, Daddy Warbucks."

I hid my face. I hadn't exactly lied when I said the fees were covered by Buffount. They would be. Eventually, when he paid up. For now, I would use my own savings to pay for everything. She didn't need to know the details. No one needed to feel like a charity case.

"That it?" The cashier smiled and started to scan each item.

Suzie's eyes grew wider with each beep. Behind us, someone whistled long and low.

"Damn, that's a fine ass," a gravelly voice said.

Another said, "I know that ass."

Suzie tensed subtly at the sound of the rough voices before placing a smile on her face and turning around. "Hey, boys. What're y'all doing here?"

Her accent grew thick, taking on a character. She leaned back against the counter so her whole body was on display. I frowned. The two men approached, clearly bikers, clearly lost, and from the looks of it, ones she knew. They were both clad in leather and frantic facial hair. One had a hawkish nose and bright red hair that stuck straight up. He took his time to scrape his gaze up and down her body.

"Damn, I miss you at the G-Spot. Don't forget I called you for some private time." He sucked in his lips with eyes focused on her chest.

The other one, who was rounder with a gleaming bald head, crossed his arms and looked me over with a frown.

"I'll be back soon. Been busy." Suzie's face looked strained. To me, she said, "This is Cueball and Rooster."

The one she pointed out as Rooster pushed his chew into his lip and stuck out his chin in my direction. His voice was slurred as he talked around it. "This your man?"

Cueball gazed at me. These names were ridiculous and a little too on the nose. His face was impassive, but gears were turning as to why Suzie was with me. I'm sure if he could do math, it wouldn't add up.

"This is Clifford Rutledge," she said. Her introduction jarred me. She hadn't called me by my full name since we met. "He's a, uh, business associate."

None of us moved to shake hands.

"Business?" Rooster snorted.

Cueball laughed. "What? The business of showing your tits?"

Anger flashed through me. I was about to step up when the cashier announced the total for all the clothes. The amount was staggering. I handed her my card.

Rooster noticed the piles of clothes being hauled into the bag and grinned. "I see now. Business associate."

"Razor know about this? Seems like you got you a good deal here. He getting his cut?" Cueball said.

I opened my mouth to point out several mistakes in those sentences, but Suzie gripped my arm and said, "He knows. I pay Occum. Occum pays Razor."

"I'll be asking." Rooster frowned and spit a brown wad into a nearby flower planter.

She nodded. I couldn't speak; the rage threatened to boil over. Suzie looked forward coolly. Taking it. Not defending herself. This was not the woman I knew. This woman was passive, her face an empty mask showing nothing real. Where was the firecracker that spoke back and stuck up for herself? Where was my Suzie? I swallowed the thought back. Not mine.

"I just dance." She spoke with wide, innocent eyes. "Occum takes his cut. Razor gets his. All's good, y'all."

I kept trying to catch her focus. None of this made sense. I thought Occum was her boss? Who the hell was this Razor character, and why was Suzie paying him for anything?

"Good." Cueball crossed his arms and nodded.

The other one shook his head at me. "Hope you know what you got here." He cupped Suzie's jaw and ran a thumb over her lips.

The edge of my vision clouded in black. I couldn't remember my last inhale. It was like being an out of control teenager all over again. Suzie grabbed my hand behind her back, hidden from view, lacing her fingers through mine with some effort and squeezed.

"UT Professor Starts Brawl at Local Mall."

I ground my teeth but kept my mouth shut.

"Your receipt." The cashier smiled stiffly, glancing between all of us. "Y'all have a nice day." As soon as she handed me the bag, she scurried away behind a rack of clothes.

"We better get going. Nice seeing y'all." Suzie moved to walk but they blocked her.

"Hold on, sugar tits. I'm still talking."

My hand was still in hers, unsure of who held tighter. I was at war with my old self and the current one. I wanted to drop her hand and bash their skulls together while pointing out they were a waste of atoms.

She dropped my hand altogether to reach for Rooster. She rubbed her hands up his arms and stood on toes to whisper in his ear. As she spoke, his hands trailed down her back. I glared at it, hatred growing to a white-hot ball in my stomach. He roughly squeezed her ass and grinned at me with yellowing teeth.

"Bye." She stepped back and tugged me away.

"Bye, Short Fuse. Have fun." When we were almost out of earshot he added, "Don't forget where you come from and who your family is."

Her pale face smiled as she twisted to shoot one more flirtatious wave over her shoulder.

CHAPTER 13

SUZIE

*W*ell, I had to give it to Ford; we managed to get all the way to the car before he spoke. He'd been crackling with rage since we left. I'd made the smartest choice in that moment. Those boys never needed an excuse to start something. You had to talk carefully, or they would make you pay for it. If not now, then later.

Not that long ago I would have gotten off on the jealous anger burning in Ford's eyes but this time it wasn't fun. He started the car and took a deep breath. The steering wheel creaked under his grip. We sat in the parking lot. Outside it poured rain and I watched the drops collect and fall down the window as his anger became an entity sitting between us.

I was about to explain all that, how dangerous Rooster and Cueball could be when they were offended, when he spoke first. My stubborn nature made me hold my tongue.

"You just let them touch you like that?" he asked without being able to look at me.

"Excuse me?"

"The way they touch you. Talk to you. It's despicable. Why do you let them?"

I saw now why he was angry. It wasn't some sort of jealousy or concern for my well-being; it was that I wasn't fitting into the image he was trying to make for me. It was one thing to know what I really was, it was different to understand it and see in person. He didn't like the reality that was Short Fuse.

"Let them?" I tapped my nails in a pattern on my knee, containing my own anger threatening to take over. I knew he always kept his emotions locked tight in his chest. I could do the same. I wouldn't be the angry banshee people made me out to be.

"Guys like that? They're bullies. You have to stand up to them. You have to tell them no. They'll back down."

"Oh really?" I couldn't help the loud scoff I made. "Please explain my options to me. Tell me how I should have handled it. Stupid ol' me forgot and I need you to remind me."

"Tell them no. That it's your body. They have no right. You don't have to stand for it."

I huffed a sad laugh. He had no clue what the real world was like, and yet he accused me of being small-minded. I felt drained at the idea of explaining what a whole life of dealing with men like that had taught me. We didn't have the days it would take.

"It's easier to just go with it. They don't mean anything."

"Suzie, you don't know—"

"No!" I screamed out in the silent car. Fine. I was overly emotional and crazy but I couldn't take it for a second longer. The word rang in the air and my ears as I collected my thoughts. He shut his mouth tight. I went on. "No. You don't know. You have no clue what it's like to be me. You think I should just tell them 'no'? Okay, so let's say I insult them and humiliate them in public in front of you, some rich guy—"

"I'm not—" He started to speak but I kept talking over him.

"That's how they'd see it. They'd grow it like a seed in their chest. They'd see me and it'd burst out of them through their fist. You won't be there though. So what'll happen? They'll teach me a lesson. They'll remind me of my place."

"But you said you were Occum's favorite." His voice had grown scary deep and quiet.

"Yeah, maybe. But this isn't about me. Those guys are Wraiths. I don't go with that MC anymore. I'm part of a rival club, the Black Demons. Every word has to be calculated. At the G-Spot, I'm protected. Anywhere else, I'm fair game."

At that, his fury seemed to grow.

I went on, "You say I don't think before I speak, but trust me—every single part of that exchange was controlled, by me." I smacked my chest hard. I was so worked up I could shake him.

"I don't understand what just happened. Who's Razor?"

"Razor is the head of the Iron Wraiths. It's a long story, but the short of it is that I'm loyal to Occum. Occum protects me from those assholes and Razor. Razor is a very, very bad man that I do not want to cross." Again.

"Why are those guys talking to you at all?"

"I'm not sure." Maybe they were sent by Razor to remind me I'm still in his debt. Maybe they just happened to be there and wanted to fuck with me after what happened at the G-Spot with Ka-Bar the other night. I didn't think it was a coincidence that they showed up though.

"If I see them again, I'm not sure I'll be able to hold my tongue." Ford's voice was low with anger I'd never heard.

I prayed that never happened because bless Ford's heart. He was a professor that hung around people with silver spoons shoved where the sun don't shine. He was out of touch. Those guys would kill him. I couldn't think about that.

The steering wheel creaked more. He released it to start the car. He turned on the defrosters to clear the windows fogged with our anger. After they cleared, he drove slow and controlled out of the parking lot and headed back home. To his house.

After a while, he said, "I don't understand why you hang around with bikers."

I chewed on my lip. How did I explain that they cared for me in their own way? They weren't all bad. Some, like Ka-Bar, looked out for us girls. The Black Demons took me in and protected me when I had nothing and was in deep trouble. It was a long story and there were some things I had to do in exchange for their protection, but that was just my lot in life. It is what it is.

"Have you already forgotten? I'm a stripper and a biker bitch. Just because you want people to see me differently doesn't change who I am."

We pulled into a free spot on the street in front of the house. I opened the car door and jumped out before he even put it in park. I ran into the house and didn't stop until I reached my room. I threw my wet coat onto the floor and remembered the clothes forgotten in the car—the clothes that would never change me. I squeezed my fists into my eyes before remembering my makeup. I stared in the mirror. A sad little girl, playing at being adult, looked back. Things would never change. I needed to remember who I was and what life waited for me.

CHAPTER 14

CLIFFORD

couple of weeks passed. I managed to avoid Suzie for the most part. She had been progressing smoothly in her training without me. I gave her books she pretended to read and told her that with midterms and tests, I didn't have any extra time for her transformation. If we saw each other in the hall, we exchanged stilted hellos.

But despite all the excuses, the truth was I hated how I felt around her. Well, not true. I wanted to be around her all the time because I loved how it felt to be the focus of her attention. I loved watching her try to coerce a laugh out of me. I liked the way she moved with clunky confidence, but I also liked showing her new things. She adapted quickly and with minimal pushback. I regretted my actions on the shopping trip. I had wanted to comfort her. I wanted to take her away from all the madness of her normal life. Her *real* life. But the words had come out all wrong. I accused her of letting people take advantage of her. I acted like I knew better. How was I any different from the other men in her life who pushed her around?

My concerns formed as accusations. Who was I to insist that she change? I knew it could make a difference. People's response to her could change. I hated how complicated it was getting.

"Suzie, are you up there?" I called up the stairs. It was the Sunday night before Halloween and fall break had begun. Midterms were over and while I had a lot of work to do, tonight I would work on my relationship with Suzie. I needed to repair some of the strain between us. She'd been gone all day, allowing me to install my surprise.

"Yeah?" She poked her head out of her room. Her hair was high in a knot on her head. She blinked at me.

"Are you busy?"

"No. Just dancing." Her face was lit up from exertion and covered in a thin sheen of sweat. She stepped out of her room and closed the door dressed in workout gear.

"Perfect. Can you come down? I want to show you something in the basement."

"Sure. That doesn't sound ominous at all." She skipped down the stairs smoothly.

Ominous? Good word. Maybe she was reading those books. She smelled deliciously of her own sweet scent as she passed. I cleared my throat.

Jack walked in the front door at the exact moment we stood there. "What's going on?"

"Ford wants to show me something in the basement." She wiggled her eyebrows and he smiled.

"Close the door. You're letting a draft in," I said sharply to Jack.

He did so before shrugging out of his coat and knit cap. "Getting chilly out there. The trick or treaters are going to be cold this year."

Suzie bounced up and down in her neon sports bra. It was…distracting.

"You guys get trick or treaters?" Her hands were clasped and eyes lit with excitement.

"Oh, yeah. A bunch. It's a historic neighborhood so parents like to take their kids to get a lot of pictures. And a lot of the people around us are doctors and lawyers too, so you know what that means."

"Big candy bars."

They laughed. I never went out on Halloween as a kid; it hadn't really been a safe neighborhood. I guess I sighed loudly because they both turned to me.

"Sorry, Ford. You wanted to show me something?"

Familiar embarrassment crept up. This was a stupid idea. I would never fit with these two. I would never belong. I was always out of place, even when I tried so hard to contain myself to fit in.

"It's nothing," I mumbled. I sounded petulant but exhaustion from the perpetual tension caused by my presence ruled me.

"I have to go up and change." Jack sprinted up the whole staircase in three steps leaving us alone.

"Come on, Eeyore, just show me."

She grabbed my hand and headed to the basement. The ceiling was lower and perfect for my purposes. Suzie beat me down the steps and gasped.

It occurred to me, belatedly, that my gift may have been considered insulting. She'd been cooped up and I wanted to give her an outlet for her excessive energy. She had mentioned she enjoyed choreography too, but now I saw how it could be misconstrued.

"You got me a pole?" Her hands clasped the back of her neck as she looked at me through long lashes.

I scratched at my beard and said, "I had it installed. I upgraded the sound system too. So that you could sync your phone and play whatever you wanted." I stepped down the last step and went to the pole. I grabbed it and shook it hard. "It's bolted to the studs in the ceiling and the cement flooring. Plenty sturdy. It's not exactly allowed with the historic homes, but I thought you might like to practice. Since you're not working."

She was silent, looking at me with a little frown. Yup. I'd insulted her.

"When I ordered it, they suggested these mats." I pointed to a stack in the corner. "I guess in case you fall. And with the cement floor, I thought that was probably a good idea. Safety and all that."

Why was she so quiet? Suzie was never quiet.

Ever since she moved in, she stomped around the house or sang loudly in the shower or shook the chandelier when she danced. It was never peaceful with her here. I couldn't remember what it sounded like with just Jack and me.

"Look. If I insulted you—I was trying to make amends for…I can't seem to say—"

"It's perfect." She cut me off by smiling at me. A big smile. A genuine smile.

Her eyes gleamed, and it was like a balloon popped in my chest making room for air again. She stalked toward me. I tensed and lifted my arms into the air, unsure of what to do. Slowly, she wrapped her arms around my middle and lowered her head to my chest. She squeezed me tight.

"Thank you, Ford."

I relaxed and curled my arms around her back. We hugged. Simple, but wonderful. I had forgotten how nice it was to be held. She smelled so good. Her soft curves were in perfect counterpoint with all my awkward angles. I lowered my face to her hair and inhaled quietly.

"Holy shit. The Historic Homes Foundation is not going to like this." Jack's voice came from the stairs.

Suzie stepped back and I swore she wiped a tear away. "Ford got me a pole to practice on!"

I scratched the back of my head, and put more distance between Suzie and me.

Jack nodded while a grin grew. "I see that." He snuck me a thumbs up as Suzie moved to examine the pole.

She threw herself around it, picking up speed as she went, defying the laws of physics. Jack and I shared a glance, our eyes wide. She'd just hopped up there like it was no effort at all.

"This is perfect." She twisted until she was upside down and gripping the pole with one leg, arms spread wide.

"Wait. Try this." I went to the sound system and selected a cello sonata. I assumed it wasn't her typical selection, but when this track played on my way back from Green Valley, my mind had pictured Suzie twirling gracefully around a pole. I used the dimmer to lower the lights, highlighting the makeshift stage.

Suzie held my gaze for a long moment before closing her eyes and absorbing the music. The strings moved in like a thunderstorm on the horizon. Her movements started; graceful, slow, but with an underlying tension that spoke of things to come. I backed into the couch and Jack fell in next to me. The cello grew prominent over the soft repetitive piano. She completed a slow twirl around the pole, one arm gripping above her head. Seamlessly she was off the floor, again defying gravity.

As the music crescendoed, so did her movements. Her acrobatics predicted the rise and fall of the piece. Her soul absorbed it and her body played it out through her muscles, each tragic note emphasized by her interpretation. My heart expanded in my chest. Infinity loomed before us, drawing forth futility at the same time. Her face creased with an edge of desperate emotional pain, and still, she spun.

Jack looked at me with an open-mouthed head shake, as if to say, "I had no idea." I nodded because I knew her talent, the beauty, and the strength. I'd seen it once before. The first time we met.

The passion. I'd seen it and dismissed it because my own attraction for her clouded my memories. Suzie had come alive once the music took her. This was her energy source, what drove her. Her art was ingesting the music, interpreting it, driving the power of the emotion. She was living art and an artist all in one. This woman deserved her own stage.

Her emerald eyes opened as the music gave a final gasp of intensity and her gaze locked on me. The same focus and seduction I'd seen that first night at the club ran through me. She could have been communicating with me or she could have been a million miles away. I couldn't look anywhere else.

I smoothed the goosebumps on my arm as the last note of the cello hung in the air. She transitioned into a final slow spin bringing her to the floor. She stopped, her body bent over crossed ankles like a ballerina.

Jack stood to clap, "Bravo!"

It was a minute before I remembered where I was.

Suzie

Sadness welled up in me so tight I didn't think I could breathe. If it weren't for my heaving chest I would have thought I'd died after that dance. I don't know what came over me, but the piece Ford selected was so beautiful it spoke to me immediately. It reached into my bones. I had shown too much of my soul. That dance hadn't been sexy. I had been too emotional and that wasn't what men wanted to see. That wasn't my job as a dancer. God, I could only imagine the look on the faces of the guys at the G-Spot if I tried something like that.

And yet when I lifted my head, Ford sat entranced, his fist to his chin with his usual frown in place. His expression and glassy eyes gave away the impact I'd had on him. Jack smiled and clapped.

"I like it," I said. "The pole. And the song."

"Good." Ford stood with his frown still in place. "Suzie, there's a Halloween Fundraiser on Friday. It's a masquerade ball to raise money for the children's hospital. A lot of the who's-who will be there. I thought it might be a good time to see how you'd do in a setting like that."

Okay, we were moving on and pretending like that hadn't just happened. This man gave me whiplash.

"But we haven't fixed me." I pushed away from the pole still short of breath.

His face clouded over. "You can get a dress. They provide the masks. I think you're ready."

His frown stayed in place but he didn't speak. I didn't understand his distance. I hated that I couldn't read him easily like other men. I wished he would just tell me what was going on in his head.

"Are you going?" I asked Jack. Ford stiffened next to him.

"Nah, not my bag. Plus, someone has to be here to hand out candy."

I frowned because I wanted to hand out candy and now, I was going to be put on display like a pig at the state fair. I let out a breath through puffed cheeks.

"I have to go. Feel free to practice down here any time." Ford left the room without another word.

I wasn't looking for flowers thrown at me, but a little bit of acknowledgment over that performance would have been nice. Where's a stool to throw when a girl needs one?

Jack winked. "Don't mind him. He's got a lot going on behind the scenes." Jack stretched his arms above his head. "Okay, you have got to teach me some moves."

I gave a stellar lesson and was not surprised to find he picked it up naturally. His tall and lean build gave him an advantage. After we were both exhausted and Jack thoroughly wiped down the pole and mats with antibacterial wipes, we broke for some lunch and juice. We sat eating in the cool basement, our feet propped up on the coffee table.

I was lost in thought when Jack nudged my foot with his.

"So how goes it?" Jack asked around a mouthful. "With all the stuff? You've both been quiet lately."

"It's okay. Better now I think." I gestured to the pole. "We had a spat and he backed off a little."

"Did he apologize?"

"Thank you for knowing it was his fault. Not in so many words, but I think that's what this was."

"I know he's a pain in the ass but he's a good person."

I chewed thoughtfully. I didn't hate Ford; I liked him. It was hard to know for sure because when he talked, I felt like punching him. When I wasn't around him I found myself making excuses to find him. I liked that he treated me like an equal, even if he thought I could be better. That in itself was more than anybody else in my life.

"I worry that I'm going to end up disappointing him." My thoughts slipped out. It was honest and true. "It's weird being here. Away from my life, my job, and Dad. I feel like I'm in a weird dream and when I wake up, I'll have to go back to everything."

"Does that bother you?"

"I don't belong here."

"Says who?"

I looked at him with a smirk. "Just people with working eyeballs."

"All I'm saying is, be open to change. You never know what will fit."

"Okay." I nudged him with my foot. "Question."

"Yes?" Jack grinned at me.

"Does Ford own a razor?"

Jack shook his head with a laugh. "I see an idea forming, little miss, and I don't want to be here when you see it through."

"Sure you do!" I shot up off the couch. "Now, it's time for me to give Ford a little taste of his own medicine."

"I want no part in this," he called out, but I was already on the move.

I ran upstairs and collected what I needed before trotting back down to Ford's office. I was filled with giddy excitement.

"Hiya, Ford." I popped my head into his study a huge smile on my face.

"Why do you look scary?" Ford looked up from his laptop, his glasses perched on his nose.

See now, it was times like this I couldn't possibly buy that I was older than Ford. He looked like a grandpa. His hair was salt and pepper. He liked classical music and did crosswords to relax. He wore sweater-vests for crying out loud.

"I need to borrow you for a hot minute."

He glanced at his watch. "Why?" He dragged out the word like he was scared.

"You said that ball was this weekend?"

"Yes?"

"We need to get ready."

He looked around his office as though it could help him. "Right now?"

"Yes." I sauntered up to his desk and tugged at his arm.

"I'm busy."

"Oh come on, scaredy-cat."

"I don't like the look in your eyes."

A few minutes later, I had him leaning back on a chair I put in the bathroom with a hot towel on his face.

"I did not picture this." His words were muffled.

"Nice, huh?"

He moaned an "mmm-hmm."

I squirted a large dollop of shaving cream into my hand. "Here we go."

He peaked open one eye. "Wait, wait. What are you doing?"

"You need a shave and a haircut." I leaned in and looked at his ears and eyebrows. "And a heavy pluck."

"No. No."

He struggled to sit up, but I sat on his lap. He stilled, gripping the chair.

"Sit still or you're going to get hurt."

I put the shaving cream on his neck where his beard had grown wild. I carefully rubbed it in, creating a thick lather. His Adam's apple bobbed.

"You're fine," I whispered. "I'm not shaving it all off. Just a trim."

"Okay good. I look like a baby when I shave."

I laughed.

"I'm serious. My students would never take me seriously."

"Don't worry." I made quick work of cleaning up the parts of his neck where scraggly hairs ruled and used an electric razor to start cutting back his beard.

"You need to sit like that?"

"No," I said wiggling back and forth on his lap. "But I like making you uncomfortable."

I smiled. He frowned.

"I'm comfortable," his voice cracked.

"Okay." I leaned toward the counter behind his chair and purposely brushed my breasts along his chest. It had the unwanted effect of making my nipples hard but was worth it to hear him clear his throat and feel him shift under me. "This part might sting."

It took a hell of a lot longer to get through the plucking. His eyebrows were a mess and his ears were unspeakable. "God, you need a woman around to take care of you."

"Women are cumbersome. And I resent the outdated notion."

"You and Jack sure you're not planning a spring wedding?" I raised an eyebrow at him.

"I should be so lucky." He said it so dryly I couldn't help the cackle of laughter that broke out of me.

When I stopped laughing, he watched me closely.

My heart started pounding. I was on his lap. I'd done much more crude things, been far more undressed. And yet I'd never felt more exposed to him.

"I just need to trim your hair." I ran my fingers through the length pulling it out to examine where I should trim.

He cleared his throat. "You've done this before?"

"Cut my dad's hair all the time." It was way cheaper than taking him somewhere. Though it had been a long time since he needed to keep it neat. He stopped going on interviews years ago.

"Okay."

I slipped off his lap and moved behind him. Thankfully the scissors I'd found were sharp. I only trimmed the ends, leaving it a bit long. My goal was to take him from nutty professor to just a bit wild. I ran my hands through his locks to see if I'd missed anything, feeling the warmth of his skin. I swept my hands up his neck, weaving my fingers upward. I felt myself sway forward.

"I think we're done." My voice sounded a little off. I walked in front of him, pulling the last strands to make sure everything was even. "Looks good."

He enclosed my wrist. "Thank you."

"You're welcome."

"I'm sorry about shopping. I'm sorry to have hurt you."

"You're getting better."

"Better?"

"At apologizing."

We held each other's gaze. We were so close to something. I felt it in the way my pulse thumped against my chest. I pulled back to give a professional assessment of my work. I'd only been looking at his indi-vidual components: hair, beard, eyebrows. But when I took in his face as a whole it stunned me and I gasped without meaning to.

"What is it?" he asked softly. "Is it bad? Am I going to have to wear a paper bag over my head?"

He looked damn good. I almost couldn't look at him because I was worried what might fall out of my mouth.

"Just be thankful the party is a masquerade."

"What?" He shot up to look in the mirror.

"I'm kidding."

I stood behind him to watch his reaction. He examined his face closely, running a hand over the short beard, and turned his face side to side. "Huh."

"You're welcome."

"Could be worse," he said.

He straightened. We both stood next to each other and looking at our reflections. Right now, it was almost believable that a man like that would be with a woman like me. We looked like a couple. A normal girl and her man.

I turned away, unable to look any longer.

CHAPTER 15

SUZIE

I was too stir-crazy to stay in that beautiful house any longer. I couldn't stand another moment of staring at books or working through pointless tongue twisters. The audiobooks were a good idea. I could at least do things while I listened and okay, that *Wuthering Heights* was a real kick in the stomach. But I was still going insane. I needed to move and shake. Ford and Jack were at work and I needed a dress.

Something about the smell of fall made me sentimental and anxious. Maybe it was the dead leaves and sharp air. Or maybe it was the shortening days. Whatever my deal was, I changed into one of my new outfits and made my way to the main street of town in search of entertainment and maybe a dress for the Halloween Ball.

I happened across a boutique with some nice gowns in the window but when I got there it wasn't open yet. There was a coffee shop on the corner with a small bookstore attached. It smelled like fresh coffee, vanilla, and cinnamon. The wholesomeness of this place made my skin itch. I probably stuck out...well, like a stripper at a bookstore. I waited for someone to tell me I wasn't welcome. But no one looked up.

A young, cute guy behind the counter with a beanie over scraggly hair looked up from the book he was reading and said, "Welcome. Required textbooks are upstairs. Holler if you need anything." And then went right back to reading.

He thought I was a student. I snorted and covered it up with a quick thank you. I caught my reflection in the glass of a display. And then I remembered that I was wearing my new clothes: jeans and a cardigan with a patterned scarf that covered my neck and cleavage. I hadn't bothered with makeup since it was so early and it took too much time. Never thought I'd see the day where I thought makeup was too much work.

Damn, that man was rubbing off on me.

A weird thing had been happening when I thought of Ford lately. Like drinking champagne too fast, I felt giddy and bubbly. After I cleaned him up yesterday, I couldn't stop looking at him. He was handsome before, but now he was damn sexy. I didn't like it. Every time I saw him, I found myself staring.

I focused on the present and the anonymity that came with my new identity. I could be a totally different person. I could be anybody else. The idea thrilled me.

"Suzie?" a woman's voice called.

Ah, cluck. So much for that.

I turned to find Gretchen - Fashion Consultant, Landlord, Driver, and all-around Badass. She dropped a short stack of books on the counter and headed to where I hovered near a rack of paperbacks. Today she was dressed equally fabulously in a retro navy dress, Mary Janes, and a leather jacket. Her cat eye makeup was a perfect flick. She managed to be sexy without revealing much skin at all.

"It is you." She picked up the end of my scarf and ran it through her fingers. "Cute scarf."

"Thanks," I said cautiously. I was thinking of a way to insult her in case that was some sort of a judgmental comment.

"Fancy meeting you here. Shopping?"

"Killing time. There's a dress shop next door I want to check out, but it's not open."

"Oh yeah, Tracy's Place. They've got some nice things. How's it going with the complicated relationship?"

"I don't even know," I answered truthfully.

"You seem different." Her gaze studied me astutely. Astute is a word I learned in my lessons and I loved the way it sounded.

"I'm just me." I shrugged.

"'Just', huh?" She nodded toward the counter. "I was going to get coffee, if you want to join me?"

I took too long to answer because she added, "It's not a big deal if you don't."

She shrugged and I genuinely believed it would make no difference to her. It wasn't insulting. It was oddly freeing. I got the impression I could say just about anything to her and she'd take it in stride. I thought of Ford's list of "to-dos" and on that list was make friends with women. Well, I couldn't guarantee anything, but I could at least tell him I tried. Then he could shut up about it.

"No plans. That sounds good," I said.

"Cool. I'll meet you over there after I check out."

I made my way to the little coffee shop counter and waited to order but as it turned out the guy behind the bar pulled double duty. So after he finished bagging up Gretchen's books, he jogged over to help me. With the counter in the way, Gretchen was at my side before he tugged his apron on.

"Geez, the service in this place is appalling." Gretchen softened her tease with a wink.

"What'll it be, ladies? We have coffee or hot tea," the cute guy asked.

"Starbucks it is not."

"Easy, Gretch, or I'm changing the Wi-Fi password on you again."

"You'd never." She leaned toward him over the counter and his gaze flicked to her cleavage and then away. I bit back a smile. "Lucas, this is Suzie. Suzie, this is Lucas, the love of my life. He just doesn't know it yet."

The cute man held out his hand to mine and shook it but his ears burned furiously red. He was large and imposing but his gentle hand-shake was at odds with all that. Gretchen was such a shameless flirt.

We ordered two coffees and chose a little table by the window. "Better for people watching," Gretchen said.

I sat with my hands tucked between my knees, trying to think of something to say.

"It's cold out there—"

"No. Don't do that. Don't talk about the weather with me. We've moved past that. I've threatened your dad. No bullshit talk." She said between sips of plain black coffee. "Or don't talk at all. Just don't waste time talking about nothing."

I chose to focus on my coffee. This was weird. Wasn't it? People don't just go to get coffee and talk. This wasn't a 90's sitcom. But I guess people had to meet some way. I noticed her bag of books and was about to ask what she had bought but then questioned if she would consider that small talk too.

I was saved from thinking too much because when I looked back to her she was studying me. "I thought you looked familiar in the car but now I'm sure I know you."

"You live in Green Valley, right?" I had thought she seemed familiar too—but that was Green Valley. Shit, we were probably third cousins or something. I had no doubt we had at least had fifty Face-book friends in common.

She shook her head. "Not anymore. But I lived there for a little while."

She took another swig of coffee and asked, "What do you do when you aren't moving in with a single man?"

I had a feeling this was coming. Here comes the judgment and the awkward excuse to leave.

I lifted my chin and said, "I'm a stripper."

She didn't even blink, just bent to blow on her cup. "Pink Pony or G-Spot?"

"G-Spot. I worked at Pink Pony for a while but had a falling out with the owner."

"Hank Weller? That guy's an odd duck. But that's gotta be how I know you. I worked there for a hot minute too."

"You danced too?"

"No, bartended." She waved her hand like it wasn't important. "What did you do to piss off Hank?" Her eyes lit up like she was looking forward to the answer no matter what it was.

I smirked. "He's Team Winston. I dated one of them. It didn't end well."

"Shut up. Which brother?"

"Jethro."

The coffee stopped halfway to the table. I'd seen this reaction before too. People thought I was trying to get some claim to fame.

So I quickly added on, "But this was a while back. Way before he married freaking Sienna Diaz. Before he got straight, even."

"I had a feeling about you." She sat back and shook her head. "I knew as soon as we met, we were going to be great friends."

"Did I miss something?" I had definitely never given off that impression before.

"I dated Jethro too."

"Seriously?"

She laughed with a little shake of her head. "Yup. PS Jethro."

"PS Jethro?"

"Pre-Sienna. That or Piece of Shit. Depending on my mood that day. That's how we refer to him."

I studied the skin of milk on my cooling coffee then sat up straighter. "Wait. At the same time? When?" Was this some sort of weird trap? Was I about to be ambushed for shit I did almost a decade ago?

"We need to compare notes. Actually, we probably need a spreadsheet. There are a lot of us and I'm sure some of our timelines overlap."

"Wouldn't that not make us friends then?"

"No way. Enemy's enemy and all that. We're sisters in battle. I don't know about you but those months with Jethro were not my finest hours. I was changed."

I nodded. I had almost gotten caught up in a life I wasn't ready for when I realized I didn't mean shit to him. But some other girls weren't so lucky. I heard a lot of ugly rumors. Splitting from Jethro probably saved my life.

Not that I was exactly winning Oscars or writing movies.

"This is unreal." Gretchen slapped the table.

"It really is. I mean, I guess it's not so hard to believe. Jethro was a bastard back then. I bet we could start a club."

"We could track down some of the others and compare notes."

I snorted. "Yeah, but who has that kind of time."

She kept on with the joke. "We could meet every other Thursday at seven to talk crap and scheme petty revenges."

"That's oddly specific. Wait. Why are you making that face?"

She tapped her lip thoughtfully. "Club is a strong word. We like to think of it as a society. A causal get-together."

"You're serious? 'We'?"

"And it's just a few of us. Not all of us. Exes I mean."

"You have a club."

"A society," she corrected with a sniff. "The Scorned Women's Society. 'No ex left behind.' And usually we don't talk about Jethro at all, we hang out or try something new like Wine and Paint or talk about a book we've read."

"Seriously?"

"If you happen to be free you could join us. We meet different places each time. Sometimes up at Kim's house pretending to be a bible study group."

I raised an eyebrow in question and she waved me away.

"That's a whole other story for another time. But we always have fun. You gotta meet Roxy and Blithe. They're riots."

I bit back a smile. She knew about me, who I was, and she still wanted to hang out.

"That sounds nice," I said. Look at me, out here making friends and being open to change.

CHAPTER 16

CLIFFORD

I sat on the couch and waited as the doorbell rang for the tenth time in half an hour. Each time it jarred my exposed nerves.

"Just leave it open already." I snapped to Jack who was dressed as a pirate, complete with a hook, balancing a bowl of candy in his normal arm.

"Calm yourself. She'll be down soon."

"I don't care."

"Aye, liars walk the plank, matey." He threatened me with the plastic hook. "And stop shaking your leg. It's an old house. You're giving me motion sickness."

I glared but stilled my leg, which had been bouncing unbeknownst to me. As Jack handed out candy to mini monsters and ghouls, I paced in front of the sitting room windows. Costumed children carrying plastic pumpkin buckets ran screaming with delight down our street as leaves swirled at their feet.

My nerves were inexplicable. Suzie would be fine. I wasn't worried about her. So what had me so worked up?

Suzie's door shut upstairs. I turned on a dime to find her at the top of the stairs. Time stopped.

Lined heavily with dark makeup, her eyes glinted like emeralds and immediately caught me in their gaze. Her hair was slicked back and spun into a loose twist exposing her shoulders and long, graceful neck. I tore my gaze away to study the midnight black gown that was a few shades darker than her hair. It cinched tight in the waist and then fell into massive skirts. The top was composed of thin straps trailing down to a heart-shaped bodice that emphasized her perfect cleavage. The vision of her robbed me of my words. I had expected her to be beautiful, but this was unfair. She descended carefully, the dress needing the entire width of the staircase.

"Breathe," Jack leaned in next to me to whisper.

"Do you like it?" She looked squarely at me as she asked.

You're beautiful. You take my breath away. I couldn't find anything good enough to say. "Will you be able to fit in the car?"

She blinked and I swear the light diminished from her eyes. What the hell was wrong with me?

"I should be okay," she said.

"You look amazing." Jack took her hand and spun her in a circle.

"Yeah, what he said," I mumbled.

"Well, I'm ready if you are. God, I hope I don't have to take a piss. I don't know what I'll do."

"Suzie," I chastised.

"Sorry." She slipped into a proper British accent. "My apologies, good sir. It is only that I find I'm quite unable to breathe in this contraption. I do not know how one is expected to..." She faded out. "Yeah, I got nothing."

The last part was in her own voice. Jack laughed.

My mean comments needed amending, so what did I do? I added on, "Maybe just keep exclamations of bodily functions to yourself."

"You mean I shouldn't show anybody how I can play 'Old MacDonald' with my armpit?" She tucked her hand into her armpit like she planned to show a demonstration but quickly snagged it back. "Good gravy, I'm sweating like a sinner in church."

I took a deep breath and let it out slowly.

"You kids have fun." Jack slapped a hand on my back. "Don't drink and drive, and don't be out too late."

"Yes, Dad." Suzie accepted a kiss to her cheek. Turning to me, she asked, "They have the masks, right?" Her hand trembled slightly as she reached for a small black purse.

I forgot she was all bravado when she was nervous. We were so similar in that regard.

"Yes. They provide them as part of the admission."

"You had to pay to go?" she asked.

"You have to pay for your seat. That's the fundraiser."

"You pay for your chair?"

I shook my head. "No. You purchase the right to attend and then that money goes to charity."

"Ah. How much?"

"A thousand dollars a chair."

"Good Lord, they must be made out of gold."

"No, it's not the chair you're buying…" I started but stopped when I saw her face. "You were teasing."

"I was." She looped her arm through mine. "Bye, Jacky. Save me some Reese's."

"Bye." He closed the door after us.

I led her carefully through the bushes that lined the entrance to the front yard. A little girl passing pointed and said, "Mommy, look! A real princess."

Suzie placed a hand to her chest and smiled so big it illuminated the whole street. She was still beaming when I opened her door and lowered her into the car, careful to arrange her skirts to avoid damage. I cleared my throat and hesitated. I wasn't sure why it felt like it cost me something to say nice things. Or rather, why it felt like sharing would put me at risk for humiliation. But I wanted to make progress with Suzie. I wanted to be better for her.

She was smoothing out the volume of skirts when she looked at me with her bottom lip caught between her teeth.

"If you haven't figured out already, I'm not great with words."

She released her lip and smiled. "You don't say."

"I think you look very…sufficient."

"You can do better than that, Ford." She frowned.

I squeezed my fists and on a whoosh of breath said, "You take my breath away every time I look at you." I gently shut the door and jogged around to the driver's side.

I started the car and pulled into the street without a glance in her direction.

After a few minutes, she relaxed back against the seat. "You don't look so bad yourself."

Suzie

I let out a slow breath, watching how it moved the little fuzzies on the feather I held. I had found the feather on the tablecloth when we sat down, like it fell out of a boa. I puffed it into the air and tried to keep it from falling back down.

"Suzie." Ford stood uncomfortably straight next to me.

I let the feather fall. "Sorry."

We had been at this shindig for over an hour and I had yet to be introduced to anybody. Ford looked damn fine in his tux and I obviously looked like a million dollars, so I wondered why we were hiding at a table on the outskirts of the room. This was supposed to be an opportunity to test my conversational abilities but we were basically decoration.

The ballroom was something out of a fairytale. The amount of money that must have gone into every detail blew my mind. Each table was decorated in heavy crushed velvet black tablecloths and tiny votive candles and sculptures made of wire and crystals shaped to look like scraggly, old trees. Every surface was covered in black or crystals so it was both perfectly spooky and classy as cluck.

"What're you thinking?" he asked.

Ford must've been watching me closely because when I turned to him he blinked rapidly and looked away. I wondered how long I'd been staring around like a slack-jawed yokel.

"It's magical," I said.

He nodded then studied his drink.

"How did you afford this?" It wasn't just the gold-encrusted chairs; it was the tux and my dress. When Gretchen helped me pick it out the other day, I had placed it on hold and Ford bought it on his way home.

He cleared his throat and furrowed his brow. "It was part of the package from the investor."

"Really?"

Ford studied the couples walking by. "Yeah, he said he'd pay for a limo and all that too. But I told him that wasn't necessary."

"Phooey. A limo is always necessary." I pouted.

"Fine. Next time, a limo." Ford almost smiled.

We held each other's gaze and something folded over in my chest.

I looked away to the gowns swirling all over the dance floor. "I do have a question though. Why're we just sitting here? It's a party but I feel like I'm at a funeral. Let's go mingle. I'm ready to embarrass you—I mean meet people."

He frowned at my teasing but then said, "We are. We will. I'm working through the logistics."

"Well, you go up to people you know and say hi. Not sure that it has to be much more complicated than that."

"It's not that simple. I need to make sure that I introduce you in a way that isn't condescending but highlights the gravity of my research without sounding trite…"

I stopped listening because he tended to get lost in his ramblings. Seeing him in a fitted tuxedo was a magical thing. The thin dark mask emphasized his features. A few passing women had tried to catch his gaze until I glared at them. In so many ways, he was a mystery. So confident in standing up to Occum, but so unsure of small talk. Not that I blamed him—I frickin' hated it too.

"Are you listening? What are you looking at?" His question brought me back into focus.

I wasn't about to tell him I'd been watching how his lips moved to the side a little when he talked without a filter and there was something about the action that made my neck warm.

"I'm listening."

He made a face like he didn't believe me. "There are the implications of a relationship we have to be wary of, too."

"Why's that?" I shivered.

"Obviously we can't have people thinking." He cleared his throat. "It could potentially inhibit the, um, that is—if people assume there is some sort of uncouth behavior."

"You don't want people to think we're screwing?"

"Suzie." He blushed.

I knew I was being rude, but he was pissing me off. Lord forbid anybody thought he'd muddy up his perfection with a girl like me.

"I get it." I finished the drink, slurping it sloppily from the glass just to piss him off more before banging it down on the table. I wiped my mouth with the back of my hand. "I'm gonna go meet somebody."

"What?"

"If you ain't gonna dance with me, I'll find somebody who will."

I moved toward the dance floor. Already three guys hovering near the bar paused in their conversation to watch my next move. The handsome man in glasses looked like the best bet when Ford grabbed my wrist and spun me into his arms. The fabric of his tux was slightly rough under the sensitive skin of my arms as he wrapped them around his shoulders.

"I've got you." He grabbed my waist and snapped me right against him.

I swallowed, too stunned to speak for a minute. I loved being in his arms. Damn if chemistry wasn't a crazy thing. I couldn't tell if he felt it too. Sometimes it seemed like he did, but that it pissed him off. Other times it seemed like he couldn't look at me. His face was even harder to read behind the mask but if anything, he seemed lost in thought—and slightly worried.

"Are you having doubts?" I asked him.

His gaze flicked back and forth between mine. "What?"

"Doubts? About introducing me to someone. If it's too soon, I get it."

"No." His thumbs moved in circles on my hips. "No. Not about you at all."

"Oh, excuse me." I bumped into a couple behind me. "Your dress is amazing."

An older woman draped in a peacock colored dress and clinking beads that matched her mask glided past.

"Thank you, love. You look fabulous too." She inclined her head and they spun away.

I shrugged at Ford as if to say, "Look! My first time talking to a fancy-pants and I didn't mess it up too bad. Aren't you proud of me?"

He blinked once. Okay then. Maybe that message didn't go through.

We danced for a little while longer. His dancing was controlled, but efficient. No surprise there. The man needed to let loose.

"Relax. This isn't a waltz." I squeezed his shoulders.

"I know how to dance."

"Oh, excuse me."

I could have danced all night, but he took me back to our table for the speeches that were supposedly starting soon.

"A request for more money," he whispered as he pulled out my chair.

While he went to the bathroom, I met the couple next to us. I discovered it was the nice peacock dress lady, Kathy, and her husband John.

Ford returned and I was halfway through a story about my Aunt Helen and her fling in the forties with a former member of the mafia when Ford returned.

"She never saw him again." I drew a finger along my neck and stuck out my tongue. "All she ever heard was he went on vacation and never came back."

They laughed and I smiled until I saw Ford's face. He was grimacing as usual.

"Ford. This is Mr. John and Kathy Carlisle. They have a house off

Bandit Lake and two purebred Greyhounds they rescued from the race circuit."

"I was gone two minutes," he said, mostly to himself.

He set down two more glasses of whiskey for us.

"And is this your Ford?" Kathy said.

Ford's eyes widened. It was just easier to say Ford was my date rather than this is the man I live with—along with his handsome and also single roommate—who was being paid to turn me into a classy broad. It was a mouthful.

"Clifford Rutledge." He kissed her hand like a gentleman from a black and white movie before shaking the man's hand. My heart fluttered.

"John." The older man nodded to Ford's name tag. "I see you're a donor as well. What work do you do?"

Rather than correct him, Clifford dived into a whirlwind of four-dollar words and didn't stop until he was loosening his tie and a little sweaty. John frowned and nodded but I could tell he had no frickin' clue what Ford was talking about. I exchanged a look with Kathy and she shook her head like men were another species she had long ago given up on.

Slightly to the side, she said, "John used to get the same way when he'd talk about his surgeries. I never had any clue what he meant."

Ford stopped and took a drink when they started speaking on stage. He was clearly not happy with his delivery either. He wiped sweat from under his mask with a fancy handkerchief from his pocket. I squeezed his hand under the table and smiled. He frowned deeper. I rolled my eyes. It was our favorite routine.

When the presenter finished asking for money, Ford made another attempt to explain his work. John scanned the crowd, looking for an escape no doubt, so I jumped in.

"The gist is that this man is going to change the world, Dr. Carlisle. His research will allow small towns to be completely rejuvenated, from the ground up."

Both men looked at me.

I went on, because it was like watching a puppy trying to jump over a six-foot fence when Ford tried to explain his research. "Public transportation and government funded programs will coordinate to provide services to communities, allowing citizens access to both educational and recreational activities. This, in turn, will allow the citizens to integrate more fully into society, broadening the tax base and jumpstarting the capabilities of the next generation. It's a win-win that improves the lives of the current citizens and the future generation." I stood up and brushed out my skirts. "Now, if you will please excuse us both. I'm owed one more dance."

"What a lovely idea." John smiled and looked at his wife. "I shouldn't waste such a beautiful date."

We all set our glasses down and slid to the dance floor. A small band played smooth jazz music. Ford pulled me close and I blinked up at him in surprise as he gently rocked me to the music.

I reached up and poked his brow until his frown smoothed out. "What's got that brain of yours all worked up?"

"How did you know that?"

"What?" I asked.

"About my research."

"You told me." I shrugged.

"Yeah, but you sold it."

"I appreciate how surprised you sound."

He smirked. "I've been committed to this idea my entire adult life and have never been able to express my thoughts so succinctly."

I shrugged and moved closer to him, using the crowd as an excuse. "Maybe you're too close to it. I'm not bogged down by the details."

He hummed and it vibrated through my body.

After a few more minutes of swaying, I asked, "So, did I pass your test?"

He gave me a look that said he was not amused. But lately, I found myself more and more interested in pushing his buttons. Using a hill-billy accent, I said, "I know I can be a little hard to talk to, what with my humble upbringing, but ever since I got shoes for my feet and a real ed-u-mah-cation, I talk pretty."

"Alright, very funny."

"I think that big fancy doctor man thought I was real special."

"Suzie."

"Maybe one day I'll be a real lady and won't embarrass you no more."

"Suzie." He was short. He was distant and thoughtful, more so than normal, but he also had this intensity I couldn't nail down. To be honest, it freaked me out a little. I didn't know what to expect from him.

I started making banjo sounds from *Deliverance*. I was two seconds from lifting my skirt and slapping my knees like at a hoedown when he placed his hand over my mouth and pulled my body close to his. "Stop. Just stop."

I blinked up at him with his hand on my mouth and his hard body against me. My things touched his things, our middles pressed tight, and I swore he'd be able to feel my heart trying to beat its way closer to his.

"You never embarrass me. This whole thing…it isn't about trying to change you. I just needed to show other people…" He trailed off as he tucked a loose strand of hair behind my ear.

I stayed stock-still afraid he'd realize how close we were and add distance, like he was so in favor of doing.

"I told you, I'm not great with words, but I thought I made it clear from the beginning that I only wanted you to feel better. I wanted the world to see the real you, how you're just as capable as anybody else. That your accent doesn't make you trash. If I ever made you feel like less than anyone else it was only because I can't communicate my thoughts clearly. Obviously." He pointed his chin to the place he tried to talk to the doctor.

I couldn't breathe. It had nothing to do with him, or rather, everything to do with him. At some point in his speech, he dropped his hands to my shoulders and off my mouth, but I still couldn't fill my lungs completely. He gently massaged the exposed area like he couldn't keep his hands still. I couldn't wrap my mind around what he said.

"Oh." I swallowed down my heart, which had squirmed its way to my throat—and still tried desperately to get out of my chest. "I thought you wanted me to make something of myself."

"I think you could do anything you put your mind to. I'm not doing a good job in this experiment. I keep trying to help but you already know what I have to teach you—clothing, your accent, and even your small talk. You could live a totally different life and nobody would ever know, or care, where you came from."

My heart finally caught up with what he was saying and crashed back down to where it belonged. I nodded.

"Ah." He thought I could be something but that I lived short of my potential. He still thought my dancing was garbage. That I was garbage but he held out hope I could change.

It wasn't his fault he couldn't see the truth. He was surrounded by opportunities and I was surrounded by reality. I forced a smile onto my face. He frowned and tried to speak again but I cut him off. I didn't want to talk anymore. I didn't want to hear how I was wasting my life. I didn't want to explain how my path had been laid out since the day my momma walked out. Dancing was all I had and I worked hard for it. He had dreams about communities, education, and business. I had dreams about family, choreography, and losing myself to the music.

"I have an idea," I said.

"Hmm?" He still looked lost in thought.

"You need to be here any longer?" I asked.

"No. I think I've shown my face to the important people."

"No offense, but this party sucks."

He held my gaze. I wished he wouldn't look at me like that. I got so confused when he did. How could he look at me like I was the most interesting thing in the room but also think I was not living up to my potential? I was done with thinking. I needed to drink and forget.

"I want to go dancing," I said. "Real dancing."

"I don't know where—"

"No worries. I happen to know just the place."

CHAPTER 17

CLIFFORD

This was not a good idea. This was in fact, a very bad idea.

"This is a bad idea."

Suzie waved my comments away. We sat in the car as people moved in and out of the front door of the Green Valley Community Center. Those who weren't in costume were in jeans or equally casual clothing.

"We're overdressed," I added.

"Don't worry. It's Halloween. We're in costume." Though she sounded breezy as she gnawed at her cuticle.

I wondered her reasoning for bringing me here of all places.

"This is a jamboree or something?"

She rolled her eyes at me. Sometimes one eye roll from her made my whole week.

"Yeah, complete with milk jugs and tin washboards. Come on, let's go in before we miss the bands."

I was pleasantly surprised by the entertainment as we explored the building. For such a casual title, the "jam session" had been organized by music genre and each room was in full swing. There was evidence that food had once filled a banquet table near the entrance, but that had been fully picked over by the time of our arrival. The crowd seemed to be thinning out; families headed home and younger couples warmed up. There was a looseness in people's bodies that spoke of alcohol flowing, though I didn't see any outright. It wasn't until we reached the biggest room, what Suzie called the main stage, that I realized how many glances we were getting.

Whispers of "Who is that?" and "Damn, they aren't from around here..." followed us as we made our way to the center of the dance floor.

Suzie pulled me along until she bumped into a group of girls her age, maybe older. Dressed in cowboy boots and plaid shirts, they could have been copy/pastes of the same person.

The one in the front scanned Suzie up and down. "Little over-dressed," she said to her friends, obviously wanting to be overheard.

Suzie squeezed my hand tighter, her long gown swishing along a dirty and scratched wood floor.

"Wait, isn't that that crazy stripper Jethro dumped forever ago?"

"How pathetic."

"Right? How can she show her face after he got engaged to Sienna? Trying to use a fancy dress to hide her loss."

"Desperate much?"

Mean girls were symptomatic of most patriarchal cultures. Their appearance had always boggled me, as women had enough odds stacked against them. You'd think they'd band together rather than tear each other down. But then again, I'm sure the roots were based so deep in our patriarchal society, that it sought to do exactly that—keep them fighting. That might make interesting research actually—

"Come on, Ford. Don't worry about them. Let's just dance." Her voice was tight with tension.

I had stopped walking when I heard them talking about her. It occurred to me, embarrassingly belatedly, that Suzie was hurt by those words. I assumed Suzie to be impervious to the thoughts of small minds because of how she always stood her ground to me. And I was on the more difficult side of the scale. However, it made sense—as Green Valley was where she hailed from—that she'd be more sensitive. Roots settled deep and were hard to break.

"You realize we can hear you speaking, right?" I addressed the question at the clear leader of the four women.

"Ford. Don't worry about it." Suzie tugged on me but I remained unmoved.

"Sorry," the leader said without sincerity. "I was talking to my friends."

"I don't think you were. It seems as though you wanted her to hear."

The other girls started to look uncomfortable, but of course, the leader had to prove herself to keep her pride intact.

"She's the one that came here." Her face twisted with mock pity. "You know this is a family event. We can't have the likes of her here."

"Meaning?"

She stage whispered with a cupped hand. "Strippers." Her face scrunched up in a way that told me she practiced it in a mirror to make sure it was cute enough. "Sorry, but she should probably go."

"Does it make you feel better?"

"Her leaving?" She blinked. "Sort of. I mean the Reverend is here." She tilted her head to look me up and down. "Look, you seem like a nice guy. You should know that she has a nasty past. Done some unclean things."

"Ford." Suzie tugged harder.

I ignored her and kept my face neutral even though I seethed on the inside. "You misunderstand my meaning. Does trying to put her down make you feel better about your own life? Are you bored with your life or feel like you don't have sufficient accomplishments? Are you that miserable you feel compelled to make others feel bad? Or are you just mean-spirited?"

She opened her mouth but didn't speak.

"Because I've spent plenty of time with this woman. I've seen her help people who don't deserve it. I've seen her try to better herself. I've seen her take care of people who don't deserve it. Not once have I heard her say mean things to someone just to hurt them."

The mean girl's face paled. Her posse mumbled excuses and began to scoot away from her.

"People are not their occupations or their pasts. They're a culmination of a thousand different things and worthy of respect until they've lost it. You have lost my respect based on your actions. Suzie, the stripper you seem to look down on, has nothing but esteem in my eyes. To me, that tells me you should think about your life and your actions."

"Ford. It's okay." Suzie was pulling me but she was laughing now. Not a "that's funny" laugh; more like, "oh man, you're crazy." But either way, I would take it, because her laugh was as soothing as a creek rolling over pebbles.

We were several steps away when Suzie stopped, straightened her shoulders and looked to the main girl who stood dumbfounded.

"I hope you have a good evening." She appraised the other woman. "And I like your boots."

Pride swelled in me. I had thought Suzie might take a swing, or use one of the patented insults we'd been working on, but better than that, she took the high road. She wouldn't allow that trash to bring her down. I never wanted to show her off more than at that moment. I took Suzie to the dance floor and held her close and inhaled her. The smell of her soothed my frayed nerves and the beast inside. For once she was my savior instead of my tormentor. Her body shook and I squeezed her tighter to me.

"I can't...nobody has ever...there is literally..." She gave up trying to speak and shook her head.

She couldn't find the right words when I had. It was an unparalleled moment on all accounts. I wanted to savor it.

"I didn't say anything but fact. I've learned to pity people like that. They're obviously dealing with low self-esteem that has driven them to make life choices that result in them being deeply unhappy."

Her mouth twisted to the side. "I've never had anybody defend me like that. Without fists."

"You're a good person, Suzie. Don't let small minds make yours up."

Her face held something back. I couldn't tell if she was happy or sad. After a few minutes, she slid something into my hand. "Here," Suzie handed me a flask.

It was small and metal, and from the warmth still clinging to it, I could tell it had been tucked somewhere discreet. I took a swig and didn't react to the burn that watered my eyes. The metallic zing of the flask smelled of Suzie's curves and I thought of what it might be like to inhale her there. Suzie held my look longer and blinked slower.

I shook the flask hearing a faint splash at the bottom, "How much of this have you had?"

"Not too much." She winked from behind her mask.

Couples and groups of girls danced freely to the fast boot-stompin', hand-clapping beat coming from the band on stage. It was a group of hairy, flannel-clad men; one playing guitar, another playing upright bass, and one on the banjo and singing. They could be related, or they could all be part of that lumbersexual craze I saw on campus with the hipsters. Didn't matter. The music was damn catchy and soon Suzie and I were rocking around the floor.

I loved the surprised smile she couldn't contain after I twirled her smoothly and led her around the room a few times.

"You really can dance," she said through laughter.

"I told you."

"You keep surprising me, Ford."

Suzie surprised me every day. I spun her out again and she handled it expertly. Despite our formalwear, we were two-stepping with the rest of them. It helped to hide the feelings that kept trying to bubble up out of my chest. If Suzie was beautiful before, seeing her truly free and happy was like staring at the sun.

The tempo changed into a fast, almost swing jailhouse rock and so we stopped twirling around the floor and leaned toward each other to join the spontaneous clapping that broke out as the bearded singer wrenched out guttural tones.

"Cletus is a heck of a singer." Her shoulders rocked as she moved effortlessly to the music. She couldn't help herself. All music spoke through her and was made for her. She was a beautiful conduit.

I brought her close to me again, sliding the empty flask into my pocket. I had grown exhausted of not touching her. This amount of touching was safe. This was okay. The song came to an end and shifted gears to something slow. Her laughter dissolved into somber, uninterrupted eye contact. A banjo slowly strummed an even beat and the singer sang until the bass came in to strengthen the tempo. The simple melody and instrumentation were deceptively soulful and sent shivers down my neck.

"Lend me your eyes, I can change what you see, but your soul you must keep totally free," he sang. The singer's appearance was unkempt but his gaze was intensely focused as it swept the audience.

Suzie and I came together and rocked slowly to the words that spoke to something deeper than my analytical brain. Her scent enveloped me. I held her tighter to mask the feeling growing and duplicating inside me. I was present in this moment. In the way she felt pressed against me. In the heat of shared exertion. In the animalistic response to holding a beautiful woman. In the harmonizing voices.

It was all real. This was living.

She looked up at me and I swore she was about to tell me something I wouldn't be able to wrap my mind around. At that moment the bass, guitar, and banjo picked up the beat and a drum joined in. We were forced to change to keep up with the quickening pace.

"Awake my soul," he sang.

My soul was awake around Suzie. More than around anybody else. She drove me crazy. She shook me up. I had no idea who I was around her anymore.

"Come on, sour britches," she said.

I must have been frowning again. I couldn't help my default mode.

"Let's keep up."

We danced and danced. It was a miracle the song ended because my self-control was threadbare. The general tone switched to some up-tempo country folk dance songs. Eventually, she lost some energy and we stopped to get water.

"That's what I'm talking about, Ford." She wiped her mouth on her arm as she polished off the bottle of water.

I smiled as I deposited a dollar into the jar. There was only one thing hanging over this night. I tried to ignore it as best as I could, because while I had chosen to be present, it was clear Suzie wasn't.

I tensed with my next question. "Suzie, who do you keep looking for?"

Her face stayed neutral but her response was too fast. "I'm not looking for anyone."

"Your head is on a swivel." She had glanced toward the door for the countless time that night. I used a finger to gently bring her chin back towards me. "Are you worried about that Razor guy showing up?"

She frowned. "No, the MCs know not to come here. Not with Chief James and the Winstons crawling all over." She gestured to the stage. She gave me a bright and totally insincere smile. "Honestly, I'm not looking for anybody."

"Winston. That name sounds familiar."

She shrugged but wouldn't look at me.

"Suzie?"

She let out an exacerbated sigh. "I used to date one of them. Jethro. A thousand years ago."

My insides went icy. I actually felt the blood freeze all the way to my fingertips. "Okay."

The sudden realization that this side trip had been a ruse to get back at her ex made me feel sick. How could I once again be so caught up in a moment, only to find I was totally alone?

"Hoping to make him jealous?"

She glanced at me and frowned. "No. Nothing like that. I don't care about that man."

I waited in silence for her to tell the truth, hating how this stung.

"Plus. He's not even in town, I don't think. He's too busy attending movie premiers."

And there it was.

"Ah."

"Don't 'ah' me. I was just thinking maybe if his brothers were here they would pass on how…"

She trailed off probably realizing whatever she was about to say was going to piss me off.

"You wanted them to see how hot you are? How you had another man wrapped around your finger?"

Unexpectedly she laughed a loud crack of a laugh. "First of all, you couldn't look more miserable right now if you tried. I'm pretty sure you're incapable of being wrapped around anybody." She kept talking without seeing how deep those words cut me. "If I'd wanted to show them that then I'm failing worse than a turkey trying to fly south for the winter."

Was I that hard to read? I worried my emotions were written all over my face but she made me sound dead on the inside. Hell, I'd been having fun.

She went on, "No. I just look...better tonight. I look sophisticated."

"You want him to think that you've changed."

She shrugged and studied a couple dancing. I balled my fists and ground my teeth.

"You want him back?" I growled.

Her head snapped back to me. "It's complicated."

"I need some fresh air." I walked away without another word.

I knew it was a bad habit of mine to leave the room when I couldn't speak. But better to leave than stay and say the wrong thing. I went out a back door that led to a small back parking lot. Only a few cars remained. I sat on a short stack of cement stairs feeling the cold seep in through the thin material of my tuxedo. I tore off my mask and scrubbed my face. I focused on gulping down the cool air and pushing it out slowly in white puffs. I was angry and humiliated. This was everything I knew I would eventually feel from the first second I laid eyes on Suzie Samuels.

"Ford?" Her hand squeezed my forearm as she came to a stop at the bottom of the stairs so she was in front of me, almost face-to-face. "Hey? Look at me."

"I'm ready to go." I tried very hard not to, but her eyes were magnetic.

She rubbed her hands up and down her exposed arms. "Just wait a minute. Can I explain something?"

"I don't care." I shrugged like a petulant child. In my defense, I never had the chance when I was young.

"Oh Lord, you're too much sometimes." She tugged at my arm again until I looked at her. "You have to understand. Jethro was my first." She blushed and looked away. "I was in love with him. I assumed we'd end up getting hitched and having some kids. That's what you do around here."

I didn't want to hear this. At all.

"When we met, we had fun. We were suited, I thought. And sure, I was young and a little wild, but I was always his, even though we broke up and fought all the time." She stopped for a second when her words became a little strangled. "We got together when we were kids. I figured he just needed to sow some wild oats and eventually he'd get around to asking me to marry him.

"I didn't know that the whole time he was just stringing me along. I was one of many, turns out. I did things to keep him around. Things I'm not proud of. I'm not a good person." She looked lost in her thoughts for a second and shook her head. "It wasn't his fault. I made the choices. But he's changed now. He changed for her."

My ire faded. I stood up and stepped down so we could remain on the same level. I removed my tuxedo jacket and wrapped it around her shivering shoulders. She held it tight.

"I thought that maybe, I dunno, if people saw me like this, all fancy, and with someone like you, they'd tell him about it."

I wasn't sure how to take that.

She quickly amended, "I could be Suzie Samuels again, not Short Fuse Suze. Not 'that stripper who burned Jethro's motorcycle.' Someone bigger than this place. Someone smart." Her throat caught on that word for some reason. "Then maybe people'd realize that I'm a serious person too. I'm not just a good time."

"Suzie."

"I know what people say about me. All my life they have. I'm gorgeous but nothing going on upstairs. Down for a good time but not good enough to meet mama." Her nose wiggled back and forth like she was trying to stop tears. "I just don't understand why nobody ever thinks I'm good enough. I don't know where everything went wrong. It's like they look at me and only see..." She didn't let herself finish.

My heart thrummed loudly in my chest. I thought she must be able to hear it. Anger bubbled up in me, it boiled over the words I tried to comfort her with. It wasn't her fault. She was labeled early on, and from there on she had no choice. I understood how it worked.

"I just thought he was my person, you know? Even if the rest of the world thought I was trash at least I had my man." Her chin wobbled and my control was barely tethered. "But I was wrong. I was so wrong. He never thought of me as anything at all. Despite what everybody has told me my whole life..." She hiccupped. "I never felt stupid until the day I realized I was nothing to him."

That confession broke her. She took off her mask and tossed it aside. Her face fell into her hands and her shoulders shook. My arms brought her to me before my brain could convince me not to. I couldn't talk but I could hold her. I could hold her like I always wished I could be held. She grasped the coat tightly around herself but she shook into my arms. I got the impression this was the first time she talked about something that she obviously dwelled on. She nuzzled as close to me as she could.

"I'm sorry," she mumbled into my shirt.

"Shh. No. Why are you sorry?"

My heart was beating so hard my chest rose and fell, essentially rocking her.

"I know you hate displays of emotion." She sniffled a laugh and looked up at me.

I smiled down at her. I dug out my handkerchief from the jacket she now wore. "You really are making a scene." I softened the tease by wiping away a tear that ran down her face. Her black makeup was a mess but she never looked more beautiful to me.

She laughed and took a deep, steadying breath before she stepped back to wipe away her ruined makeup. "Man, that must've been building up for a long time. Sorry. I think all the dancing and memories here, it just unlocked something."

To both of our surprises, I gripped her closer and squeezed her until she relaxed back into my arms. "Don't apologize for feeling things freely. Just because I'm bad at it, doesn't mean I don't envy it."

She sniffled and looked up at me. She shook her head and frowned. "Your issue is not that you don't feel, Ford. Your issue is that you feel too much." She smiled and put her head back on my racing heart.

I froze at her words. Despite my best effort to hide everything, she'd seen right through me. She saw everything. All my control was pointless.

I held her an appropriate amount of time to hide my existential crisis. "I'm going to go to the restroom, then we'll get going."

"Okay." She smiled at me and I fought to keep from sprinting for the door.

Why did she look at me like that? One second she couldn't see the truth about my feelings at all, and the next she saw everything. I turned and left her standing on the stairs of the community center as I ran away from my feelings. I left everything I felt on those steps. By the time I came back, I would be in control again.

CHAPTER 18

My soul was lighter. As I swiped at my makeup with Ford's handkerchief, I felt cleansed like I had just taken a long, hot shower after a perfect performance. Poor Ford got the brunt of my emotional breakdown but it was so nice to get it out. Being back in this town after being at Ford's place and living a different life was harder than I expected. I drank too much. I felt too much.

Seeing Cletus Winston on stage reminded me of a different life and of all the ways I wasn't Sienna. It wasn't that I was hung up on Jethro; it was just that I never knew when I would feel like a woman. Not a good time girl.

But Ford had held me. He'd even made a little joke. A smile split my mouth. I looked up to the stars sparkling bright. I did miss this view back in the city. The air smelled crisp and fresh like fall. I was changed. Reborn. What a silly thing to think just from a good cry. Ford needed like twenty good cries—poor guy was so pent up.

"Look who it is."

My head snapped back down and immediately my instincts went on edge. Fear pulsed from my toes to fingertips. Out of the tree-lined darkness, appearing like ghosts, came two dark figures.

"Who's there?" I stepped back toward the light of the community center.

They stepped under a street light. It was the same two bikers from the Iron Wraiths, Rooster and Cueball. The same two that found me wherever I went. My heart raced. Now I knew it wasn't a coincidence. My first thought was, "Please, God, don't let Ford come back out here." I wanted to run up the stairs but too much movement too fast would trigger them; I just felt it. I took one slow step backward up the cement stairs.

"Just us. Don't worry," Rooster said. Soft in the face with his red beard growing in patches, his eyes had that gleam of someone who wasn't quite right.

I took another step backward, smile fixed in place, but they came forward suddenly. Cueball moved behind me blocking the door and Rooster put a hand on my arm. The scent of cigarette smoke and stale whiskey overwhelmed my panicked senses.

"Hey, boys." I smiled sweetly despite the fear screaming in my head to run.

Best to not upset them. My other hand felt around to open the door but Cueball grabbed it. What if Ford came back? What if he wasn't coming back for me at all? What if my display of emotions made him cagey? My palms grew sweaty.

"Short Fuse. This is getting out of hand." Rooster picked up some of my skirts and fisted the material. "Who you tryin' to fool, honey?"

Cueball spat behind me.

"The music's only playing for a little longer. If you want to go dance, y'all better go in now." I kept my voice light.

"Dancing sounds great." Cueball yanked my waist from behind and ground against me. "We wanna see what we've been missing."

It was violent and vulgar. His belt buckle and hardening cock pressed into my bottom. I wanted to scream. They weren't teasing at all. This time they were here to prove a point. They weren't about to leave until they got what they wanted.

Rooster's breath was vile as he said to my face, "Come on, now. We just want what's owed us."

Cueball flipped me to face him.

"Far as we see it, you owe Razor. We get to collect," he said.

I was spun from one to the other as they each ground their pelvises at me. I was dizzy. Too much dancing and whiskey and terror. Bile crawled up my throat. I didn't want this. I didn't like this. There was a time when I could go with the flow just to get it over with…but not now.

"Get her, Cueball. Remind her where she belongs."

"I'll teach her a lesson."

"You can take the trash out the trailer park, but you can't take the park out of the trash."

"I'm here with someone." I was running out of options. New fears flooded me. I tried to push myself out of Cueball's grip.

Rooster stepped closer now, holding me still. "Come on, Short Fuse. We can share."

"We have before." The other laughed.

I felt shame then. For my spiral out of control after Jethro. For using bodies and drugs to forget the emptiness inside me. Before I told myself it was my choice, but to see it through their eyes…it was too much. I needed them to leave. They had to go before Ford came back. Ford wouldn't be able to talk to them, wouldn't be able to try and rationalize with them. He'd make it worse. I couldn't let him see the person I really was.

Rooster didn't let me go. Instead, he gripped my hair, pressing bobby pins into my skull from the fancy hairdo that only hours ago had made me look sophisticated. How ridiculous to think I could ever be more than this. My eyes watered as I shook.

"Oh, you like that? You getting all wet for me baby?"

"I need to go back in." I hated how small I sounded. How weak I was. I wasn't this person. I was Suzie Samuels. I was…what?

I was a stripper. I was trash to be passed around. I was nothing. Ford kept trying to change me but here I was again. Maybe this was my place in life.

I closed my eyes and let my head fall back.

"There you go. Good girl." Rooster's breath was rancid in my face as he spoke.

I turned my head away. I studied the stars and thought how the moment would pass. How I would get over it. If they'd just hurry. I wasn't proud but I knew my place.

I conjured thoughts again as four hands groped at me. A hand cupped my breast. I squeezed my eyes shut tighter. Just a little longer. I shut down my connection to my body. I had done it with booze and drugs before, but I could do it now. I would just let them get what they needed to leave.

My skirt was lifted. The cold air on my body snapped me back to the present. Adrenaline flooded me. A sob broke from me.

"No!" I screamed. And flailed my arms. I pushed away the limbs. I couldn't do it. I couldn't be this person. "No, stop!"

They were so much stronger than me. They were two determined men and I was one woman. I stomped a foot. I bit a hand. I kicked and punched and fought for everything.

"Come on, Suzie. Be a good little slut."

"Shut your mouth and open your legs."

"No! Stop!"

I screamed louder, praying someone would hear me. Deputy James left a while back but there were still people. Somebody would hear me if I screamed loud enough. A hand clasped over my mouth and panic made me go wild. I flailed with every muscle I ever danced with. I was strong. I could do things these men could never do. I kicked and jabbed and punched and refused to stop. I shouldn't stop. I wouldn't make it easy. I would show that I never wanted this.

"Jesus, stop it woman. It'll be over soon." The hand on my mouth squeezed so hard I thought my jaw would snap. He covered my mouth and most of my nose. I couldn't find a breath.

"We were promised an easy time," aggression made Rooster sneer.

I bit down on the hand holding me. "Help!" I screamed and it ripped from me, making my throat raw. I was a wild animal.

Tears mixed with the taste of blood in my mouth. I fought and struggled but I was losing. They dragged me from the stairs and toward the trees lining the center. A rougher hand covered my mouth and nose this time. I couldn't breathe. Panic. Pure fear and panic. I wouldn't stop fighting. I wouldn't. But the gray was closing in. My muscles weakened. If I could just catch a breath...if they brought me to the trees, I would be dead. I knew it as sure as I knew anything.

"Get off her!" Ford's voice cut through like a light turned on in the middle of the night.

There was a loud snap and the arms that held me slackened. A body crumbled to the ground, taking me with it. The deadweight pinned me, crushing my chest. My lungs couldn't fill. I couldn't see. Shouts and grunts and punches were all I could hear.

"Please don't have a weapon," I prayed over and over in my head. "Please. Please." I sobbed. My eyes grew hazy. The throbbing pulsed with my heart. My vision clouded. The last thing I saw was Ford, white as a ghost and bleeding, bent over me. His eyes were black and a look I'd never seen before transformed his features.

"Are you okay?" I asked before I let go to the darkness.

***

Clifford

I was not okay. I was the furthest from okay I had been since that last time. Over ten years of control. Gone. It was barbaric, ridiculous, and humiliating. My entire body shook, pumped full of pure rage as I pried the biggest attacker off Suzie. Rapist.

Those men were about to...

I couldn't think. No. Suzie. Focus on Suzie.

She wasn't responding and terror pulsed through me; it gave me inhuman strength. I shoved the man who had toppled onto her when I attacked. I wasn't safe. I wasn't careful. I could have hurt her. The biker fell over with a loud crack as his head hit asphalt. I hoped he broke something.

I didn't waste thoughts on him. Protect Suzie. Save Suzie. I had to get Suzie out. That was my only goal. I squeezed my eyes shut tight against the image that accosted me when I stepped outside. I wanted to stop to throw up but I had to haul her limp form over my shoulder. I felt nothing as I carried her to the car. I managed to buckle her in but by the time I got to the driver's seat I couldn't see through the anger that blurred my vision. I shook so hard I couldn't get the key in the ignition.

I screamed. It was raw and burned out of my throat. The animal within me was unleashed. There was no caging me back up. Pure survival.

"Ford?" Suzie placed a hand on me. "You're shaking."

I couldn't look at her with anything more than quick glances. She sat up and her fogginess cleared away the longer she looked at me.

"I can't...get the...car started." My words halted between gasps for breath.

"Okay. It's okay. I can drive." Her palm moved up and down my arm.

Aside from the shaking I couldn't control, I was frozen solid. Muscles in my neck and shoulders were so bunched with tension I sat like the Hunchback. I looked over her face. It hurt me. It made my blood burn faster. Her beautiful cheek was scratched, a tiny bit of blood trickling down. The edges of my vision went black.

"You can't drive. You were just—"

"I sure can." Her voice was cool. How was she so cool? After what happened? How could she even breathe? "My...I was taught by Duane. He's a damn good driver. Scooch on over."

"You could be hurt."

She laughed once. "If that's your excuse then I call bull."

I shook my head, staring straight ahead.

"Ford, your whole face is covered in blood. It's getting in your eyes."

That explained why I couldn't see very well. It was hard to know what was emotion and what was physical at this point.

"I can't move." Some of the adrenaline drained and I started feeling weak. Spots on my head and body began to thrum with pain.

"Okay, okay. No worries." Her voice was still so cool and cautious.

I turned and scooped her into my arms. She gasped at my sudden action. She was probably in pain. She was probably scared of being touched but I couldn't stop myself. I was already so far gone, better to let the beast inside run the show. Before he left.

I nuzzled into her neck. My hands clasped the back of her dress before moving over her exposed skin. Feeling every inch while I could. I studied her face. I checked her body and hugged her again. How do I convey the fear? How do I show her how terrified I was seeing her…I pushed those thoughts away. Inhaling her deeply, I memorized her warmth against my cheek.

"Oh, Ford," she said my name on a sigh, and I thought I might have died. "It's okay. I'm okay. You're okay." She petted my head, her nails lightly scratching my scalp. "But we have to go. Right now."

Distantly the sound of deep rumbling motors filled the silence between us.

Suzie climbed over me, straddling me for a moment to cup my cheeks and pull my gaze toward her. She was in danger, teasing my control like this. She didn't know that I was gone and the beast was in control. Only the scene I had just witnessed kept the lust contained. I wouldn't be another man in her life hurting her for selfish needs. I would never hurt her.

"Everything is fine." She smoothed my hair back and lifted my face to hers. "I'm gonna drive us out of here. You're okay." She grabbed my hand and placed it over her heart. She was very much teasing the beast. "I'm okay." She swallowed and dropped her forehead to mine. "You saved me."

I closed my eyes and took a deep, shuddering breath. With each inhale in I regained control but other feelings started to stir. Harder-to-control feelings.

"Now we've got to get the heck out of Dodge."

I slid to the passenger seat and Suzie adjusted the driver's seat.

"Buckle up." She was all seriousness as she adjusted the mirrors and started the car. "We're gonna go fast."

I thought I couldn't be surprised anymore, but this was Suzie.

She dropped the clutch and shot us out of that parking lot like a pinball shot off the plunger. Gravel kicked into the air and the backend fishtailed. She shifted smoothly, glancing in the rearview mirror occasionally. She handled the dirt and sharp curves of the unlit back roads expertly. Her focus was written over her face. We were on the main road and heading back home before I could speak.

"You do know how to drive."

She smiled over at me. "Told ya."

<hr>

Suzie

Ford didn't speak the rest of the way home, but eventually, some of the rigid tension relaxed out of his body. I was worried about the Iron Wraiths coming after me. I was worried about what would happen to Ford now. But mostly, I worried if what he saw back there changed his opinion of me. His face was bleeding and swelling fast. I couldn't stand the silence anymore.

"You should know something about me," I said.

Ford turned from where he leaned on the door frame to watch me. I kept talking.

"I'm not a good person. I've said it before but for some reason, you seem to think I'm better than I am. Especially after how you defended me to those girls."

I glanced at Ford, it was dark but I felt him studying me. "Girls?"

"At the dance. The way you stood up for me."

He huffed an annoyed puff of air. "Not even worth the energy it takes to think of them again. They're nothing."

"Well, it still meant a lot to me." I cleared my throat. "I've done bad things. I got mixed up in a world that I'm not proud of. I've tried to clean up my act a little but after I was kicked out of the Iron Wraiths, I went a little mad. I didn't tell you about all this. But I think you should know who I really am."

"I know who you are now. That's all that matters." His voice was thick and deep in the quiet car.

"You think you do. You think you can dress me up and change who I am. But I'm ugly on the inside, Ford. My whole life I've known the path I'd be on."

"How's that?"

"I got pretty when I was young. I developed young just like my momma. I got my looks from her and everybody said it was only a matter of time till I got knocked up at sixteen like her. She ran away, but I didn't. I stayed for Daddy and then Jethro and now for the Black Demons."

"You like living here?"

I shrugged, not sure if he saw or not. "I don't have a choice now. I never did. My momma's leaving set my path."

He remained quiet.

"The thing is Jethro got me mixed up—no. I got mixed up with drugs and a wild life with the Iron Wraiths for a while. I can't take that back."

"That's true. You can't change your past. It doesn't define you. It's only part of you."

"It's easy to say that but you can't understand what it's like. I'm not trying to get into anything right now. You were so amazing back there. I just wanted you to know. People are gonna say stuff like that and expect me to be a certain way because that's how I've always been."

"Is that what you want now?"

"Just ask anybody in that town. Where else could I go? After all this, where would I go?" I thumbed back to where we left.

"Just because everybody says things about you, doesn't make them true. You get to decide who you are."

I thought about that. He'd been spouting out the same nonsense since we met but he didn't get it. Even after seeing me with those men, he still thought that. When was he going to realize that not everybody could change who they were at heart?

I shook my head. "Anyway. I don't know why I said all that."

"Thanks for telling me about your past."

I twisted my mouth to the side. There was a little more to my reputation but I was suddenly so tired. I had to focus on getting us home safely. Eventually, I slowed to a stop in front of our house. I sighed, feeling a hundred years old. The night had been long—and strange.

"Thank you again for saving me."

He frowned and then winced.

"Come on, let's go inside so I can clean you up."

***

Clifford

The counter in the bathroom was cluttered with bloody washcloths and cotton balls. I sat on the toilet seat, head leaning back and eyes closed, processing the events of the night. A headache, caused by bad choices and adrenaline, pounded behind my eyes. The full impact of my wounds wasn't hitting me yet but based on her expression, it wasn't good. Her face was clear of makeup, revealing smooth, creamy skin and long eyelashes that swept her cheeks as she examined me. Her full lips pursed in concentration.

I closed my eyes because being this close to her, her breath on my lips, was torture.

Her car-ride confession replayed in my head. If she thought that she was a bad person, I couldn't imagine what she'd think of me if I told her the truth of who I was. She was scarred by a mother who left her with a man who didn't care about anything but where his next drink came from. The only other man she loved seduced her into a life she never wanted. A panic rose in my chest. There had been moments dancing with her when something bigger than me grew and bloomed in my chest but now I clamped that down.

"Damn, Ford." Cold rubbing alcohol dabbed another cut on my cheek.

"What?" I rasped through my raw throat.

"You took down two grown men. Bikers." She clicked her tongue.

"I'm not proud of that. Resorting to violence makes me no better than them." I didn't remember much from what happened. I came outside and Suzie was gone from the steps. Two men were holding her and she was fighting with the wild strength of total fear. One of them was yanking up her beautiful skirt when red began to bleed across my vision. It wasn't a decision. I attacked. I didn't stop until Suzie was safe.

"Maybe," she said with a smile when I squinted one eye open to look at her. "But it was still pretty badass."

She cleaned a spot on my forehead that burned. I sucked in a breath.

"Sorry," she whispered.

"That person out there wasn't me."

"I'm not so sure about that." I was going to argue with her but then she let out a breath that heated my neck. "I like you, Ford." I opened my eyes and she was right there in front of me, looking back and forth between my eyes. She said the words like they surprised her.

"I like you, Suzie."

She raised her eyebrows like she never expected me to say it back. "Oh."

I swallowed. I wanted to say more. I liked her so much. I liked everything about her. I liked her dangerous, scary amounts.

She blinked a few times. Her gaze moved over my face and she nodded. "Okay, I think that's as good as it's going to get."

"Are you okay?" I gently examined a red mark on her cheek.

"It's nothing." She nuzzled into my hand and shrugged.

She went to stand but I tugged her back down.

"It's not nothing." I studied her green eyes for the truth. "Are you okay?"

"I am now." Her smile was shaky.

We watched each other. I stood and took her with me. I hugged her again. Once I started touching her freely, I couldn't stop. I liked her so damn much.

"Oh," she said surprised again but wrapped her arms around me. "I know it was tense. But usually, I can handle myself." I leaned back and she shrugged under my skeptical look. "Well, normally I can. I don't know. I just…I can sort of check out. This time—"

"What do you mean?"

"Well, you know when things are kind of out of control. You sort of need to retreat into your brain. Detach from your body. When I was partying a real lot I would do that sometimes if the guys got a little too crazy."

She laughed it off. I was so drained from the fighting, but anger seeped back anyway. How do you tell someone they didn't have to live like that?

"You like partying with those guys?" I asked.

"I used to. I dunno. I thought I did." She collected the soiled towels and debris to dump in the waste bin. "It was easier than being sad." She smiled. I watched her closely. She was so broken and abused. Her whole life she had been made to be nothing more than an object—a means to an end.

Sort of like I was using her.

"Anyway. You gonna tell me what happened back there?" She locked her gaze on me.

She leaned back against the counter. I stood inches apart from her.

"I guess I sort of check out too sometimes. But I go in the opposite direction." I scratched the back of my neck. "When I was younger, I'd get mad and it was like a switch flipped. The anger just took over."

"Wait, are you serious? *You* lost control?"

I huffed a laugh. If she knew even half the truth. I was nothing more than the rest of the trash in her life. "Yeah. I had—my home life growing up wasn't great."

She raised an eyebrow. "I know you were a foster kid but for some reason," she shrugged, "I got the impression you were rich."

"Hardly. Look, it's late." I glanced at my watch. "Well, early. We should get some sleep. I have a lot of work to catch up on today."

"Okay." She studied me until I fidgeted.

I let out a breath, afraid she was going to pry. I appreciated that she told me about Jethro, but that story was rainbows and kittens compared to my childhood. I was half out the door when she grabbed my hand. She stood on toes to grab my face gently. She pulled my head down to hers and kissed my cheek. She ghosted a kiss on my forehead, then my lips, soft and quick. I felt it. Everywhere. Instantly.

"Thank you again. I don't know what I would have—"

I cut her off. "I'll always protect you if I can." I closed my eyes for a second to think. "I'm sorry I left you alone out there. If I hadn't left…"

"If you hadn't come back." She corrected. "That's all I care about. You came back."

She needed to know that people should fight for her. People shouldn't call her stupid. Labels were a self-fulfilling prophecy and she hadn't had a chance from the start.

"Okay."

"Goodnight, Ford." She walked out of the bathroom and turned off the light, leaving me in the darkness.

"Goodnight." A thought jumped into my head. "Suzie, wait." She was just a shadow in the dark hallway but her footsteps came to a stop. "Jethro Winston is an idiot."

"Unfortunately, he's not. Him and his kin are good people. It would probably be a lot easier if they weren't. I hate that I got him at his worst, but I'm glad he found happiness." Her steps retreated until I heard her door close softly.

I closed my eyes and shook my head. I wanted Suzie to have everything. I wanted her to have somebody who could give themselves to her one hundred percent. I could never be that person for her. I could never let go of control completely.

"UT Professor Arrested for Felony Assault and Battery."

The night could have gone so much worse. We were lucky to get out of there while we could. I was losing focus, getting distracted. It was time to be better and get through this so I could get back to my life.

CHAPTER 19

CLIFFORD

hump. Thump. Thump.

I knocked my head softly but repeatedly on yet another grant proposal. Maybe if I did it long enough, I would stop thinking. I would be completely spent of brain cells.

"This is not a good sign."

I didn't lift my head. Only Jack would come in without permission. It was fall break and only teachers were here.

"Hi." My voice was mumbled by the desk.

"Hello, Ford's head." His use of my new nickname caused me to resume my penitence.

Thump. Thump. Thump

"Okay, okay. Let's just stop that." He put his hand on my shoulder. "I did knock, but you probably didn't hear it over the sound of your self-flagellation."

"Self-medication."

"My mistake." I heard the familiar shuffle as Jack popped into my other office chair. "Things are good then?"

"Peachy." I looked up.

"Holy crap your face." Jack did nothing to soften his horrified reaction.

"It feels worse than it looks."

"What the hell happened Saturday night?"

I sat up but only because I didn't want to re-open the wound on my head. "Oh, the usual. Went to a ball with a beautiful woman. Danced with millionaires. Then went to a jam session in Green Valley where I beat the shit out of two bikers, berserker style."

His eyebrows rose. "Maybe I do need to get out more."

I slouched back in my chair and rubbed my eyes. It hurt. Everything hurt. That's what I deserved for losing control. I picked up a pencil and gripped it.

"Seriously, man, what's going on? You beat up two guys?"

"Suzie helped a little." He waited with expectant eyebrows. "These bikers. They cornered her when I was inside and—"

I found I still couldn't think about it, let alone talk about it.

Jack wiped a hand down his mouth. "Shit."

"I barely got her out of there. She wasn't fully conscious when I did." The pencil in my hand snapped in half.

"But you did. You got her out."

I nodded, but felt more culpability than I could let go of.

"Did you call the police?" he asked.

"Suzie says there's no point. Any more trouble will just make it worse. She keeps saying 'her guys' will handle it."

He nodded like he got it but didn't like it.

"She said they were a rival with her boss's gang or something."

"Totally different world down there."

"Yeah." I scooped up the pencil remains and tossed them into the garbage next to my desk.

Jack sighed. "Is she okay?"

"I think so."

"She's tough."

I agreed—but I also knew how tender she was. I learned what she held inside her. The fact that she could still be so optimistic, so loyal at all was a miracle.

"She seems so immune to the injustice. That feels more hopeless than if it was hard for her. It kills me," I said.

"It's terrible. All of it."

"I can't do this anymore."

"Do what?" He straightened with a frown.

"I can't keep up this charade of research. What have I even done in the weeks she's been with us? What am I proving?"

Jack stayed quiet. He must have been holding his tongue for some time.

"I've grown to care about her," I said softly.

"Me too."

"When I'm around her—my control hangs by a thread." I shoved my chair back to stand and tried to pace behind my desk. It wasn't a big area, so it didn't take long to traverse the distance. My movements were like one of those little carpet cleaning robots stuck in a corner. "And when I saw those guys hurting her…" I closed my eyes and saw a rough hand shoved up her skirt and the look of absolute terror on her face. I couldn't stop seeing it. "I can't explain it. It's like something broke. I was watching from a distance as my body was on autopilot. I could have murdered someone."

"But you didn't. And Suzie would have been raped or killed. You saved her. Don't forget. Men like that, they aren't trying it on. Their intentions were clear."

"They held her down, Jack. Telling her to just go with it. Like she owed them something." I stopped because emotion clogged my voice.

Jack's nostrils flared and fists clenched. I saw my own look of helplessness reflected in his eyes. "You stopped them. She's so strong."

I pushed up my glasses to rub the bridge of my nose. "I haven't snapped like that since I was a teenager. I'm not normal when I'm around her."

Jack frowned. "What's normal? You defended her. What other choice was there?"

Jack knew my past, to some extent. We met in juvie but I don't think he ever understood how unstable I was.

"I don't know what to do now. But I know I can't keep this up. She can't live with us, live this life, only to go back to that…mess. What do I do?" I asked him with pleading eyes.

"You have to talk to Suzie. She deserves a say in what happens now."

I nodded because he was right. I was afraid to talk to Suzie. I was afraid of what truths might come out, but there was no other way to move forward.

At the moment there was another knock on the door.

Jack stood. "I'll leave you to your self-abuse. Maybe go climbing today. The day is young. You don't need to be here."

"I have a lot of work."

"If that work is avoiding Suzie, then I'm sure you do." He went to the door to let in the visitor as he walked out.

Dean Lucero was dressed in her standard uniform of khaki pants and a brown paisley-print sweater, wearing a flat-mouthed frown.

"Mr. Jones, how goes the math world?"

"Calculated." I'd heard Jack respond with the joke before. He flicked a last wave and went on with his day.

Dean Lucero clasped her hands low in front of her. "Mr. Rutledge, is this a good time?"

"Sure. Have a seat."

"No need. I won't be long." She held her chin up, but her face was a mask. I couldn't discern the nature of this visit. Dread transformed into a different level of anxiety entirely.

"Is everything okay?"

She pointed to my face. "You tell me."

"An accident."

"Right." She hovered just behind the chair Jack had just been in and clasped the back. "I spoke with Ted Bouffant this morning. I hadn't realized he was your donor."

"You know him?"

"Of course. He's one of the biggest donors to the school. I had never spoken directly with him before. Typically, his donations go to the sports departments."

"I didn't know that."

"I'm not sure what you did to convince him to donate to your cause, but the stipulations of his donation were clear. One hundred percent goes to your research, to be divvied up however you see best."

My heart hammered against my chest. Of course. The words I'd been desperate to hear for months and instead of relief, I felt renewed dread.

"That's terrific."

"It is." She smiled a genuine smile. "This must be a huge relief to you."

"Yes." Tension pounded at my temples.

"This is a huge deal. I'm very proud of you, Dr. Rutledge."

I swallowed a sour taste back down my throat.

"He mentioned a contingency in your research—that the money will be deposited in December after the conclusion of a social experiment?" Her voice lifted in question. Her own concerns flashed on her face. It's all just a little too good to be true, wasn't it?

"Yes. I'm confident that the research will prove conclusive. My assistant has been extremely helpful."

Images of Suzie dancing flashed into my mind. Of her quirked mouth and teasing eyes.

"Is this assistant a grad student?"

"No. She's not a student of the university at all."

Dean Lucero thought this information over, gently tapping the elbow of her sweater.

"Well, it all sounds very exciting. You keep doing what you're doing and everybody wins. This is a great boost to this department's reputation, as well as your own. I had a good feeling about you when we brought you aboard."

"Thank you."

I fought to keep my face blank. What could I do now? How could I stop when I was so close? But Suzie...what did she want?

She patted the back of the chair as though she wanted to say more but gave a curt nod.

Once the door was closed, I dropped my head to the desk.

I took Jack's advice and came home after the discussion with Dean Lucero. I was too distracted and worried to fill out any more grant proposals anyway. I hoped Suzie would be out for the rest of the day. She'd been enjoying the company of new acquaintances lately. From what I gathered from our bits of conversation, it was some sort of intellectual society with shared interests where they discussed world news and volunteered their time. Everything and anything to help elevate the mind, that's what I'd said. I was happy to see she took my advice and found a better group of people to hang around with.

I walked into the den after setting down my stuff on the hall tree. Suzie bent over in front of me and smacked her ass loudly.

My mouth fell open. All my chairs had been moved to the front room and were occupied with a group of women writhing around in spandex as hip hop blared from the speakers.

"There you go. Really work it." She snapped up and her hair flipped out all around her. A whiff of her sweet scent flew to me. Her back was to the doorway so she couldn't see me standing there watching helplessly. "Don't be afraid to get into it. The more turned on you are, the more your partner will feel it."

What had I done to deserve this? Had I offended the gods? But no, I knew exactly why I was being punished. Suzie moved her hands up her body. The women in the background mimicked her, tossing their hair and rubbing themselves. This would be a good time to go.

I turned on a dime and made for the stairs.

"Ford?" The music quieted. "Hey, wait."

I cursed my loud walking and turned to her and the ladies. "Hello." I waved.

They all spoke at once. "Oh, this is your Ford?" "Wow, that's a shiner." "He's a looker."

I stood still and intently studied a distant point somewhere on the wall behind them all as they waved from their chairs, spread-eagle.

"Ladies, this is Ford. Ford, these are the gals." Her face was lit up like after she went downstairs to practice on the pole. Like she was lit up from the inside out. "Ford hurt his lovely face saving my life. And I told you. You weren't allowed to say anything about it."

"I know, but damn." This came from the redhead who came to stand next to her. She appraised me with arms crossed, like my mere existence had already offended her. "Thank you for protecting her."

"Ford, this is Gretchen, my friend I told you about."

I shook her hand. She crossed her arms immediately and frowned at me. "I want to ask you some questions about this 'research.'" She uncrossed her arms long enough to air quote me.

"Gretch, I told you all about it. Leave him alone."

The redhead walked backward and collected a bag. When Suzie turned to face me, her back to her friend, Gretchen pointed two fingers to her eyes, then pointed them to me and then back again. Threat received loud and clear. I kept my face impassive.

She and the other women chatted as they collected their things. Suzie wiped off sweat as she came up to me. Her eyes were bright and her cheeks full of color.

"Need something?"

I decided my talk with her could wait. I couldn't talk to her now. Not when she looked so distractingly full of joy. Instead, I took the coward's way out.

"Can you turn down the music? I'm going to go work in my office."

"We're done. Are you okay? How's your face feeling?" She pressed her cool fingers to my cheek and I fought from purring into them.

"I'm fine. I have to go work."

"Weren't you supposed to talk to Suzie about something?" Jack, who had the world's worst timing, appeared out of thin air to ruin my life. He spoke through a mouthful of cereal as he leaned coolly in the doorway.

I hoped he choked on his Frosted Flakes.

"What's up, Ford?" Suzie asked as the room cleared of women.

"It's okay. It can wait." I ground out, glaring at Jack.

"I'm free." She waved to a chorus of goodbyes at the front door.

"Fine."

"Why don't you show her Obed or Clear Creek?" Jack had to tilt his head back to slurp around his words.

I glared at Jack again. The bastard smiled.

"Thanks, Jack. That's a great idea," I gritted out.

"I'd been wondering if you'd show me your secret life." Suzie grinned with such eagerness there was no way I could dampen her spirits.

"We can go for a walk," I said. "It's too late to climb today."

"Let me make sure the girls got off okay and I'll go get ready." She hopped up and down with a little clap.

She was gone before I realized what was happening.

"You're smiling," Jack told me. "I wanted to let you know in case it hurt."

I scratched my beard. "I hate you."

"I hate you too, buddy. Go have fun. Talk. Thank me tomorrow." Jack disappeared into the kitchen.

Suzie and me, alone, in beautiful nature. No pressure. I could handle this. I'd be too distracted watching the trails and not her lips. This would be fine. I would be fine.

Suzie

For someone who wanted to talk, Ford spent most of the drive in his usual stony silence. I'd grown used to quiet drives with him though so I didn't usually take it personally. Today his silence felt extra loud. I ignored it. He needed to figure out what he wanted to say and how. That part made me a bit anxious, because it meant he was in knots over something related to me. He'd talk when he was good and ready. I watched the passing forest grow denser as the roads got windier.

I, on the other hand, was looking forward to spending some time with him outside the house. I needed to get out. I needed to not think about trying to make myself better for a little while. I especially needed a break from reading.

I'd been thinking about our kiss a lot, too. I had barely brushed my lips against his skin. Yet I couldn't get it out of my mind. Every time I caught a whiff of his scent or remembered the heat of his body next to mine, my insides got all squishy like I might collapse into a pile of pudding.

Ford pulled into a parking lot with a wood sign that said Obed River Trailhead. He reached to the back seat, causing his upper body to come close to mine. I blinked, stupidly thinking he had been about to lean in for a kiss. Well, in my defense, it's all I'd been thinking about. How I wanted it. How it was a bad idea. How he may or may not want it too.

"Let's walk to the trail and I'll show you where I typically like to climb. Maybe sometime we can come with my equipment and I'll show you the ropes?"

"Was that a climbing pun?" I sucked in my lips to keep from smiling.

Ford twisted back around to the front again, a fleece pullover in his hand. "I guess it was. I'm going to pretend it was on purpose." He smirked.

Call the media! Ford Rutledge smirked at me. I must have been too quiet because his gaze faltered and fell to my lips where they were parted in a stupid grin.

"Let's get moving before it gets too late. These short days can get cold fast."

I was glad for the extra coat he grabbed, but after a few minutes of walking on an incline through heavy forest I was plenty warm. The trees were beautiful and the air crisp. Sometimes I forgot how beautiful it was just right outside my door. It sorta reminded me of the trails I'd gone on with Jethro. We'd hike out to go fool around away from his brothers and my daddy. The thoughts of Jethro took me by surprise only because it was nice to find that I felt nothing. Maybe a little sentimental thinking about being so young and having a whole life ahead of me, but not that clawing ache in my chest and not the humiliation of rejection.

I'd probably still key his stupid car if I saw it though.

We rounded a corner and I was met by the sound of rushing water where the creek joined a larger river and a couple of tiny waterfalls trickled down like a soothing fountain.

"This is Clear Creek. Eventually, it leads to Obed River. It starts as a tiny trickle and then eventually becomes a massive river that's formed some amazing landscapes. It's pretty incredible."

"It's beautiful."

"Just wait until you see the rock faces. Perfect for climbing."

"How'd you get started in climbing? I still can't believe I didn't know this about you. It's like you lead a double life."

He cleared his throat. "I discovered it when a few kids in my class said they were coming up here. I was trying out new ways to burn some energy. I had tried sports and different types of self-defense but I didn't like the violence. Something about physically touching nature and the effort required to scale a wall appealed to me. And if you do it right, nobody gets hurt."

This wasn't the first time Ford alluded to a dark past and an aversion to violence. I loved that he shared this with me. I smiled and we continued on. My cheeks and nose were cold but the cool fall air and a good hike made me feel invigorated. Eventually, the trail widened. One person was bouncing down the rock face on a rope held by another. They waved friendly enough. Ford and I waved back. I wondered if they thought we were together.

He noted me watching them and shared, "That's called rappelling. Some people call it abseiling."

"It looks fun."

"It is. You know what I like about all this?" Ford asked.

"Huh?" I studied his profile as he spoke, his gaze tracking up the cliff face.

"I like rock climbing because it seems straight forward and relatively simple but it requires all your attention. You have to think about your foot and hand placements in advance or risk getting stuck and having to backtrack. Or worse. It's exhausting and highly physical but still requires focus. I can't think about anything else when I'm up here."

"That sounds nice."

I loved when Ford spoke about things he loved. His mouth moved freely and his hands got involved. It was such a nice change from the stiff, contained man. Also, imagining those intense muscles in his arms working as he wedged and jammed his fingers into the rock face did some weird magic to my girlie parts.

"You'd be good at it," he said. "You're very athletic."

"Right. I can already see myself as a climber. I'd shoot right out the gate and climb until I got stuck then fall back down and give up. Hell, I'd probably just stay at the bottom and watch everyone else climb."

"That's not true. I wouldn't let you." His words were almost flirtatious and my goodness, if this was what Ford was like in nature, I'd put up with it a hell of a lot more to see this side of him. We held each other's gaze until he broke away. "Next time we can try. It's already getting kind of late."

I was still thinking about how he said "next time." I wondered how much of the future he thought about. After December, did he think of an "us" at all? I couldn't help how joyous I felt with Ford right now. I was at peace.

We stepped through some scraggly small trees breaking through large grey rocks onto a precipice. The world dropped away before us, falling into a pit filled with color. My stomach went with it. I wobbled.

"Careful now." He grabbed my hand to steady me.

The air was chillier with the wind whipping at us. The sweat from the climb dampened my hair and sent chills through me.

Ford frowned. "You're cold."

"I'm okay. It's beautiful here."

We surveyed the changing leaves below us. A massive valley exploding in fireworks of red, oranges, and yellow and decorated with pops of green pine lay below. A thick river wound its way through it all. I felt small in comparison.

"I can never get enough of this view."

I turned back toward his voice. His expression, usually so stern, had softened. There was something about being close to Ford that I didn't feel when I was around other men. Other men, they were just bodies or sometimes more like different animals. When Ford was this close, I was more aware of every touch. Almost to the point of fixation. Like now. If he would just take a few steps closer, our hands would brush.

Ford had a way of treating me with his own particular brand of sour, but at least it was as an equal. If he didn't stop looking so sweet and treating me so well and talking to me like an actual person, I was bound to do something stupid. It'd been a while since I had done something stupid.

I'd changed lately. The thought of getting the VIP stage held less allure. I wanted out of my house and I wanted to live on my own but had no idea how I could do either without hurting Daddy and with no money. I hadn't allowed too much thought about it. I couldn't. The attack by the Iron Wraith guys really shook me. I was used to guys getting rough. Something about being all dressed up and feeling so good about myself and looking classy had made me feel untouchable to the scum. Yet it hadn't mattered. One look at me and they treated me the same. It wouldn't matter how I changed on the outside. I would always be Suzie Samuels. Short Fuse. Best to get through this without feeling too much more.

"Now I'm the one who smells burning." Ford's voice broke me from my thoughts.

"Just woolgathering." I smiled to see he had stepped closer to me.

He cleared his throat and inched closer yet. "You can have my coat if you want."

"I don't want your coat, Ford." I was sad and wallowing in self-pity. It made me reckless.

His frown was back. I couldn't help but huff a little laugh.

I stepped slightly in front of him so that his heat warmed my back. I couldn't face him for the silly thing I was about to say.

"I don't want your coat because I want you to hold me."

The heat coming off his body took my chills away but I still shivered. My knees felt weak and I licked my lips.

He cleared his throat again and I waited for his rejection. My heart skipped a beat when his arms came around me, wrapping me up from behind. I leaned back and rested against his chest. He was a few inches taller than me and we fit just right. I melted into him. It was the most comfortable place I'd ever been, like staying in bed on a winter morning.

"I have to tell you something." He squeezed me tighter and took a deep breath that made the little hairs at my neck stir.

At his words, I prepared myself. Things hadn't been going too well with his attempts to change me. I knew I wasn't what he expected. I wasn't trainable like he'd thought.

I said, "Okay," in a small voice.

"I'm having conflicting feelings."

"About?"

He had to feel how my racing heart shook my whole body.

"This experiment. It's not going according to the plans. I don't know what we're doing anymore." As he spoke his deep voice rumbled down my back and I felt it everywhere.

I closed my eyes. "Am I disappointing you?" I hadn't meant to say it. I especially didn't want to sound so damn pathetic but the words just slipped out. I kept trying—in my own way—to make him happy, but time and time again I messed up. Or maybe I didn't mess up, but I certainly wasn't progressing quickly enough.

"I—what? No. Suzie, No." He took a deep breath and I knew he was trying to find his words. "My dean came by today. She was checking that I was doing everything to maintain funding. But I'm having doubts."

My heart raced faster. This was it. He was kicking me out. I knew it. I wasn't ready. I couldn't go back to my old life in Green Valley. Not yet.

"Are you kicking me out?"

"Do you want to leave?"

"No."

Ford turned me gently by the shoulders until I looked at him. "I don't want you to go."

"Okay."

We stared at each other a long time. I smiled first. He followed my lead and I thought his smile was the best thing I'd ever seen.

"I thought maybe you were kicking me out because I'm too stupid or something."

Ford huffed a breath. "Have people been telling you you're stupid all your life?"

"I guess. I think people want me to know my place."

"Suzie." He shook his head. "You aren't stupid. You are... People shouldn't be allowed to tell others that. Especially not children." He fisted his hands and stomped away. "It's not okay."

"I appreciate you, Ford, but I know what my strengths are—"

"You tell someone they're one thing their whole life, of course, they're going to believe it."

I frowned. "But I'm not smart. I never got good grades."

"Not having access to information does not make you stupid. And schooling isn't the only way to have intelligence. I've watched you read a room the second you walk into it. You obviously have far more social sense than I ever will. And you are so supremely gifted with your body."

"Now that I've been told before." I flipped my hair with a showy wink.

"I'm serious." He waived away my comment, frustration growing. "With music. You feel it in your bones. And you teach people too. Not everybody has a gift for teaching, let me tell you."

I smiled down at my muddy sneakers. I did love dancing and teaching. "Today, Gretchen told me that she hasn't felt that hot in years." I had to admit, it sorta felt nice to lift women up and give them confidence. I was teaching them to dance for themselves. Not for men or money.

"You have a gift of making people feel like they're the most important person in the world."

I shook my head studying the valley below.

"I'm serious. The first time I saw you, I thought it was part of your routine. I thought maybe you made your money that way. But you have an energy about you."

"The first time you saw me you'd just busted Occum's balls. It was great." These compliments made me itchy. "I still can't believe you told him off the way you did."

"Were you eavesdropping?" he asked.

"I had to hear who was pissing Occum off so much, didn't I?"

Some of the tension released from his shoulders and he shook his head with a laugh. "That guy. There's something off."

"He's not nice, but he protects his own."

Ford looked like he was about to say something but thought better of it.

"So if you aren't kicking me out, what are you going to do?"

I was so afraid of his answer and afraid of how much his answer meant to me. I didn't want another man to have this power over me, and yet he had found a way to worm right in.

"First I wanted to give you this. We're done with it." He pulled the worn notebook from his back pocket.

It was the one he'd been tracking my to-do list on. He handed it to me. The way I clutched it, it could have been a diamond ring.

"Okay." It felt like a grand gesture. Only I wasn't sure what kind. The middle finger kind of gesture, or what?

"No more lists. No more changes. Do with it what you will. I don't need it. You decide if you want to do anything or nothing with it."

"Okay." I studied him. He was watching me so intently. His focus flicked all around my face. I wanted to lean into him.

"Also, I'm not sure what to do next. That's why I wanted to talk to you. I wanted to provide you with all the information to allow us to make the best choice. So that we're both okay with the next course of action. I'm worried that my reasons for keeping you are entirely selfish so I want to make sure you decide what we do next."

It was like a giant bag of down feathers burst inside me. Instead of answering I wrapped my arms around him. I brought my lips to his and showed him what I thought of his plan to talk to me first.

I thought it was clucking brilliant.

CHAPTER 20

CLIFFORD

I don't think I even realized how badly I needed to kiss Suzie until her lips were on mine. It was a physical release of tension in my muscles. I'd been twisting and squeezing tighter and tighter since the moment I met her and now everything released. Her lips were even softer than the brief pecks she'd given me. Her smell was all-encompassing and hypnotic and sweet and, God, her body against mine…I couldn't even think straight.

I had been surprised, as always, by her actions. That was Suzie for me. Surprising.

It wasn't until she started to move away, her body stiffening, that I realized I had been too stunned to move. I had to remedy that.

My arms enclosed her, one hand reaching up to still her head from its retreat, the other holding the small of her back more firmly. I tilted my head to deepen the kiss. I needed more. I explored and shared and gave and took all with my tongue and lips.

She moaned. It undid me. My hands itched with the need to find relief on her body. I explored her curves. I squeezed a healthy handful of her ass and caught her surprised gasp with my mouth. I pushed her hair back and shirt down to kiss her neck and shoulder.

The forest was around us, the light fading, but I couldn't let go of the salty-sweet flavor of her. Her hands seemed equally unable to be still because they rubbed over my chest, down my shoulders to squeeze my biceps. I flexed her harder to me, preening over the compliment of my muscles and not giving a shit about how ridiculous I was in the moment.

I was lost in her. There was only right now. Right, wrong, ethical could all go to hell. This was pure, and the closest thing to a religious experience.

"Ford," she groaned my name with her head thrown back.

I nipped and kissed, and eventually, found a fraction of a brain cell to stop. Eventually. I slowed and she did too. We pulled back to blink at each other in stunned shock.

"Wow." Her word was a laugh that sounded like awe.

"I agree."

"Okay." She blinked a few times and took a deep breath. "Wow."

"Yes. Now that that's taken care of…" I swallowed with difficulty.

Her fingertips were exploring her lips as though they had an explanation of what just happened. It was…distracting. Her eyes were lit from within and hard to look away from.

"Glad we got that out of our systems." She nodded seriously. She added, "We should make a plan."

"I agree." I nodded, going for serious composure. I hadn't gotten anything out of my system. I had just introduced my system to a stimulation it had never known the likes of before, and it craved a repeat. Even my hands, which should have been resting safely at my side, still held her, albeit not so intimately.

"Stop smiling. I'm trying to think," she said.

I sucked in my lips but the smile wouldn't be wiped away. "Well, stop your eyes from beaming. Then maybe we can get somewhere."

She laughed and shook her head, blushing as she turned her gaze toward the ground. I made Suzie Samuels blush.

"Something you should know about me. It's critical that I understand cause and effect. I'm known to fixate sometimes until I understand fully why a certain behavior produces particular responses."

Her dark brows furrowed. "Okay. Thanks for sharing."

I stepped closer again and found my hands rubbing up and down her arms beyond my control. "That's why it's imperative for me to understand what I said that caused that reaction in you." Understanding dawned; a slow smirk spread. "Not that I'm complaining," I added quickly.

"I didn't think you were. Though if anyone were to kiss me like I'm going to war and then complain, it would be you." She softened the tease with a touch to my nose. She flushed a little more. "It's silly and..." she paused for the right word. "Impetuous?"

I nodded with a smile. That woman was a sponge for knowledge. "There's little about you that's not impetuous. I envy that about you."

"Short Fuse has always felt like an insult to me."

I didn't like to think of other people insulting her or claiming to know who she was when they obviously had no clue. I frowned. "They meant it as one. Or at best, a way to remind you of your place. I meant that I admire your courage to do what you feel is right in that moment, instead of overthinking it until it's too late."

"Oh. Well, it's not always great."

"There are pros and cons to both sides."

She thought for a minute and said, "True."

"Are you avoiding my question, Ms. Samuels?"

She laughed a little and shook her head. "I'm really not. You just sidetracked me."

"Cause and effect." I waved my hand to say, out with it.

"It's so silly. I just...you just... You asked me." She blinked in a rapid flurry. "You waited to make a choice about my life until you talked to me." Her eyes gleamed with a hint of extra moisture. Almost to herself she added, "I knew I was about to do something stupid."

I processed all that. Something so simple and seemingly obvious—though I had needed Jack to remind me—had been so thoroughly nonexistent in her life that she'd wanted to show me gratitude for my paltry offering. It was heartbreaking and a little unnerving. I wasn't sure what answer I had even wanted. I would have been okay with "I couldn't keep my hands off you," but not something like this. Everybody should be treated with a minimal amount of respect and consideration. That's a right, not a privilege. It somehow tinged the kiss with a cast of solemnity. But God, it had been a great kiss. Kiss felt like too shabby a word for what we just shared. It was an experience. A cleansing.

"Noted," I started again. "You should always be consulted about your life."

"I know."

Sometimes people said "I know" but then never acted like they knew. I found that response odd.

"Anyway," she said. "Nothing's changed. We are still on track. I want to impress that man with my transformation." She looked to the side, her eyes going hazy. "I *am* transformed."

"Are you sure?" To me, it felt like everything had changed. I was a different man than I was ten minutes ago. My pants were certainly tighter.

"Yeah. You need your research money. " After a brief hesitation, she nodded with determination. "I need my stage. We'll keep on keeping on."

We shook hands and I laughed at the formality, as my hands had just been roaming her body. Then I was thinking about my hands roaming her body some more. She had kissed me out of gratitude. I kissed her back because there were no other options for me. I could—and would—contain myself now.

"About the kiss," I said.

"I know. I wasn't thinking. I'll behave." She seems abashed and I hated that.

"It's not that I didn't enjoy it. I did enjoy it. Tremendously." She chewed her bottom lip while I spoke. "We have to be careful. The eyes of the school are watching now. This donation is a big deal."

She nodded with consideration. "Gotcha. No more handsy-fun-times."

Even though I knew it was the best option, I wanted to know more about what handsy-fun-times might entail. Maybe a bed would be involved—or at least a comfortable surface—and not the side of a pine tree for support.

"Okay. So one more question." Her tone had grown serious.

"Hmm?" I was lost in thought and looked up to find her standing in front of me.

"You know how you're making me read all that philosophy stuff?"

"Yes?" I memorized how full her lips were and how her green eyes almost glowed in the dusky lighting.

"If two people kiss in the woods, and there's nobody around to see it, does it still count as unethical?"

"Interesting hypothesis." My nostrils flared and I bent to be closer to her. My hands slid behind her, hauling her closer to me. "We should test it."

"But then no more," she said on a whisper.

"Right." I was so close I felt the warmth of her breath tickle my lips.

And then I kissed her. With more luxuriousness than before. I savored every detail knowing we'd have to be strong after this. We were protected by location, but after we left this haven we were done. I wished I had years and not just minutes. I needed more. She gasped a hot little sound that drove me crazy, so I found the nearest tree and backed her to it. I wasn't smooth about it and the tree could have been poking into her back, so I used my arms to shield her. Suzie tested my control. I wouldn't be another man to hurt her. Ever. But enough to remind her that I was a man who wanted her desperately.

"Ford," she gasped as I moved to inhale her smell and drag my lips up and down the smooth column of her neck.

I decided then and there that I very much preferred her nickname for me over anything I'd ever been called. I wanted to hear her scream it. I wanted to make her cry out my name until she couldn't breathe anymore.

I finally broke away. "I can't kiss you anymore. I can't blur the lines. My whole future rides on this. I can't kiss you. I can't." I kissed her. "After this."

"Okay."

I kissed the area where her chin met her ear. "Okay." I kissed her cheek. "After this, I'm stopping."

"Yes."

"I am." I kissed gently next to her eye.

Her hands were twisted in my shirt under my jacket. "So stop."

My lips weren't kissing hers but they moved back and forth over hers, soft against soft, nuzzling them. "I thought I had."

She laughed deep and sensual.

I groaned and dropped my forehead to hers. We grinned big goofy smiles at each other.

Belatedly, I registered that the sun was almost down.

She seemed to notice too. "We should head to the car."

"Okay." I took a deep breath in and counted the rocks I saw in my direct line of sight.

We grabbed our water bottles and headed back. I held her hand the whole way. Maybe because of the encroaching darkness. Maybe because I needed more time before breaking the connection. Either way, I held her until I was forced to release her, to allow her to get in the car. We smiled at each other again before I closed her door.

As soon as we had driven a few miles and our phones had reception, Suzie's began to ring.

She frowned as the screen lit up her face in the dark car.

"What is it?" I asked.

"I don't recognize the number. Local." She chewed her lip then slid her thumb across the screen to answer. "Hello?"

The person on the other end was loud enough to be heard but not clearly. It was a masculine voice. Wherever they were the background noise came through. With each second that ticked by her body tensed.

"I'll be there as soon as I can." She hung up and said to me, "My daddy's in trouble."

Suzie

The second I saw the number my body tensed for bad news. First of all, anybody calling me and not just texting was usually bad news.

Secondly, deep down I knew that number. It was a place I wanted to forget from a life that was no longer mine.

Anaconda-sized dread coiled in my gut and got comfy. All the warm fuzzies I had after my make-out session with Ford evaporated away. As soon as I told him where I needed to go, he started driving that way. It wasn't even a question that he came with. I couldn't process what that meant right now, too twisted up as I was.

"Ford, you can't come with me to an Iron Wraiths bar. They'll kill you for what you did to Rooster and Cueball."

"Going by yourself is not an option." He held up a hand when I started to speak. "They have no idea who attacked them. They were too focused on you. Even if they did, it changes nothing." His voice was scary and deep. "If you're going, I'm going."

I didn't answer. Not because I thought he would leave me to handle it, but because of the exact opposite. I didn't know if he'd go all guns blazing or with a sharp tongue if trouble stirred up. I studied the trees the headlights illuminated as we drove the winding roads toward the Dragon Bar.

"You're worried about your father?"

I made a sound that wasn't a yes or no. I wasn't worried about him. He'd probably gotten sloppy drunk and ran out of money, but was mostly harmless. I was worried about the Iron Wraiths bar filled with mean and vile men. Mean and vile men who did not like me—especially not after events that may or may have been caused by my temper.

"Suzie." He gently pulled my hand from my mouth where I'd been chewing my cuticle without realizing. "Tell me what's up. Is your dad in trouble?"

He didn't let go, instead driving with his left hand. He laced his fingers through mine. I wasn't about to let go either. He tethered me and kept my thoughts from spiraling.

"Probably not. It's the bar. The Iron Wraiths go there and they don't like me."

"You mentioned them before. Because of the rivalry with the Black Demons?" He flicked a concerned glance my way.

"Partly. And maybe a little because a long time ago, I made a stupid mistake. One of them decides you're on their blacklist and they all follow suit. Pack mentality."

"What did you do?"

"Well, most people would tell you that I set Jethro Winston's motorcycle on fire in a fit of jealous rage."

"You set a motorcycle on fire." It wasn't quite a question because he didn't quite disbelieve I could do something like that.

"Yup. And burned it. To the ground." I had made sure of it.

"Was that premeditated?"

"As much as anything I do is thought out in advance. At the time it seemed like my best option." And it had been.

"You said that's what other people would tell me. What would you tell me?"

The darkness of the car and his hand in my mine felt like it gave me the courage to be honest and tell him something nobody else on this planet knew outside a few people. It was important for him to know about what he was getting into.

"When I was with Jethro, he was mixed up in some heavy shit. Including, but not limited to, drugs—buying, selling, and using, to some degree."

The hand in mine squeezed tighter.

"One time he said that he wanted to go to the Dragon Bar to drink. I hadn't been feeling like he was serious about me at that time. I had almost broken it off a few times but I didn't. I kept hoping that maybe I could just..." I shook my head once. "Well, anyway, I was still with him and eager to please. We showed up and had some drinks. I was a little drunk when he tells me he has to go take care of something. A few minutes later a bunch of the Wraiths come running out and leave the bar in a big hurry. The rumble of all the bikes booking it at once was intense." I rubbed down my arm to soothe the goosebumps forming.

"I told him I thought we were on a date and I was sick of him putting those bikers first. He made a face and said something about us not dating. I couldn't believe it. It had been almost a year of on again, off again. We *had* been dating but with one comment he made me seem like I was crazy for feeling that way. Then he started to drag me to the exit. He was freaking out. He was hollering, 'We need to go now.' I got angry. I was sick of him dicking me around and I was sick of feeling stupid. I said, 'No, fuck you.' He took one look at me and dropped me like I was nothin'. He said, 'Suit yourself.' He left me where I stood. That's when Razor said the cops would be there any second and he needed to get the fuck out."

Ford let out a long breath. "He's the head of the Wraiths, you said?"

"Razor, yeah." I couldn't stop now so I kept on. "That was when we heard the sirens. Jethro was freaking out. He looked terrified. I knew why we had to leave. I knew that Jethro hid drugs in his bike. He never told me outright, but I'd seen the secret compartment near the gas tank and the one under the second seat. I wasn't an idiot. If the cops showed up and caught him in possession of all those drugs, he'd go to jail for a long time. Razor would've easily let him take the fall.

"In my mind, I only had one option. I was steaming mad, on so many levels. I never wanted to be mixed up in any of that sh—stuff and he had pushed me more and more. So finally, I snapped. I killed a few birds with one stone. I grabbed two bottles of Bacardi from behind the bar and ran outside. The whole time I swore and called him every name under the sun. I made a whole scene of it. He was yelling at me to stop, telling me I was crazy. Outside I started pouring the booze all over his bike. He swore up and down but he didn't stop me. He could have easily pulled me off. But he didn't. We both knew what I was doing."

I took a deep breath.

"By the time the cops showed up, the bike was far past being saved. I probably could've been arrested for that, but Jethro made some excuse about a gasoline leak and honestly, the cops were eager to ignore it and happy to see him hurting. They ran inside to search for whatever they thought they'd find. They didn't find anything, of course."

I thought too often of Jethro's face when I got out that lighter. The anger—but something else. That something else is what stuck in my head for years. That something else had me hoping beyond hope that there was a good man under there, a man who might fight for me and protect me. Turned out there was. Just not for me. For a better woman. A familiar pain clamped my heart.

"Jesus."

"I know." I quickly wiped away a tear that escaped before Ford could see. "But that was the last time I saw him, at least on purpose. Green Valley is a small place so he was around, but I was done. I knew I'd never be enough for him. After that, the Iron Wraiths put a mark on me because of what I did. I had to run for protection somewhere else."

"Black Demons?"

"I was young and terrified. Razor is dangerous. Nobody crosses him. And I wasn't really a Wraith girl, just a piece for Jethro. Jethro wasn't about to stand up for me. When I came home and told my dad what happened, he added to the fear. Told me how stupid I was to cross Razor. I found out that the Wraiths had broken his leg when he couldn't pay back a loan he took from them. My whole life until that point I'd thought it was an accident from work. But no. He started drinking after mom left and ran up a debt with them. When he didn't pay up, they taught him a lesson.

"My dad terrified me. He couldn't believe I'd crossed Razor. I was nineteen. I had no idea how bad it was. I was young and scared stupid. I ran to the G-Spot where I was working. I thought maybe I could find help. I found Occum. The Black Demons took me in. Occum took me in. He protected me."

I stopped to take a shaky breath. The words were spilling out so fast I couldn't keep up. Ford was so silent. I continued.

"At first it was just because I owed them money. They're paying off my debt to the Wraiths. It was a motorcycle and who knows how much drugs. I assumed it was a ton of money, not to mention the pride of Razor. Then I realized they're my only family. They're the only ones who accept my lifestyle. The rest of the town wants nothing to do with me. Not with my daddy being the type of person everybody sees as a bottom-feeder and me and my career choices. I have nowhere else to go. I've been dancing, stripping. Most my money goes to Occum and he pays the Wraiths. But dancing and stripping is all I do. Nothing more."

I couldn't look at him for that last part but I had to be clear about that. I was a lot of things, but I was not a hooker. "But I want to be done with the stripping part. I'm so tired. I just want to dance. I don't want to party with bikers or be passed around. I've done so many ugly things, Ford." My voice wobbled. "I don't want you to hate me but you need to know the truth going into this place. There could be trouble. You need to stay in the car. I'll get my dad and get out. But if anybody starts something, in their mind, they have good reason too."

He released my hand to grip the steering wheel. I knew it wasn't going to be good. His initial impression of me had been proven true. I was crazy, a biker whore, and good for nothing. I suddenly felt so tired I couldn't hold up my head. I rested it against the window even though it was cold and hard and each bump shook my skull. Maybe it would shake some sense into me. I closed my eyes.

"We aren't our pasts," Ford said a few minutes later. "We all have to do things to survive given the circumstances we're in." He seemed so sure of his words, like it was a mantra he'd said time and time again. But he held an undercurrent of silent fury.

I closed my eyes. He was distant and cold, like the Ford I first met. I wondered if he would say anything else. Maybe tell me a different course of action I could have taken. The silence grew up like a wall between us.

As we pulled up, Daddy sat swaying on a curb out front. One arm gripped the ground as though to keep from spinning, the other tucked around his hunched middle. He was once such a large man, a force to be reckoned with; now, he was just a sad hunched figure on the curb. It was pathetic and heartbreaking, but also infuriating. I hated this town. I hated that this was my life. I hated that there was no way out of it.

"Let's get this over with. Stay here." I unbuckled my seatbelt before Ford had even put the car in park.

CHAPTER 21

CLIFFORD

I was too furious to be hesitant about walking into a bar full of pissed off bikers. Suzie had given up any freedom she may have had to save a man who treated her like an object. Less than that. He treated her like trash to be discarded when it got too cumbersome.

I was close to the precipice of rage. I should have made a plan. I didn't. I secretly hoped somebody would cross me. It would provide an excuse to punch their lights out. The thought of violence gripped me so suddenly I couldn't fight it back down, quickly followed by a shame I couldn't rationalize away.

"UT Professor Loses Funding After Bar Fight."

I was no longer this person. I was a good man—a man in control.

I followed Suzie out of the car where she crouched down to her father.

"Daddy? You okay? Let's get you out of here." She kept shooting glances to the entrance. "Get back in the car, Ford."

A loud, twangy country song rumbled behind the heavy wooden entrance. A line of bikes surrounded the bar, but nobody was outside.

"Let me help you with him." I wasn't going to argue with her, but I wasn't getting back in the car either.

I grabbed the old man's arms and helped Suzie pull him to his feet. He was so far gone he wasn't responding, just mumbling gibberish. There was a little dribble of vomit on his chin and the front of his shirt. I leveraged his weight to help him stumble forward. Thankfully, I had a lot of experience.

Suzie was uncharacteristically silent but her stressed glances from me to the door had me wanting to soothe her. We moved as fast as we could, but the man walked with a bit of a limp. It took us a minute to get him situated. I fought the urge to see if I could track down a towel to clean him with. It must have taken a long series of events to bring this person to a point in life where he was comfortable covered in his own vomit.

He sprawled out in the backseat and I positioned his legs inside so the door wouldn't close on them. He was a big man. I was surprised. He must have been formidable in his prime. Now, he had the signs of an alcoholic too far gone; broken blood vessels covering a puffy face, a heavy, almost distended middle, and a permeating odor. Suzie took off her coat and made a pillow for his head. Her mouth was twisted to the side as though she fought back angry tears.

I wanted to punch something. I wanted to scoop her up and cradle her from everything bad. Mostly, I wanted to throw back my head and scream. This situation, this bar, this part of town, all these things reminded me of a place and time I fought so hard to block out.

After we shut the doors on either side, we made eye contact above the car. Her shoulders heaved up and down with a great sigh. She opened her mouth to say something but was stopped short by a gravelly male voice.

"Short Fuse? That you?"

Whelp. Maybe I'd get to punch someone out after all.

She widened her eyes and gave me a "be cool" look before turning toward the voice. A large bearded man, clad in leather, stood with arms crossed on the threshold of the bar. A cigarette hung from his mouth and the beard surrounding it was stained yellow. I didn't recognize him, but his leather vest had the same insignia as the men who kept harassing Suzie, that I now understood to be the Iron Wraiths. I balled my fists and went to her.

"Hey, Ka-Bar." She sighed and made her way over to him. She didn't seem scared of him or hesitant.

I remained glued to her side and ready to maim, as needed.

"This is Ford. Ford, this is Ka-Bar. He bounces here and at the G-Spot sometimes."

I recognized him now from that first night I met Suzie.

He crossed his arms and his leather creaked at the action. "I miss seeing your sweet face."

Suzie mumbled something indistinct and looked at the ground. I put my arms around her shoulders.

"No offense, brother." He chuckled at my action.

I blinked once at him.

"Thanks for calling. How much do I owe?"

"One fifty."

"How long was he here?" Color drained from Suzie's face.

Ka-Bar shrugged. "He bought a few rounds for the house."

"Sounds like from the house." Suzie squirmed and checked her pockets. "I think I have like twenty-eight. Can I—"

"Here." I got out my wallet and handed over a few bills.

"Ford, I'll pay you back." Her eyes were full of embarrassment when she looked at me.

I shook my head once.

Ka-Bar took my cash, counted it, and thumbed toward the bar. "Wanna come in and have a drink? The guys would love to see you."

"We're leaving." I realized my voice was at its lowest setting with no emotion behind it.

At the same time, Suzie snorted, saying, "I doubt that."

"Why? I'm serious. Come in and say hi." Ka-Bar flicked his cigarette and lifted his chin with a confused smile.

"I can't." Suzie shifted on her feet. "I don't want to cause drama."

"What drama can a pretty face cause? Your man can come too." He seemed genuine.

Suzie looked at me confused and then back to Ka-Bar. "After how I left things, I'm not welcome here." She looked pointedly at the bikes. "I'm probably not even supposed to be within a hundred yards of your bikes."

The biker laughed. "Suzie, that's all in the past. Nobody cares what you did to Jethro Winston. That guy's dead to us now anyhow."

Again, Suzie looked to me. I frowned. I didn't like this. Maybe this was some sort of trap. I squeezed her arm and nodded my head toward the car. I could tell she wasn't sure how to handle this news.

"Maybe next time," Suzie settled on. "We gotta get Daddy to bed."

"Alright, gorgeous, you have a good night. See y'all later." Ka-Bar dropped his cigarette to the ground and stomped it out.

With that he strode back in the bar without another glance.

Suzie and I seemed to be in agreement that we should leave as fast as we could. Like it was too good to be true. We half-jogged to the car. In a blur, we got in, buckled up, and I pulled out. With each quick action, the seconds crawled. We kept checking to see if we were going to be followed or someone was going to run out shooting at us. But nobody came. Nothing happened.

It was only after a few miles of driving in silence, save for the louder-than-an-engine rumbling snore of her father, that her shoulders relaxed from her ears.

"Huh." Suzie looked at my profile. "That was weird, right?"

"I have no frame of reference. "

"The Wraiths hate me. But Ka-bar, he seemed genuinely surprised by me saying that stuff."

"I agree."

"Huh," she said again, frowning out the window.

"Maybe they've moved on?" I said.

"Not likely. Razor never forgets." A little twist of dread filled me. I was about to voice my concerns but then she added, "And those Wraiths keep harassing me. Telling me I owe Razor."

I hadn't forgotten about that. I thought about it all the time. "I don't like any of it." I took a deep breath and started, "I wish that—"

My words were cut short by a groan from Suzie's father, who shot up from the back seat. His head popped in between us, looking at her, looking at me, and then back again.

"Suzie?" He seemed confused. Understandably.

His breath could curdle milk. I cracked the back windows just enough to suck some air out.

"Yeah, it's me." She turned in her seat and I caught her frowning at him. "Daddy, what in the hell were you doin' at the Dragon Bar? You know we aren't welcome there."

"I've run up my tabs at the others." In the rearview mirror, he shrugged.

"Don't go to a bar at all. How'd you get there?" she asked then held up her hands. "No. I don't want to know. What about the forty dollars I gave you two days ago?" Her temper ratcheted up with each word. Then she glanced at me sheepishly. "Take the next exit. Head toward the trailer park."

I nodded.

Her father squinted with one eye closed out the window. "Hey, can we stop at the Piggly Wiggly on the way?"

"No," Suzie snapped. "They don't sell Jameson."

"Get me a six-pack then."

"No. You're having some tea and going straight to bed."

He grumbled and sat back.

Suzie crossed her arms and sat stewing in silence for a whole minute before she spoke again, "You can't ever go back there." She had turned all the way around in the seat. "You look at me and promise me."

"Fine, fine. Don't get all worked up. Just like your mother with that temper."

I gripped the steering wheel.

"Did they hurt you?" she asked with a softened voice.

"Why would they? They don't care we're kin. Their beef is with you and not me. It was your temper that ruined things."

Suzie positioned herself forward facing again. "It doesn't matter. You don't have the money and it's not safe. Just don't go there."

"Well, what am I supposed to do? You left me all alone to fend for myself."

"That's not true. I come and bring you food every week."

"Yeah, but when you aren't there…" he seemed to think better of whatever he'd been about to say.

"Then you can't steal my extra cash? Yeah, I know."

I was seething at this exchange but it wasn't my place, wasn't my family.

We drove the rest of the way in silence except the quiet instructions Suzie gave me to find their home. "The one up here on the left."

The trailer park was familiar in its depression. It was like the last home I lived in with my parents. I put the car in park and moved to help her. The faster we moved her father, the faster we could get out of here.

She put a hand on my arm to stop me. "I'll get him. He's sober enough to walk back."

"Okay, if you're sure." If she didn't want me to go into her house, I wasn't going to force her.

Her dad began his bumbling process of leaving the car and heading for the steps. I realized belatedly that he and I hadn't shared any words and that unsettled me for a reason I couldn't define. Maybe it was that she kept this whole part of her life so closed off to me. He was this mysterious figure I'd heard about but never met. I still didn't feel like I'd met him. I'd met a drunk alter-ego of a man. I was getting itchy being here. I wanted to leave and take her with me.

Suzie hesitated before quickly grabbing my hand and squeezing it. "Thank you again. I feel like that's all I ever say. Thanks for helping with Daddy and earlier." She blushed a little but her eyes were downcast.

"Earlier" felt like a thousand years ago. She was closed off now, distant. She didn't touch me as freely or hold my eyes. Maybe I should have done more, said more.

"Okay."

She frowned but smoothed her features quickly.

I didn't know how to formulate what I wanted to say. I had so many thoughts. I hated that she was stuck in a cycle of men using her.

I wanted to take her home and talk to her in the comfort of our quiet and clean house.

We turned in tandem when the screen door slammed shut.

"And, I think I'll probably spend the night here. Maybe a of couple nights. Make sure things are okay around here."

She wanted to leave me and go back to this life. I couldn't handle it. I didn't want her to go. I was irrationally upset by this news. After the surprising events of this morning, it had been such a wonderful afternoon, followed by this shit evening.

Inside a TV blared to life followed by the crash of something.

She closed her eyes and took a deep breath. "I better go check on him."

It wasn't fair. That man didn't deserve her. She shouldn't be bending backward for all these people. I wanted to express to her all the things she deserved. But because my mouth and brain were never on the same page…

"He's never going to be better if you keep enabling his behavior."

I knew it was a dick thing to say. I knew it was reminiscent of the Clifford she had met and not the Ford I was around her. But the words slipped out and I regretted them immensely.

Her jaw clenched, nostrils flared, and her eyes burned with fury. But then the rage that twisted her face melted into a laugh. "Wow. Thank you."

"For what?" My chest heaved from frustration with myself.

"For reminding me that all men do think they know what's best for me." She chuckled sardonically and shook her head. "For a second there I actually thought you were different."

She got out of the car and slammed the door, leaving me to my stunned silence.

Suzie

I was spitting mad. I was seeing red. I was about to burn everything to the ground. I was all the ragey things. But really, the truth was, I was humiliated. I was humiliated that Ford saw my father like that. I was humiliated that my real life was a pile of garbage and he couldn't wait to get out of this heap.

Oh, but not before telling me exactly how to live my life.

I slammed the car door so hard Mrs. Albensi and all her cats probably sprung up from sleep but I didn't care. I stomped up to the house and was just about to go in when Ford stopped me.

"Suzie, wait." He slammed his door and jogged to me.

I should've slammed the door in his face. I still might.

"What?" I crossed my arms and tilted my head. "Forget some more sage advice you have to share?"

"No. No." He held up his hands. "Now just wait. I'm sorry. I got it all wrong."

"I don't get you. How can you go from being so thoughtful one second and then tellin' me how to live my life the next?"

"I am being thoughtful. Addictions are black holes and he'll pull you in until there's nothing left. I didn't say it right, what I meant."

"You didn't mean that?" I gestured to the car.

He frowned. "No. I meant what I said. But it was the timing. I got all mixed up. Can we please talk for just a second before you go stomping off again?"

I shoved a finger in his face. "Don't you talk to me about stomping off when things get tough."

"I know. I know. Please. Let me just try and explain myself. It's been a long day and my thoughts are muddled."

"You think I didn't have a long day too?"

"I didn't say that!" he yelled. His voice was deep and coarse with anger. Noticeably so. I had to say I was weirdly getting off on it. He was always set to calm, quiet, or some setting in between. I liked kick-starting his engine.

But I was still mad.

He took a deep breath and lowered his voice. "We both had long days, okay? I know that. Let's talk before we separate saying something we don't mean."

I made a sour face because there he went making sense again, not wanting to shout and scream. I guess it was the mature thing to do. But dammit, I wanted him riled up.

"You don't get to do that. You don't get to say mean things and then make me feel like I'm being emotional and overreacting."

He started to speak but I cut him off.

"You don't get to come to my home and lift your nose at the way I live. I didn't ask you to come here. I didn't ask for your opinion or judgment."

He fisted his hands and punched the air so fast I would've thought I imagined it.

"Goddammit. I know that! I'm trying to tell you I'm sorry but you aren't letting me get a word in edgewise and now I'm shouting for your whole goddamn neighborhood to hear!"

He really was shouting now. He was red in the cheeks and his voice cracked. Maybe I was a drama queen because I'll be damned if it wasn't hot.

Instead of admitting it, I tossed out a hand. "So talk."

"Y'all better do something," Mrs. Albensi shouted through the screen of the window. "You're upsetting my kids."

Ford turned on his heels to look in the direction of the voice before looking back to me. Moxy sat on the window flicking her tail and eavesdropping. That cat was always getting out.

"Go back to bed, Mrs. Albensi, we'll quiet down." I gave a tired wave.

"Y'all better. And who is that? I don't know that man."

"He's a friend."

Ford lifted a hand and waved tentatively.

"Mm hmm, friend, I'm sure." Judgment was clear in her tone.

"Goodnight, Mrs. Albensi."

"Night. Make sure you tell your daddy to turn down that television."

"I will."

"Don't make me call Sheriff James. His boy and my nephew are friends. He'll be here if I call."

"I know, ma'am. We're going in."

Ford stepped toward me and whispered, "I know I'm tired, but is that cat talking?"

I couldn't help but smile when I saw Ford's eyebrows rise in confusion. He frowned at my smile and that made me start laughing. I was laughing so hard I couldn't breathe. And Ford's face went from confused to smiling to chuckling with me.

"Come on." I pulled him up the stairs and into the trailer.

He hesitated at the door. "Are you sure?" He flicked a glance behind me. "What about your father?"

I pointed to where my dad was passed out in his chair. I walked in and shut off the TV as I headed to the back of the trailer where my room was. I glanced back to make sure he followed. He was tiptoeing and frowning, as always, past the snoring beast.

"Close the door." I sat on my bed and pointed to the fiberboard door.

Ford swallowed. He took off his coat and folded it over his arm. He hovered with his back to the door. His throat made a weird sound. He refolded his coat and shifted on his feet.

"What's your deal?"

"It's your room." His cheeks reddened.

"Oh my god, do you think I'm gonna try and seduce you with my dad two steps away?"

"No." But he looked to the left.

I rolled my eyes. "Oh Lord. Want me to ask Mrs. A. if one of her cats can be your chaperone? I don't want to upset your delicate sensibilities." I did one of the accents that made him laugh.

And it worked. I sucked in my lips because I wasn't ready to forgive him but dammit I loved his laugh. I wanted to make him laugh every day.

"No, it's not that." He moved and sat next to me on the bed. "It just feels intimate. Seeing where you sleep."

He blushed again. I would have paid a month's worth of tips to know what he thought in that moment.

"I've lived here my whole life. It's really not much." I shrugged and examined my room through his eyes.

I had a vanity that used to be Momma's covered in old stickers and makeup stains. A white three-drawer dresser missing a handle with one drawer lopsided because it broke forever ago sat next to the door. I had at least closed my closet so he couldn't see that madness. The walls were wood paneling that had warped in places where the rain leaked in. It looked junky and old. I couldn't remember what color the carpet used to be. If cleanliness was godliness, no wonder I was labeled a fallen woman.

I should have stayed and talked with him in the car. "It's not much…I know it's not."

Ford held my hand. "I like it."

I huffed out a breath of disbelief. "Right. It's basically the Ritz."

He turned my chin toward him and my heart skipped.

"I do. I like it because it's all you. I like it because you're sharing it with me."

I swallowed. "You're crazy."

He shrugged. "I know." He relaxed back on the bed, balancing on his hands. "What are those for?" He nodded towards the old dance trophies.

"Those are nothing. When I was little I did some competitions. They give them to everyone."

"They all say first place."

I shrugged.

He squinted his eyes to read them better. "What happened after 2001?"

I chewed my lips. "Mm. That's when Momma left and Daddy lost his job."

He nodded. "The thing is. What I said, it wasn't from a place of judgment. I said it from a place of experience." He held my gaze. "Enabling isn't love. It only delays the inevitable."

"What'm I supposed to do? Just abandon him? Like Momma did? Like everybody else does? Like everybody expects me to?" I snapped. I didn't mean to. I could tell it cost him something to admit that to me.

He shook his head. "You could get him help."

"Oh sure, with all my extra cash. I know you said you know but you can't possibly understand. This didn't happen overnight. It's not like I enjoy seeing this version of him. It crept up slowly over the years. A little worse each day. Things weren't always so bad. He was... he is a good dad. He's just having a hard time. He couldn't keep his job. I didn't realize until it was already too late. Bills had piled up and I didn't know how bad it was. But he couldn't work. Thankfully I could at that point. He took care of me, so now I'm taking care of him."

"But you aren't."

"Stop it." I spat. "I work so hard for him. You have no idea."

He couldn't know what I'd been through to keep the trailer. To keep money for groceries and heat. He had no clue.

"I understand."

"No, you don't, Ford. Don't say you do when you have no idea what it's like for me. Like I can just fix it by working harder to change myself."

My voice was rising again. I grabbed my old stuffed bear from my bed and hugged it to me. I didn't care if it was childish. Lately, I'd been letting myself imagine a different life; a life outside the G-Spot, where I wasn't up till three a.m. most days. Where maybe I was more than a dancer, even. Those thoughts were dangerous though.

"I do understand. Maybe not exactly. But well enough." He tugged at his collar. "I was born in a town almost exactly the size of Green Valley. A few hours south of here."

I blinked. There was no way. "Yeah, right."

"Really." He sighed and rubbed his palm against his beard. "I had ten people in my graduating class. Not that I graduated. I was already moving with a fast crowd by junior year and dropped out."

This had me sitting up. With a sniff, I asked, "No shit? I dropped out junior year too."

"Yeah. I...well, I was headed on a very different path. But that's my whole point. I changed who I was. I believed I could and here I am."

"That simple, huh?" I snapped with extra saltiness.

"No. Not simple at all." He lifted his chin and his eyes got a sort of faraway look. "I had a teacher who believed in me. After I dropped out, she tracked me down. Found out I was mixed in with the local gang. We were just kids, but we were desperate to prove something. This teacher told me to get my shit together and she'd give me a real job. She was moving and so I went with her."

I didn't like the way that sounded. "Were you supposed to sleep with her or something?"

He looked genuinely appalled. "What? God. No. Why would you —" He stopped short, looked me in the eyes so hard that I had to look away and then went on. "No, she was married. Happily. She and her husband sort of took me in as a foster kid through the system. They did that with a lot of kids who needed a chance. Jack too."

I must've made a face because he shook his head. "Nothing weird."

"What about your parents? Weren't they worried?"

"No." His face grew dark. "They weren't concerned."

"Your parents didn't care that you left home?"

"Suzie, my birth parents only cared about their next fix. I think by the time I hit puberty they forgot that I was kin." His nostrils flared. There was a story there. A story I wasn't sure that I wanted to hear. "My foster parents are the only parents I acknowledge now. They're my mom and dad. To Jack, too."

"Oh." I couldn't help but pick at the invisible wall he had built up around him. I wanted to know more. I knew my daddy had his troubles but deep down he loved me and didn't want me to leave. "Your birth parents were addicted to drugs your whole life?"

I couldn't imagine.

"No." He cleared his throat and then picked up the raggedy blanket on the end of the bed. "When I was young I think I was lower middle class. I have memories of a bigger house. Cleaner. My mom and dad were always partiers though. They always drank and had people over that I didn't know. It was a revolving door of strangers." He frowned. "My dad worked in a machinery factory. They made giant machine parts for tractors and stuff. One day he got hurt. The doctor gave him opiates for the pain. He got hooked. Got my mom hooked. Then when they realized they could get the same high for a fraction of the price, they switched to heroin."

"Jesus."

He had started fussing with the end of the blanket, running his fingers through the fringe, avoiding my eyes as he spoke. "It's actually an appallingly common story. I found all this out later from my foster mom. Heroin is an epidemic in small communities right now. She also told me when they found my parents." He stopped here. His face didn't change. He just stared like he was focusing. "They OD'ed together on some filthy mattress in a crack house. Bad heroin."

My hand covered my mouth. How does somebody survive that? How does a child lose both parents? I thought of his coldness in a totally different light now. A child alone in the world. My throat was tight as tears blurred my vision. It was a sickening, horrible thing. I couldn't believe this was Ford's life. I couldn't believe somebody could come back from that. I didn't know how to act.

He'd shared with me. So I'd give him what he needed.

I scooted closer to him on the old mattress. The action had us sort of falling together. "That's absolutely horrible." I wrapped my arms around his middle and rested my head on his chest. His heart thumped like crazy against my ear.

He was stiff as I hugged him. That was okay. I'd give him all the hugs. He didn't have to hug back.

I swallowed. "Is this why you do the work you do?"

He hummed a yes. "If I could help kids from growing up like I did... But these towns have to change. All these small towns are dying. People are searching for something to escape; major changes need to be made. It's not like I think I'm capable of changing the world. But if I could save just one kid from the childhood I had, it would be worth everything. Every child deserves to have one person believe in them, to have the access and opportunity to want more for themselves." His eyes grew dark and I could almost hear his internal counting. "I don't like to talk about my past."

"Okay. We don't have to."

He let out a breath and fell back to the bed. He seemed happy that I let it go. I fell with him. I rested my head on his chest and looked up to him.

"But," I added.

He raised an eyebrow at me. Our faces were very close again.

"I think that right there, the reason you just told me, that's what you tell people. That's how you get your funding."

He let out a sigh and focused on the ceiling. "People can't know the sad truth of my life. I worked hard to present my best self to the world. If I shared the truth I'd be treated differently. I don't want the pity or the judgment."

I could tell this wasn't the time to press, so I sucked my lips in. After a few more minutes of replaying our short history together, I said, "Well, that explains some things."

"Like what? What do you mean?" His voice was guarded.

"Like that dancing. And your accent."

He looked offended. "The dancing, yes. I went to plenty of bars and clubs when I was living fast. I knew the ladies liked it." He actually blushed when he said it. Once again I could not connect this Ford to the man of his past. "Wait, what accent?"

"After you beat the shit out of those guys. You swore like the dirt-iest biker I ever met." I couldn't help the laugh that bubbled out. "Sometimes when you get worked up you slip a little. I thought I was rubbing off on you." I smiled and nuzzled into him.

He frowned. "And that's why I don't let that happen. It scares me."

"What does?"

"Losing control."

"It's okay. I liked it." I smiled and kissed his neck. It didn't count here. We could be us here in my bedroom, away from prying eyes.

I breathed him in. My vision was blurring as my heavy eyelids fell closed. I snuggled closer to him. I should tell him to leave so there were no lines crossed. I should, I thought sleepily. I grabbed the blanket without moving off it and tucked it around us, making a Ford and Suzie burrito.

After a few minutes when our breaths evened out, lulling me to sleep, he whispered, "That scares me too."

CHAPTER 22

SUZIE

"Well, well, well. Look at you." Gretchen whistled low.

I twirled around to show off my khaki colored apron already stained with coffee and then propped my hands like I was a little teapot.

"I know. I'm very official," I said.

"I'm glad you got it. Lucas is a fair guy."

"I didn't have much of an interview. He asked if I could pour coffee and if I would show up. Next thing I know, I'm filling out my first W-9."

She smiled coyly. "Very nice."

There wasn't a lot of business at The Coffee Shop right now but I wanted to make sure I didn't upset the owner, Lucas Olsen. Thankfully, with the way Lucas snuck glances at Gretchen I didn't think I had anything to worry about. Lucas was a very quiet artsy type for being such a large man. I knew almost nothing about him except that he owned the aptly named The Coffee Shop and The Bookstore and he always wore a beanie to cover his caveman hair and beard. He could have been anywhere from twenty to fifty.

"Does this mean you're sticking around for a little while?" Gretchen leaned onto the counter.

A heavy weight filled my stomach at her question. "I'm working on a new image. You know that."

Serving coffee in a college town was small beans compared to what I made dancing but getting out of the house each day was nice. Being in the college environment only helped my transformation. Already today I'd heard noteworthy conversation I could try out on Ford later.

She crossed her arms. The other ladies were already at the table and gave me a thumbs up when I looked at them. I had gotten their drinks mostly right. Though Roxy added a lot of sugar to her tea and I'm pretty sure Blithe dumped hers out in the planter, unless she drank it in one gulp when my back was turned.

"I don't see how it's anyone's business how you earn your money."

"People think I'm a hooker. Plain and simple." I shrugged.

"Still isn't any of their damn business."

"I know. But it's important to Ford. He's got a reputation to uphold. His work is real important."

She gave me a look.

"What, Gretchen? I know that judgy eyebrow by now."

"I'm just sayin' don't go bending over backward for a man and changing who you are. Unless bending over backward is what you're into." She grinned.

"It's not like that with us."

"What's it like then?"

I shrugged.

Sometimes we were so close to something, especially after our talk in my trailer last week, and then other times I felt like he wanted to run to Mexico to get away from me. Getting together with Ford was a bad idea, but my body hadn't gotten the memo. We'd been good about keeping physical distance from each other. But we talked all the time. All day we checked in with each other. He called me just to talk while I walked to and from work, sharing the drama of his students and the stress of looking for additional funding. I hadn't known about all the work involved when trying to get tenure. Hell, I didn't even know what tenure really meant until he explained it to me. I'd learned so much about him but no matter how much he shared there was still a part of him he locked down and kept hidden.

Gretchen took a sip of the coffee I made her. "Holy crap. That'll put hair on your chest."

I took the cup and dumped it in the sink. A thick river of grounds stuck to the side of the cup. "It's complicated."

"You measure the grounds and add water. It's really not—"

I glared at her. "With Ford and me."

"Hmmm." She held her tongue though and I took the chance to change the topic.

"Anyway. What's going on with you? Something happening with you and Lucas?"

"Sure, we can change the subject." Her innocent smile was canceled out by a mischievous glint in her eyes. "It's complicated," she mocked me.

"Wait a minute, are you the reason he hired me?"

She winked at me. "It certainly wasn't your barista skills."

"Thanks, girl." I beamed. "What can I get you? I'll try again."

"No offense but I'm good with water."

"Don't give up on me yet. I'm learning. I'll be a real barista in no time."

"And that's what you want?"

I wasn't sure what I wanted anymore. "It doesn't matter. It's only temporary anyway."

She gave me a look before heading back toward Blithe and Roxy. "Hurry and take your break. We need to have an emergency meeting of the SWS. We can't get a hold of Kim and we're worried."

The Scorned Women's Society had been meeting regularly but I had yet to meet the allusive Kim. "Isn't she sort of on lockdown? I thought she was always hard to get a hold of?"

"Yeah, but something is up. Normally we can see her at least once a month."

"No ex left behind." I nodded seriously as I spoke our motto. "Give me five minutes."

As I wiped down the coffee machine, my stomach twisted with a dread I couldn't identify. Then I realized it was my instinctual reaction to the sound of a bike rumbling in the distance.

"Shit." I glanced toward the ladies but they didn't seem to notice anything.

Maybe it was just driving by, no big deal. Nothing to worry about. I tried to breathe as I waited for the rumble to pass the large windows of the storefront, gripping the rag in my hand.

Then a bike pulled up in front of the store, parking sideways to take up two spaces. Instant dread flooded me. I knew that bike too well. Occum cut the engine. The silence was deafening. I could go to the back and hide but obviously, he knew I was here. I didn't want him talking to anybody else. He took his time getting off his ride and striding to the door. He took in the sign that hung above the door and shook his head. He brought so much chaos with him. The racing of my heart. Heavy boots and squeaking leather. The thick smell of cigarettes and grease. He was so out of place here.

His gaze moved around the store, snagging on Gretchen.

"Nothing for you to see here, friend," she said.

He smirked before finding me behind the counter.

I plastered a smile on my face and quietly said to her, "He's here for me. Let me get rid of him."

She crossed her arms. "There's a bat under the counter. You just say the word."

"It's best if I handle it."

She nodded once and turned back to the girls who all spoke in low voices.

"Hey, Occum." I wiped the sparkling clean counter to hide the tremor in my hands.

He flicked a rack of postcards and sent it spinning. "They got you working in a bookshop, Short Fuse? Don't you have to know how to read?"

"What do you want, Occum?"

He came to the counter that separated us and leaned over, taking up way more than his fair share. "Is that how you talk to me now?"

"I'm at work." I glanced to Lucas who had come out from the back when the bell on the door rang. I didn't want to get him involved. I called to him. "I'm just gonna take five. I'll be right back."

Lucas was built like a heavy-weight fighter but spoke with the gentleness of a librarian.

"Five minutes." Lucas looked torn about letting me go with Occum. He shot Gretchen a look who gave him a quick shake of the head.

"Sure thing, boss." I slid my apron off over my head and laid it on the counter along with the "be right back" sign.

Occum scanned me up and down when I came out from behind the counter. "Why you dressed like that? Covering up the goods." Occum smacked my ass so hard it stung.

I wore jeans and a long sweater. This had been my outfit of choice since the weather turned. I was so close to lashing out, but this was Occum and him being here was bad news. I had him follow me up front. I figured he was less likely to try something in the middle of the day in the center of town. I smiled at Gretchen as we passed but all the ladies had solemn looks on their faces.

"I don't have a ton of time." It was chilly outside and I wrapped my arms tight around myself.

"You have time enough." He glared. "Don't you forget who you're talking to."

In the light of day, Occum looked like shit. His long beard was tangled and his bloodshot eyes were sunken with heavy bags pulling down the lower lids. He reeked of smoke but the instant we were back outside he lit up a fresh cigarette. I tucked my hands into my sleeves and made a "so tell me" expression with arms out.

He stood with his legs spread wide and arms crossed. "Heard you were at the Dragon bar."

"I had to get my daddy. Nothing happened."

"You weren't talking to the Wraiths?"

"I talked to Ka-Bar but only 'cuz I had to pay him." There was no point in lying as he already knew everything.

"You aren't allowed to go there. And you sure as hell aren't allowed to talk to them."

I balled my fists tucked under my arms. "I know. The circumstances were outside my control."

He laughed. "Oh shit. Look at you trying to talk all fancy now." He stepped closer, spewing his putrid breath in my face. "Don't fucking forget who saved you, who protects you. Don't go stirring up shit because you're bored."

"I didn't." My teeth were clenched tight.

"You're on thin ice, girl. You have no idea how much it took to keep the peace after you started shit with Rooster and Cueball. They were gonna come after you but Razor stopped them. Cost me though."

"They attacked me. What was I supposed to do?"

"Watch your mouth." His face contorted with rage and his bald head splotched.

My chest heaved. Occum was supposed to protect me. Yet, he had come all the way down here just to tell me to mind my business. I knew the second I said it, it was a mistake. I'd been getting too bold. Forgetting myself. Ford never filtered me; he let me speak plainly. I needed to stop that. Most men didn't like that.

"Lord, girl, you've lost your goddamn mind." He shook his head. "If I knew this whole thing was gonna change you I would have never allowed it."

"You don't control me." I straightened my spine and glared.

I didn't have a chance to brace myself. The hand shot out and slapped me before I could prepare. I gasped from the shock and pain.

"I warned you. But you can't keep your mouth shut, can you?"

I couldn't speak. The shame burned my cheeks. I knew everybody inside had seen that.

"You're lucky I don't do more, but you make me too much money."

I scowled.

He added just to hurt me, "But don't push me. You aren't that valuable."

My eyes stung with tears. From the slap. From the words. My body shook from the control it took to keep my composure.

"Is that all you wanted?" I asked with a shaking voice.

He crossed his arms over his chest. I didn't recognize this man.

This was not the father figure who took me in when I was scared and running for my life. This man was a creature from hell. The hatred and ugliness changed his face into something scary.

"Just make sure you don't get too caught up in all this." He gestured to me and then the bookshop. "You remember who your family is."

"I won't forget." I wanted to press my hand to my burning cheek but refused to give him the satisfaction of knowing it hurt.

"We protect you, Suzie. We care about you. Razor is pissed you hurt his men. He's asking for revenge. He wants things." He lifted a hand to my cheek but I flinched, so he ran his hand through my hair instead. It was in a loose braid over my shoulder so it got tangled and snagged.

The world around me hummed. I couldn't hear anything but his words. I knew there would be repercussions for hurting the Wraiths who had attacked me but Occum was supposed to protect me. That was what I danced for. For protection.

"Is there a problem here?" I didn't hear the bell of the door ring, but there stood Gretchen and the girls in the doorway behind her. Gretchen had her bat. Lucas shot concerned glances from where he helped a customer.

My pulse jumped. If there was anything Occum hated more than women, it was women who tried to stand up for themselves.

"Everything's fine." I smiled a watery smile and implored with my eyes. "Go inside. I'll be right back."

"I don't think so," Roxy said, her eyes never leaving Occum. "I think you should leave."

He chuckled and popped his knuckles in his leather fingerless gloves. "Oh yeah? You gonna make me?" He laughed with a shake of his head. "I recognize you, Gretchen LaRoe. I know who you are. Cast-offs from a fucking pussy who couldn't hang with the Wraiths. You think you can fuck your way out of this?" Occum looked at me and there was something in his eyes I couldn't identify. "You gonna get your sluts club and little professor to beat me up?"

"Leave," I said.

He lifted his hand and I flinched. He smiled.

"I don't have time to deal with this shit with the Wraiths. I don't know how long it'll take for you to pay off this debt now. But you don't go near the Wraiths. You don't talk to them. If I find out you talked to them again, there won't be any more warnings."

I shuddered.

"You need us, Short Fuse. You're dead without us. Your daddy too."

I hated that I was kowtowing to him. I hated that he was here in my town, with my friends, ruining the one piece of happiness in my life.

"It's time to leave." Roxy pulled me toward the door.

Occum stepped after her with his arm raised and a lecherous smile. I grabbed it with all my strength, digging my nails into his flesh.

"Don't you touch her."

"You're changing, girl. You're making a mistake." He dropped his arm and looked at me with unadulterated hatred.

I didn't care what he said because he was moving back toward the bike and leaving. That was all I cared about.

"This isn't where you belong. You can play dress up and pretend for now but this isn't real."

"I know that." I was too angry. I was too scared for my new friends. I couldn't handle this mess bleeding over to my other life.

"You better get your john to sign off on those papers. Or all your whoring around is a waste of fucking time."

Occum got on his bike and drove off. His words rang in my ears louder than the engine long after he left. Heat burned my eyes and neck and cheeks. I wanted to be swallowed up by the ground. I couldn't turn around and look at the girls. I couldn't handle what they had learned about me. I couldn't see the truth of who I was in their eyes. That was the thing though, wasn't it? What I really was. I was a biker whore. I was Short Fuse Suzie, stripper and nothing more. That's all I'd ever be. This whole fake life was a joke. In the end, I was going to have to go back to Occum. I was going to have to live the life I belonged to.

"Come on, doll. Let's get inside." Gretchen placed a hand on my shoulder gently.

I faced the girls. "You heard him. What I am. You don't have to pretend anymore that I'm any better. You don't have to be seen with me."

A cold emptiness filled me. An acceptance at the reminder of who I really am.

Gretchen glared at me, her face angrier than I'd ever seen it. "You think that's what friends are? Just here for who we want you to be?"

I held her gaze. I was angry. She was too. We glared at each other.

"No ex left behind." Her words sent chills down my arms. "It's not some cutesy saying. It's an oath."

I nodded, breaking our staring contest first.

"Who was that man?" Blithe asked.

Roxy gently tugged me back into the cafe. When we were back inside, Lucas walked the only customer out and locked the door, turning the sign to "Closed". Gretchen whispered something to him and he nodded once. His gaze moved over my face before he returned to the back of the store and out of sight.

Blithe placed an ice pack on my cheek. I didn't realize until the cool hit it how badly it burned.

"He's my boss." I didn't want them to know the truth of my past and what I'd done to survive.

"He don't treat you like a boss," Gretchen said.

She was quiet with rage. I realized that her and Ford had that in common. Under an overall level of toughness, they were actually pretty similar. She stewed quietly with her thoughts.

"That's not how anybody should be treated." Blithe said. Her hand moved to a small scar on her chin.

The other women tutted their agreement sadly.

Blithe removed the ice and pressed a gentle finger to my face. "I know it feels like that's normal. That's just how they show their love. But love is never violent. It can sometimes feel like there is no way out…"

I shook my head. They didn't understand. Occum was the boss. He controlled everything. My whole life was wrapped up in the Black Demons. They didn't understand that there was no other place for me to go. I burned my bridges everywhere else. The Black Demons protected me. I didn't have the money or knowledge to run away. I wasn't as strong as they were. It was too late to change.

"Do you need help?" Gretchen asked flatly.

I didn't need help. I needed to stick to the plan. I needed to get the signature. And remember where I came from and more importantly where my life was. The universe had sent me a reminder just when I had been thinking that maybe I could change.

"No. I'm good." I held her gaze before I eventually had to look away.

I didn't feel like I had won the argument though. I felt I'd lost something in Gretchen's eyes.

This was why it was better to let people think nothing of you. It doesn't hurt to never have their respect, but it hurts like hell to lose it.

CHAPTER 23

CLIFFORD

*A*s the calendar flipped its pages toward Christmas, Suzie and I fell into a comfortable companionship. She'd flourished at The Coffee Shop with the locals. Part of me wanted to jump up and down and say, "See this is where you belong, this could be your life," but then I'd remember that this wasn't what she wanted. This was just a way out from under the thumb of Occum. It caused such an ache in my chest, so I didn't let myself think about it.

But I thought about kissing her again all the time. It occupied my brain more than anything else. It was…unsettling. I never acted on it. I think my blowup on Halloween and subsequent actions had released some of the tension in me. Now I doubled down and focused on my work as much as I could while I still had grad students and a classroom. Dean Lucero and Bouffant checked in frequently as if I'd forget my goals without their reminders. No other grants had come through and the clock was ticking like the Tell Tale Heart, ever present in the back of my mind.

Thanksgiving arrived without warning. Jack was going to see our parents over the long weekend, but I couldn't leave with him. I had three grant applications to complete and two construction sites I needed to visit, but most of all, I was worried about Suzie.

Jack stood in the doorway, his overnight bag over one shoulder as we saw him off.

"Have fun in Washington." Suzie kissed his cheek.

My blood didn't boil with jealousy anymore. It was clear any feelings between the two were different from what Suzie and I shared. I'm not sure what that meant exactly, but at least I didn't feel like an outsider around them anymore.

"Tell Mom and Dad I'll try to visit them over the winter break," I told Jack.

"I'll tell them. You kids behave yourselves," Jack said with a smile as he made his way toward Gretchen, his ride to the airport. She waved to Suzie but stopped to glare at me.

"As if I know any other way," Suzie called out innocently.

"Right," he laughed. "See you Sunday."

Back inside the house, Suzie closed the door and leaned against it. "I can't believe it's Thanksgiving."

"Do you need a ride to Green Valley?" I shifted.

I didn't want her to leave, but it was a holiday. I'd grown so used to talking to her every day about everything. All the little nuances that I had always thought were too much work to share with anybody else flowed easily off my tongue. It wasn't work getting to know her; it was as effortless as daydreaming.

A shadow fell over Suzie's face. She waited a beat before answering. "Nah…" her voice trailed off.

I had thought she might say more but she remained quiet. She hadn't brought up her father since the night in the trailer. She didn't want my judgment. It made me feel like an ass. I never wanted her to filter herself.

"Do you want to order food and stay in?" I asked.

She smiled instantly. "That sounds wonderful."

I ordered Vietnamese and we slurped pho as we watched reruns on TV in the basement.

She pushed her bowl away and relaxed back into the couch. "Sorry I didn't make a big dinner. The meals I cook for Daddy usually involve cream of mushrooms soup or bologna."

"I thought I was going to be on my own. And this is delicious."

This was as close to happy as I get. Except maybe being alone. Lately, I'd gotten so used to her company it'd be weird not to have her around. And sometimes being alone felt, well, lonely.

As much as I enjoy silence, I couldn't ignore that something had changed in Suzie recently. It wasn't her clothes, or flourishing vocabulary, or her new job. There was a subdued aura around her, like someone used a dimmer switch to turn down her energy. It had only been the last few weeks and coincided with her avoidance of me. Maybe she wasn't happy here at all. Maybe I was totally wrong. Maybe this life was too boring for her. There were a hundred questions to ask. I turned the volume down on the TV.

"Do you want to decorate? For Christmas, I mean." That was not one of them.

She looked around, the green of her eyes more than brilliant against her purple sweater. Her hair was in a long braid over her shoulder and I thought about tugging it free to run my hands through it. I settled for tucking back a strand that had come loose.

"Right now?" Her softening gaze followed my hands.

"Yeah."

"It's still Thanksgiving. Don't you have some high opinion on waiting until December at least?"

"Normally Jack and I decorate this weekend because it is the longest break before the madness of finals. The HOA requires some sort of non-denominational decorations in December." I shrugged. "Plus, I like it."

I liked making new memories around this time of year to compensate for all the years of shit I had behind me. I'd been thinking about the holidays a lot lately. I'd imagine what it would be like to decorate the tree with Jack and Suzie. This would be the only Christmas I got with her.

"Will Jack mind if we do decorate without him?"

"For as cool as Jack is most of the time, he turns into a downright diva when untangling Christmas lights."

She laughed. "I could see that." She popped up excitedly. "Okay. I'm going to go make hot chocolate. Let's get festive!"

She sprinted into action before I could respond. I was glad that for once I hadn't tried to talk it out and just did something that made her happy. Her whole demeanor was brighter already. My soul swelled.

By the time I brought down all the boxes from the attic she had the cocoa made. Bing Crosby crooned from the old record player and the warm crackling of the music filled the air with romance.

She gestured to the fire she built. "I hope you don't mind."

"Nice job." It burned bright and evenly. "Mind what?"

"I know men like to make the fires." She twisted her hands through the long sleeves of her shirt.

"Right." I scoffed. "Now take off your shoes and go make me a sandwich."

She started to slip off her shoes. "Suzie. Jesus. I'm kidding." I thought by now she could recognize my particular brand of deadpan humor. This was why I shouldn't try to be funny.

She smoothed her braid over her shoulder. "Oh, obviously." She brought me a mug of cocoa. "Here. Cheers."

"Cheers."

We clunked the mugs and took tentative sips.

"The boxes are labeled, so anything marked tree we'll have to wait on. I hope it's okay, but I like getting a real tree. I know it's a little more work, but the authenticity is worth it in my opinion."

I started sorting through the boxes. We didn't have a ton of stuff, but Jack and I had made a decent holiday collection since college. When I glanced up, Suzie was chewing on her lip and nodding.

"That sounds nice." There was something about her tentative posture that conveyed she was holding back.

"Are you sure? If you prefer a fake, I'm sure there will be some sales tomorrow. We can go buy one. Though honestly, all those Black Friday sales are scams. They either mark down garbage or mark things up just to put them on 'sale' at regular price. It's a whole racket." As I rambled her face was unreadable. "But if you prefer to go out tomorrow, we can."

"No. I don't mind at all. Thank you for asking what I wanted." Her words came out tight at the end. Her hands were clasped behind her back. "Come here."

I stood from the box I had been digging through and cleared my throat. There was something about her behavior that caused my heart to pick up the pace. The closer I stepped, the bigger her smile grew. She stopped herself by catching her bottom lip between her teeth. The color and sight of it dragging between her perfect teeth was hypnotic. I wanted to explore the softness there.

I stopped right in front of her. "Yes?"

"Hiya, Ford." From behind her she produced a little bunch of plastic mistletoe and held it above her head.

She looked up innocently when the attached silver bell rang once. Her gaze dropped to my lips and her tongue flicked out to wet her own. Jesus.

"Suzie, I thought after last time... Maybe it isn't the best..."

She closed the distance between us, her breasts pressing firmly into my chest. "This doesn't count. It's mistletoe. It's basically a law. You don't want to kiss me, Ford?"

Her thick eyelashes blinked slowly. Her free arm dropped to my shoulders. She rocked her hips slowly as Bing Crosby crooned about a white Christmas. Of course, I wanted to kiss her. Day or night, sick or healthy, dressed up or dressed down. I wanted to always be kissing her. How could she not see it written all over my face?

"It's not that. I'm not explaining myself well."

"So just stop." She rested her finger against my lips. "Stop trying to explain all the things you want and feel. Stop trying to talk and ratio-nalize and contain yourself and just show me."

"Show you?"

She kept moving slowly, sensually. "Show me what you want."

"I think—"

"We're running out of time." Her words sunk into me. Her look, the sadness, it made sense. The clicking tock of the next coming weeks. She was sad. "I need to know what you want. Don't talk or think or rationalize or debate with me. We're running out of time," she repeated.

Her eyes squeezed shut like she was silently praying for something. Could it be possible she didn't understand how much I felt for her? I felt like I was a flashing neon sign of sexual turmoil.

What I wanted? All I wanted was to never move from this moment. I wanted to feel her perfect hips under my hands, rocking gently, until the end of time. I wanted her to look up at me like I was the best thing in the world. I wanted nothing to change or be ruined. I wanted to bring her light back. I wanted to make her happy. For forever.

That's all.

I didn't know when that had become my most important goal in life. Perhaps her diminished light over the past few weeks had reminded me to never take for granted the beautiful things in life. I moved my hand to her neck, so long and smooth and beautiful. I was obsessed with the area above her shoulders. My thumb moved tentatively up and down. She was uncharacteristically still and quiet, her playful mood slipping away. She was sad and afraid. I had done that to her. I made her doubt herself.

What the hell was wrong with me? I managed to take the most beautiful, most confident woman in the world and reduce her to this. My throat tightened with emotion. Her throat moved with a swallow under my thumb. My head lowered to inhale her. I couldn't tell her all the ways she was beautiful. I couldn't tell her how much she had come to mean to me over these weeks. I couldn't tell her all the stupid rules and boundaries I set were only there for protection—her protection, as well as mine.

But she was right. I could show her. While we had the time.

I moved her hair off her shoulder and pulled her sweater and bra strap down to reveal her silky smooth shoulder. I let my lips graze her skin and watched in amazement as tiny goosebumps formed. I rubbed away the mark the bra left, massaging her until some of her tension melted away. Her breathing grew rapid. A small pulse point raced in her neck. I lowered my mouth to it and sucked it softly.

Her knees buckled but my arm had snaked around her, holding her up. The only thing that fell to the floor was the mistletoe. Her hands went to my head, fingernails scratching through my hair. I was rock hard already. I showed her that too.

She moaned.

I worked my way slowly up her neck, lavishing her, showing her. As I kissed and tongued, my hands roamed up her body, moving from hip to ass to waist to breast, never stopping, memorizing as much as I could. Not having to talk helped. If I spoke now, I wouldn't be able to hide how I felt. If she wanted me to really show her how I felt, then I'd fucking show her.

Suzie

Passion. Oodles and oodles of it. I always knew it bubbled just under the surface of Ford and now that I had gotten a sneak peek of it, I knew I was right. I'd had good sex before. Well, at the time I thought it was good. But I was closer to coming now with Ford caressing my shoulder than I'd been after hours with other men. This side of Ford was addictive. He was attentive to the point of obsession and it made me feel sexy. More than that, I felt cherished.

I was afraid to make noise or move and wake him from whatever magnificent monster had taken over. We were panting as he backed me to the wall and braced me there with his strong arms.

Cluck. Yes. Wall sex—tricky in practice, but epic levels of hot if pulled off correctly.

I threw my head back. I wanted to please him. Kiss him. But he was in control. I reached for his hardness and inhaled sharply.

"Oh, Ford." I couldn't wait to feel the full weight of him in my hand.

"Shh." He gently moved my arms above my head, clasping my wrists with one surprisingly capable hand, before trailing kisses on the underside of my arm.

Who knew the underside of the arm was so fucking erotic?

His subtle strength was one of the things I liked most about him. My knees shook with want, threatening to give out. We were still in the living room, in front of the giant bay windows where the Christmas tree would go. The Christmas tree that we would get together. I smiled and hid my expression in my arms. He'd asked me what I wanted. He had from the get-go. Always claiming that he never knew what to say, but always saying exactly what I needed to hear.

"Wait." His voice was firm.

The smile fell from my face. "Noooo," I whined.

He braced the wall like he alone was responsible for keeping the house from crumbling in. His breathing was ragged. His shoulders hunched in concentration.

I grabbed his face and made him look at me. "No, Ford. No. You don't get to talk yourself out of this." I grabbed his hand and put it on my breast. He'd been grazing and tracing all around those poor breasts without giving them the proper attention they deserved. "You've been giving me lady blue balls for weeks. You're not about to take this away from me." I moved his hand to massage my breast. He collapsed into me and laughed into my neck.

Wait, laughter?

"Are you laughing?" I shoved him slightly back, to see his face.

Sure enough, a smile I'd never seen split his face wide open. A breath whooshed out of me. Good golly, Miss Molly! He was hot. It always surprised me how attractive he was. Those little glimpses of his passion were like catnip to me. But still. This was no time for laughter.

He laughed harder.

"Ford." I shoved him harder this time in outrage.

"Sorry...sorry. Hang on."

His shoulders shook and soon a deep barreling laugh I would have never expected came out of him. And goddammit, it was sexy too. Only now was so not the time I wanted to discover his sexy smile and drop-dead gorgeous laugh. Now it was handsy-fun-times.

"Fine. Have your little laugh fest." I shoved past him and made for the stairs. I mumbled to myself. "I'll just go take care of things myself. What else is new? Like a freaking nunnery in this house."

I made it about half way up the stairs when I was captured from behind.

"Not so fast."

His voice had a light, playful tone but his actions spoke louder. His large arms encased me. The force of him caught me by surprise. I fell forward on the plush carpet, not hard enough to hurt. He made sure of it when we tumbled forward. Ford pressed into my body, making his want clear for me but not crushing me. I was trapped beneath him and so happy about it.

"What are you doing?" I arched myself into him and he groaned. "I thought you wanted to stop."

"Suzie." He ground into me. We were like teenagers! "The very last thing I want to do is stop."

We were rocking against each other in tempo, though the music stopped a long time ago. His nose nuzzled my neck and hair. I turned my head to taste him. He was braced on his forearms but he wouldn't give me what I wanted. He teased me with more kisses and his short beard. The contrast between his rough beard and gentle kisses was almost too much. I clenched and relaxed, building and building.

I wanted him inside me.

"I didn't want to fuck you against the wall in front of the window for God and everyone to see." That accent was back. Southern, dirty, and so very hot. Damn this man.

"Oh," I said. After a beat, I added, "I'm fine with that."

He laughed again but this time it was mixed with a frustrated growl. "Then we will do it another time." He whispered into my ear as he rubbed his rock-hard package against me. I met him motion for motion. "We will do it on every fucking surface of this house."

"Imagine Jack and his Lysol after that."

He cracked up again into my shoulder. "Jesus, you're funny."

My nipples were getting no satisfaction at this angle. The steps dug into my ribs and hips despite his attempt to not crush me. I pushed up a little and he rolled off to the side. I rolled over to face him.

"And you're so handsome when you laugh. I want to make you laugh all the time."

He pushed the hair behind my ear. "You make me feel...so many things."

I blushed into my arm holding me up.

"Suzie?"

"Ford?" I looked up and his eyes were as dark as the night of Halloween. I wondered how much of that inner beast was in control now. Was it wrong that I hoped all of it was? I hoped he had no rational thought left.

"I just want..." He frowned and shook his head. He tried to speak again but I held up my finger to his mouth.

"Show me," I whispered.

He leaned over me until I was on my back. If there were stairs digging into me or neighbors watching or the world spinning outside, I didn't notice any of it. All I saw was the way Ford looked at me as he lowered to kiss me.

And the man could kiss.

He took his time; he caressed and teased and invaded and retreated. He drove me to the brink with his kiss. I was overwhelmed with the emotion I felt, with the arousal I felt.

After a minute he stood up off me. This time I didn't protest. I reached for him and he hauled me to his chest. Without speaking, he led me to his bedroom. He closed the door and suddenly I was as nervous as a teenager. You'd thought I'd never been with a man. I guess I never had been with a real man—at least none like Ford.

I walked backward towards the bed, arms crossed. I relaxed them down and then crossed them again. I never worried about being good before. I just had to be present and sexy and easy. But this was Ford. I wanted to please him. What if I wasn't what he wanted? What if I was too used up? What if—

"I lost you." Ford lifted my chin to his face.

"I'm nervous."

"You're nervous?" His eyebrows lifted in surprise.

I played with the ends of my hair. I wondered if I should take it down. Did he like it better up? Some guys like the ponytail for when they—

"Hey." He prompted me to look at him again. "We don't have to do anything."

"I want to." The words came out on a rush. So much for playing it cool. "If you want to?" Who was this person? I was Suzie frickin' Samuels. I should be blowing his mind by now.

"Oh, I want to." His mouth quirked. "Since the moment I saw you."

"What?" This had me baffled. He never showed interest, just annoyance and disapproval of my lifestyle.

"It's taken every ounce of self-control to..." He started then took a deep breath. Normally, he'd start counting but now I only witnessed his resolve. He stepped toward me. "I'm showing you."

"Oh." I swallowed.

He pushed me softly onto the bed and slid off my leggings.

"God bless leggings," he mumbled against the skin of my thighs.

I squirmed as chills spread over my legs. He lavished kisses up my ankles. He cherished every inch of my legs with his mouth and hands and breath as he worked his way up from my feet, past my ankles, and calves and thighs.

"Oh, sweet Jesus." The zings were everywhere.

He chuckled a hot laugh over the core of me, through my panties. I shuddered in uncontrolled delight. I squirmed, desperate for more. His beard tickled against my thighs as he slowly slid the panties down my legs. Every inch the fabric grazed was alive with nerves. I studied the ceiling before closing my eyes.

"Shouldn't I be helping you?"

"Shhh." He kissed me lightly once. Right on the core of me.

"Oh-okay."

"Suzie. Relax."

I did. I closed my eyes and focused on feeling. I let him show me everything.

CHAPTER 24

CLIFFORD

 y head rested on Suzie's flat stomach, rising and falling to the gentle rhythm of her slowing breathes. I smelled her, tasted her, felt her. My senses were overrun by her. To be honest, I was a little in shock that I could bring her that amount of pleasure. My inflated ego was as big as my—

"Why did you start laughing earlier?" she asked breaking through my thoughts.

I waited a beat. That felt like a lifetime ago. A person ago. I was a changed man. Being with Suzie had changed me. I was sure of it. It felt crucial to only give her pleasure. To show her that not all men take and take. I wanted to give. To show her.

"I think I was relieved. You've been so out of sorts lately. I thought maybe I did something or said something. Or that living here had changed you."

My head shook when she laughed. "The whole point of this was to change me."

I lifted up to look at her before making my way toward her. "There was and is nothing wrong with you." In my mind, it had never been about changing her. It was about showing her she was capable of growth. There was a difference there that I had never been able to express accurately.

"I wish you wouldn't say stuff like that." Her eyes grew distant.

"Like what?"

"Stuff that makes me think...never mind. Hey, stop frowning." She rubbed away my creased eyebrows in the way she was so fond of doing.

"I'm sorry if I ever made you feel like you needed to change."

She waved my words away. She seemed conflicted. "Hey do you, uh, want me to... I mean, it's your turn." She gestured to my very demanding and very hard cock still tucked safely away in my jeans.

"I'm perfect." I genuinely felt more satisfaction in being responsible for her pleasure than I could have possibly gained any other way. I was a king.

She frowned now and sat up. "Oh. Okay. I guess I'll just get going."

She made to slide out of the bed covering her perfect breasts. Breasts, in hindsight, that I did not spend near enough time with. I grabbed her hand and tugged her back toward the bed. "Where do you have to be?"

Her hair had loosened from the braid and now the dark waves fell over her smooth skin. She tucked strands behind her ear.

"I figured you wanted to be alone now. Since we...um. Since we're all wrapped up here."

"I don't want you to go. Do you want to go?"

"No." She answered immediately. When she spoke honestly my man-pride swelled. "So, then I'll just get back in bed then." She looked uncomfortable, like she didn't know what to do with her hands.

I knew what to do with her hands. I placed one above our heads and held it as I traced over her skin. Now that I had access to her, I probably wouldn't ever be able to stop touching her.

"Much better." I pulled her close to spoon her and inhaled her neck. She always smelled so amazing. Even after she'd worked out. Especially so. It defied logic.

"Thank you," she said over her shoulder. "For that. That was... unexpected. But so good. I've never...I'm going to stop talking."

"You never what?"

She flushed, even from behind her, I could tell. "I've never come that way."

If I thought my man-pride was inflated before, holy shit, I wasn't going to be able to leave the room at this rate. My head wasn't going to fit through the door.

"Really?" I wondered if this was something she told all men. And then I swore at myself for thinking that way. Suzie was many things, but she was honest to a fault.

"Yeah. I mean some guys have tried." She hid her head in the pillow. "Oh my God, this is awkward. I mean, they tried but they sort of mashed…and there were teeth, and I never relaxed enough. I'll just say I get what all the fuss is about now."

I kissed her exposed shoulder and my dick grew angrier with me every second that went by. It was important to do this for her. To show her that men can give without taking too. I mean. I loved tasting her and bringing her to climax and yes, I would have loved to slide into her very wet…

I cleared my throat. "You're welcome."

With my arm that lay on top of her, she laced our fingers and kissed my knuckles.

"You should not talk more often. It suits you." She grinned mischievously.

I huffed a laugh into her neck.

"I'm just saying if ever you're like 'hmm what should I say?' Just don't. Just go ahead and ravage me instead."

I growled and rolled her onto her back. I nuzzled her breasts. "That is a very good plan."

"Everybody wins." She gasped as I sucked her nipple into my mouth.

Turned out those breasts needed my attention now. They practically begged for it. "You have no idea how long I've thought about touching you like this." I was talking to her breasts, but I also talked to her. I was drunk on her. I had no filter.

"So why didn't you?"

"It's hard to let go, when I've held on this long."

"Let go?" Her long nails gently scraped along my back and shoulders as I licked and sucked her amazing body.

"I'm afraid to let go. I'm afraid of who I'll become," I said between tasting her skin.

"I don't know what makes you say that, but you don't have to be afraid of that. Not with me. I'm here too now. I'll always bring you back."

I dropped my head to the space between her breasts. I held her close to me. How was she so damn intuitive? How did she always say so much just right? I trusted her. If she said I could lose control with her maybe I could...maybe I could allow myself to just relax a little.

"Although if this was any indication of what you are like when you lose control, I might not want to reel you in." She laughed and yelped when I bit the area right above her ribcage, just below where the fullness started.

I growled and went lower, deciding in that moment to show her just what happened when I took what I wanted without thinking.

Suzie

I had no idea men were capable of so much giving and so little taking. I lay in Ford's arms for hours, completely dazed by what had just happened. He'd given me orgasms. Plural. Multiple. A LOT. All different ways and took nothing for himself. I offered too. But he seemed to be proving some sort of point to himself.

We were on our backs, holding hands. At some point, he joined me under the covers as the chill set in. He kept his pants on though. He made it very clear how important it was for him to keep his pants on. Something about lying in bed and holding hands and not having sex was the most intimate thing I'd ever done. I'd had sex when I was fourteen. I never got to experience innocent romance.

I really, really liked it.

"So. Tell me how engineering has anything to do with what you want to do?" I broke the silence to ask.

I could almost hear him frown in the darkness. I had no idea what time it was, but somewhere between ten p.m. and three am.

"Are you familiar with Maslow's hierarchy of basic needs?"

"Remind me," I teased.

"It's this pyramid of items humans need to survive. The base is formed by the physical, the things we need to survive: shelter, water, food. Sex. And above that, there are safety needs and so on, so that at the very top there is self-actualization. This means that in order for anybody to have passion for education or desire to better themselves, they have to have their basic needs fulfilled, like a place to live, clothes on their back, food in their bellies."

"Huh." I thought of how run-down my trailer had gotten since Momma left. I was working too much to make ends meet and didn't have the time or energy to care about having a flower box or fresh paint. I interrupted him after it was clear he'd only just started. "Ford, I know you know your stuff. You know you know your stuff, but you need to give me the elevator pitch. We need a quick, punchy line to help sell you."

"You make it sound like a business transaction."

"It is. That's the world we live in. At the party, people will want to know what you are about, and I want to be able to give them the quick pitch."

He groaned.

"No offense," I squeezed his hand, "but you don't want them to glaze over from boredom and look for the quickest exit."

"That never happens."

I waited a beat. "Sure. Never. Still, let's think of one anyway. Pretend it's the Winter Ball and you have thirty seconds or less to get my attention. In this scene, I'm an old, wealthy white guy whose time and money are way more important than anybody else's." I sat up and clicked on the light next to the bed. When I turned back, I've lost Ford. I could be using the sexiest of engineering lingo and he'd not hear me. He stared at my chest, unblinking and fuzzy eyed. He leaned forward and sucked a nipple into his mouth.

"We are not off to a great start." I gently shoved him away.

"I'm sorry. If all investors were you, I'd be screwed. I can't talk to you. I can't think straight around you."

I laughed but pulled the sheet around my shoulders. "Okay, okay seriously. Sell me. Tell me how to understand so I can say it right if anybody talks to me."

"I'm not good at this."

I thought for a second. "Just explain it to me then. Why do you do what you do? Who are you trying to help?"

"The children."

I blinked my surprise. "What?"

"Kids, all kids, deserve an equal start in life. We aren't all equal in our circumstances and it's not fair that some are born into the lives they have. They deserve a fighting chance. Their basic needs have to be taken care of. Somebody should believe in them. Then they'll have a shot at life."

There it was. That passion for his work that was so damn appealing.

"Well, why didn't you just say that?" I whispered.

"I thought I had."

I snuggled back down into him, deciding sitting up was too much distance. "You've never mentioned children. I mean a little at my trailer, but this clears things up." I wished I could see him like that all the time. Aflame. I wanted to see it again. All the time. I wanted to let his beast out for forever.

"Sometimes I forget to say the most obvious things," he said softly.

I twirled my fingers in his chest hair. "You're hairy."

"Thankfully, you never do." He rumbled a laugh.

I laughed into his ribs and looked up at him. "I like you."

"I like you too." He added, "Even when you play music so loud it shakes the house."

I jabbed him in the ribcage. "I like you even when you're a crabby paddy."

I rested my head on his chest. I inhaled him. I loved his smell. I laughed a little to myself because he still had a massive boner. We had sat here discussing important topics and Little Ford was screaming for attention. I wanted to reach out and stroke him so badly. But I wanted to respect his desire to wait, too. We were running out of time but I could take things slowly. I liked the idea of it. The idea of moving slowly and taking the time to explore each other's bodies appealed to me; it caused a warmth to spread within me. So long as I didn't think about the after.

"I had a terrible childhood. I was lucky to get out. I'm not typical. I need to help them. I need to make sure I change things. I need to pay forward what was given to me. The world is stacked..." He trailed off as his voice grew tight with emotion.

I pulled him tighter to me, my cheek pressed snug against him. He squeezed me back.

"I promise I'm going to melt the faces off those rich SOBs. They won't have any clue what hit them. "

His laughter jostled me. "Oh, I don't doubt that for a second."

"I ordered my dress. Gretchen and the girls helped me. I think you're going to like it."

"Will it be on you? Then I'll like it."

"And you say you're not good with words."

I let out a long breath and we settled into a more comfortable position as sleepiness seeped in. "I can't believe it's already almost December.

"It's gone fast." His voice was quiet. The air was heavy with all the things that we weren't saying.

That I'd be moving back to my old life. That'd I be dancing the VIP stage for men who may or may not appreciate my artistic talent. He'd be doing the work he loves. We wouldn't be together. We were from different worlds and the chasm was too wide between us.

I closed my eyes and allowed myself to forget for a minute. I chose to lay there in his arms and just breathe in the moment. I knew what I was getting into when we started all this. I would be fine. He'd be fine.

There were no other options.

CHAPTER 25

CLIFFORD

I wanted everyone to shut up. The house was full of people. Suzie's new friends clucked away loudly upstairs, stomping around, laughing and wasting all our time. I wouldn't yell. I'd be patient. I wouldn't go upstairs and kick down the door and tell them to hurry.

"I'm having déjà vu." As Jack spoke, he covered my watch with his hand. "You have plenty of time."

I dropped my arm and crossed to the bay windows to look outside. It was pitch black even though it was only eight. The Winter Ball was just about to start. Every single person in *my* home had told me that nobody shows up to a party on time. I sighed.

Jack rolled his eyes and said, "I'm going upstairs to help. You're making me jittery."

I hadn't explicitly told Jack about Suzie and I getting together while he was gone. It turned out Suzie was an openly affectionate person and since our, um, connection last month, she'd spent every moment we were together touching and kissing me, as though she needed constant reassurance. I didn't mind. I liked it. The few times Jack walked in on us embracing in the kitchen or cuddling on the couch, he always acted like he saw nothing and never commented on it.

I glanced at my watch. It had only been a minute. I paced in front of the bay window and smiled when I spotted the tree decoration boxes stacked in the corner. We still hadn't bought a tree. We'd been so busy and the days were going too fast, but we would. I'd already imagined taking her to pick out a tree.

I'd even invite Jack to come with.

I drew the line with the Scorned Women's Society.

The boxes on the floor reminded me of my favorite night. Well, that first night had previously held the honor, but the last few nights had tied it for first. We were taking things slow. I was enjoying the journey with her. I wanted to sleep with her. God knew I did, but the second I did, I'd have lost control. I couldn't lose control. If I opened that door…there'd be no going back. I didn't want to feel things I had no right to feel. I didn't want to have to try and shove all that back down when she went back to her real life and forgot about me.

I pressed my hand to my chest to ease the perpetual heartburn I had lately. After tonight, I could relax. After tonight, after I knew the funding was secured, I would relax a little. I would re-focus.

"Ahem." I turned around to the sound of Gretchen clearing her throat. "May I present Miss Suzie Samuels of Green Valley."

I was so lost in thought I'd missed that everybody had come down. Everyone except Suzie, who stood at the top of the stairs. The room went silent. That woman could make an entrance.

I couldn't breathe. She was a vision in winter white, fresh like the fallen snow. I'd never seen anybody look so beautiful. It was truly hard to look at. Her beauty burned too bright. Her long elegant neck was stacked with pearl strands and her midnight hair was twisted up elegantly off her neck. Intricate lace covered her neck and shoulders. The dress then transitioned into a hectic combination of lace and pearls which flowed elegantly down the curves of her body. Long white satin gloves covered her hands and arms. She smoothed her skirts and flicked glances to the people all around me.

She was breathtaking.

"This is when you speak," Jack reminded me.

Suzie began her descent down the stairs. The delicate beading swished and clicked in an oddly satisfying cacophony with every move she made. A thousand insufficient phrases came to mind and tangled on my tongue, not one of them good enough to express how I felt. How I *felt*. Because she could come down in a potato sack and I was sure I would feel the same.

I swallowed and tried to speak. "I—you are…"

She stopped in front of me. Her eyes flicked between mine and she smiled. "You like it?"

"You are beautiful." Painfully insufficient. Not nearly enough and yet, her face lit up with a smile.

"Oh. Thank you."

I frowned. "You act like you've never heard that before." Suzie had been told she was beautiful her whole life.

She leaned forward and kissed my cheek. "I've never heard it from you." She blushed and fussed with her dress.

Meanwhile, I replayed our every interaction. I know I had told her she was beautiful. I thought it every time I saw her. There was no way I would have forgotten. When I finally came back into focus, Jack and Gretchen stood in similar positions, with arms crossed and shaking heads.

"I sometimes forget to say the most obvious things," I added to the room. And then more quietly I said to her, "I've thought it a million times. Every time I've seen you."

Her eyes lit up but her smile was shaky. "Oh, Ford."

The group sent us off with a loud announcement from Jack that they were going to have a party while we were gone. He'd grown quite close with these ladies, insisting he'd learned more from them in a few weeks than all of undergrad.

"Use coasters." I frowned.

Gretchen glared at me. She did not like me. I may not have social sense, but I knew well enough when I was vehemently disliked. But I wouldn't back off on coasters.

"It's antique wood," I defended.

She continued to glare at me as she hugged Suzie goodbye.

A car had been sent for us. It was very chic, and Suzie's reaction to the stretch limo was almost enough to make this all worth it. I still had my doubts.

In the car, we were silent with tension. Suzie had seemed distant since she came down the stairs. She must have been nervous. I could help her. She was going through all this for me.

"Suzie." I cleared my throat. She looked up at me with her big green eyes. "God, you're beautiful." Now that I had said it once, I needed to make sure I said it every time I thought it.

"Thank you," she whispered.

"Tonight. I want you to just be you." I closed my eyes in an effort to try and get these things right. Talking was easier if I wasn't distracted by her face. "You have shown me that I was wrong about everything these last few months. Well, not everything. I still think my research is valid and I still plan to pursue that avenue. What I need to do is find a measurement stick. I think where the experiment got off course was—"

A hand softly squeezed my knee. "Start over."

I opened my eyes. She was smiling expectantly at me.

"Seriously gorgeous."

"Ford. Focus." Her head shook with a laugh.

"I just want you to be you tonight. You're perfect as you are. You didn't need to change your clothes or accent to be respected by me. Or anybody else, for that matter. You're funny and charming and an exceedingly quick learner. You just be yourself tonight. Don't worry about accents or pretending to care about my research—"

"I do care about your research." She was listening intently but a small line of worry had formed between her brows.

I needed to make sure I got this right.

"Of course. As much as you can with what you've learned. I know you care in your way." Why did everything I say sound condescending? Luckily she knew me by now. "I know I said all that stuff when we started about changing and opportunity but you have shown more than enough these last few months that my original hypothesis was right all along."

As I spoke her smile fell off and I worried once again that I had muddled the words. But no—she was perfect as she was. That was what I meant, and that's what I said.

"I've shown you what?"

"That you're a product of your environment. Your whole life you've been valued for your looks. For the sexual gratification you could provide. You've been told that you're an empty vessel to be filled. That you were stupid and unworthy of love."

In the soft light of the limo, her shoulders tensed.

"You never believed you were capable of more because you were never told you were. You tell a person they're one thing their whole life, they'll believe it. It's similar to the Pygmalion Effect. This was never about changing your clothes or accent. This was about making you believe you're capable of more."

She sat still, despite the bumpy car ride. Her eyes wide with a fear I didn't understand as they took in my words. Why was the world shrinking around me? Why did it feel like I had said the wrong thing?

"You said all the things you've said because you were...wait, the experiment wasn't the clothes, it was how you spoke to me?" Her arms shot out when we hit a particularly big bump to grip the seat for balance. "You only said those things to prove a point?"

We passed under a streetlight and her color was gone. I had messed up. I moved to sit next to her on the bench and gathered her hands. They were ice cold through the satin.

"No. Suzie. No. I wanted you to see what my research was about. If you treat someone one way their whole life, they will act that way. Time and time again research has shown that. But if you believe in someone and show them that they are worth more, then they believe it. Everybody believes it. There are four pillars to this: climate, input, response opportunity, and feedback. That's what we were doing. Yes, we were changing things but that was just to help you understand that you were capable all along."

She didn't relax. "Ford. I don't want to talk about theories or pillars. I want to know what you feel for me."

I held her gaze. Her eyes implored me. What I felt for her was superfluous to this whole experiment. What I felt for her couldn't be summed up adequately and saying anything more would only make our inevitable separation all the worse for both of us. I couldn't tell her what I felt for her. I couldn't break that last thread that held me together. We were going back to our separate lives after this. Better to not open Pandora's box.

"Please, tell me how you feel." Her swallow was audible even with the low hum of the moving car.

God, if only I could be the person she needed. I would love to be the person she deserved. She deserved a man who could be totally free around her and protect her and enrich her and lift her up. All I ever was around her was tense and on the edge of control.

"UT Professor Wins Historic Alumn Funding for Research."

I was so close now. I had my plan and my path, and she had hers. Paths that were worlds apart. Why did it feel like my insides were tightening? Why did my mind, the one that was supposed to be rational, want me to yell out and tell her all the things I felt for her? I couldn't.

"I feel that you are an amazing person. I admire you. I want you to know that you are capable of whatever you want. These last weeks have been a treasure to me." God, even as I said the words it sounded like a bad break up. I didn't want to sound like I was feeding her lines.

Her smile grew wider with every word. Her cheeks straining, her eyes glistening but she nodded. "Yeah, no. Thank you." She nodded rapidly. Her dangling pearl earrings bobbed. "I guess you've been saying that from the beginning."

"Yes. I was never trying to deceive you. Ever. I wanted to be honest through this whole process. I was worried about what this might do to you."

"How's that?" She let out a shaky breath.

"Well, living here and all that. And then going back to Green Valley. I knew it might be hard." Why did I sound like such a tool? I shook my head. "I just mean, from the start. I always wanted to be clear about expectations."

She nodded once. "That's true. You did."

"Have I upset you? What aren't you saying?"

She gave me another watery smile and sniffed. "No. It's just that… I appreciate what you're saying. That I can be myself. Thank you. You have made me feel okay to be myself."

She looked out the window, straight ahead and not at me.

"You're sure you're okay? You still want to do this?"

She nodded stiffly. "Of course." She turned and looked at me with a squeeze of my hand. "We've got this."

But I had lost her. I had said the wrong thing. I couldn't say what she needed to hear.

***

Suzie

I understood so much now. I understood the expression "hindsight is twenty-twenty." I wish I could go back in time and shake myself and say "It doesn't matter. He's not worth it!"

I totally got it now. Everything I thought I felt for Jethro at the time felt so big but looking back, it was nothing. A hot and fast fling as hollow as a glass ornament and as easily broken. It felt nothing like this. You couldn't help who you loved. Just look at my father, who still loved a woman who left almost twenty years ago. And once you loved someone nothing else mattered. That's why love was scary and terrifying and stupid.

I didn't know how I made it through the rest of that limo ride. I was in a freaking limo in a ball gown with free booze and I couldn't even enjoy it. All I could think about was how stupid I'd been. How I'd let myself fall in love with a man who couldn't feel the same about me. He said he respected me and that I was fine as I was but when tonight was over, he never wanted to see me again. A reminder of the endgame. I may be fine as I was but I still wasn't enough for him. Never enough.

He admired me. What a load of shit. He *admired* me. I didn't understand. It wasn't like he'd only wanted to fuck me and leave me, he hadn't even done that. Did he think that low of me that I wasn't even worth a fuck?

I closed my eyes against the pain.

My attempt to rally the familiar anger to help with the hurt, failed. My time with Ford had been special. He obviously did care enough about me. He just didn't love me. He couldn't love me. I had to accept that. I needed to remember that. I'd never felt like maybe there was something bigger than me in this world until Ford. And now I had to go back to the G-Spot and live my old life.

Ford squeezed my hand, breaking me from my rambling thoughts. When I looked at him smiling tentatively at me I knew I was right.

"I'm so glad you're here with me," he said.

Sometimes he said things that drove me crazy with confusion but now I understood. He was a good man. He wanted me to feel value and self-worth. He was showing me how a man should treat me. He had gifted me with self-respect. I was the fool that fell in love with a man that could never love someone like me.

"Me too." The door opened. "Let's go knock 'em dead."

He smiled and frowned with his face at the same time. Only Ford could pull off such a feat.

"Wowza," I said and the driver who had helped me out of the back seat smiled.

The mansion was bigger than anything I'd ever seen in real life. It was the size of a hotel but looked like a ranch. A hundred giant windows were covered in perfectly aligned Christmas garland and lights, glowing from the party within. Every manicured hedge was wrapped in twinkling white lights. Ford emerged from the car behind me.

"Incredible," he said.

The driver gave us a nod and said, "Enjoy," before leaving with the line of cars to go wherever cars go while rich people party.

The inside was decorated in rustic white linens and pine boughs. A grand staircase by the entrance had pine garlands wrapped around the banisters that looked like they were made of real pine and not the plastic stuff. The air smelled of savory foods and cinnamon. Next to the stairs, some musicians played classical Christmas music. I'm sure my jaw hung open like the yokel I was.

"I've already counted four Christmas trees. Real ones." He winked at me and my heart crashed against my chest.

It hit me that we'd never decorate a tree together. Because even though I loved Ford and I wanted to help him tonight, I was never going back to that house. His house. I couldn't. I was relieved that Gretchen had agreed to pack and store my things at her place. I wouldn't stay with her either. I wouldn't be able to see anybody from this brief vacation from my real life. Not for a while. I needed to get back to reality. The trailer park and G-Spot were where I belonged. What I was enough for.

I wanted to claw this high lace collar away so I could breathe.

Each room was more crowded than the last and the house never ended. Heads swiveled toward me as we moved forward. I smiled and nodded. My cheeks twitched from forcing a BS smile for so long. Stripping had taught me well. I wanted to be done with this farce. I wanted to leave and be gone. Feeling Ford next to me was too much. If only I could stop smelling him and aching for him, somehow stop my insides from collapsing in on themselves.

Ford succinctly explained his research and got several intrigued looks and compliments on his work as we worked the room meeting people. I smiled at him—real ones—to encourage him. I threw in my two cents from time to time as people asked about what I did. I said I was a student and research assistant. Not a single person called me out or challenged us. Seemed we'd passed the test so far. Yet, I'd never felt more dishonest in my life. It was like I was playacting or watching a movie. I was so far removed from myself.

We stopped in a doorway that led to the back of the house, away from the crowds. We were blocked from sight. Ford's thumb rubbed the small area of skin exposed between my long gloves and capped sleeve.

"I feel great. I'm on fire."

I laughed because he really was. He glowed. His passion ignited him, lit him up from the inside out. If only he saw how compelling he was when that part was free, he'd never lack for funding.

"You're doing great."

"It's you. You're my lucky charm. My muse."

The soft look in his eyes and the smile teasing his lips cut to the quick. He brought me in for a hug and I could finally let my smile drop.

"I guess people see you on my arm and they assume I must be worth something," he whispered.

I closed myself off against his words. I fortified my insides against those little comments. Those were like the tiny rivers that made canyons. They wore me down, ripped a hole through me over time.

"Suzie, look up."

We were under a giant bouquet of what must be actual mistletoe. I'd never seen the real stuff before. It was like the first time I realized cranberries weren't naturally can-shaped. The bunch of mistletoe was wrapped in satin and hung a few feet above us at the crest of the archway.

"I see your ways." I stepped up on my tip-toes, hoping to get away with a chaste kiss.

Ford pulled me firmly to his chest and kissed me with passion. I was powerless against his energy. I melted into him. I was an idiot who'd never learned, allowing myself this moment. Then I would tell him I was leaving. He would be sad in his way, but relieved too.

For now, I'd remember this. This would be the new memory that I would bring up when I needed to get away from my reality. If men got too rough or things moved too fast, I would remember this moment. Ford holding me and kissing me like I was worth something, because in this moment I *was* worth something. His hands shook as they held me close and I could tell he was barely controlling himself.

A sad ache re-emerged as I realized I'd never see him totally let go.

Not for me. Maybe someday he'd meet someone who was worthy of his full passion. His hands moved down my back and he leaned back from our kiss. I was proud of myself for not getting emotional. I had a mask in place like the masquerade ball, but this time it was all me.

His hand rested on my neck, his thumb grazing over the skin there, bringing happier memories to the surface. I would think of those moments too when the darkness threatened.

"You're so beautiful."

I wanted to scream. I wanted to tear off my dress. I didn't want to be beautiful anymore. It meant the world to me when he finally said it but now it was a new barrier. I wanted to be more than that. I wanted to be everything to him.

"She is indeed." A large man approached that I recognized instantly as one of my regulars.

Titty Teddy approached and my insides went icy. Ford's smile grew when he saw the other man. The world slowly tilted around me. Something was registering but hadn't clicked into place. Dread settled in.

They'd been speaking that night…

Ted's gaze took me in and he shook his head with amusement. "Well, well, well. Look at you." He grabbed my hand and gave my glove a gentle kiss. "Transformed indeed."

"Thank you, Mr. Bouffant. Thank you for having us," Ford said.

I was speechless, knowing I should say something.

The party hummed loudly a thousand miles away. I felt Ford look at me. I couldn't look at him. I was sure my face gave me away.

"Of course." Ted's gaze moved over me again in an appraising way.

"Teddy," I whispered. "This is your party?" I asked louder.

"Indeed, it is. Welcome to my home. That's my wife over there. Normally, I'd ask you to steer clear but since I've heard from many of my peers that they were quite impressed with you, I'm not worried about her guessing how we know each other."

Anger firmed the frown on Ford. He studied me, his concern deepening. I couldn't hold his gaze.

"You two know each other?" Ford asked.

"Yes." My voice was too quiet. "Teddy's a G-Spot regular."

His brow was so creased with concern but I couldn't smooth it out. Another thought clicked into place and ice shot through me. My feet were cemented but my body floated away.

"I didn't know he was the investor," I said.

Ford's frown smoothed into an emotionless mask. Ted's gaze moved between us. He held up his hands and gestured toward a door.

"Let's go to my study, the three of us, and talk," he said.

Ford needed a little shove to get moving after Teddy led the way. He didn't speak and when I reached for his hand, he didn't hold mine back, so I eventually dropped it again.

CHAPTER 26

SUZIE

"Have a seat." Ted gestured to the large leather sofa in his study.

Ford and I moved stonily to sit as directed. He went to his desk and leaned against it, one leg propped up, balancing off the edge.

"I can see that your theory has proved true, Mr. Rutledge. You've done a great job convincing myself and the guests of Suzie's status and class. Suzie herself seems changed. I haven't seen her stripping lately." Ted looked to Ford and then to me. "Is he always this chatty?"

"Is this some sort of joke? Were you toying with us?" I asked through a raspy whisper.

The man looked affronted. "A joke? No, ma'am. I'm a man of my word."

"You'll fund my research?" Ford's voice was rough and low.

"I said I would, didn't I? I said if you showed me a new woman, I'd believe all that mumbo jumbo you were spewing."

The tension was thick and hot enough to fry biscuits in. I pointed to the desk. "You write him a check now. He did his end."

"Of course." Ted stood and ambled around his desk. He rifled in the drawer before pulling out a large checkbook. He bent over with a grunt and the only sound that filled the silent room was the pen scratching across paper. "Make this out to Clifford Rutledge?"

Ford cleared his throat. "However you discussed it with Dean Lucero." His tone remained guarded but he started to relax.

I couldn't blame him. It still felt like the other shoe needed to drop but hearing that it had been coordinated through the school offered some relief.

Ted signed with a dramatic flourish. He ripped the check from the book with a sound that seemed to echo long after he was done. He held it out over his desk toward Ford. Ford reached for it. My heart raced like they were handing off grenades.

"There is one thing." Ted snatched back the check.

Ford balled his fist and sat back down. I closed my eyes, dread cementing me to the chair.

"I recently invested in the entertainment industry. I'm branching out. I'm now a partial owner of the G-Spot. Perhaps you're familiar?" He smiled at me. "We know Suzie is. Brings in the most revenue. I've seen her dance. I get it." He licked his lips. I studied the wall behind him as my body began to shake.

He continued without waiting for a response. "The thing is, my partner informed me that this money was contingent upon your review of some documents."

Ford growled out instantly, "You and I never discussed this."

"We did not. But as I'm invested in the club it is in my best interest to make sure the operation is running smoothly."

"In that case, you need to tell your partner that the building is one huge safety violation. I'm sure he doesn't want me going to the police to report the design elements on some of those secret rooms."

I frowned. I knew Occum was a cheap bastard but I didn't know about any secret rooms. Did he mean changing rooms for the stage? I couldn't focus on thoughts of renovations because of the storm brewing next to me. The air vibrated with Ford's growing rage.

"No need to get defensive." He held up his thick hands, a giant gold ring on the pinky of his right hand looked like it was cutting off circulation in his finger. "And we definitely aren't getting the police involved."

Ford sat silently next to me. He wouldn't look anywhere but straight ahead, his jaw muscles working as he kept his mouth clamped shut. I wanted to grab him and shake him.

"What's the matter with you, son? I'm giving you the money you want. You proved your point. I'm very impressed with Suzie's transformation. I heard you were getting a little something extra in this arrangement too, so what's got you bent out of shape?"

I gasped.

"Come on, you know we had to have an eye on you. Made sure things were progressing. Now, we've been more than patient. It's been months of this waiting game but the time has come. You need to let this renovation move forward. No more bureaucratic bullshit."

"This has all been a setup from the beginning?" Ford asked with no emotion.

"Here's the thing. This is the real world. Sometimes you have to do some ethically questionable things to get what you want. You were being too self-righteous. Occum saw that. Suzie was too damn stubborn, too. You both needed to think you were saving the other, feel okay about it all. Fine. We get it. Now you can sleep at night."

"He never agreed to sign," I said. I wanted to shout. "He said he'd work with Occum, but he never said he'd sign."

Ted's gaze settled on me and he looked at me like he just realized I was there. "You saying Occum lied? He told me this gentleman agreed to sign off in exchange for having you three months."

"No. I—" I grabbed Ford's hands, shook them until he looked at me. He blinked slowly as though trying to reconcile all the information being thrown at him.

"Why did he think that?" This came from Ted.

"Occum must've lied to him. I never promised any of that." Ford looked at me without really seeing. I wanted to scream that it was me. He knew me now. I wanted to remind him of the last few weeks and all that we shared and were.

"We might have alluded to it. I—I thought we'd cross that bridge when we got there. I wanted Occum off your case." I grabbed his ice-cold hands and squeezed, but he remained unmoved. "I thought we'd have more time."

"Time's up." Ford closed his eyes and it was like the air went out of him.

"No!" I stood up. "You aren't doing anything for Occum. This is just a misunderstanding. I'll get us out of it." I put my back to Ford and pointed a finger at Ted. "He needs that money. People are counting on it. You promised him."

"And you promised Occum a signature. We are at an impasse."

I was in the other man's face now, panting, I was so worked up. He chewed his lip as I spoke, not even remotely ruffled by the situation. There was no way I was letting Ford sign off now, not after everything he shared with me. I was stuck with Occum anyway, so I'd make it right.

I held my arms out like I could keep Ford safe. "I'll go to Occum. If I have to work double shifts for a year, I'll do it. He'll listen to me." He started to talk but I went on. "I make more money than any of the other girls. I'll strip. I'll do what he wants. I don't care. I thought we had more time. I thought I could—"

"Suzie—"

"No. Please. You don't understand what this money means. Just give him the check."

Ted leaned back and crossed his arms. "Looks like it's a little too late." He gestured his chin behind me. Everything moved in slow motion as I turned around. I knew what I'd see but I was desperate to be wrong.

Ford was gone.

"Where did he go?" I asked, feeling my heart shatter into a thousand pieces.

He shook his head once and tore up the check. "You better find that man before Occum does, or there'll be hell to pay."

Clifford

Get away. Get away before you do something stupid. You can't go to jail. These were my only thoughts. I moved without thinking, bumping people.

"Excuse me," I half mumbled without caring. A few outraged gasps followed me but I didn't care. I didn't care about any of these people. I just needed to think.

"UT Professor Jailed After Attacking Alum."

It was a setup. All along I'd been playing right into that man's hands. I couldn't stand there and listen anymore. I had been conned. I was losing my mind.

I needed to be alone, needed to clear my thoughts. Then, I could go back and explain. Explain what? Do what? Take the money? All this had been a waste of time. A joke. They had been laughing behind our backs. Playing us. And I'd been desperate enough to buy it all.

I pushed my way through the crowd until I found an empty bedroom. I closed the door behind me and took deep breaths. Followed by more counting. My vision was still blurred. I couldn't go back there. The darkness edged in. I thought of my perfect place. A lonely cabin in the woods. Nobody for miles. Soothing thoughts that typically calmed me weren't working. The silence was deafening and Suzie wasn't there. Instead, Suzie flashed through my mind. Her stupid cockney accent and goofball antics. Her startling beauty. Her athletic ability. All of her, like snapshots, they consumed.

"Fuck." I punched the air. And calmed my breathing. No. No. I gripped my hair. No, focus. This wasn't about Suzie. This was …

The money. It had been right there, literally inches from my grasp. My whole future secured. Tenure. Success. All the things I had always strived for. I fell forward, gripping a chair in front of me. What the fuck would I do now?

What a fool I'd been. To think the funding would fall into my lap like a wish granted by a magical fairy godmother. God! I'd been so stupid.

I punched the chair. What was I going to do? Where would I go now? I could just take the money, a dark voice whispered. We'd all get what we wanted. But I'd seen those blueprints. I'd found the hidden room. It was clear what those new additions would be used for. I couldn't sign off on that. I'd be signing off on the loss of life and innocence and who knew what else. Doors that locked from the outside? My stomach roiled as I thought of all of it.

Suzie would never let me be a part of that. There was no way she knew what that man was building in there. I believed her when she said she didn't know Buffount was the investor. And yet she offered to dance more, to strip, to save me from signing. She'd give up everything for me. Like I would ever let her do that. I didn't deserve her.

I needed to talk to her. I needed to see what she thought we should do. I know she wouldn't let me take the blood money but maybe she would take me to Occum so we could talk…

I looked up and around the room remembering she wasn't with me. I had walked away in a rage. I had walked away. My heart raced harder in my chest.

Where was Suzie? What was the last thing I said to her?

"Time is up." Was that what I said? I wasn't thinking clearly.

No… Belatedly, I recalled in my mind her face as she registered my words—the crumble of her beautiful features, the color draining from her face. But I'd been too self-absorbed to see the hurt. She'd been defending me and I left her. Again. I left rather than stay and fight.

I raced back into the party. Searched the crowd for a white gown and dark hair. But she was gone. I was too late.

CHAPTER 27

SUZIE

J had made it about twenty steps down the gravel driveway
when rough hands grabbed me from behind.

"Ford, thank God." I gasped as I turned to find a man that was not
Ford.

"Think again, Short Fuse."

Rooster shoved me roughly into a car before I had time to think or
even scream. Cueball sat in the driver's seat.

Razor had finally caught me, was my first thought. Quickly followed
by *fight*! I didn't have time to scream or fight this time. A second later
a hand at my throat pressed until darkness took over.

I awoke as I was dropped roughly into a chair. My heart raced in
my burning throat. I didn't move a muscle. Instinct told me to play
dead.

From a distance, Occum said, "Leave her there."

I remained perfectly still except for the shaking caused by my
racing heart.

"Now get the fuck out of here before anybody sees you."

"What about her?" Rooster asked.

"Just lock her in. I gotta go take care of some shit. Now fucking
go."

I didn't move, my head slouched over like I was still passed out. A million thoughts raced. Rooster and Cueball. But...they were Iron Wraiths. They worked for Razor. My head throbbed. I pricked my ears to see if anybody else was in the room. A door slammed shut and as far as I could tell, I was alone inside.

After another minute of trying to calm my breathing, I slowly squinted open an eyelid to ensure I was alone. My head lifted next, causing the muscles in my neck to burn with pain. Occum's office was abandoned. What the fuck was going on? I rolled my head around to relieve some of the tension in the muscles of my neck. Fear flooded me. First Buffount and now this. Did I have any understanding of who controlled my life?

I wanted to curl into a ball and cry. But now wasn't the time. I ran to his desk looking for a phone, fully knowing nobody had landlines here. Papers fell to the floor as I roughly shoved things around looking for a weapon or anything.

"What are you doing?"

I shot up. "Nothing."

"Find anything interesting?" Occum came into the room and locked the door behind him.

"I was just—"

"Oh, Short Fuse." Occum's face was pale green and shone with sweat. His hands shook as he ran them down his yellow beard. "You screwed up. You had one job. Now Razor's coming to collect—"

"Are you going to give me back to Razor?"

The world spun around me. This whole night had been too much.

"Razor doesn't give a shit about you."

I shook my head not understanding.

"Actually, that isn't totally true. You started stirring shit up. Now he's asking questions. I had everything going smoothly, but you had to beat up his men."

"If Rooster and Cueball are his men, why're they helping you?"

"You're asking a lot of questions." He stepped forward. "I warned you what would happen last time."

"I didn't cross you. I just thought maybe—"

His gaze snapped to my face. "We talked about that. You thinking."

He walked farther into the office, forcing me to stumble backward until I backed into the chair. His eyes flashed with something I couldn't identify, almost like excitement. That scared me more than the anger.

"Your VIP stage is done. Would you like to see it?" His hand struck out like a snake to grab my arm, just above the glove. His dirty nails bit into my flesh.

"Let me go."

"No. You need to see." He pulled me toward the door. "I've worked so hard on it."

The dress constricted my movements, weighing me down. I didn't want to see the VIP stage. I didn't want to go anywhere but away from here. I fought and screamed, but the music was too loud and I was too weak.

We moved past his office and rounded a corner. He opened a door to what used to be a closet. A small staircase now led upstairs. All of this was new and not part of the rumors I'd heard. It occurred to me as we moved up hidden stairs that this was exactly why Ford wouldn't sign off. Hidden rooms meant nefarious activities.

Occum came to a sudden stop and pulled out a set of keys. A small key triggered a secret door to open.

"Get in." He shoved me roughly up into the opening.

Once I was in, he followed. The door closed revealing a room that would hardly fit both of our bodies if we laid down end to end. It was floor-to-ceiling mirrors, except for one pole in the middle of the room. In the reflection, a million versions of me and Occum went on forever. It was a dizzying effect. I couldn't take a full breath. The heavy fabric of my dress suffocated me. The look in Occum's eyes was terrifying. He'd been on edge the last few times I saw him but now his eyes were wild. He wasn't fully here, like part of his mind was somewhere else. I didn't know this man.

"What is this place?" I backed away into a mirror. I saw my reflection everywhere. Pale and wide-eyed.

"This is your VIP room." He smiled.

"This isn't a stage...this is...are those two-way mirrors?" I touched one behind me.

"It's brilliant. Each person has to pay for exclusivity of watching in each of the private rooms." He pointed to each frame of glass in the octagonal room. "Each booth will cost at least a thousand, depending on the show. And that's just to watch clothes come off. Maybe I'll throw another girl in there with you sometimes, I haven't decided. But then—and this is really the brilliant part—"

My stomach churned and the room around me spun. Our reflections all around us taunting, like a carnival ride. I tried to keep my face under control. I could keep it together. Just give him what he wanted. Get out of this cage. I couldn't breathe. I couldn't work in this. I only half listened to the words until he said the next part.

"Then we'll have a bidding war. Whoever pays the most will get to take you into the champagne room."

My head shook back and forth as he spoke. "I don't do that...I told you."

"Yeah, you keep saying that. At first, it was hilarious." His face was scarily still. "Now it's getting old. You make me the most money. But you're a lot of trouble. And you're getting old."

My knees threatened to give out. "I'll find a way to—"

"It's too late." In a flash, he was behind me. One arm was around my waist. The other held my chin roughly, forcing me to look at my reflection. His long beard tickled my exposed skin. "What do you see?"

"You're hurting me. Let go. Let's go talk." I struggled futilely to get out of his grip, my heart racing. I dug deep for happy memories to help keep me calm and in control.

"What. Do. You. See?" He gripped my jaw so hard it might've dislocated.

"Me?"

"More specifically?"

"A d-dancer?"

"Was that 'a dancer'?" He laughed without smiling. "You're funny. I thought you were stupid at first, but I know better now. I see through your little act. Somebody so funny couldn't be stupid. Try again."

I didn't speak. I couldn't.

"Okay, I'll help you out, since for once, you're at a loss for words," he spat the words with wrath I'd never seen. "I see a pretty piece of ass. I see a girl who works for me. For the club. I see a whore for the right price."

With every sentence my body shook more and more, I saw the strain in my muscles as I tensed in fear.

"I see a whore in a fancy dress." The hand that had been holding my jaw disappeared out of sight for a second and appeared again with a knife in hand. With a fast flick of his wrist it opened, revealing a long blade.

I gasped and tried to get out of his grip. "Occum, what're you doin'?"

I fought him, but he was standing over the trap door and he was so strong. God, he was so strong. I needed to stay calm.

"I'm sorry I messed up. I'm sorry I talked back. I'll dance. I can strip if you want."

"Shut up. I won't tell you again."

The blade in his hand glinted as he moved it toward me, reflecting on a thousand different surfaces. I froze. He wouldn't hurt me. I would have no value if I was bleeding.

He brought the knife to me and I couldn't look away as he slowly used it to cut down my satin gloves. Starting at the top of my arm and all the way down. When he tried to cut the second glove, it bunched and snagged so he reached across my body in a twisted embrace to hold the glove in place as he used the other to cut the material. It wasn't steady; it was barely controlled rage. There was a demon writhing under the skin of this man.

"Short Fuse Suze." He half hummed the words to himself like he was lost in the pleasure of torturing me. "So pretty. You make me so much money. It's a shame."

Next, he gathered bits of my gown in his fists and cut them off chunk by chunk. The sound of the beads hitting the floor as he destroyed my couture gown would forever echo in my head.

I stood holding my shivering arms.

"I see a scared little girl who thinks she's better than her roots." Slice. Another chunk fell to the floor. "I see a slut with nobody to give a shit about her."

Another chunk. I wouldn't collapse. I would stay standing. I closed my eyes and took a fortifying breath. It's just words. It's just words.

"I see someone who owes her real family. Who thinks she can pull a fast one."

"No. No, it wasn't like that," I whispered.

"I've taken such care of you." He pet down the side of my face with his calloused hand that smelled like rusting iron. "I put you on the main stage and this is how you repay me?"

He continued to cut off another layer as he held my gaze in a mirror, the pure hatred immobilizing me. My dress was completely cut away. All that remained were my thong and strapless bra.

"You don't take from the Black Demons."

I gasped when the knife cut off my bra. He nicked my skin in the process and a drop of blood moved slowly down my back.

"Occum," I moaned, hating how weak I sounded.

"I've been more than patient with you. You've cost me too much."

The blade sliced off my thong roughly, cutting a small line in my flesh above my hip. I bit back a scream. The sight of my own blood on my skin and his dripping blade did something to me. Something snapped.

"You're a stripper. A hooker. My bitch. Whatever I tell you."

Until that moment I'd truly thought Occum wouldn't kill me. That I had too much value. But there was darkness and pure evil in his eyes. I was nothing to him. I've never been anything to him. I was a way to make money. An object to please his boys. Never a person. And now, I didn't serve any purpose. The realization came too late. I was in too deep.

This is how I die.

He placed the blade at the base of my throat, near my shoulder. I had to squeeze my eyes shut now because that was Ford's spot. That was where he loved and nuzzled and inhaled me and now it was about to be destroyed.

"Open your eyes."

My body was shaking so hard now he was visibly struggling to hold me up.

"I want you to see what happens when you don't listen to me."

I gasped out a sob.

"Please…please," I begged. I couldn't keep it together anymore.

"I need to collect for my trouble." He moved the blade across my neck, not cutting, but using the back to form a cold trail along the base. "Or should I go collect from your john?"

"No," I said the word too quick. I knew it the moment I gasped it out.

His eyes lit up with the closest thing to joy I'd seen on him. "So that's it. You're saving your man? Did you go and want someone else too good for you?"

"I don't care about him. He's nothing."

"Right. Right. I'm sure that's why you're trying to protect him. This just got a whole lot more interesting." He laughed like he was genuinely excited. He thought for a minute, the flat side of the blade against his bottom lip, his tongue teasing the edge. "Let me guess, you seduced him, but he likes you for you?" He laughed. "You really are an idiot. Men will say anything it takes to fuck you. Wow, I'm gonna have men paying thousands of dollars to fuck you and that little shit got to do it for free. I'm impressed. Wonder what he'd think if he saw you like this."

He gestured to the mirror. My reflection was appalling, hunched and shaking, naked and grotesque with blood smeared down my back and legs. I couldn't look anymore. He released me and I instantly crumpled to the floor. I didn't feel anything—just a hole in my chest where my heart used to be.

Occum tilted his head side to side and the bones cracked. "I wonder if your man will want you if you're hideous."

I looked up from where I crouched and saw such evil I scrambled to get away. I called out for help as he grabbed my hair and dragged me back toward him.

"All this beautiful hair, so pretty and long."

He held my head up by a handful of hair, forcing me to my knees. The hair was fisted tight and my neck was extended as long as it could go. He moved his knife to my hair. A sob sneaked past my tight throat. He began to cut. The blade was sharp but not designed for this. He had to saw through the mass. It snagged and tugged, pulling at my scalp. Shock had me staring wide-eyed as chunks fell to the floor all around me.

He stopped when my hair was strewn all over the floor, some on my naked body. He had cropped most of it a couple of inches from my scalp, but in patches it still hung a few inches shorter than my shoulder. I was something out of a scary movie. I stared in horror at my reflection, makeup running down my face. I was hideous. I was no longer a human. I was an animal.

"Look at me."

I'd curled into myself and it took me a second to register his words. When I looked up, his face was as serene as ever.

"You *are* going to dance for me. You *are* going to strip. But most importantly, you *are* going to fuck who I tell you to, when I tell you. Because if you don't, I'll find your man and I'll really use this knife. Do you understand me?"

I nodded.

"Say it."

"Yes." I knew he would. I knew he would use any excuse to murder Ford. I knew it in my soul that he was filled with evil.

"Good." He crouched to the floor in front of me. He lifted my chin so I could see into his eyes. He squeezed my chin hard and it might have hurt if I wasn't so dead inside. "I'm not kiddin'. I will fucking kill him and while I do, I'll tell him about every single man who passed you around and used your body like the slut you are."

I saw the death in his eyes. Any bit of my soul that remained was snuffed out with that thought.

He kissed my forehead. "That's my girl. You're my number one, you know that. And the VIP room is yours until you pay off what you owe me. See, I'm fair. I kept up my end of the bargain, even though you didn't keep yours."

I huddled on the floor.

"Oh, one last thing." He grabbed my arm and lifted it until the soft inner flesh of my arm was in front of his face. "I need people to remember you're mine."

The edge of the blade sliced into my skin and my vision blurred as I screamed. My blood. I couldn't take this. Unable to cope with this new torture, I instinctively pulled away from the physical pain. My body and mind separated, both shutting down.

It took a minute for me to register the sound of shattering glass all around me over my own guttural screaming. A black square appeared where my reflection had been and I belatedly realized I was seeing into one of the sitting rooms. A man stood panting, with something raised above his head.

"What the fuck?" Occum swore and thrust his knife forward.

"Ford," I sobbed out.

Ford's face was contorted in rage. He swung a crowbar down on the next window. I crawled to the back. My hands covered my head from the rain shower of broken glass.

Occum swore incomprehensibly and lunged at Ford. I huddled in the back, flinging glass shards off me. Occum and Ford fought for the crowbar. Occum's knife was on the floor a few feet away. They struggled. Occum grunted. Ford screamed a primal sound. I watched the scene play out like I wasn't there, unsure of my role.

Ford was so strong; he fought so hard. Here he was again fighting for me. The surreal crunching of bones. Rapid punching. Kicking. Thrusts. Blood.

Occum brought his knee up and Ford crumbled forward. I thought I was powerless, but a scream ripped out of me as I moved into action. The knife was in my hand. I sliced it across Occum's calf.

Occum reared back for me.

I stabbed upwards, the knife hitting somewhere around his stomach. He fell forward, barely missing me.

Ford lunged, punching Occum's unconscious body. Eyes black, mouth dripping blood, he kept punching. The snaps and crunching of bone. He wasn't going to stop. He was going to kill Occum.

I threw myself forward, grabbing his arms. He didn't stop. He didn't see me.

"Ford!" I yelled grabbing his face.

Finally, he registered me. He stopped his assault, looking first at me and then at his hands.

"You can't go to jail for murder. People need you."

He blinked. Blinked again. And stumbled backward. I was still naked and shivering. I let go because I couldn't hold on any longer. I let go because I was done fighting.

CHAPTER 28

CLIFFORD

*S*uzie wasn't talking. She was conscious. Mostly. But she wasn't talking. Her clothes were gone. Her hair was gone. She bled from a few spots. But what had me shaking with terror was that she refused to speak. Her eyes were open, but she wasn't responding.

I glanced to the unconscious man. He was passed out, not dead. I wanted him to be dead. But Suzie stopped me. Suzie. I blinked back into awareness. She needed me. She had saved me. Now I had to save her.

"Suzie, we've gotta go. Look at me. Are you okay?" I hugged her close to me. I rubbed her cheek. She blinked at me but said nothing.

I shrugged out of my tuxedo coat and wrapped her in it. Thankfully, I had known about this secret room from that initial inspection. I had left her and she hadn't been okay. My Suzie. The driver who had taken us to the party had seen two men forcing her into a car and had just maneuvered the car out of the line when I came running out. We followed it to the G-Spot and called Jack to meet me there. I knew Occum had taken her. Especially after I refused Buffount.

Suzie was a sack of flour as I scooped her into my arms. I threw her arms around my neck and she made a sad attempt to wrap them tighter. I stood and followed the stairs to a hall and a series of back rooms and hallways that weren't on Occum's blueprints. I had to get her out of here before Occum's bar full of pissed-off bikers figured out what was going on.

I knew the man was planning something evil that first night I came. I knew it. I should have shut it down. Why didn't I go to the police? I was stupid. Fucking stupid. To think I ever considered…

"I've got you."

She held on tighter and my hope grew.

I found the secret back door and took her out, listening for yells or gunshots. Rage and murderous thoughts rang through me. I moved with purpose. I could burn this place to the ground once Suzie was safe.

Gretchen's car came around the building. She and Jack jumped out.

"Oh my God." Gretchen's hands flew to her mouth.

"Be cool. Be cool. Get in the car." My voice was a whisper. I wasn't sure if I was talking to them or myself.

Jack was silent as he helped me get Suzie in the back.

Gretchen's face was pure rage as she got in the driver's seat and started the car. "What happened? Is she okay?"

"We have to go. Go!" I yelled.

"Should we call the police?" Even as Jack asked, he sounded unsure.

"No police," Suzie said with a haunted look, her face going even paler.

Gretchen, Jack, and I exchanged a glance. It may have been the wrong choice but in that moment, I would do whatever Suzie said.

Gretchen nodded and pulled out of the parking lot. Nobody followed us out. There was going to be hell to pay. I would pay it and more. Whatever it took to get her out alive. I cradled her in my arms in the backseat, only vaguely aware of the last few minutes. I'd been all action and no thought. They—well, mostly Gretchen—peppered me with questions but I couldn't speak. I couldn't describe what I had found upon walking in that room. I couldn't do anything but hold Suzie in my arms and pet her face and what was left of her hair.

"Let's get her home," Jack said.

"She's going to my place," Gretchen said the words as facts.

I shook my head. "Not a chance."

"Ford. This is not your choice. It was hers. She's already packed."

"What?"

"Before the party. She wanted me to get her."

Suzie remained quiet when I looked at her, unseeing and seemingly unaware of the conversation happening about her.

"No. She belongs with me," I said, but my voice was weak.

"What, so you can leave her the second things get hard? Again?"

"That's not fair."

"No!" Gretchen yelled out in the silent car. "This isn't fair. Look at her. You left her and this happened."

Her words reflected the guilt I felt. She was right, but I couldn't leave her now. I couldn't leave her side when she needed me most.

"I'm glad you got there to save her from who knows what. But I'm stepping in now. I'm taking over. You've done enough," Gretchen said.

I looked to Jack but he shook his head and said, "It should be her choice."

I held Suzie tighter. They were right. I didn't deserve her. All I could do now was let her go.

CLIFFORD

*S*uzie was in hiding. Gretchen and the rest of the SWS had taken it upon themselves to hide her from the Black Demons until we could make sure she was safe. We hadn't heard anything from Occum or his thugs but it was only a matter of time.

I wasn't eating or sleeping. I couldn't focus on work. In the week since Gretchen took her away, I'd gone through the motions of my life. I texted Suzie all the time asking after her. She'd responded, "I'm fine," every time until yesterday she finally said, "Please stop trying to reach me. Gretchen will tell Jack if anything happens."

I was gutted but I had to respect her wishes. I had to do what was best for her. Rationally, I understood that. I only wished that my heart would get the memo because it ached with pain every fucking minute of the day. I missed her so much. I missed her clomping around the house and singing and dancing like she was perpetually on the set of a musical. I missed her goofy and often adolescent attempts to make me laugh. I missed her.

I stood behind the desk in my office staring out the window when Dean Lucero cleared her throat to get my attention.

I jumped and turned to her. "Sorry, I didn't hear you come in."

Her hands were clasped, instantly filling me with dread. My face must have betrayed my growing alarm. Her features softened but the thin line of her mouth spoke of unpleasant business. "Please, let's sit."

We both did so, facing each other across my desk.

"I have good news and I have bad news."

I nodded for her to go on.

"Mr. Bouffant pulled his funding from the school. All of it. He made it clear that this was due entirely to your actions and that if the school ever wanted additional support, we'd basically have to beg for it."

I closed my eyes. I knew what was coming. I tried to muster the outrage but I couldn't.

"I'm sorry," I said.

I wished she'd just fire me so I could get on with my life. Or lack thereof.

"I hate to say it but his offer always felt a little too good to be true." She sighed. "These things happen. These alums can be touchy. The board will make it right. However, due to the circumstances…"

Here it was. Fired.

"You are going to be put on a probationary period."

I blinked at her.

"The good news is, one of your other grants came through. Last minute, as always, but it should get you through another semester. Congratulations." She smiled.

Her news should have provided relief and yet, something shifted. I looked around my office. I looked back to her.

"I'm resigning," I said. I hadn't known until the words were out of my mouth. "Thank you for your support and I'm sorry."

Her jaw dropped open.

"There's nothing more for me here."

When Jack found me, I was decently drunk.

He must have come home without me noticing. I did have the music up loud, like Suzie liked it—until the windows rattled from the bass. I listened to the playlist she'd made for me. She was right. I loved it.

"Hey, Ford. Whatcha doing?" Jack was behind me.

I winced at the nickname. "I don't like nicknames."

"Sorry. I know." He apologized before taking the Christmas tree from my hands. "But seriously, what are you doing?"

"I'm putting up the tree. Duh." I struggled to stand up after he took away my support beam.

"Are you drunk?" He looked at me with a judgmental face.

"Judgy face," I grumbled.

"Yeah, well, welcome to how the rest of the world feels when you look at them." Jack leaned the tree in the corner.

"Nobody puts tree in the corner." I cackled a laugh and looked for Suzie. But she wasn't there.

"Okay. You realize it is still wrapped in the net, right? And where is the tree stand? Lord, man, go sit down. Or go drink some water."

I did as he said. The sitting. Water was too far.

After fighting with the tree, Jack turned to me and asked, "Why are you here? Don't you have finals?"

"I quit."

"What?"

"I quit my job. Got Funding. Lost Funding. Got different funding. Put on probation. Got different funding. Resigned. Ruined my professional reputation. Burned my bridges at UT. I'm pretty much screwed on all accounts." I burped. "Don't care."

"I can't wrap my mind around all this."

"'Former UT Professor Lost it All After Being a Dumbass'. How's that for a headline?" I sat back on the couch scrubbing at my face. Putting it all out there at once had a decidedly sobering effect. "I lost it all. And I just can't find it in me to care."

"Obviously you do or you wouldn't be reacting like this."

"I have nothing."

He sat down next to me, head back and staring at the ceiling. "That's not true. It feels that way right now, but you know it's not true."

"I mean I could be in jail." I looked up at him.

He raised an eyebrow at me. "Don't say that."

"That night when we got her. I thought I was going to murder him and go to jail. I was okay with it."

Jack pursed his mouth at my words. "I'm sure."

"I did. I wanted to kill him. If you could have seen—how he hurt her. I was okay with going to jail. Just to stop him forever." My eyes were watering. "I don't care about the other stuff. The research. The bullshit. Nothing else feels remotely important now. Which is insane, because what is the point of everything I've done these past years? I'm losing my mind and I don't know what I'm saying. I'm rambling."

"It's okay. Get it out."

"It all sucks. I miss her so much, it hurts. Here." I rubbed the area of my chest where the pain never dulled. "When I first wake up, I'm okay. Then I remember everything. It's like someone died. Part of me, I guess. I can't tell her. She's gone and hates me. I screwed up everything for a fucking career that I don't give a shit about."

"You'll care again. You just need time. It's important work. You do important work. Or you could—"

"Maybe I'll just murder Occum and go to jail. Then I won't have to worry about anything. My days will be planned for me."

"Right. Because prison is a vacation."

I held his gaze for a minute and looked away. "I shouldn't joke about it."

"You shouldn't. But sometimes you have to. You're not going to murder him," Jack said. "Not without my help. And I think Gretchen wants in on it too."

I huffed out a sound. Not quite a laugh. I was nowhere close to laughing. I didn't know if I could ever laugh again. Suzie wasn't here.

"I'm serious." I held his gaze. "I'm going to go down there—"

"You can't murder him. You aren't a murderer. You aren't the person you think you are in your head." I felt his gaze on me as he spoke.

"I've done it before." My voice was low.

"That was different. You were a kid. You were..."

"Defending someone I loved," I finished for him.

"You were a kid." His put a hand on my knee to stop it from shaking. "You're not a murderer by nature. There's a difference."

I looked up into his eyes. "How do I fix this?"

"You need to talk to her."

"Talk to her? She won't look at me, she won't be in the same room as me."

"Then show her. She's hurting. She's not feeling like herself."

"I know. I know it's not all about me. But I don't know where to start."

Silence filled the room as I stared down at my hands. Finally, I said, "The thing that sucks most is, when she first got here, she was so loud. She took up so much space and sound. She brought chaos. A tornado of strewn clothes, dirty dishes, and thumping music. I couldn't wait for it to stop. I couldn't wait to go back to the way things were." I let out a long breath. "And now the house is big and cold. And quiet."

"It's weird. Empty."

"The light went out of here. I'd do anything to get it back. What I wouldn't give to hear her call me a nerd again."

"She did love to hate you." He sighed. "I miss her too."

"I've grown so used to having her around. I don't know how I can live without her." I sighed. "I'm in love with her," I said. My voice was filled with awe because I said it. I admitted it out loud and the world didn't end. That's because it already had.

"And?"

I frowned at him.

"You've loved her as long as she's been here. The first night you got all weird about me and her hanging out I could see it all over you. There were feelings. I just don't understand why you've been so reticent to tell her. Or yourself."

I stared at my hands. "Because I'm not in control. I would have murdered him. If I didn't have to get her out of there so quickly, I would have. And before that, Buffount, and before that, those fucking rapists. Suzie makes me out of control. It's not safe or fair for her to be with someone like me."

Jack let out an annoyed sigh and my head snapped up.

"Are you sighing at me?"

"Yes, I'm sighing at you. What the hell is wrong with you? Suzie is the best thing that's ever happened to you."

"I didn't say—"

"All this other stuff with work and Occum and all these excuses, they're just that. You didn't murder anybody so stop saying it. And you wouldn't ever hurt Suzie in a million years. They're excuses. There's nothing wrong with caring about people. People are life. If something happened to me, would you just say, 'Oh well, get back to work'?"

"No, of course not, but that isn't the same. Suzie…she's distracting and makes me…"

"She what? Makes you uncomfortable? Makes you feel? Good. You need someone to push you out of your comfort zone. You're so stuck up your own ass you can't even see light."

"Please. Don't sugarcoat it."

He stood up. I almost tipped over trying to look all the way up at him.

His arms were crossed as he paced. "No, I'm pissed. Suzie's my friend too, and my friend is gone."

I'd never seen Jack like this. Never. It reminded me of myself when I came unhinged. I kept quiet as he continued to lay into me.

"I don't get you. You were given a gift. A fucking gift. And you're too afraid to see it for what it is."

"I'm not afraid," I defended.

"Then why not just admit how you feel to her?"

"Because I can't let go."

"Why not?"

"Because I'll hurt her!" I yelled at him.

I had hurt her. She went to Occum without any thought for herself. I thought of her sacrifice to save her ex. How she danced to keep her dad safe. She did it all without thinking of herself. Because she didn't think she deserved better. Because she thought that was her role in life.

"You're being an idiot. Man, you've got to let go of that shit from your past." Jack paced in front of the tree. "You know, we all have shit that we deal with. You think I'm just all good now? No, it fucking sucks. I still think about that old shit. That stuff before juvie. You didn't know me then. I still have nightmares. But it doesn't define me. Doesn't make me a miserable person. I work every day to move on. And it *is* work. Staying focused on where I am now and not wallowing in the past, is hard work. But you've got to, because that shit is toxic. You keep swallowing it down every day like medicine. Like you're some hero for holding on to it. But it's killing you. And admittedly, you have some fucked up shit in your past. But so do I. So does Suzie. Hell, so does Gretchen. It shaped who we are. It's part of who we are."

"I didn't—"

"I'm not done." He held up a hand and I shut my mouth. "You're always talking about labels and how damaging they can be and equal opportunities and making the most of life and yet you aren't doing shit to prove it. All you do is talk and research and hold on to these convictions that you're some crazy out of control motherfucker, but you don't actually do anything or move forward. It's like the harder you try to escape your past and prove you're not the same person, the stronger you hold on to it."

I blinked as he unloaded on me, trying to absorb his words and think of my own defense. Finally, I landed on, "I don't want to hurt her."

"How would loving somebody ever hurt them?"

"Because I can't do it a little. If I let myself love Suzie, admit that to her, it would be all-consuming. There would be no moderation. I would suffocate her. My passion for her would overrun everything. I can hardly convey my thoughts to her now. If I let loose, I'd never get anywhere." I thought of my parents. How they'd loved each other but it was a destructive, hurtful love that eventually destroyed them both.

"Oh, man that's bullshit and you know it."

"No." I ground out. "It's not."

"Yes, it is. You're just scared. You don't think you're enough for Suzie. And trust me. Right now, I don't know that you are. You think because she's sharp as a damn tack and resilient as fuck and you are the boy from the broken home, that she won't have you. You're too damn afraid to let her know how you feel and who you really are because you don't think she'll have you. That's what this boils down to. You just don't want to admit to her the things you've done because you think she'll leave. Trying to protect her, my ass."

"Why are you telling me this now?"

He slumped down onto the couch at the end like he ran out of steam. He turned to face me. "I thought you were just a grumpy fuck by nature. But now that I've seen you with her and know your potential, I can't go back. You can't go back. You're a changed man. You can't go back to being Clifford. You'll suffocate."

I couldn't speak because he was right. The months with Suzie were the few times in my life I felt truly alive.

"You're a good man. I don't know why you fight it and act like you aren't. But Suzie deserves to know how you feel about her. Respect her enough to let her make an informed decision about what she wants."

"What, just tell her I love her? It's not that easy."

"It's exactly that easy. Just be brave enough to let go of this lie you're living." He snorted. "Or not living." With that, he stood up and thumped up the stairs. "And hurry up because I miss her."

CHAPTER 30

SUZIE

It was easier this way. To be decided. To know for sure.

No more toying with emotions. I knew who I was and what I was supposed to be doing. I was Suzie Samuels, stripper for the G-Spot and now prostitute for the Black Demons. Or at least whenever they found me, I would be. Hiding out at Gretchen's was like waiting in purgatory. Every day I waited for the rumble of bikes to come and take me to where I belonged.

Hooker. Slut. Whore. The words flash through my memory as painful as the day Occum spat them at me. I had been staring at a water stain on the ceiling that looked like a bunny when Gretchen stomped into the room. I didn't move. I was too numb to be surprised.

"Okay, get up," she said.

"Go away."

She threw a pillow at my head. "Girl, it reeks in here. When did you last shower?"

"Go away." I left the pillow where it landed and used my arm to secure it over my ear.

"Nope. I'm done. A week is more than enough time to wallow. This is shameful," Gretchen said.

"I know. This place is trash. I'm trash." I lifted the pillow to yell. "Go away."

"Not this room, your attitude," said another voice from the door.

I lifted the pillow enough to see Blithe and Roxy waving from the corner.

I sat up. I was dressed in an old hoodie and laundry day underwear that went up to my bellybutton. I tucked my hair off my face into the hood. Or at least what was left of it—a few long, greasy strands on top.

"What're you guys doing here?"

"We heard you're having a hard time. We came with reinforcements," Roxy's peppy voice said.

"Like what?" I sounded wary.

"Food, drinks, makeup, movies."

Blithe jumped in, "Cleaning supplies." Blithe worked at the Donner Bakery and liked things neat and tidy. She'd come to the wrong place.

I grumbled.

Gretchen propped her hands on her hips. "Don't sound so pleased. We want to help."

"But why?"

"That's what friends do."

"No ex left behind," Roxy added.

I blinked. Frowned. Blinked again. I guess I hadn't thought about it much. I'd spent a lot of time with them. At first, because Ford made me. And then I'd started to like it. I liked being girly and not having to worry about being sexy. I liked that we were all so different but had things in common and could talk about anything. I guess I thought they were all above me and took me in because Gretchen made them. I never thought they saw me as one of them. Not for a second.

"Oh," was all I could manage.

"I don't like seeing you like this." Blithe's voice was full of worry.

"I'm having a bit of a hard time at the moment."

"Well, get over it," Gretchen snapped.

My mouth fell open and then I got angry. Really angry. How dare she come in here and invade my space and tell me that I just needed to get over it. Who the hell did she think she was?

"Oh, okay. Why didn't I think of that? Wow. Thanks. I'm better." I pulled the pillow back over my head. "Go. Away!"

"We'll wait outside," Roxy said.

Steps retreated down the short hall.

Gretchen poked my side. "Please sit up."

"I'm mad at you."

"I'm mad at you too," she snapped.

I sat up but kept the hoodie secured so only my face poked out. I knew she'd already seen my hair, but I didn't want to see the pity on her face again. I just wanted to be alone and sleep. "You're mad at me?"

She crossed her arms and sniffed. "Yes. You're freaking me out. You aren't taking care of yourself and I don't like to see people I care about treated like crap. Especially when they're doing it to themselves."

"Sorry, I've had just a little bit going on."

"I know. Listen, I know. And it was horrible what happened. But I care about you, you crazy person. I like that you lit a motorcycle on fire and that you pole dance. I like you. I don't like what all these men in your life are doing to you."

"What's to like?"

"Seriously? Normally, I wouldn't indulge this pity party but I'm starting to seriously worry you don't know what you bring to the table."

"No, I know. Bad manners."

"Shut it down. No. Can you look at me? Listen. You are a fucking badass. Time and time again life has knocked you down and you've gotten back up. You've got compassion for people who don't deserve you. You stand up for what's right. You've got gumption I've never seen in anybody else. I knew we'd be kindred spirits the moment I swung a bat at your daddy."

Her words settled in. She liked me. For me. I'd assumed she hung around because she liked the dance lessons and maybe because of our shared history. I didn't think there was much to like about me. I was so sad and lonely and now with her here I wanted to unload all of it.

"I don't know what to do. I feel like nothing matters. It's only a matter of time before the Black Demons come for me and I have to start...it's not going to be good."

"That is not going to happen." She tried to push back my hood. "We'll figure something out."

I smacked her hand away.

"You don't have to do anything you don't want to do. I promise you that. Just don't shut me out. That's not cool."

"I'm sorry. I honestly didn't think of it."

"Well, I know that. That's why it sucks. I don't expect you to add me to your will or anything. But at least think of me. Like I think of you."

My nose burned. "Okay." It came out more a squeak than a word.

"We're friends now. More than that, remember? Sisters in battle." She grabbed my hand. "What happened sucked. It did. But you got out. Ford got you, we were there. You got out."

I didn't though. Not really. A part of me was still curled on the floor of that VIP room. That room that I thought I wanted so badly. A room that might be the death of me, because how could I ever go back there? Not after feeling Ford's touches and knowing how it felt to be cherished.

I settled on saying, "I should've never trusted Occum."

"Oh, honey. You didn't know."

"He's so awful. So much worse than I ever thought. None of the other guys were ever like that to me. You should have seen his face."

"I'm glad I didn't. I'm glad you're okay." She squeezed my hand again.

"Am I?"

"You are. You're here and you're whole."

I held her gaze. "I don't feel whole." My free hand squeezed the fabric over my heart. "I feel *a* hole."

"I don't think that has anything to do with Occum."

I closed my eyes and it was such a relief I decided I'd keep them shut.

She hugged me. "You'll be okay. You don't have to live a half-life. This is our one chance at it. But it's up to you. You have to change your life. You can't rely on anybody else."

"I don't know where to start."

She took a deep breath in. "To be perfectly honest, you should probably to talk to someone—a professional—about the trauma you've been through. Obviously, I'm here if you want to talk, but someone with better tools for coping wouldn't hurt either. I only have so many bats, you know?"

"Thanks." I huffed a sad laugh.

"And then define who you are and what you want to be. Don't let anybody else do that. Own it."

I thought about it. I'd never allowed myself to think about a whole world of possibilities. "I want to dance. I want to be free of the bikers and clubs. I don't want to go back there. I don't want to be under anybody's else's thumb." Even saying the words out loud made me realize how deeply I wanted freedom. I was tired of that life. Tired of late-night shifts and coming home dead on my feet. I'd been tired of it for a while.

"We'll work on that. I have an idea actually. But for now, we need to think of a way to get you out of there."

"I'm so afraid they'll come back for me. I don't understand why they haven't yet. Ford hurt Occum. He isn't going to take it."

"Something's going on there… I've heard rumors. For now, keep living with me. You can't go back to work at The Coffee Shop yet. Don't worry about that. Lucas knows you're still healing."

"Okay."

"We'll figure this out together. You're not alone."

Emotion had me biting my lip. "Thank you."

"You survived a lot of shit these last few months—rapists, asshole millionaires, sociopaths with knives—but you keep getting back up. Girl, you are full up on star-power. I'm here to tell you don't let this be the thing that keeps you down. You have to keep getting back up.

You keep your eye on the prize. Decide what you want and go get it. Don't stop until you do."

I nodded, feeling slightly rallied.

"I'm glad I found you. Even if we are both Jet's rejects."

"Is that how you see it?" She tilted her head at me. "You're missing the point then. For all his faults, Jethro did do one thing right. Jet brought a group of badass women together. He must've seen something in all of us. We all have a bit of awesome. Don't you feel it? That's the reason we found each other."

"We are pretty cool..."

"People change, if they really want to. Jet changed and then he fell in love. Real Love. Capitol L. It's transformative."

"I didn't think you believed in all that."

"I don't. Not for me. But I've seen it. Loving means putting someone else first. It means wanting them to be their best selves. Are you doing that for your loved ones?"

"I try."

"Do you? What about yourself? You love yourself? You give yourself your best chances? Nobody else can change your life but you. Nobody. Even if Ford and your daddy always put you first, you'd still have to do the work. Support only goes so far."

I ingested her words, let them stew.

"Think of all those assholes out there." She squeezed my hand. "The ones that have been telling you who you are and who you aren't. Don't let them win. Don't give me the stink eye—I'm serious. Don't let anybody tell you who you get to be. You gotta dig deep and define that yourself.

"That's what Ford kept telling me."

"He wasn't all bad. He had his moments. He did save you."

"Twice," I said.

She nodded. "Fair point. And he paid for all that stuff. And he calls to check on you like, three times a day."

"What?"

She avoided my gaze. "Hmm?"

"He calls to check on me? What stuff did he pay for?"

"The whole time, he paid Occum your wages. He paid for your clothes. I guess he had been taking it out of his savings. According to Jack."

"What? Why?"

She shrugged. "I guess, in his defense, he really did see you were special." She frowned. "But it doesn't matter. That's what I'm tryin' to say. It was nice that he did that, but nobody else is going to fix your life. Others can support you and make you feel loved, but you gotta make your own choices."

I was still reeling from learning the truth about the money. It was a lot of money. And he was still checking in on me? Even after I sent him away?

I focused on the here and now. "I do try and change, and life keeps knocking me down."

"So get back up. But you have to want to change. You're holding on to things…like your daddy."

My mouth opened.

"He's not gonna stop drinking no matter what you do. It has to be his choice. Just like your life is your choice."

I wasn't ready to think about that. I knew I had to change. I didn't know where to start.

"It all feels too big."

"Start small. Little choices. Just for you. For example, if you wanted to shower…"

"Yeah, yeah."

I smiled at her and she smiled back and damn if I didn't feel my heart for the first time in days.

And she was right. Not two hours later and I felt a little better. And while makeup didn't feel necessary for life anymore, it was something I enjoyed. And staring at my reflection I saw why. I felt pretty.

Roxy had managed to make a super cute style out of my hair. The one side was shaved short and the longer hair on top fell over for a cool, edgy bob. I looked badass.

"Now, there's my girl," Gretchen nodded approvingly in the mirror.

"Wow, I look damn fierce."

"You always do."

These girls were beginning to mean something to me. Something big. I never thought I'd be the type of girl to have friends. But I liked it.

CHAPTER 31

SUZIE

The only way things were gonna change is if I changed. And I was ready. I couldn't sit idly by anymore. I had to do something, even if it was stupid.

"What are you doing with my bat?" Gretchen's question didn't slow me down.

I looked in the mirror to check my makeup—flawless, obviously—and zipped up my leather coat. "I'm going to Green Valley. I need to find out what's going on with the Black Demons and Occum. See if anybody heard anything. I'm losing my damn mind."

"And you think you're going down there by yourself?" She reached for the bat.

"Nope. I figured you'd insist on coming along." I winked at her in the mirror.

"Damn right." She grinned. "My swinging arm is out of practice. Should we call the girls for backup? I have bats hidden all over the damn place."

"No. I don't want any more people involved. This is just a fact-finding mission, anyhow."

Five minutes later we were on the road. The sun shone high overhead. Unfortunately, there was only one highway to Green Valley and it went right by the G-Spot. I didn't want to look at the building where fear had consumed me.

But of course, I did.

"Stop!" I yelled out.

Gretchen snapped her head to where I looked as she braked sharply. "Jesus, woman! Don't do that!"

"That's Ford's car. Ford's car is at the G-Spot!"

"Shit." We were past the G-Spot by now, but she stopped quickly on the shoulder, tires sliding in the dirt.

My thoughts zoomed around a million miles per hour. "Oh my God. What if Occum got him?" My palms slapped the dashboard repeatedly. " Quick! Turn around. Pull in!"

"I'm going, I'm going. Hang on, it's gravel. Gotta be easy on my boo."

All at once, the courage I'd been feeling drained into utter terror. I had to go into the place of my nightmares. Mirrors and blood and nasty words.

"Should we call the police?" I gnawed on my finger and didn't give a flying fig about my manicure.

"We don't know what's going on. Let's just take a breath and calm down. Did I say breath? I meant a bat. At least one. I'm also packing but probably shouldn't bring that in. Technically, I'm not legally allowed to have it."

"Oh my God, Gretch."

"It's a technicality."

I shook my head. "Let's go in the back. Sneak in. See if we can see anything. I don't want to get shot before we even get in."

"So I shouldn't bring—"

"No guns." I worried my thumb a second longer, then added, "We can always come back for it if we see something fishy."

Gretchen's face hardened in determination.

We left the car on the shoulder a little way past the G-Spot. Bats in hand, we sprinted across the road like foxes into a hen coop and to the back of the building. The back of the building smelled like grease and the rot from the dumpster that sat right outside the back entrance. We crouched low and waited, watching each other with wide eyes. There were no windows to peek in. We'd have to go in.

"Occum's bike isn't here." My voice wasn't as steady as I wanted it to be.

"Small blessings."

"I can't be sure, but that could be Ka-Bar's." Made sense. It was the middle of the day—nobody was on staff yet. Wasn't sure about the other bike. The only car was Ford's.

"Okay, we go in quietly. See what we can see," I said. "First sign of trouble, you get the cluck out."

She gave me a look like I just asked her to sing the alphabet backward.

"Yeah, yeah that's what I thought you'd say."

She held up her fist for me to bump. "No ex left behind."

I bumped her with my free hand, the other wrapped around one of her bats. I held her gaze and sucked in my lip to keep from grinning. "You're a damn fool." I took a deep breath in. "I'll go in first."

She nodded once, eyes narrowed with determination. "Let's go get your man."

The door was unlocked—thank God, because I had not thought of an alternate option—and no noise greeted my ears as it slowly opened. I stilled with just an inch cracked. Though it was dark, there was no movement inside.

I opened it all the way and slipped in. The last time I was here—

No. I pushed the thoughts away. I was Suzie clucking Samuels. I was Short Fuse. The world knocked me down and I got back up. I was making my life choices from here on out.

I crept along the dark hallway, heading toward the bar and away from Occum's office, slowly until my eyes adjusted. A second later I about peed my pants when Gretch grabbed my hand.

I squeezed it hard. "You scared me."

She squeezed it back harder. "You literally just told me to follow you. Who the hell else would it be?"

We were whisper yelling when we both shushed each other, fingers to mouths. Voices had reached us.

"Ford," I mouthed.

She nodded. A second later, her head tilted with confusion. She mouthed back, "Jack?"

It had sounded like Jack's deep and jovial voice. What was Jack doing here?

I made my way past the backstage and dressing rooms, Gretch's hand still in mine. When we rounded the corner to the bar up front, three figures came into view. She dropped my hand and sprinted to crouch behind the bar to listen. I followed a second later. The voices hadn't called out, so we must have made it.

"Just tell me where he is," Ford demanded.

I smiled because I remembered the first time I'd heard him use that tone. A lifetime ago. I peeked over the counter. Ka-Bar stood with crossed arms and a menacing scowl. I rolled my eyes. Bikers. Ka-Bar was dressed as usual, leather head to toe. Ford and Jack tried to match his body language but it was a little less convincing in khakis and button-ups.

"I don't know what to tell you—"

"Tell me where Occum is or I'll call the police."

My heart stopped. No. Ford couldn't. The police would just make everything worse. We were still alive and that might be because we hadn't gone to the police.

I shot up from my hiding place and jumped the bar like I'd done a thousand shifts before.

"Ford. No!"

I rushed toward the men, watching as Ka-Bar reached for his hip, then relaxed.

"Short Fuse?" he asked.

"Suzie?" Jack and Ford said in tandem.

"What the hell are you doing here?" I asked Ford ignoring the commotion my sudden appearance caused.

A moment later Gretchen was at my back.

"What are you doing here? You need to leave—it isn't safe for you," Ford's forehead crinkled and I had to make myself not smooth it back down.

"For me? Ford, you need to leave." I grabbed his arm to tug him away.

Ka-Bar held up a hand. "Short Fuse, where you been? We were worried."

He scooped me into a hug that cracked my back before I could answer.

After I was set back on the floor, I focused on Ford. "I don't want you talking to Occum."

He re-crossed his arms and looked to Ka-Bar. "I'm here to buy your freedom."

I looked around in disbelief. Gretchen frowned but looked intimidating. Jack did a good impression of an imposing figure.

He went on, holding my gaze like he'd been preparing to say this. "You can dance if you want. You can strip. You can do whatever you want. But I want it to be your choice. I don't want you doing anything you don't want to do anymore. I don't want you indebted to anybody else."

I shook my head slowly. I had been about to speak when Ka-Bar spoke up. "What are you talking about? Debt? You said that the other day too. Short Fuse, we don't got beef with you."

My brain throbbed trying to process all this information.

Belatedly, I responded, "Not with the Black Demons. The Iron Wraiths. I was paying off the debt. Giving my tips to Occum and he paid Razor." As I spoke, different pieces were sliding around in my head. The comments about Razor but never seeing him. The hauntings from Rooster and Cueball. The fact that I worked for years and my debt was never paid.

I clutched my stomach.

"Short Fuse, you don't owe the Wraiths shit. Your money is your own. Your tips, they're yours," said Ka-Bar.

I shook my head. They didn't understand. That wasn't right. For years... "But Occum—"

"Occum's missing," Ka-Bar said. "And with a shit ton of Razor's money. Why I'm here.

Haven't seen him in at least a week. There's blood and broken glass upstairs in some area I didn't know existed. We thought maybe… We found out he was skimming money. God, you're a sight for sore eyes, Short Fuse. We thought the worst."

"He was working with Razor. For Razor," I said. My lips were numb. The world spun. The rest of the pieces fell in place. "He was never a Black Demon. He never protected me. I was played."

Distantly, I was aware of Gretchen and Ford on either side of me. "Sit down."

A chair appeared behind me and I was lowered into it.

"But I've been dancing here for almost ten years." I swallowed down the sour liquid filling my mouth. "He's been taking my money."

"Razor had Occum come here to take over this place. Keep an eye on things. Then he got greedy. Started taking for himself," Ka-Bar said.

My hand covered my mouth. "All for nothing. Nothing."

I checked out of the conversation all around me. I couldn't process anything else. I couldn't think anymore. The things Occum had said to me. The way he made me feel. Like I was worthless without him. All these years… I'd been an idiot.

Rage like I'd never felt boiled my blood.

"Gretchen," I said. She was crouched in front of me in an instant. I lifted my gaze to hers. "Where's that bat?"

Clifford

As we argued on the legalities and indications of Occum's disappearance, Suzie rose in my periphery. She moved like a person possessed.

There was a bat in her hand.

"I'm going upstairs," she said.

Gretchen and I were in tow. I wasn't going to stop her. I would only support her from here on out.

"Now, wait just a minute. I know you're upset, Short Fuse. But let's not—"

I glowered at Ka-Bar. "Suzie gave her wages for years. Way I see it, she can do whatever the fuck she wants." I reached toward my pocket. It only held my phone. He didn't know that. "Now I suggest you back the fuck off."

Ka-Bar nodded.

We followed her down the hall. Occum's office looked as though it had been ransacked. Suzie just kept heading toward the back stairs. I motioned to Gretchen and we scurried farther along the corridor to a wider staircase. I lead her to the room where I had broken through the glass. Suzie stood in the center of the room where I'd found her as Occum's prisoner. The trap door was flipped open next to her. The glass had been swept toward one of the walls but dried blood still stained the floor. Her face was unreadable.

"This door locks from the outside?" she asked me as she motioned toward the trap door.

I nodded.

"It wasn't in the blueprint?"

I shook my head. "When he gave me the tour, he had the light off in that room. But the dimensions didn't add up. At first, I thought it was a movie booth or something. But then I saw the hidden entrance."

Her eyes closed for a minute. Under her breath I barely heard her say, "Locked in against their will."

Without warning, she screamed like I'd never heard anything—like a wild animal crying out in pain. She kicked the trap door closed then lifted the bat above her head. The bat connected with one of the remaining mirrors. It shattered with an ear-splitting cacophony of sound. A small cut seeped blood on her cheek.

"You asshole!" Her screams were muffled, instantly absorbed into the padded soundproofing of the outer rooms. "You sick son of a bitch!" The bat swung in wild arcs.

More glass shattered. Suzie screamed another war cry.

I stood motionless by the mirror I had broken as she took out her rage. I felt Gretchen's presence next to me. But my eyes were glued to Suzie, watching for additional cuts, knowing that her rage needed to expend itself before she'd allow me to look after her. Suzie's face was twisted with fury as she made sure every mirror in the room was broken. And then when there were no more glass walls, she hit the frames and even the trap door.

By the time she crouched in the middle of the room, hunched over and spent, the whole area was obliterated. She panted as tears streamed down her face.

"I'll take Jack home. You take care of our girl." Gretchen left.

Only Suzie's ragged breaths filled the silence of the room. I stepped forward, shoes crunching on broken glass. I bent to scoop her into my arms but she stopped me.

"No." When she lifted her face to mine, I was surprised to see her smile through tear-streaked cheeks. Blood dribbled lightly down one of them. "I'm walking out of here. On my own."

She grasped my proffered hand and stood with effort. She lifted her chin, straightened her shoulders, and walked out of what was left of that horrible room. At the threshold to the stairs she said, "I'm free."

CHAPTER 32

CLIFFORD

After I cleaned her cuts, we wordlessly got in my car and left. I wasn't sure if it was too soon to go back to my place, so I drove through the winding country roads of the Great Smokey Mountains without any direction. Suzie sat with her head propped on the window.

After a long while, when I had thought she might have fallen asleep, she asked, "You went to the G-Spot to buy my freedom?"

I cleared my throat. "It was the least I could do after I fucked up so bad."

She sat up with her arms wrapped tightly around her. I clicked up the heat. "With what money?"

"I have some savings. I'm sorry about that night. I'm sorry I couldn't say what I should have said."

"And what should you have said?"

I couldn't do this without looking at her so I delayed answering her until I could find a pull-off. With the car in park and the engine running to keep us warm, I turned to her.

"I should have told you I loved you. Because I did. I do."

As I spoke, her mouth formed an "o" and her eyes widened.

I had planned everything I wanted to say but the whole day had taken an unexpected turn the second she jumped out from behind the bar, surprising me like always.

"I love you. I have for some time. I'm sorry that I was too late in figuring it out. I fucked up so bad. The thing is, I know I'm a cold man. I know I don't say what I mean. I know I can be difficult to read. But there's nobody else for me. There never has been, and there never will be. I know that about myself. I forget to say the obvious out loud. I assume everybody sees it as clearly as I do. The moment I fell in love with you, it was obvious. Or so I thought. I kept all the words locked up. But you are it for me. I don't deserve a chance, but I'm asking for it anyway."

She started to speak but I pressed on with a shake of my head.

"I was living in fear, bathing in it. But now I know that fear wasn't real. I found out what real fear was when I saw you with Occum. I can't risk not spending every available moment with you. Life is too precious. I was so afraid of being like my parents and letting life pass me by but that's exactly what I ended up doing. I lived with extreme focus—blinders, really—which is no different than living in the haze of drugs. I used my goals as an excuse to miss out on everything around me. Not anymore. I'm not wasting a moment that's given to me. I want whatever you'll give me. I want to hold your hand in bed every night—at least until you roll over and take all the covers—but I'll sleep in the cold next to you. I don't care. I want to live with my eyes open now."

I took a deep breath in. Her eyes were as wide as salad plates.

"Jesus, I think that's the most I've ever said at once. I need a lozenge." I rubbed my throat. "I mean every word."

"I want that too, Ford. I want to be enough for you too. I was so afraid you always saw me as backwoods trash. I would never in a million years have thought I was enough for you. That you felt this way the whole time is a little mind-blowing. I think I need a minute."

The smile on her face grew and my heart hammered against my chest.

"I love you, and more than that, I value you," I said. "As you are. No changes. I want to be your person, the first person you think of when anything happens. Anything."

"You already are that person for me." She held my gaze. "Do you trust me enough to be that person for you?"

"Yes. God, yes. You're a miracle." I couldn't help the grin that split my face.

She shook her head like she couldn't believe it.

"You are. You are the most tenacious, stubborn, loyal, beautiful person I've ever met. You astound me all the time. See? That right there. I think that all the time, but I bet I've never said that."

"I astound you. Very fancy."

I hauled her to me. I inhaled deeply. "God, I love the way you smell. That's another one I think all the time. It never fails to amaze me how you can always smell so good."

"Gretchen might disagree with that…" she trailed off. "Please don't stop. Keep 'em coming. Tell me everything as you drive us home."

We spent the drive back to Knoxville hand in hand. I was on top of the world. I was with Suzie.

My Suzie.

"Hey, I was just thinking…" she hesitated.

"What? Tell me."

"Um, remember you were telling me about that Maslow's hierarchy of needs?"

"Yes. What about it?"

"You said that in towns with high poverty—where those basic needs aren't met—that there is no interest in things like education and art and stuff."

"Right. If you don't feel safe to sleep and your stomach is always growling, chances are you aren't going to take time to plant flowers or go to the theater."

"Exactly. I guess what I'm wondering is, pretending money isn't an issue, what would you do? Like to change the world? No money issues, just funds and go."

"Well, I'd want to research…"

"Ugh. No. No research. What would you *do*? Would you still want tenure?" Suzie sat watching me, with her new short hair emphasizing her beauty even more. Her green eyes were brilliant and on full display without the hair to hide them.

"I don't think so. I thought I did. It was my plan for so long. Now, I'm not so sure. I started on a path to help and it got derailed. I quit, by the way."

She gasped and looked at me.

"It's okay. I wasn't okay at first. But I am now. I don't think it was ever what I wanted. I just wanted to help."

"Tell me how you would do that. Remember, all the money in the world."

I gripped the steering wheel. "I guess… Well, I'd start a program. For kids of parents with addictions. I would want there to be a place where those basic needs are met, to allow room for a desire for more. Take them outside of that bubble kids can get stuck in. I'd show them what's out there, what they could reach for. I'd want someone to believe in them. Give them hope."

"So why not start there? I think it's safe to say enough research has been done. Why not just start helping and do that?"

"I guess…I mean, start a program myself?"

"Yeah. You have the brains, and the know-how. You could just start, and maybe the government could help. You know how to write a grant request." A grin grew on her face. "You said you were going to buy my freedom with your savings. I don't know how much it is, but it could be a start."

I told her what I had been prepared to offer.

Her eyes went wide. "Ford!"

"What?"

"You have that much money? But you're a teacher. You have a roommate."

"I'm naturally frugal. I guess I was always afraid of going back to poverty."

She smiled. "You were going to give all that up for me?"

"I still would."

She smiled at me so big. I meant the words. I'd give up everything for her.

"You're crazy. With half that money you could do something. At least start something. Other people might join in. I could help you. I know some people."

"Huh." I turned her words over in my head. Could I be responsible for all that? Didn't I need to find the person who would do that? But I'd need a person that cared like I do. A person that would make sure that every detail was right. Somebody had to do it, so why couldn't it be me? I could be enough.

"Suzie?" I asked when we were almost home.

She blinked up at me with sleepy eyes. "Hmm?"

I loved her new hair. I kept meaning to say that but wasn't sure if—

"I love your hair." No overthinking and overanalyzing, I told her how I felt. No more confusion.

"Really?" She ran a self-conscious hand over it.

"Yes. It makes your features even more breathtaking. You're beautiful. I love you."

She bit her bottom lip between her teeth. "Thank you."

"Will you please move in with me? And stay with me for forever? I miss you."

I focused on the road, but her stare was tangible. "I'm not too loud? I don't make too much of a mess in my room? I still chew with my mouth open."

I kept my face serious. "That's the other thing. I'm going to need you to move into my room. For the foreseeable future. For safety."

I stole a look from the road.

She beamed at me. "Hmm. You're probably right."

I laughed and grabbed her hand to kiss her knuckles.

Suzie laughed and then sobered instantly again. Her emotions were written all over her face and were giving me whiplash. God, I missed that. "I forgot something else," she said.

I slowed to a stop in front of my house—*our* house. "What?"

She gripped my hand and stared at me so hard I thought the worst was coming. "I love you too, Ford."

And just like that, my last thread of control snapped as I scooped her into my arms and my lips took hers. She was mine, and I fully intended to show her how much.

Ford

I'd been an idiot. Worse than an idiot. Losing control was amazing. And freeing. I lost control on Suzie for a week straight and every second of it was better than the last. Day or night, bed or couch. I had no intentions of ever reigning in that side of me again. Control had been a made-up form of protection for my heart that I no longer needed. I simply loved.

I pulled her into my arms and tucked her under my chin as we both stared at the big pine tree proudly displayed in the front window. It was the day before Christmas Eve, but we'd finally gotten our tree. Turned out the one I started putting up in my drunken blur wasn't ours and needed to go back to the neighbor's before they noticed it missing from their back porch.

Jack's finals were over, and tomorrow the three of us were flying to Washington to be with our folks for Christmas. She couldn't believe how thrilled I was to bring her to meet them, and so in preparation she had asked a thousand questions on how to dress and act.

"Be you. That's all," I'd said.

She'd not stopped smiling since. I was so proud of her; there wasn't a thing I'd change.

Suzie's father was trying to quit drinking. Mrs. Albensi was all but living there to make sure he stayed that way. Three days since he last drank. A start. Suzie had cried the whole time as he called Alcoholics Anonymous. He was going to his second meeting tonight.

I had spent the week setting up several exploratory meetings set with the local school board and businesses for January, looking for investors and people to share my ideas for an after-school program. Suzie helped me develop a strong pitch that we'd practiced day and night. It shared the details of my life and the difference a helping hand had made. I would spill it all if that was what it took. I was done pretending to be something else, someone else. My past didn't freeze me in place anymore. Come hell or high water, I would start making a difference in at least one child's life.

Suzie let out a contented sigh and said, "You were right."

"I typically am."

She pinched my thigh. "Real trees are amazing."

I turned her around and kissed her with all the love I felt for her. It was a long kiss.

"Oh, get a room." Gretchen walked in carrying a bowl of popcorn with Jack right behind her, shaking his head.

"This is my life now. I live with two rabbits. In an old house. With very thin walls," Jack said with an annoyance that his smile betrayed. "There's not enough Lysol in the world."

Next into the room came the rest of the SWS. I had grumbled my disapproval when the small holiday get-together was suggested, but was promptly overruled. The name Scrooge had even been thrown about.

"Come on. At least use coasters. It's antique." I gestured to the classic oak bar where the peppy one just set down her drink.

"Sorry," she giggled. "Let me just wipe that up." Only that pint-sized brunette could actually giggle a word.

Suzie tickled me and whispered, "Be nice."

Our home was filled with warmth. Warmth of soul and warmth of comfort. Soft holiday jazz played on the record player and fresh pine, cinnamon, and now popcorn filled the air.

We all set to work unpacking the tree boxes and decorating every branch with whatever we could find. It was cramped and chaotic but when I saw the giant smile on Suzie's face, I wouldn't change a thing—except maybe to purchase more coasters.

Jack scooted next to me under the guise of placing an ornament on a branch towards the top. Of course, Jack did the top foot of the tree.

"Hey, man, I think something's wrong with your face." He said it so discreetly that I was sure a bit of lunch was stuck in my beard. I checked smoothly but found nothing. When I looked up again, he was smirking. "You haven't stopped smiling in days."

"You should go on a stand-up tour."

"I'm not appreciated in my own time."

Next to me, the ladies discussed their next meeting. Something about the art of kintsugi.

"I found some boxes of teacups in the basement here. I'm sure we could smash those up," Gretchen said.

I looked over at her in horror to find her watching me. "Kidding, kidding."

It was pick-on-Ford night. Normally, the ostracizing would have raised my hackles but now I saw it for what it was—good-natured teasing between friends. We were all friends. What a weird and wonderful life.

"Still no word?"

"Nobody has seen her. I'm starting to worry." This came from one of the twins. I still couldn't remember who was who even though they weren't identical. I didn't remember most of the names of the group of women who traipsed through my house. Suzie's studio could not open fast enough.

Suzie and Gretchen frowned.

The redhead said, "We're going to have to step in."

"It's between her and her parents. What can we do?"

Their conversation moved toward the hot toddy stand and I couldn't hear the rest. I frowned at Suzie, but she shot me a reassuring smile from across the room. Whatever was going on there, I'm sure she'd fill me in on later.

When the boxes were empty and the tree was plump with senti-mentality, everybody started to make their excuses.

Gretchen put on her heavy coat and wrapped a scarf around her neck. "I got a hot date."

"Do I know this person?" Suzie asked.

Gretchen shrugged coyly then smiled. "Oh look! It's starting to snow."

"Sure, you can change the subject," Suzie teased.

We all went to the window to confirm. It didn't snow much here, so the few flakes that fell from the sky quickly melted. But it was perfect for the festivities.

"Beautiful," someone whispered.

It was a picture-perfect scene. A warm house full of friends and laughter. My heart was thumping in my chest but not from fear or rage, just pure unadulterated happiness.

"I'll drive you all home," Jack said.

"Ladies man," Gretchen teased, and we all said our goodbyes.

Suzie and I sat in the loveseat that faced the large window, holding hands watching the snow collect in contented silence.

"Did you ever think you could be this happy?" Suzie asked.

I waited a beat and thought. "No. I don't think I ever allowed myself to dream this big."

She nuzzled a smile into my shoulder as I slipped an arm over her. I felt the warmth through my whole being.

"You, here, in my arms. It's more than I could have ever dreamed of."

"Me too." Suzie sighed. "I'm not great at many things, Ford, but I'm going be so damn good at loving you."

I held her gaze and felt my love expanding in my chest. Every day I loved her more in ways I never thought I could.

"I never thought a woman like you would love me."

"Mmm, a woman like me?"

"So full of life and passion."

"Ah. I see."

"How is it possible you see anything worth the effort in me?"

"Well, some guy once told me that I would have to work at the things that were the most important to me."

"He sounds condescending."

"He's alright." She shrugged, pretending to think it over. "I wouldn't kick him out of bed."

"Lucky bastard." I inhaled her neck before leaving a soft kiss. "I love you, Suzie Samuels."

"I love you, too."

EPILOGUE

SUZIE

The following Spring

"'Anonymous Investor Funds Ford's Fosters,'" I looked up from the newspaper to check on Ford, who hadn't stopped shaking his head in disbelief. "'An anonymous investor has donated one million dollars to the local start-up, Ford's Fosters, based out of Green Valley, Tennessee this week. The start-up was created by former UT professor Dr. Clifford Rutledge as a way to help at-risk youth gain access to higher education.' It goes on. Ford, this is incredible. I can't believe it." My eyes scanned the page, greedy for more.

Ford hid his face in his hands. Emotions colored in his cheeks and ears.

"'Ford's Fosters focuses on free, safe public transportation for youth from all over the region looking to participate in various outdoor activities, like rocking climbing and hiking. "Our goal is to encourage learning while providing an outlet for all that pent-up teenage energy in a safe, chaperoned environment. Everybody deserves somebody to believe in them," Rutledge said about his dream charity.' This is fantastic. This just came out in the Knoxville News this morning!" I hopped up and down as my voice wobbled with joy.

The whole room broke out in applause. Jack had brought the paper in with the cakes and getting all our attention by hooting and hollering—understandably so. As soon as I saw the headline, I started reading it to the whole room.

Ford, on the other hand, remained stunned silent. Eventually, he said, "I still can't believe it."

"Oh, it's real, my friend." Jack slapped him good-heartedly on the back before shaking his shoulders. "You wanted it, you got it. You worked damn hard trying to find investors. You earned this."

"I just wish I knew who to thank… I can't imagine who it was."

"We probably won't ever know. We know who it wasn't." I made a face to Gretchen, referring to Ted Bouffant, who had been convicted of insider trading charges in March.

Ford stood and gingerly took the newspaper from me. Behind him, the room broke out in applause. "Okay, enough. Enough." He motioned everybody to be quiet. "I'm blown away and honored, but today isn't about me or Ford's Fosters, it's about Suzie. She's the reason we are all here today. The light of my life." He grabbed one of the many plastic champagne glasses and raised it to me. "Cheers to the most courageous, beautiful, wonderful woman I have the honor of calling my life partner."

"Cheers," the crowd sang.

I felt my eyes getting glossy so I waved at my face. I would not ruin perfectly amazing makeup. I would not. He stepped back with a bow to me and I stood up to face the crowded space.

Now I felt the full force of embarrassment as a room full of people looked to me, clapping. I lifted my chin and held out my arms. "Welcome to Stripped. Green Valley's newest—and only—full-fledged pole dancing studio." Gretchen and the rest of the SWS waved and gave me thumbs-ups from the crowd.

More people than I'd ever imagined in a million years were here; including, but not limited to, the most church-going, pearl-clutching ladies of Green Valley. Despite the fear of complete and utter rejection, I kept my voice strong.

"If some of you out there are worried about starting on the pole, I offer a variety of classes for all skill levels. The point is to come out, shake your booty, feel sexy, and have fun."

A few women blushed at the word sexy, but most clapped loudly.

"Our first class is tomorrow at ten a.m. for anybody looking for chair dancing basics. For now, enjoy the snacks and refreshments provided by Donner Bakery."

The room clapped and I headed to Ford, fanning myself along the way.

Gretchen and Jack joined us, bringing me a piece of banana cake.

I pressed the backs of my cold fingertips to my cheeks. "I still can't believe this many people showed up for fitness classes. Honestly, I half expected to be chased out of town with pitchforks."

"Nah." Gretchen waved her hand. "Green Valley is sexually enlightened and surprisingly woke."

"Love is everywhere. It's the fresh mountain air," Jack said, surveying the crowd, possibly looking to get enlightened himself.

"Geez, girly, you may have to hire more than just me part-time," Gretchen said as she flipped through the sign-up sheets. "Your first month is booked solid already."

"I know. Talk about champagne problems."

Ford squeezed me close to whisper in my ear, "I'm so proud of you."

I looked into his eyes and felt the familiar tingles of love. "I'm so proud of us. Look at us going after our dreams and shit."

He lifted his chin. "Damn, it feels good."

I nuzzled his chest, loving the smell and warmth of him. He was mine. All mine, mine, mine.

I studied all the people who had come to my little open house from the safety of Ford's chest. I was still just a little overwhelmed by it all. People who I assumed hated me had shown up. People I didn't think even knew I existed. Some even shook Daddy's hand as he went around with Mrs. Albensi. Daddy beamed with pride. I was proud of him too. Ten weeks sober. It hadn't been easy but he'd been working hard at it. All by himself, with our love and support—and, of course, Mrs. Albensi and his sponsor.

Excited whispers broke out all over the room and I lifted my head to see what caused the commotion. In walked Jethro Winston and Sienna Diaz. To my complete surprise, I felt nothing. Well, not *nothing*, nothing. I felt a little thrilled to see THE Sienna Diaz in my studio.

Jethro scanned the room as Sienna nodded politely at the crowd that immediately descended upon her. When he found me and our eyes met, he lowered to whisper something in her ear. Sienna freaking Diaz looked up at me and smiled so dazzlingly perfectly I could only smile back.

"Is Sienna Diaz smiling at me?" I asked through clenched teeth.

"Yup," Gretchen answered. "Good gravy, she's gorgeous. Oh shit, Jet's headed this way. I'm out." Gretchen grabbed Jack by the wrist and dragged him away, obviously using his height as a shield. The coward.

"Want me to stay?" Ford asked me. He brushed back my hair from my face and rubbed a thumb over my cheek.

I'd kept the half-shaved look for a while and now had a messy bob. I missed my length some days but liked this style a lot, too.

"Just give us a minute," I said.

"I'll be checking out that German chocolate cake if you need me."

I smiled at him and took a deep bracing breath as Jethro Winston came to a stop in front of me.

"Hey, Suzie," he said tentatively, as though he was bracing himself for a screaming rampage.

In his defense, it was possible that once or twice, maybe, after the motorcycle incident I had cursed him out loudly. In town. For everyone to see.

"Hey, Jet," I chewed the inside of my lip. This wasn't awkward. Not at all. I certainly wasn't thinking about the fact that I was a member of a society that had been founded specifically to talk shit about him.

But now, truthfully, with him standing in front of me, I truly didn't feel anything but...neutral. If anything, I felt a little bad that he was obviously so nervous. Part of me wanted to scream 'Boo!' just to see what he did. But that wouldn't be nice… Maybe later.

"The studio looks great." He glanced around, hands deep in his pockets.

"Thanks." I followed his eyesight. It wasn't much. A room surrounded in mirrors, ballet barres and some poles, a few stacked chairs in the corner. But it was all mine, and I was damn proud. My therapist told me it was important to celebrate all the little wins.

Turned out all my lost wages had been calculated by the new owner and the G-Spot gave what was due to me. It was enough to buy rent for at least a year on this studio in downtown Green Valley.

"There were a few things I wanted to tell you." Jethro squinted as he spoke, not quite able to meet my eyes.

"Okay."

"I heard about what happened with Occum and those guys, Rooster and Cueball. I know they've been missing for a while but it looks like their bodies were finally discovered."

I gasped. It'd been months since we'd heard any news about Occum. Right after the incident, the police used a warrant to search his house, but it looked like they weren't the first. The place had been ransacked and there was evidence to suggest that Occum had booked it out of town.

Not surprisingly. Everybody knew he crossed Razor. Nobody crossed Razor and lived to tell about it.

"It's probably not going to be in the news so I wanted to let you know in case you were worrying at all. "

"Wow. Okay. Thanks, Jet. I appreciate it."

I felt a weight lift off me that I didn't know was still there. I didn't mourn them. Not after what they did to me. I only mourned the time I wasted thinking about them.

"Also, I wanted to congratulate Ford on his program. And the funding. That's great news."

I beamed with pride for my Ford. He'd stepped up and was already making a difference in people's lives.

"I'm real proud of my man." I shot Ford a smile where he stood watching our conversation.

"It sounds like a great program. Wish there had been something like that for me, when I was young. Might've saved me from hurting people who didn't deserve it." His eyes were full of meaning with those last words.

I nodded with a sad smile. It all felt so long ago.

Jethro took a deep breath and seemed to decide something. "I never thanked you for what you did. With my bike."

I glanced around, cheeks burning.

"You don't have to thank me for destroying your bike—" I shook my head once and gestured with wide eyes to where the sheriff's wife stood.

"We both know what you really did. You saved me from what could have been a very different life. Thank you."

I held his gaze and nodded once.

"Lastly, thank you for never going to the press when I first got with Sienna. I know they hounded you like crazy for dirt. They probably offered you a lot of money. But you never did. I didn't deserve that. But thank you. And I'm sorry I was such an ass back then."

"Stop. It's in the past. We were both kids. Different people. I forgive you."

And I did. I meant it. I had no ill feelings toward Jethro Winston at all.

"Thank you." He ran a hand over his beard. "Well, anyway, I'll let you get back to your celebration. Congratulations again."

I waved to him and as I did, Sienna looked up from her crowd. Her eyes took in Jethro as he walked away and I recognized that look of pride and adoration. I knew it because that was exactly how I looked at Ford.

Ford came up and hugged me from behind. I turned in his arms to study his handsome face.

"Everything okay?" he asked.

"Yeah, he was just eating crow."

"Good."

"He said congrats to you and on your fund—"

I looked back just in time to see Jethro and Sienna as they left the building. It hit me that the funding hadn't become public news until today. I guess there was a chance that he had read about it but the article had just come out and they hadn't been here when I made the announcement. There was almost no way of knowing. Unless…

"They couldn't' have…no, they wouldn't…"

"What? What am I missing?"

"Nothing," I shook my head to clear it. "He just said congrats."

"And you're okay?" He lowered his head so I would make eye contact.

"Better than okay. I'm great."

"You look happy. Lighter."

"I am. You too?"

"I'm the happiest guy that ever lived." He reached into his pocket and pulled out a little velvet box. My heart started hammering. "I'm hoping you might make me a little bit happier…"

ACKNOWLEDGMENTS

As I sat down to write the acknowledgments for "My Bare Lady" I thought of all the wonderful people in my life and with each one I would think, "none of this would be possible without you." I was worried that it would start to sound insincere. Without all the supportive people in my life, I can't imagine where I'd be. Probably in a cave of sadness, not living out my wildest dreams, and eating my weight in ice cream. So really YOU are amazing and I truly wouldn't be here without you.

J.R., how can I properly thank somebody who has always had unwavering faith in me and sacrifices so much of their own life to support my dreams? I still haven't figured it out, but you bet your booty that I will show you my gratitude and love until the end of time.

Lauren, my sister from another mister, but also my actual sister-in-law. President of the Piper Sheldon fan club, established 2008. Current members: one.

Tracy, you have read this book more than anybody else, you sweet, patient soul, and for some reason you still want to read my writing. Please except this coupon for free chai lattes for forever.

To the state trooper in Georgia who pulled me over on my way from researching "Green Valley" in Tennessee as I headed back to the airport. I was a mess. You were patient and kind. I made it to the airport on time.

To the Sharks of Awesome, who are totally Penny's people, but who I found when I needed them the most and where I met so many strong, amazing, and hilarious people. My only regret is that I didn't ask the Georgia State Trooper (see above) if I could Kinnear him because we would have all agreed that he was the Jackson James of our hearts.

To the Smartypants Romance authors and Fiona. Getting to know you and being welcomed into the coolest crew ever has literally been life changing for me. I sincerely love you all.

And, of course, to Penny. Whose amazingness has brought us all together. You are endlessly inspiring. ALL OF THIS is because of you and your willingness to put your book out there in exchange for a free dinner.

ABOUT THE AUTHOR

Piper Sheldon writes Contemporary Romance and Magical Realism books that hope to be NYT bestsellers when they grow up. For now, she works as a technical writer during the day and writes about love the rest of the time. Of course she also makes room for her husband, toddler, and two needy dogs at home in the Desert Southwest.

Find her online:
Website: www.pipersheldon.com/
Facebook: www.facebook.com/piper.sheldon.39
Goodreads: www.goodreads.com/PiperSheldon
Twitter: @piper_sheldon
Instagram: @pipersheldonauthor

Find Smartypants Romance online:
Website: www.smartypantsromance.com
Facebook: www.facebook.com/smartypantsromance/
Goodreads: www.goodreads.com/smartypantsromance
Twitter: @smartypantsrom
Instagram: @smartypantsromance

www.ingramcontent.com/pod-product-compliance
Lightning Source LLC
Chambersburg PA
CBHW051638180726
48284CB00006B/1776